D0959556

THE BLOOD OF CAESAR

OTHER BOOKS BY ALBERT A. BELL, JR.

Mystery
Death Goes Dutch
All Roads Lead to Murder
Kill Her Again

Historical Fiction
Daughter of Lazarus

Children's Mystery
The Secret of the Lonely Grave

Non-Fiction
*Perfect Game, Imperfect Lives: A Memoir Celebrating the
50th Anniversary of Don Larsen's Perfect Game*
*Exploring the New Testament World: An Illustrated Guide to the
World of Jesus and the First Christians*
Resources in Ancient Philosophy (with James Allis)

THE BLOOD OF CAESAR

A SECOND CASE FROM THE NOTEBOOKS OF PLINY THE YOUNGER

ALBERT A. BELL, JR.

INGALLS
PUBLISHING GROUP INC

INGALLS PUBLISHING GROUP, INC
197 New Market Ctr. #135
Boone, NC 28607

www.ingallspublishinggroup.com

© 2008 by Albert A. Bell, Jr
all rights reserved

This is a work of fiction. Although loosely based on historical facts and possibilities, the characters and events are entirely a product of the author's imagination.

Illustrations by William Martin Johnson from the 1901 edition of *Ben Hur,* by Lew Wallace, from the 1978 reprint by Bonanza Books, and from *Costumes of the Greeks and Romans* by Thomas Hope, the Dover edition.
Text design by Judith Geary
Cover design by Ann Thompson Nemcosky

Library of Congress Cataloging-in-Publication Data

Bell, Albert A., 1945-
The blood of Caesar : a second case from the notebooks of Pliny the younger / Albert A. Bell, Jr.
    p. cm.
ISBN 978-1-932158-82-3 (trade paper : alk. paper)
1. Pliny, the Younger--Fiction. 2. Tacitus, Cornelius--Fiction. 3. Rome--History--Domitian, 81-96--Fiction. I. Title.

PS3552.E485B56 2008
813'.54--dc22
                                        2007051907

First printing, June 2008
10 9 8 7 6 5 4 3 2

Acknowledgments

This has proved to be, without a doubt, the most difficult book I've ever written. The first book in this series, *All Roads Lead to Murder*, appeared in 2002. My editor and I planned to have the second one out a couple of years later and subsequent books on a regular schedule. I knew what the second book was going to be about. I even knew approximately how it would end. I just didn't know I would have so much trouble writing it. I had to stop work on it several times because I wasn't getting anywhere. During each hiatus, I wrote another book, then returned to this one. For a while, when I spoke at mystery conferences, people would ask when the next Pliny book was coming out. When they began asking *if* the next Pliny book was coming out, I knew I had to stop looking for ways to sidestep this project.

So, here is the next Pliny book. Writing it has given me some sense of what a woman goes through when she's in labor for thirty-six hours. I just hope the result is as satisfying.

Many of the characters in the book are historical persons. Further information about them can be found in the glossary. My biggest problem with terminology has been what to call the emperor. I wanted to stay true to Pliny's usage in his letters, and he does not begin to use the term we translate "emperor" until at least the mid-90s AD. This book is set in the summer of 83. At that time Pliny, like most people around him, used the term *princeps*, or "first citizen," when speaking of Rome's ruler. Although other writers of Roman historical mysteries use the term "emperor" indiscriminately, I felt I ought to use *princeps*, in spite of the awkwardness of an unfamiliar, italicized word appearing so often.

I am extremely grateful to my editor, Judy Geary, for her patience and encouragement during this long and trying gestation. I also owe much to Bob and Barb Ingalls, of Ingalls Publishing Group. My writers' group at the Urban Institute for Contemporary Arts in Grand Rapids, Michigan, has encouraged me even when I felt the book was going nowhere. Few writers, I daresay, are blessed with the kind of support I've gotten from the long-term members of that group—Steve B., Steve P., Patrick, Jane, Roger, Paul, Greg, Dawn, Nancy—and from the more recent members— Diana, Liz, Carol, Nate, Karen, Vic, Michael, Norma, Christine, and even from a few who have just passed through. All have had their impact.

For my aunt Betty,
in appreciation of her support and encouragement

THE BLOOD OF CAESAR

THE FIRST TO DIE under the new regime was the proconsul of Asia, Marcus Junius Silanus. His death was treacherously contrived by Agrippina, without Nero's knowledge. She was not provoked by Silanus' ferocity of temper. He was lazy, and previous rulers had despised him ... But gossip in the streets widely suggested that Nero, who was hardly more than a boy and had come to power only as the result of a crime, was less fit to rule than a mature, blameless aristocrat who, like Nero, was descended from the Caesars. For Silanus was a great-great-grand-son of the deified Augustus—*and this still mattered a great deal* (italics added).

Tacitus, *Annals* 13.1

I

"**This feels like a trap**," my friend Tacitus said, putting his hand on my arm.

He and I stopped beside the House of the Vestals and the dozen slaves accompanying us came to a halt.

"A trap? What are you talking about? We're in the middle of Rome." I looked around, fearing that I would see a gang of thugs emerging from the shadows. But surely not within sight of the Praetorians who guarded the steps leading up the Palatine Hill.

"There's nobody else here." Tacitus pointed to the foot of those steps, twenty paces or so ahead of us on the Nova Via. "Nobody else is going up to dinner. There's something wrong."

"Maybe we're just early," I said, glancing at the length of the shadows around us.

"Are you sure we've got the date right?" Tacitus asked.

I signaled to Aristides, my *nomenclator,* who handed me the invitation I had received that morning. The broken wax seal reading CAES DOM AUG GERM around the figure of a defeated barbarian still clung to the single sheet of papyrus. I unfolded it and read it over again:

> *G. Plinius Caecilius Secundus is invited to dine with Caesar Domitian in his house on the Palatine on the Ides of July at the tenth hour.*

"That's what mine says, too." Tacitus held his invitation next to mine. The same scribe had written both. "But where are the other guests?"

Just as one frightened soldier spreads fear through the ranks, Tacitus was undermining my confidence. From our vantage point I couldn't see much of the Forum, only the Lacus Juturnae and the temple of Castor and Pollux straight ahead of us. They lay almost deserted in the shadows cast by the late afternoon sun. By now most people had gone off to bathe and prepare for dinner. The prostitutes who plied their trade in the shadows of the temple showed no interest in the few unfortunate sycophants who'd failed to cadge an invitation to dinner somewhere.

"I don't like the looks of this at all," Tacitus said. "I tell you, it feels like a trap."

"By the gods, man. We've been invited to dinner with the *princeps*. You act like the Cyclops is beckoning us into his cave to devour us. What do you think is going to happen?"

"I don't know, and that's precisely what worries me." He craned his neck to look down the side street leading to the Via Sacra. "Caligula used to invite men to dinner after he had killed them. Then he'd pretend to wonder why they didn't answer his invitation."

I didn't see the connection. "Are you suggesting Domitian is as mad as Caligula was?"

Tacitus looked around at our slaves, who were making no effort to disguise their interest in our conversation. "No. No, of course not." Taking my shoulder, he drew me a few steps away from the slaves and lowered his voice. "But what if Domitian has invited us here to arrest us?"

"That's a bit far-fetched."

"No, it's not. He doesn't dare arrest Agricola, but he could arrest Agricola's son-in-law."

In the three months since we returned from Syria, where we became friends, I had learned how much Tacitus despised Domitian. He hated, on principle, anyone who ruled Rome like a king. And then Domitian recalled Tacitus' father-in-law, Julius Agricola, from the governorship of Britain and made it clear Agricola would receive no further appointments. Agricola's popularity, with the army and with the people, guaranteed his life, but everyone knew Domitian was insanely jealous of him.

And why not? Agricola had proved himself a better general than Domitian and, in the opinion of many, would make a better king, if Rome must have a king by whatever name and if that king could come from some family other than Caesar's. Vespasian and his sons had shown he could, even if he had to usurp the name of Caesar along with the power. The line of Julius Caesar and Augustus had to end sooner or later, just as so many noble families in Rome are dying out. I was my late father's only child and my uncle adopted me in his will because he had no children.

"You can't seriously believe Domitian intends to arrest you," I said. "People who are going to be arrested don't get invitations to dinner. They're rousted out of bed in the middle of the night by the Praetorians."

"If he's not going to arrest me—or worse—then *where are the other guests?*" He waved his invitation toward the empty street ahead of us.

For that I had no answer. As I stared up the Nova Via, a scrawny-legged plebeian in a ragged tunic made his way across it. The wretch would trade his wife and children, I knew, for the note I was carrying. And I would happily be relieved of something that suddenly felt more like a summons than an invitation.

Tacitus was right. There ought to be other people coming to dinner. I could not imagine any reason why Rome's ruler would want to have an intimate dinner with two obscure young equestrians, recently returned from holding minor provincial posts.

"I don't want to go up there," Tacitus said. "I'd rather leave Rome right now. Cross the frontier into Germany. Or maybe Parthia. Anywhere but the top of that hill."

"Are you mad? Where have you gotten such a strange notion?"

With his hand on my chest Tacitus pinned me against the wall of the House of the Vestals. Although he's nearly a head taller than I am, I don't usually feel that he looms over me. But at that moment I felt like I was facing a cut-throat in a dark alley. "You know I put no stock in religion, Gaius Pliny." His voice sank to a whisper and he put his face closer to mine. "But Julia consulted an astrologer this morning, to ask about us coming here. The seer said, if we climb that hill, our lives will never be the same again. I scoffed at that message until we got here and saw no one else going up to dinner."

The desperation in his voice frightened me. I pushed him away and tried to laugh it off. "Your wife wasted her time and your money. That response is as vague as any the Delphic oracle ever gave. It could prove true in several ways, not all of them bad."

"But few of them good."

"Be reasonable. We can't ignore an invitation from Domitian." I was trying to convince myself as much as Tacitus. "If you aren't on his list of enemies already, you would be after such an affront. And so would I."

"I'll wager your name has already been added. You're a friend of Agricola's son-in-law. That assures you a spot near the top of any such list Domitian draws up."

I must admit I had never thought of my friendship with Tacitus as posing any danger for me. "You're being overly dramatic about this. Perhaps the other guests have been invited to come a bit later. Domitian may just want to get acquainted with us."

"Why would he want to do that?"

"Why not? ... My uncle served his father loyally. Your father-in-law has enjoyed a distinguished career, even if he's out of favor at the moment. That could change."

"So you think this is Domitian's way of making peace with Agricola."

Like a drowning man, I grasped at anything that might keep me afloat. "Why shouldn't he want to get to know the next generation in both our families? He may have some new appointment in mind for us." I knew I would never win a case in court with such weak arguments. "In any event, we dare not ignore this invitation. And we can't be late."

I stepped out of the shadows and took a few steps up the Nova Via, waving for my slaves to follow me. Tacitus' slaves assumed they were being summoned as well. He could do nothing but fall in with us.

The street ran into the Forum at the point where the steps leading up the Palatine began. That was where we stopped. One of the Praetorians guarding the stairway approached us, his hand resting on the hilt of his sheathed sword. "May I help you, sirs?" The words were cordial, but his face—which had all the charm of a clenched fist—and his tone of voice said, 'You'd better have some business here or be on your way.'

We held out our invitations, as though offering a sop to a snarling watchdog. "I'm afraid it may be a mistake," I said.

The Praetorian looked up from reading the notes. "Not at all, sir." The menace was gone from his voice, but his expression had not softened. "You and Cornelius Tacitus are expected. Please, go on up. Someone will meet you on the stairs to escort you in."

Once we were on the steps I said, "See, we got past the guards with no trouble."

"But will they let us pass when we're going the other way? What do you suppose would happen if we tried to leave right now?"

I rolled my eyes in disbelief at his unreasoning suspicion, but I knew we didn't dare turn around.

The marble steps up the hill were slick from the rain of the last two days and the morning's drizzle. Although the sun was trying to break through the clouds, the sky threatened more rain by evening.

"Let's hope the rain holds off until we can eat and get home," I said, hoping to keep any conversation on a safe topic, if one can find such a thing in Rome.

"You don't like traveling *in* the water any more than *on* it, do you?"

"As I've told you, my friend, water belongs in two places—in a bath and mixed in wine."

We fell silent as we concentrated on negotiating the steps. If we had been wearing just tunics, as our slaves were, it would have been less difficult. But our dining gowns threatened to trip us and fling us face-first on the stone. We finally gathered them up like women do to avoid dragging them in the filth in the streets.

We were halfway to the landing when Tacitus asked, "Have you been up here before?"

"Only once, ten years ago. My uncle brought me with him when

12

Vespasian appointed him procurator of Hispania Tarraconensis. It looks quite different now from what I remember."

"I would expect so. Domitian has turned the Palatine into the busiest building site in Rome." His tone made the statement an accusation.

"But every *princeps* has built something up here—a new house or an addition to an older structure."

Tacitus said nothing. What could he say? I was right. Augustus, our first *princeps*, lived atop this hill in a house no grander than any other Roman nobleman's. Domitian, by pushing all other property owners off the hill, had made room for what would be the largest house in the city, complete with its own arena for games and shows. With the workmen done for the day, the scaffolding and the unfinished walls of his edifice loomed so high into the mist that we could barely make out the tops.

"Look at that," Tacitus said in disgust. "He's extending the Palatine into the very heavens. This reminds me of the giants that Ovid talks about, piling mountains together to reach the kingdom of the gods. Someone should read that story to Domitian, to remind him of the disaster that struck them at the end."

"Someone should remind you of how unwise it is to talk like that—anywhere in Rome, but especially here."

We finally reached a landing where three or four people could stand. A slave—the most perfectly proportioned dwarf I've ever seen—greeted us there. His voice was high, child-like.

"Welcome, my lords. If you'll follow me, I'll take you to the dining room."

The Palatine is not much higher than any of Rome's other hills, but it is steeper. We were breathing hard by the time we reached the door of the house. My uncle had difficulty with his breathing throughout his life, perhaps because he was so heavy. On those occasions when he had business on the Palatine he was carried up the steps in a chair, as I was when I accompanied him. Now that I had made the climb myself, I felt sympathy for the slaves who bore such a burden all the way up here.

"Please, rest here for a moment," the dwarf slave said.

Tacitus was panting as he put his hand on my shoulder to steady himself. "That little imp's not even breathing hard," he whispered. "How does he do it?"

The dwarf did seem unaffected by the ascent. "My lord Domitian knows the approach to his house is arduous," he said. "He suggests that his visitors pause here, have something to drink, and enjoy a splendid view of the city."

He clapped his miniature hands twice and two slave women appeared from somewhere behind us. One carried drinks for our slaves, who were sitting on the steps below us. The one who approached Tacitus and me carried a tray with two cups of wine on it. She must have been German, with her blonde hair, broad hips and full breasts. Tacitus eyed her appreciatively as she served us. She was the type of woman he prefers—when he prefers a woman.

"If you don't require anything else, my lords," the dwarf said, "I will make certain everything is ready for your arrival."

As he and the slave women disappeared into the house Tacitus sipped his wine and shook his head slowly. "Something is very odd here. Don't you feel it yet?"

I grabbed his gown and pulled him over to me so I could lower my voice to a whisper. "Yes, you've convinced me. There is something odd going on! I would even call it downright peculiar. But I wouldn't discuss it in an audible voice right on the *princeps'* doorstep."

"Who's going to hear us? There's no one within earshot except our slaves."

"My dear Tacitus, you know as well as I do that in Rome there's always someone within earshot."

I released my grip on his gown and he straightened it. I took another sip of my wine, the best Falernian I'd every had, and raised my voice. "We were given an opportunity to enjoy the wine and the view. Let's do that. You must admit, both are superb."

Spread out below us lay the Forum, the heart of Rome since the city's foundation. I had looked down on it from other hills. My own house sits on the Esquiline, which is farther from the Forum but about as high as the Palatine. The Palatine, though, offers a view of the Forum that only the most privileged birds enjoy. The sun, low in the sky behind us, managed to part the clouds for a moment and lit up the glistening, red tile roofs as though they had been polished by a legion of slaves.

"A panorama of Rome's history lies at our feet," I said firmly enough that any eavesdropping imperial spy could hear me. "The temple of Saturn—as old as Rome itself. The Senate house across from it. And the Basilica Aemilia, where old Cato used to pontificate." I pointed at each structure as I named it. "The house of the Vestal Virgins here below us and the temple of Jupiter Stator at the other end of the Forum—they're ancient but just as solid as the day they were built."

"I agree," Tacitus said. "The Forum is Rome's history written in stone. And its future as well."

"What do you mean?"

He pointed to one structure after another, jabbing his finger angrily. "There's the Basilica *Julia.* Behind the Senate house is the Forum of *Julius.* And down that way is the temple of the deified *Julius.* Oh, and let's not forget the Forum of *Augustus* across the way and the arch of *Augustus* below us. Do you see the pattern emerging?"

I grasped his point, but I was more concerned about someone emerging from the doorway to our left and getting it as well. He was not being subtle.

"There," Tacitus went on, warming to his topic, "is the temple of the Penates, the city's ancient household gods, but it's now overshadowed by the Forum of *Vespasian*. And at that end of the old Forum are the arch of *Titus* and the baths of *Titus* and *Vespasian's* amphitheater. Look at it, Gaius Pliny! Rome's past is surrounded by the buildings of our rulers, just as surely as the army lays siege to a city."

I looked at him as though I'd never seen him before. He was speaking with a fervor I'd heard only in some of the religious fanatics we encountered during our time in Syria.

"Am I too old-fashioned, too *republican*, for you?" he asked.

I took a sip of wine to calm myself. "You know that, on some level, I sympathize with you, but my uncle taught me to be a pragmatist. Since the time of Augustus, Rome has been ruled by a king, even if no one dares to use that word openly. We've lost the freedom to speak our minds on some subjects, but we live secure from the chaos of the late Republic."

"And you're content with that bargain?"

"What would life be like without a *princeps*? You're old enough to remember the fighting that erupted after Nero died and there was no one to succeed him. If we'd been standing here then, we would have seen part of Rome itself in flames. Vespasian restored order and we've enjoyed fifteen years of peace."

"Under an iron-fisted dynasty."

"Things have changed. No one denies that. But can't our future be as glorious as our past?" I turned to gaze back out over the Forum. "I think if our enemies were to stand on top of this hill, they would be so overawed that all resistance to us would cease."

"I think our greatest enemy lives on top of this hill," Tacitus said softly, raising his cup to his lips to keep our slaves from hearing him.

I gasped. "Great Jupiter, man! If you keep talking like that, you won't have to worry about whether you're connected to Agricola or not. You'll bring disaster on yourself and everyone around you."

As I stepped away from Tacitus I noticed one of my slaves pointing unobtrusively to something behind me. I turned around, expecting to find myself staring at the point of a Praetorian's sword. It was a relief to discover nothing more alarming than a man with a gray beard. He looked foreign, although his dress was entirely Roman. The narrow stripe on his tunic placed him in the equestrian class to which Tacitus and I belong. From his dark skin and hooked nose I guessed his origins to be eastern. From the tiredness—or was it sadness?—in his eyes I placed his age at about fifty.

"Forgive me for startling you," the man said, his voice deep but soft, the voice of a man who has learned that it's safer not to speak loudly. "I am Flavius Josephus. I assume you are Gaius Pliny and Cornelius Tacitus."

"I'm Pliny," I said, wondering how much of our conversation he had overheard.

Josephus stroked his beard. "Ah, Pliny! I greatly admire your uncle's work. I hope we'll have a chance to discuss it during dinner."

"I'm always happy to talk about my uncle's work." Especially if it would draw attention away from Tacitus' reckless comments. "Do you know how many others have been invited tonight?"

"Only one."

I waited to hear a name, but he didn't offer one.

"Do you dine with the *princeps* often?" Tacitus asked.

"Not as often as I did with his father or his brother, but on occasion."

I knew Josephus only from my uncle's discussion of his history of the Jews' rebellion against Rome in Nero's last years. Josephus took an active part in the war until he deserted his troops at a critical juncture, surrendered to Vespasian, and, like a manumitted slave, took on the family name, Flavius. His own people despised him as a self-serving coward who abandoned his homeland, his religion, and his family for the security of life as a lap-dog. He now lived in an apartment in the *princeps'* house.

"Is Ajax escorting us?" Josephus asked. "He's the dwarf, my lord Domitian's newest and most exotic pet." His voice betrayed the resentment of a displaced favorite.

I nodded as the door opened and the dwarf slave reappeared. We followed him inside. As in any Roman house we entered an atrium, but a far grander one than I could ever imagine. The walls were the height of a basilica. Scaffolding stood in place for the artists who were repainting the frescos in the bolder, darker colors so popular now. I could hear the slaves whispering in awe behind us. My own atrium, which had just been repainted, looked like a smoke-stained peasant's hut by comparison.

"This was built by Caligula," Josephus said, "when he enlarged Tiberius' house. It had to be on this scale because that wall"—he pointed to our left— "is part of the temple of Castor and Pollux. Caligula incorporated it into his house and cut that door in the wall to pander to his delusion that he was a god himself. The walls have been repainted several times. As you can see, our lord Domitian is putting up scenes of his recent triumph across the Danube."

Tacitus snorted derisively and I glared him into silence. Everyone knew Domitian had sat on the Roman side of the Danube while his troops massacred a few disease-ridden German villages. The Senate awarded him the name Germanicus and voted him a triumph. All of this so he could rival Julius Agricola.

"Are you going to write a history of that German campaign?" Tacitus asked Josephus.

Josephus smiled modestly. "I'll leave that to someone who was there to see it."

Tacitus leaned over to me and whispered, "Well, that eliminates Domitian."

With Praetorians at every door and at strategic points in between, we passed from the atrium into a peristyle garden that was on a scale with the rest of the house. The center of the garden was decorated with a fountain instead of a *piscina*. Sea nymphs cast in bronze spewed water from every possible orifice, a memorial to Caligula's crudity. On the other side of the garden, in what would have been the rear wall of a typical Roman house, we went through a door into another atrium, this one of more human proportions.

"This is Tiberius' original house," Josephus informed us. "I'm sure you know the story of the antagonism between Tiberius and his mother, Livia."

At the mention of some juicy historical tidbit Tacitus stopped gawking like the country mouse in Horace's fable. He reads more history than I do. My tastes run to rhetoric and poetry. I've not even read all of my uncle's historical works. Tacitus has, along with some of his notes, since our return from Syria.

Now my friend was eager to display his knowledge. "When Augustus died," he said, "and his step-son Tiberius took power, he built this house because his mother, Livia, was still living in Augustus' house."

"Yes ... Exactly." Josephus' face showed pleasure at finding someone who enjoyed historical gossip as much as he did, mixed with disappointment that his listener could rival him at his own game. He went on quickly. "Tiberius couldn't force her out because of her status as Augusta, the widow of the deified Augustus. So he built his own, much grander, house next door."

At the rear of this atrium we were led into a *triclinium* of normal size where three couches were arranged around a single table. Tacitus and I exchanged a glance. It looked like we were going to have a most intimate dinner—us, Josephus, the mystery guest, and the *princeps*. The only thing that puzzled me more than our presence was Josephus'.

Without being told, Josephus took a place on the lower couch. Tacitus and I started to join him there, but the dwarf stopped us.

"If you please, my lords," he said, pointing to the middle couch. He directed me to the low place on that couch.

I eyed the guest of honor's position with increasing apprehension. "There must be some mistake," I said.

"Those are my instructions, my lord. You and Cornelius Tacitus are to have the middle couch and you are to have the low place."

Tacitus and I reclined on the couch, looking at each other like men who know a trap is going to be sprung but don't know whether it will happen sooner or later. Nothing so obvious as the sword of Damocles hung over our heads, but the prediction of Julia's fortune-teller rang in my ears. Our slaves stood behind us as a flock of imperial servants entered the room. Some took their places around the spot Domitian would occupy. Others brought bowls of water, removed our sandals and washed our feet. Josephus was tended by a single slave, a woman almost as old as he was. Two slaves placed silver platters of bread, cheese, olives, and mushrooms on the tables in front of our couches. Our slaves gave us our napkins and we began to eat.

A few minutes later the dwarf escorted another guest into the triclinium and showed him to the middle place on the high couch. His height was somewhere between mine and Tacitus', but he was already showing the girth of a man who had spent his life in self-indulgence. His hair was blacker than it was a month ago, the last time I saw him. A group of the most handsome and beautiful slaves one could imagine, clothed in tunics of linen and silk in a rainbow of colors, trailed behind him. I had considered my dining gown the rosy red of dawn until I compared it to his slaves'.

At the sight of this man, Tacitus choked on an olive because he recognized the one person in Rome whom I regarded as an implacable enemy—Marcus Aquilius Regulus.

Regulus, one of the most powerful—and, to my mind, most sinister—men in Rome, employs a web of spies in other people's households and in any public place where useful information might be unearthed. He wielded enormous influence under Nero, who let Regulus do the dirty work of destroying anyone who posed the slightest threat to his regime. Regulus and my uncle frequently found themselves on opposite sides in court as my uncle tried to defend Regulus' victims, who were usually guilty of nothing more than being rich. If they were convicted, Regulus received a quarter of their confiscated wealth. In spite of all my uncle and others could do, Regulus became a wealthy man.

When Vespasian came to power my uncle managed to convince him that Regulus was a pernicious influence. Finding the *princeps'* door shut in his face, Regulus never forgave my uncle. I inherited that enmity and I prize the legacy. Vespasian's older son, Titus, kept the door barred to Regulus during his short reign. But it looked like Domitian, the younger son, had forgotten the lesson. Regulus was back in his accustomed place at the *princeps'* elbow.

Now I knew Tacitus was right. We had walked into a trap.

Regulus lives on the Esquiline hill, but higher up than I do and his house fronts on a different street, so I can avoid running into him. He greeted me the way he greets everyone, as though I were his oldest, dearest friend. The man was so unctuous I was surprised he didn't slide right off the couch.

"Friend Pliny, it has been some time since I've enjoyed your company."

I've never enjoyed yours, I thought, but I said, "Service in the provinces drew me away this past year, Marcus Regulus. But I'm sure you knew that."

He popped a mushroom into his gaping maw. "I hope we'll have a chance tonight to hear about your year in Syria. Perhaps sort out all the rumors surrounding your exploits. I seem to hear something new at every dinner I attend, especially about your return trip." His lowered eyebrows emphasized the menace in his voice.

I glared at Tacitus. "Are you encouraging the growth of these rumors?"

He smiled slyly. "A man has to pay for his dinner. I can't compose witty epigrams like your friend Martial, so I deal in what coin I have."

Before I could say anything else, Domitian entered, walking unsteadily and followed by a dozen Praetorians, who dispersed themselves around the room, except for two who remained immediately behind him. He brought only three slaves with him—all female and all wearing diaphanous gowns that emphasized, rather than concealed, their bodies. We started to stand, but Domitian waved us back down.

"Please, no need for formality tonight," he said with a belch.

He was taller than I'd expected, having seen him prior to this only at a distance. Or maybe it was just in comparison to the dwarf at his side. His complexion was ruddy and his face not particularly imposing. Large, weak eyes in an oversized head were his most remarkable feature. He reclined next to Regulus, in the host's place on the high couch, and picked up the cup of wine that a slave had waiting for him. The dwarf sat on the floor in front of the couch, getting a pat on his head from Domitian.

I almost froze when I realized I was close enough to the *princeps* to reach out and ... By the gods! I was actually thinking about what I could do if I had a knife hidden under my gown. And I could have one. No one had searched me. I was as close to Domitian as Brutus had been to Caesar. *This is what comes from spending so much time with Tacitus.*

Domitian drained his cup. As he held it out for a slave to refill he turned his face full on mine and smiled. "If you were to kill me, Gaius Pliny, you wouldn't get off your couch alive." He waved his cup broadly toward the Praetorians at attention around the room, sloshing some of his wine.

I could hardly breathe. Surely I hadn't been thinking aloud! Was there something in my expression? "My lord, I assure you— "

"Relax, my dear Pliny." He reached over and patted my arm. "It's what everyone thinks the first time they get this close to me. I can see it in their faces. I'm very good at reading people's faces, almost their very thoughts. It's a gift, a life-saving gift. Someday I may encounter a man crazy enough to sacrifice himself to rid the world of me. Someone with a grudge. Someone like ... the son-in-law of Julius Agricola. But not to-night. I can see it in his face."

Tacitus went rigid, but he kept his voice controlled, calm. I could tell he was measuring his words as carefully as a stone mason chipping away at the last block that must fit precisely, with no margin for error. "Caesar, my father-in-law has never spoken or acted disloyally toward you. He cast his lot with your father before the outcome of the civil war was clear. You've never had reason to doubt his loyalty or mine."

Domitian waved his hand. "Pssh! If I thought for a moment that I was in any danger from either of you, you would never have set a foot on that first step coming up from the Forum. But perhaps my attempt at humor was strained. Please, let's relax and enjoy our meal."

He snapped his fingers and slaves brought in the *gustatio*—boiled eggs, oysters, and radishes cut into delicate patterns. I was pleased to see his tastes, like mine, ran to simpler, lighter foods, although—being the *princeps*—he couldn't resist showing his power over even this most basic part of life. The oysters were served in bowls of ice, brought down, no doubt, from the peaks of the Apennines. It would never have occurred to me to serve them in this odd way, but I couldn't refuse to eat them. I was surprised to discover that the chill enhanced the flavor.

"Now, tell me," Domitian said as we began to eat, "how do things stand in Syria?"

"My lord," I said with great hesitation, "I'm sure you've had reports from the governor. He would be able to see the situation in its entirety much better than Tacitus or I. We held the most junior positions."

I knew that Domitian, once a year, held a large dinner to welcome back higher-ranking provincial officials and to thank them for their service. I had never heard of him questioning two men of such low rank as

Tacitus and I. Tacitus must be right. Domitian had set a trap and he was driving us closer to it.

"The governor of a province," Domitian said, "is primarily interested in convincing me that he's the best governor since Rome first set foot on conquered soil. I think you and the son-in-law of Agricola might have a more disinterested view."

I didn't believe him for a moment, but I saw the futility of further protest. "I would describe the province overall as tense, my lord." Tacitus nodded his agreement.

"And what is the source of this tension?"

"Refugees from Judaea are not well accepted in Syria, my lord. The provincials, especially the Arabs, seem to despise the Jews as much as the Jews dislike them."

"Though an outsider," Tacitus put in, "cannot distinguish one from the other, Caesar, except in the baths."

"How curious," Domitian said. He turned to Josephus. "Why do the Jews and their neighbors dislike one another so much?"

Josephus stroked his beard. "It goes back to the origins of both peoples, my lord. The Arabs claim descent from Ishmael, an illegitimate son of Abraham, founder of the Jewish nation. They resent the Jews for being the genuine heirs and the Jews resent them as usurpers."

"Usurpers of what?" Domitian asked with a laugh, which Regulus echoed. "Some arid patch of land without even one navigable river?"

"I believe you've just described Greece, my lord," Josephus said. I barely suppressed a smile as he continued. "Whatever it looks like to an outsider, Judaea belongs to the Jews and they have given their lives to hold on to it against Assyrians, Egyptians, Babylonians, Persians, and Greeks."

"*Some* of them have given their lives," Regulus said, provoking a smirk from Domitian and a deep blush from Josephus.

"But, in spite of their 'valor'," the *princeps* said, "now we Romans have it." He clenched his fist.

"Others have held it for a time, my lord, but the Jews always get it back," Josephus said in a softer voice. Even the lap dog could nip at his master's fingers now and then. "King David reigned in Jerusalem before Romulus and Remus were born. Time has taught the Jews patience."

"Patience," Regulus snorted, "is a mask behind which the defeated hide their cowardice."

Domitian patted Regulus' shoulder clumsily in approval. "Oh, a neatly crafted aphorism! Now, my dear Josephus, you saw with your own eyes the devastation which my father and brother unleashed on Jerusalem. Not one stone of your temple was left standing on another. Surely you don't think the city can rise again."

21

"My lord, when Rome in its infancy was still ruled by Etruscan kings, the Babylonians conquered Jerusalem and left it in ruins. And yet, barely two generations later, before Rome established its Republic, the city had risen from the ashes."

Domitian took another drink, something he'd apparently been doing for a while before he joined us in the triclinium. "A city rises from the dead," he muttered. "Fascinating concept."

I glanced over my shoulder at Tacitus. His expression told me he was also wondering why we were pursuing this topic of conversation.

"What do you think, Marcus Regulus?" Domitian said. "Can we construct a syllogism?"

Regulus' mouth dropped open, showing us the egg he was chewing. "I'm sure you can, my lord," he sputtered. "You are the *princeps*, after all."

"Yes, so I am." Domitian giggled. "Dear Regulus, how do you endure to have the smell of my arse in your nostrils all day? Now, let's see. A syllogism we must have." He stroked his chin and looked at the ceiling for a moment. "First proposition: People make up a city. True?"

We all nodded.

"Second proposition: A city can rise from the dead. True?"

Again we all concurred, not daring to look at one another, lest we have to admit what we all must have been thinking: this drunken lout was the ruler of the Roman world, the man who held our destinies in his hands.

Domitian pointed to spots in the air. "City ... city. The middle terms of the syllogism agree. Ergo, people can rise from the dead!" Beaming, he turned to me. "What about you, Gaius Pliny? Do you think people can rise from the dead?"

"That would be ... a valid inference from the ... premises you've stated, my lord." My chest was so tight I could hardly breathe. He was driving me closer to the trap, I was sure, but I still couldn't tell what it was or why he wanted me in it. "I can't disagree with your logic."

"No one can, dear Pliny. I'm the *princeps*." He slapped his hand on his couch, making us all jump. "But your uncle was a student of nature. He recorded extraordinary events. Did he ever hear of a man rising from the dead?"

"I'm not sure, my lord. I haven't yet had time to read all of his work."

"I have," Josephus said. "Your uncle recorded a few instances of people presumed to be dead but who awoke or were revived during their funerals. Including one poor man who woke up after the pyre had been lit and no one was able to get him off, so he was burned alive."

"Now *that* would have been something to see." Domitian flopped on his back and pretended to be wrapped tightly in grave clothes. "Help me! Help me!" he squeaked.

Regulus was the only one who laughed.

Domitian rolled over onto his stomach and took a sip of wine. "But someone being mistaken for dead is not quite the same as someone being indisputably dead for a lengthy period of time—say, cremated or the body tossed into the Tiber—and then being alive again, is it?"

"No, my lord, it's not," I said.

"There are cases in the Jewish holy books," Josephus put in, "of people rising from the dead. For instance, the prophet Elijah—"

"Speak to me when you're spoken to," Domitian snapped. "Like my other servants."

Josephus' shoulders slumped, the gesture of a slave who'd been cuffed repeatedly.

"The Jews' holy books should have perished along with their holy city," Regulus said. Tacitus cleared his throat.

"What is it, son-in-law of Agricola?" Domitian asked.

"Well, Caesar, don't the Christians claim their leader was raised from the dead after being crucified?"

"The Christians?" Domitian looked addled, whether from the wine or from this unexpected turn in the conversation, I couldn't tell. "Aren't the Christians some sort of renegade Jew? Josephus, on this topic you have permission to speak."

"Thank you, my lord." Josephus washed down his pride with a large gulp of wine. "Yes, the Christians began as part of Judaism, a school not unlike the Pharisees. But they have broken off from the main body because of the claim that their prophet was resurrected."

"Do they offer any proof?" Regulus asked.

"Some witnesses say they saw him, mostly hysterical women and illiterate fishermen."

"Can we even be certain he was dead?" Domitian asked.

"He was crucified, Caesar," Tacitus said. "How could he not be dead?"

"Men have been known to pass out from the pain," Domitian said, "then come to after they're taken off the cross. They have to be dispatched by the soldiers conducting the execution."

"I suppose that could have happened in this case, Caesar," Tacitus said. We all nodded in agreement.

"So," Domitian said, "although it seems logically demonstrable that a man could rise from the dead, we can't seem to find any sure instance of such a thing happening. Would that be a fair assessment?"

"Certainly, my lord," Regulus said. The rest of us murmured our agreement.

"Then why," Domitian said in a petulant voice, "have I heard stories, since I was a boy, of Nero returning from the dead?"

Silence.

"Why is that?" Domitian's voice rose. "I want someone to give me an answer."

"It may be, Caesar," Tacitus ventured, much to the relief of the rest of us, "because the only witnesses to Nero's death and the burning of his body were a few of his personal slaves."

"The young man is correct, my lord," Josephus added. "Nero did not have a public funeral. Under such circumstances rumors find fertile ground. The common people will believe anything. A few months after Nero's death a man who strongly resembled him appeared in the province of Asia and stirred up quite a tumult until he was captured and executed."

Domitian started to say something but was interrupted by a man appearing at the door of the triclinium. When the Praetorians blocked his way, Josephus said, "He's from the archives, my lord." Domitian signaled for the man—a low-ranking servant, to judge from his clothes— to be admitted.

"Forgive me, my lords," the man said, "but something awful has happened. Nicanor requests that Josephus come to the archives at once."

"What's the matter?" Regulus said with a chuckle. "Somebody knock over an ink pot?"

"No, my lord. Someone's been hurt. I believe he's dead."

"Dead?" Josephus' alarm seemed genuine. "My lord, if you'll excuse me ... "

"Yes, of course," Domitian said. As the slave attending Josephus helped him put on his sandals, the *princeps* added, "For that matter, why don't we all go? This sounds more interesting than the entertainment I had planned for the evening."

As we sat up and slipped on our sandals I whispered to Tacitus, "You were right. This is a trap, and we're being driven right into it."

II

THE FIVE OF US, accompanied by a troop of Praetorians and slaves, hurried back the way Tacitus, Josephus and I had entered. The colorful silk of Regulus' slaves caressed the leather and silver of the Praetorians. Even Ajax the dwarf tagged along, running to keep up with us. Domitian's steady stride showed no trace of the influence of the wine he'd been drinking. Or had appeared to be drinking.

We turned right as we came out of the house and followed a walkway to the temple of Apollo. A passageway beside that temple opened into the portico in front of the libraries that Augustus built on the western edge of the Palatine, which we were now approaching.

Each *princeps* has added to the archives which Augustus established, separate from the public records stored in the Tabularium at the base of the Capitoline hill. Exactly what the imperial archives might hold I could only speculate, since access to them was closely guarded. It seemed safe to assume they would contain personal correspondence. Beyond that ... Did imperial spies file reports, like provincial administrators?

Could there be something in there worth dying for?

The rain had resumed but we kept dry under the colonnade. Even the small trees, which added a sense of height to the buildings, seemed weary of the rain, their branches drooping from the weight of the moisture. The air itself felt like a heavy blanket draped on my shoulders. If the rain kept up at this rate, the lower parts of the city would soon start flooding.

I couldn't have walked with Domitian and Regulus if I had wanted to. The Praetorians encircled the two of them. Even Regulus' gaudily dressed slaves had to fall back. I found myself walking between Tacitus and Josephus. My slaves and Tacitus', out of habit, formed a ring around us, even though there was no crushing throng from which to protect us, and they could offer no protection against the Praetorians.

"I don't understand," I heard Josephus say, more to himself than to me, the way older people sometimes start talking to themselves. I've even noticed my mother mumbling under her breath recently.

Since I didn't understand what was happening either, I decided to turn Josephus' musings into a conversation. "What don't you understand, sir?"

He looked up in surprise. "What? Oh, I'm just not sure why I was summoned. Nicanor is in charge of the archives. I do spend most of my time there, working on my books, and he sometimes asks me about things, but I have no official position. If someone's been hurt, it's Nicanor's responsibility to look into it. There was no need to interrupt our dinner. And certainly no reason for this ... this parade."

That term was appropriate, I thought as I looked around me. We had soldiers, we had people in bright costumes—all we needed was a crowd lining our route and waving to us.

Our procession came to a halt in front of Augustus' library. The building is actually two basilicas side-by-side, with a double clerestory. A row of Corinthian columns runs along the front, their green acanthus leaves tipped with gold. Two of the Praetorians swung open the outer doors, which appeared to be made of solid bronze. Scenes from the lives of Julius Caesar and Augustus were portrayed, one on each door, as though on the shields or breastplates of heroes in an epic poem. I caught glimpses of battles on land and sea—Pharsalus and Actium?—and of barbarians prostrate at the feet of Roman generals.

Homer or Virgil would have described these doors as hammered out by the gods. Before hearing what Tacitus had said outside Domitian's door and before meeting Rome's *princeps* in person, I might have enjoyed that poetic conceit, even though I don't believe in gods. Now, like a man finding it painful to open his eyes against the sun, I was squinting directly into the glare of imperial propaganda. I wanted to look away.

As we stepped into the library that feeling was reinforced. The vestibule was lined with statues and portrait busts of emperors and gods, as though one could not—should not?—make a distinction. A fresco on the far wall showed the founding of Rome by a Romulus who bore an unmistakable resemblance to Augustus.

Tacitus leaned over to me. "Funny, I'd always heard that the other twin's name was Remus."

To fight down the wave of anxiety sweeping over me, I took a deep breath. The smell of freshly rubbed papyrus and ink, mingled with the slight mustiness of the older documents, is as gratifying to me as culinary aromas to most people. Directly in front of us and to our left were the openings for the main rooms of the library. As in any library, they were long and narrow, with boxes stacked along each wall, open ends outward, holding the documents. Nailed to the top edge of each box was a list of the works contained in it. At the far end of the room closest to me I could see work tables and materials for the copyists.

But we weren't going into the main rooms. To our right was a door, which the slave who had summoned Josephus now unlocked. On a signal from their officer the Praetorians formed a line in front of the door. Only Domitian, Regulus, Josephus, Tacitus and I were permitted to enter, followed by the Praetorian officer. The slave locked the door behind us.

We stepped into a vestibule containing a table and writing materials. To our left opened two rooms of documents, running parallel to the main rooms in the public part of the library. I use the word 'public' advisedly. Only members of the Senate and other favored persons can get permission to use this library. No one outside the imperial household, I was sure, ever set foot in this part of it, the *princeps'* own archives.

So, why was I here?

"He's down there," the slave said, pointing down the last aisle of shelves, the one on the exterior wall of the building.

With Domitian and the Praetorian leading the way, we turned a corner. At the end of this row of bookcases an apse opened to our right. I could see the feet and lower legs of a man protruding from the apse. He lay face down, with scrolls and stray pieces of papyrus scattered about him. When we reached the end of the aisle we were met by a man anxiously wringing his hands. About forty, dark-haired and with a broad, flat nose, he bowed his head to Domitian.

"That's Nicanor, Domitian's freedman," Josephus told me. From his tone of voice he might as well have added 'officious ass.'

"Well, let's see what we have here," Domitian said. He motioned with his hand and the Praetorian kicked some of the scrolls aside and started to turn the man over with his foot.

"Please don't move him yet," I blurted out. Domitian and the Praetorian turned around, as surprised as I was by what I had said. I felt like an actor who had stumbled into the wrong play and was trying, without any notion of the plot, to make up lines that fit what he saw happening on the stage before him.

"What difference does it make?" Domitian asked irritably. "He's obviously dead."

"In a situation like this, my lord," I said slowly, "it is helpful to have the scene undisturbed."

He cocked his head, like a dog that doesn't understand something its master has said. "Helpful to whom? Certainly not to this poor wretch."

"To someone who's trying to understand what happened, my lord."

"Are you such a person, Gaius Pliny?"

I had no idea what my next line should be. Tacitus inserted one that made me cringe. "Pliny is practically a necromancer, Caesar," he said. "He can learn so much from a dead body that you'd think the victim had sat up and told you how he died."

A bully's smile played around the corners of Domitian's mouth. "That's what I've heard as well. Mestrius Florus says in his report that you have an uncanny ability to ferret out the truth in a case like this."

"And to make the most outrageous accusations," Regulus said from behind him, like a little boy who feels safe shouting insults over his big brother's shoulder.

Without looking at him, Domitian raised a hand to silence him and then motioned for me to approach the dead man. I caught my first glimpse of his purpose in staging this little drama, for I was certain that was what was happening. He had heard from Florus, governor of the province of Asia, about my part in an investigation in Smyrna a few months earlier. Now, for whatever reason, he was testing me to see if the report was true.

As the *princeps* looked from me to the dead man this trap began to feel like the mythical labyrinth. I had been drawn in far enough that I could no longer see the entrance behind me. Ahead of me I could hear the raspy breathing of the Minotaur, who looked for all the world like the *princeps*.

To give myself a little time I walked around the dead man. Domitian's and Regulus' eyes followed my every step as I took note of the man's position. He was short and heavy-set, his age difficult to determine. Clad in a workman's dirty tunic, he lay on his stomach, with his right leg straight and his left knee slightly bent. His left arm was under him, his right straight down beside him. His left cheek was on the floor. His mouth hung open, and his wide-spaced eyes were rolled back under the lids. With his puffy face, he wasn't a handsome man, even when alive. The back of his head displayed a sizeable wound, and his hair was matted with blood.

When I felt I could keep my voice steady I started with the most obvious question I could think of. "Who found him?"

"I did, sir," Nicanor said, stepping forward and bowing his head.

"This is my freedman Nicanor," Domitian said. "He oversees the archives."

I wished I could ask the *princeps* to step back and not interfere, but I had as much chance of doing that as I did of telling the dead man at my feet to rise and walk.

"Who is he?" I pointed to the body.

"His name is Maxentius, sir. He's a freedman."

"Please tell me how you found him and exactly what you saw."

Nicanor thought for a moment, looked at Domitian and then down the aisle, as though visualizing the scene again. Or trying to remember his lines. "I was making sure everyone was out before I left for the day. He was lying under a couple of the bookcases. I guess they toppled over on him."

That would account for the scattered scrolls, if that was what happened. "You set them back up, I gather."

"Of course. I had to see if I could help the poor man."

I could understand that impulse, but I wished he had left things where he found them. In some of his unpublished writings my uncle described his own investigation of a couple of murders, one among his slaves, another among his soldiers. He concluded that everything about the scene of a crime, even the placement of seemingly incidental objects, could help him understand what had happened there. Once objects were moved, that information was lost.

"What were Maxentius' duties here?"

"He did ... whatever he was told to do." Nicanor glanced nervously at Domitian.

"Why does that matter?" the *princeps* asked.

"I'm just wondering, my lord, why he was here, in this particular spot."

"Because, my dear Pliny, this is where the bookcases fell on him," Domitian said in exasperation.

"Yes, of course, my lord." What better logic could I expect from the mind which concocted that atrocious syllogism a few moments ago? "What's contained in the bookcases in this apse?" I asked, glancing at the lists of contents on the bookcases that hadn't been toppled. Claudius' name appeared on most of them.

"Letters! Reports!" Domitian snapped. "The same as in all the other damn cases."

Clearly I was trying the imperial patience, and I was not going to be able to conduct my inquiries the way I wanted to. Just as a trained animal in the arena must perform at its master's pace, I would have to do what I knew how to do within prescribed limits, stumbling where I might otherwise have moved gracefully. The result would be clumsy and inane, but that was the fault of the man holding the reins, not the animal.

I turned back to Nicanor, "So you saw Maxentius lying here and came over to help him."

"Ran over, as a matter of fact. But he was already dead."

"How did you know that?"

"He wasn't breathing or moving." Nicanor seemed insulted. "He was just lying under the bookcases. He wasn't making any effort to get out from under them."

"He could have been unconscious," Tacitus said from behind Josephus.

"Oh, does the son-in-law of Agricola have something to contribute?" Domitian asked over his shoulder.

"We have worked together before, my lord," I said. "One of us some-times sees what the other misses."

Domitian took Tacitus' arm and pulled him forward. "Son-in-law of Agricola, if you two are accustomed to work as a team, then get to it."

Tacitus, with his back to Domitian, gave me a rueful look, rolling his eyes. I wanted to tell him he should have kept his mouth shut, but, like an ox welcoming its yoke-mate, I was relieved to have someone alongside me to share this burden.

I knelt beside Maxentius and took a deep breath. The death smell, though not yet overpowering, was becoming noticeable at close quar-ters—not a stench yet, but an unpleasant staleness. I touched his face and his left arm. His skin was cold, his arm stiff. I examined the fingers of the hand which I could see. They told me this man had not led a pampered life. Lifting his tunic, I looked at his back and shoulders.

"I may not be a necromancer," Domitian said, looming over me, "but I do recognize the marks of a whip."

"Yes, my lord. From some time ago, before he was freed, no doubt." What Domitian didn't recognize, but I did, were the livid blotches on the man's back, especially on his shoulders and buttocks.

Tacitus knelt beside me, reluctantly. Although he had helped me a great deal in our earlier investigation, he prefers to keep his dead bodies at a safe distance—to be precise, the distance from his seat to the floor of the arena.

"See this?" I said, trying to bend the dead man's right arm.

Tacitus nodded and raised his eyebrows, acknowledging the signifi-cance of that stiff arm.

I knew what it meant because of what I had found in a collection of 160 scrolls I inherited from my uncle. In those scrolls he recorded things he felt it would be impolitic to publish, among them scientific obser-vations that run counter to the wisdom of our day. He recorded what happened to the bodies of soldiers and slaves after they died. Bodies cool and stiffen at a regular rate, he noticed, allowing for how cool or warm their surroundings may be. After about four hours, the muscles begin to stiffen. After a day and a half, they begin to relax again.

Although my uncle observed this phenomenon numerous times, he could offer no explanation for it. An old slave of mine, while prepar-ing my uncle's body for his funeral, told me it was because the spirit of the deceased was terrified by the monsters of the Underworld and could not relax and feel safe until it had crossed the River Styx and entered the Elysian Fields. No wonder Plato wanted nursemaids and their myths banished from his ideal state.

"I'd like to have him turned over," I said.

Domitian motioned to the Praetorian and the slave who had accompanied us. They rolled the dead man onto his back. I lifted his tunic and quickly inspected his body to see if he bore any wounds.

"What was this man doing back here today," I asked Nicanor, "since he wasn't a scribe?"

Nicanor's face showed how completely off guard he was caught by what I had deduced about the dead man as soon as I looked at his hands. I didn't look at Domitian, but I felt sure he wanted to know that I knew it.

"Not a scribe? Why, uh, sir, he was ... working, like the rest of us, don't you know."

"I believe he was ... repairing some bookcases," Domitian offered.

I directed my attention on Nicanor. I wasn't about to undertake an interrogation of the *princeps*. "Wouldn't it disturb your scribes to have someone hammering on the bookcases?" Which Maxentius couldn't have been doing, since there were no tools with him.

"Well, sir," Nicanor said, "on a cloudy day like this, don't you know, it's difficult for the scribes to copy anything, since we can't use lamps or candles. They spent most of the morning smoothing and lining pages for another day's work. We stopped work at the fourth hour."

"Why so early?"

"My lord Domitian instructed us to, sir."

"So no one was in here after midday?" I asked.

"I didn't think so, sir."

"But you didn't come back until a few moments ago to lock up?"

"Oh, I locked the door when we stopped work," he said with a nervous glance at Domitian. "I'm very careful about that, don't you know. And I always check it, the last thing before going to my quarters for supper."

"And you did not see Maxentius back here earlier in the day?"

"No, sir. I found him just before I sent for help."

"Why did you send for Josephus? He has no official position here, does he?"

"No, sir. But he works here so much ... I thought he might know better than I what to do."

"Did Maxentius have a key?" Tacitus asked.

"No, sir."

Like most slaves and former slaves, he offered only the information asked for. To get more, we had to ask more precise questions. "Who does have a key?" Tacitus continued.

"I have one, sir, and my assistant, Lysias."

Domitian heaved an impatient sigh. "Gaius Pliny, I have a key. What's the point of all these questions?"

I rocked back on my heels. Domitian had set a trap, as well concealed as a net covered with brush, and he had driven me right into it. Now, like an animal in the forest which has spotted the trap, I had reached the decisive moment. If I froze in fear, he could take his time springing the trap on me. But if he saw me flinch, ready to jump, he would close the net in an instant.

Two bad choices are the same as no choice.

Domitian glared at me. "Well, Gaius Pliny?"

"Forgive my hesitation, Caesar. I'm having difficulty understanding how this man could have died some time early in the morning—around the second hour—and yet have gone unnoticed by others in the archives."

Domitian's face showed surprise mixed with fear. "What makes you think he died in the morning?"

"It's not what I think, my lord. That's what his body tells me."

"Ah, yes, the necromancer speaks. Do you reveal your secrets?"

"Only to my acolytes, my lord." I meant it as a joke—a bold one at that—but Domitian seemed to accept it as a serious response.

"Well, then, does his body tell you *how* he died?"

He wasn't asking me for just any answer to that question. He wanted to see if I knew the right answer. "It says he was struck on the head by something sharp and heavy, my lord."

"These bookcases are heavy, and the corners are sharp," Tacitus said helpfully. "And there's a bit of blood on this one."

We stood and, with Domitian looking over our shoulders, Tacitus pointed to the corner of the top bookcase on the stack. "Well, that's clear enough then," the *princeps* said.

"So it might seem, my lord," I said. I knelt again and examined the wound on Maxentius' head. "But in addition to the blood in his hair, there is a reddish dust. There's no such dust on the bookcase."

"Where could it have come from?"

"From a brick, my lord. I think Maxentius was struck by a brick."

Domitian regarded me for a moment before he said, "But I don't see any bricks in here."

"He wasn't killed in here, my lord." Since there was no escape from the trap, I might as well speak my mind. Not speaking it wouldn't save me.

"And what leads you to that conclusion, Gaius the necromancer?"

I signaled to the Praetorian and the slave to turn Maxentius back over. Then I pulled up Maxentius' tunic to show the *princeps* what I had observed earlier. "These purple splotches on his shoulders and buttocks tell me that he lay on his back for a time after he died. Then he was moved in here and arranged in this position."

"Fascinating. Now, who could have done such a thing?"

"Someone with a key, my lord." I heard Tacitus gasp as I said it.

Regulus erupted like a long-dormant volcano. "You insolent pup! You're practically accusing the *princeps* of murder."

"Is that what you're doing, Gaius the necromancer?" Domitian's voice quavered with excitement, his eyes locking on to mine and not letting me look away.

"Certainly not, my lord. I've answered the questions that I can answer. For the rest of it, that's an investigation which should be conducted by your Praetorians. I don't have any authority in this matter."

"You didn't have any authority in Smyrna either," Regulus snapped.

Domitian held up a hand to quiet Regulus. "You're quite right, Gaius Pliny," he said. "You have no authority in this matter. I will have my men look into it."

"Then is there anything else you require of me, my lord?"

"No. This has been most informative." He glanced at Regulus.

No one said anything else until Josephus asked, "Shall we return to dinner now, my lord?"

"I'm too upset over this matter to eat," Domitian said. "It's quite distressing. If you'll forgive my rudeness, my servants will see that you have something to take home." He gestured to the Praetorian officer, who herded Tacitus, Josephus, and me toward the door. Regulus stayed at Domitian's side. The last I saw of them, they were examining the purple splotches on Maxentius' back, drawing up their garments to be sure they didn't touch the body.

* * * *

As we walked down the aisle I felt like Orpheus emerging from the Underworld. As long as I kept my eyes straight ahead, I told myself, I would be safe.

And yet such is my damnable curiosity that I couldn't help but glance at the lists of contents attached to each box of documents. This would, in all likelihood, be my only visit to the imperial archives. Why not learn a little something about them while I had the chance? But a little is exactly what the lists revealed. *NERONIS EPISTULAE* several said. Letters of Nero. To whom? About what? It's a curious, and sometimes frustrating, characteristic of Latin that the possessive case "of Nero" can mean letters which Nero wrote or letters written by others which belong to Nero.

The stacks of papyrus sheets came almost to the tops of the boxes. And in some of them scrolls—most of them missing the *titulus* which bore the title and author of the work—lay on top of the piles. Had some of Nero's letters been recopied into one document? Or had something else been tossed into the wrong box?

"How do you find anything in here?" I asked Josephus.

"It can be a challenge," the historian said. "I have two freedmen working with me. Sometimes it takes us an entire day just to sort through a single bookcase, looking at every document. It's appalling how much material is out of place."

"The same is true in my library," I said. "My uncle was an avid reader and collector of books, but, because of his phenomenal memory, he didn't worry about how he organized his library. He knew where his books were and what was in them. It took me and my scribes almost two years to sort through everything."

"Did you find many documents done in Tironian notation?"

"A few." The Tironian system of rapid writing was devised by Cicero's chief scribe. It consists of over four thousand characters. I'm fortunate to have a slave who has mastered it. "I thought it was used to take notes to be transcribed later."

"Sometimes, I believe," Josephus said, "it has been used to record things that weren't meant to be read by just anyone. The most personal letters, diaries, that sort of thing. Not that it makes much difference in what language or notation a thing is recorded. We often find the papyrus on the bottom of a case is already starting to decay. But you must have observed this in your own library."

"Yes. I sometimes wonder if we'll have any records left a hundred years from now."

Our slaves rejoined us in the vestibule of the library. Three of the Praetorians escorted us back to the head of the steps leading down to the Forum, where Domitian's slaves were waiting with so many baskets of food I wished we had come in a wagon. Clearly they had been preparing the baskets while we were in the archives. Domitian never meant for us to return and finish our meal.

Josephus accepted a single basket with a heavy sigh. How often can you insult a man before he can take no more? I wondered.

"It has been a privilege to meet you, young sirs," he said. "Gaius Pliny, I regret we did not have time to discuss your uncle's work, but I think he has found a worthy successor. The way you met the *princeps'* challenge was quite remarkable. Quite remarkable indeed." He leaned over and whispered in my ear, "I knew that man, Maxentius, was no scribe. I've never seen him in the archives. How could you tell?"

"Simply by looking at his hands."

"His hands?"

"They were calloused and had no ink stains on them. Turn your right hand palm up." I didn't want to touch him because I felt unclean after pawing Maxentius' body and I had heard in Syria that Jews—if he still considered himself one—have even stronger prohibitions against contact with the dead than we Romans do.

"I'm sure you bathed before coming to dinner, sir, but your thumb and first two fingers still bear traces of ink."

He chuckled. "I scrub myself raw and it won't come out."

"A scribe, or anyone who has done his own writing for any time at all, will be as permanently marked as if he'd been branded." That was a conclusion I had drawn from my own observation, not from my uncle's notebooks. "Or circumcised," I added.

Josephus looked at me, uncertain whether I was baiting him.

"Maxentius was a Jew," I said.

Josephus nodded in understanding. "One of those enslaved after the war, no doubt." He took his leave, shaking his head in bemusement.

Tacitus and I started down the steps. "So," Tacitus said, "Maxentius wasn't a scribe. But if he was a carpenter working on the bookcases, where were his tools?"

"You noticed that, too? The white material under his fingernails was plaster. That means he was most likely building Domitian's new house." I pointed to stacks of red bricks waiting for the masons. "For me the more important question is whether Domitian had him killed just to pose this test for us."

"But ... but why would he do that?"

"I can't begin to answer that question." The Praetorians at the bottom of the stairs saluted us as we passed. "If I try to, I'm afraid I'll be walking right back into Domitian's trap."

III

THE RAIN HAD STARTED again with renewed intensity after I went to bed—but not to sleep. The sky was still leaden at the second hour of the next morning. This mid-July soaking would spawn the diseases that would sweep over Rome in the heat of August. It would soon be time to move the household to my villa at Laurentium for a while.

The rain blowing into my atrium was not hard enough to threaten the freshly painted walls. The new frescoes depicted some of the exotic locales and unusual animals described by my uncle in his *Natural History*. I was pleased with the results, except that the hippopotami didn't in the least resemble my uncle's description. Not even the added realism of the rain improved their looks.

"So you're finally up." My mother's voice took me by surprise. I turned to see her coming out of a room on the opposite side of the atrium. Perhaps the dismal light was tricking me, but she looked smaller and frailer than she had even yesterday. "You missed the morning salutation," she said. I couldn't miss the disapproval in her voice.

"I'm sorry. I had a restless night." My servants have been instructed that, if I'm not up on time, it's because I haven't slept well and I'm not to be disturbed. I take the morning salutation seriously. If my clients are expected to don a toga and trek to my house at the crack of dawn, no matter what the weather, the least I can do is walk from my bedroom to the atrium to receive their greetings. I assumed my steward had seen to the distribution of the daily dole. "Did Demetrius take care of everyone?"

"Yes. And he was far too generous with your money."

Since the eruption of Vesuvius and my uncle's death four years ago she has become increasingly anxious about our family's finances, in spite of my regular assurances that all is well.

"And he sent everyone on their way," she said in a scolding voice, "as if they didn't have to do anything for the money."

"I have no need of their services today, Mother." I turned toward my tablinum, intending to go over more accounts and try to get my affairs back in order after a year away on provincial service. "In this weather I certainly won't be going to the Forum. Only the hardiest souls would be out on a day like this." As soon as the words left my lips someone pounded on the door, like an actor on his cue.

"There is at least one of those, it seems," my mother said. She kissed me on the cheek. "I'll leave you to your business." Summoning the slave girl who had been working with her, she withdrew into the back part of the house.

The knock was repeated, vigorously. A tardy client would hardly be so bold. Moschus, my doorkeeper, groused as he went to answer the summons. The old man complains more and more of aches in his joints. He groaned as he slipped the bolt and pulled the door open.

Through the open door stepped Tacitus, shaking himself like a dog and accompanied by three slaves. He wore a broad-brimmed traveler's hat and a leather cloak coated with animal grease to ward off the rain. In spite of his best efforts to keep dry, his wet brown hair was matted to his head. The rain had even washed away his sardonic smile.

"What on earth brings you out on a morning like this?" I asked. Tacitus is a man fond of his bed, even on a sunny morning.

"I needed to get away from my wife, and I wanted to see if you had given any more thought to our dinner with the *princeps* last night, particularly the … entertainment." He glanced suspiciously at his slaves and at Moschus.

"How can I think about anything else?"

"Do you still think it was staged solely for our benefit?"

Before answering I considered Moschus too. He lowered his eyes. He had been my uncle's doorkeeper for my entire life, so I could hardly assign him another position, but I suspected that in his old age he was finding it as difficult to control his tongue as his bladder.

"Let's talk in the tablinum."

"Good idea," Tacitus said. I stepped back to avoid a shower as he tossed his cloak and hat to Moschus. Tacitus' slaves took seats on the benches in the atrium.

"Have you had anything to eat?" I asked. When Tacitus shook his head I instructed Moschus to have a few leftovers from last night's dinner brought to us and to the slaves. We entered the tablinum and, as Tacitus sank into a chair, dripping all over everything, I closed the door, which I had had installed upon my return from Syria. Before that, my tablinum, like any other, had only a curtain over the entrance. Some things that happened on that trip had sowed enough seeds of suspicion in my mind that I wanted to be able to close and lock the room where I kept my most personal records.

"You look tired," I said. "Were you awake all night, like I was, worrying about what Domitian is up to?"

He yawned monstrously. "I hardly slept last night, but Domitian was only part of my problem."

"Oh? What else is bothering you?"

"It's Julia."

"What's wrong with your wife? I hope she's not ill."

"No, she's her usual energetic self. The problem is, I couldn't satisfy her last night."

"Couldn't satisfy ... ?" Tacitus' exploits in bed were the stuff of epic, at least as he related them to me. I could not imagine him being unable to satisfy his young wife.

"Don't take that the wrong way," he said. "I couldn't satisfy her curiosity about our dinner. She kept throwing questions at me." He mimicked a girl's voice. "'What did you eat? What was the *princeps* wearing? What did his triclinium look like? How were his slaves dressed?' She wanted me to chatter with her like a couple of slave girls in a Greek comedy."

"That must have been awkward, considering how much her father and Domitian hate one another." Tacitus' in-laws were living with him and his wife until they could find a house of their own in the city.

"That's just it. We couldn't talk about it in front of Agricola, but once we were alone, she unleashed the torrent. I felt like Pyrrha and Deucalion clinging to their raft for dear life as the flood waters raged about them."

I nodded sympathetically. "At least she wasn't asking you political questions."

"My dear Pliny, for Julia the issue isn't politics; it's fashion. Did you know that the way an imperial slave wears her hair—a *slave*, mind you—can influence how every woman in Rome wears hers? And there seems to be some sort of prize for being the first in our circle to ape a new style from the Palatine. She's planning a dinner now just so she can serve oysters on ice."

Someone knocked on the door, a hard rap followed by two soft ones, a signal used by only one of my slaves.

"Come in, Aurora," I said.

Aurora, the slave girl who attends to my personal needs, stuck her head in the doorway. "My lord, you asked for something to eat?" At my nod, she brought in a tray and set it on the end of my table that I hastily cleared. She departed with our thanks and an appreciateive gander from Tacitus.

"I still can't believe how beautiful that girl is," Tacitus said. "Pygmalion's creation could not have been any lovelier, any more perfect. And she never talks. What more could a man ask?"

Aurora is easily the most beautiful female slave in my household. Tall, with dark hair and eyes and olive skin and an exquisite figure, she is the daughter of a slave woman who was my uncle's mistress for many years, but she is not his daughter. We played together as children, but I find myself now in awe of her beauty. Since we outgrew the easy familiarity of childhood, she rarely speaks to me except to answer a direct question, and I find it difficult to converse with her about anything except her household duties.

"Have you coupled with her yet?" Tacitus asked in his usual direct fashion.

"I've told you I would never force myself on a slave woman."

"I don't think there would be any force involved, my friend. You apparently don't notice how she looks at you. Your uncle was quite happy with her mother. Why couldn't you ... ?"

"No." I poured us some wine and mixed in the water to avoid looking at Tacitus. Of course the thought of making love to Aurora occurred to me at least a dozen times a day. No man, not even a eunuch, could look at her without having such thoughts. But, knowing how much my mother had disapproved of the relationship between my uncle and Aurora's mother, I did not want to prolong that kind of conflict in the house for another generation.

"So you're just content to look and dream?" Tacitus said. "You ought to at least get her one of those gowns like Domitian's slave women were wearing last night."

Without answering I slid the tray of food toward him. I usually don't have much appetite in the morning, but the stuffed mushrooms, bread, and cheese Domitian sent home with us enticed me to take a few bites. My mother would be pleased. She often expresses her concern because I'm not as round as my uncle was. Corpulence will be my fate, I suppose, but I'd rather let it overtake me gradually and not rush to embrace it.

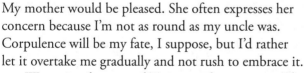

We ate in silence until Tacitus said, "I was afraid Julia would start up again this morning, so I left as soon as I could."

"Getting away from your wife is worth walking all this way in the rain?"

"Spoken like a man who's never had a wife."

"Come now. I don't know Julia well, but she strikes me as charming. You make her sound odious."

"Not odious, just boring." He wiped rain off his forehead with his arm. "A sweet but boring child. She was quite young when we married, you know, perhaps too young."

"Thirteen, I believe you said."

"Exactly. And for two of the five years we've been married I've been away on service. I feel like I hardly know her."

I had to laugh. When it comes to sex, Tacitus' only inviolable rule is that he won't couple with another man's slave. As he puts it, he won't plow in another man's field. "My dear Tacitus, you hardly know any of the women you sleep with. To say nothing of the boys."

"But that's entirely different. They don't expect anything of me."

I hated to ask, but I had to. "What does Julia expect?"

"Love notes." He grimaced. "Gifts given for no reason. I think she's been reading Ovid."

"Can't you do that sort of thing? You have a gift for words."

"What's the point? We're married. She doesn't understand that Ovid is talking about how to seduce someone else's wife, not your own. That's why Augustus banished him."

"What did you tell her about our dinner?" That question killed all the playfulness.

"There wasn't much to tell, was there? We barely had time for the gustatio before we were called away. And I certainly couldn't tell her about the dead man in the archives. Do you still think Domitian had him killed just to test you?"

"I think the whole evening was a test. What did we talk about at dinner?"

"Well, let's see. We started with the situation in Syria. Then we turned to the Jews. Then there was the business about cities rising from the dead and that ridiculous syllogism. That led to whether men can rise from the dead."

"And who turned the conversation to each topic?"

He studied the ceiling. "Domitian, now that you mention it."

"And it was all pointed toward that business of whether or not Nero was dead."

"But what does the dead man in the archives have to do with that?"

"That's what I'm still puzzling over."

"You don't think Domitian thought you could actually bring him back to life, do you?"

"Don't insult me or the *princeps*. I'm sure he's seen enough dead men to know they stay that way."

"Titus certainly did," Tacitus said.

"Do you believe the stories that Domitian killed him?"

Before Tacitus could answer Moschus knocked heavily and stuck his head in the room. "Excuse me, my lord, but three men are asking to see you."

"Do you know them?" One of his primary tasks was to be able to recognize people who have a valid claim on my hospitality.

"No, my lord. But one of them pressed his seal in this." He stepped into the room and held out a wax tablet for me to examine.

I gasped when I saw it. "Where is he?"

"Standing at the door, my lord. All three of them are."

"In the rain? You doddering old fool! Bring them in immediately!" He turned and started to walk out of the room. "Run!"

Tacitus questioned me with a look. I showed him the tablet and his eyes got even bigger than mine had when he saw CAES DOM AUG GERM encircling a figure of a fallen barbarian. "By the gods! The *princeps* is standing at your door?"

"In the rain," I said.

"What could he possibly want?" He grabbed my arm in alarm. "Do you think he's come to arrest you?"

I tried to squelch the panic that question raised. "That's ridiculous. Arrest me for what?"

"I'm sure that's what a lot of people have asked as they've been taken away."

"But he wouldn't come to my door himself, with only two men. And he certainly wouldn't knock and ask for permission to enter."

"Then what's he doing here? Did you steal any silver last night?"

With Tacitus on my heels, I hurried out to greet Rome's ruler. Three men—or, more accurately, one man followed by two others—approached across the atrium. They wore ordinary rain cloaks over tunics without even a narrow equestrian stripe on them. If I had passed them on the street I would have taken them for working men. Or a trio of cut-throats, if I looked a little closer. Domitian pushed his cloak back off his head as he stopped in front of me and the other two followed his example. One I recognized as the Praetorian officer from the archives last night. Sword handles protruded from under his cloak and his companion's as puddles of water began to collect around their feet. Tacitus' slaves huddled together in awe on one end of their bench.

"My lord," I said, "I apologize for the stupidity of my doorkeeper. He should have recognized you and escorted you in immediately."

The *princeps* beamed like a boy who's pulled off a great trick. "Nonsense. Isn't that the point of a disguise, not to be recognized? The man's doing his job. You don't want just anybody admitted to your lovely house." He looked around at the decorations in the atrium, which suddenly looked like a hovel to me. "These look fresh," he said, nodding toward my frescoes.

"Yes, my lord. Finished only three days ago."

"They're lovely." He walked over to the scene with the hippopotami and examined it closely. "Although your hippopotami aren't right. They're not really horses, you know."

"No, my lord. I intend to have them redone." Did I dare to ask him what he wanted? Or did I just have to wait until he decided to tell me? An unannounced visit from the *princeps* is unheard of. The etiquette of the situation isn't covered in the lessons given to young men of my social circle.

"But I see you have a visitor already," Domitian said. "I'm sorry to intrude."

"Tacitus was just leaving, my lord."

"Actually, I'd like for him to stay, even if he is the son-in-law of Agricola, that strutting, preening favorite of the senate and the people." His lip curled. "Let's talk in your tablinum." He tossed his wet cloak in Moschus' direction, not even looking back to see if the old fellow caught it, and headed for the room. The two Praetorians took up positions outside the door. There would be no eavesdropping on this conversation. Domitian ran a hand over the door itself.

"A wooden door? What do you need to keep hidden, Gaius Pliny? But, still, it's an innovation worth considering."

Tacitus and I followed the *princeps* into the tablinum, glancing at one another in amazement as he poked around in my shelves.

"This latrunculus board looks new," he said.

"It was a gift from a client of mine, my lord, upon my return from Syria."

"Do you enjoy the game?"

"Yes, I do, my lord. It challenges the mind rather than depending on a throw of the dice."

Picking up a couple of the smooth black and white game pieces, Domitian rubbed them between his fingers. "But sometimes the throw of the dice has more effect on our lives than all our careful planning."

"I suppose that's so, my lord." What else could I say? I didn't want to debate philosophy with the man who controlled the lives of everyone in Rome.

Domitian took my seat behind the table. Tacitus seemed as unsure how to behave as I was. The *princeps* isn't our king—although we all know he is a monarch—but Domitian insists on being called *dominus*, 'lord,' the word which our slaves use to address us. Slaves dare not sit in the presence of their masters without permission. Tacitus and I now stood before Domitian. I felt the same discomfort I had felt last night, calling him *dominus* to his face. Tacitus had evaded the issue, I'd noticed, by calling him 'Caesar,' a name that is becoming a title.

Domitian shuffled some pages of my accounts and read several. How could I ask the *princeps* not to pry into my private papers? Something on a page caught his eye. He picked it up and studied it more closely.

"A note from Musonius Rufus. Are you a friend of his, Gaius Pliny?"

"I met his son-in-law while I was in Syria, my lord. He asked me to bring a gift to Musonius when I returned. Musonius and I have been guests in one another's homes a time or two this summer." Actually, it was more like half a dozen times. I had grown quite fond of the white-haired philosopher.

"You know that man's a trouble-maker." Domitian glared at me over the note.

"I know some people regard him as ... eccentric, my lord."

Domitian snorted. "That's being kind. My father sent him into exile. Has he told you about that?"

"We haven't really spoken of it, Caesar."

I hoped Tacitus could keep his mouth shut and his face straight. Only a few days ago I had recounted to him a long conversation I'd had with Musonius about his time in exile. Musonius' relationship with Rome's rulers over the past twenty years had been stormy. Nero sent him into exile twice, once on a wretched rock of an island. Vespasian at first dealt kindly with him but finally sent him away. Titus allowed him to come home. Musonius had lived quietly for the past few years, drawing a circle of admirers and students who considered him a Roman Socrates. We hoped his future would not lead to a cup of hemlock.

"He says his return to Rome will be delayed until the kalends of August," Domitian said. "He regrets missing the dinner you invited him to."

"Yes, my lord. He's spending some time on his estate north of Rome, on the Via Flaminia." One part of me knew Musonius' whereabouts were no concern of Domitian's. Another part knew Domitian had his own ways of keeping track of someone like Musonius. The sense of panic brought on just by standing in front of the man, in my own house, had loosened my tongue. No wonder people on trial before him confessed to the most outlandish charges.

Domitian put the note down. "The farther away, the better. Be careful of your friends, Gaius Pliny. No matter how loyal a man may be, if he associates with people who foment unrest, he brands himself with their mark." He directed a long stare at Tacitus. "I'm sure you don't want to do that."

"No. No, my lord, of course not."

Domitian returned his attention to me, tilting his head back and studying me under half-closed eyelids. "Your uncle was a man my father and brother could rely on. I hope I will find you as trustworthy."

"I take my uncle as a model in all aspects of my life, Caesar. He taught me that, when someone earns my trust and respect, he should have it without question or reservation."

"Good. That's what I need to hear. Now"—he slapped his hands on the table, apparently oblivious to the subtlety of my comment—"there is something I want to discuss with you."

"Would you like for me to leave, Caesar?" Tacitus asked. I think he saw his last chance to escape before Domitian revealed whatever was on his mind. I wished I could go with him. Once the *princeps* had made us his partners, I suspected, we would not just be caught in his trap. He would have his collar on us and be leading us around like pets.

"No," Domitian said. "I think you can be of use to me as well, son-in-law of Agricola." He turned back to me and asked without any prelude, "Gaius Pliny, do you think Nero has returned?"

My mouth worked for a moment until I managed to stammer, "As I said last night, my lord, I ... I believe death is the end of our existence. And Nero is dead ... isn't he?"

Domitian put his hands to the sides of his large head, as if it were too heavy to stay up on its own. "That's the question I've been asking myself all night."

"There were witnesses to his death, weren't there, Caesar?" Tacitus asked.

"I have a freedman in my household," Domitian said with a heavy sigh, "who held the sword Nero ran on. He has stuck to that story, even under torture. But only a few slaves saw the body before it was burned. And they're all dead now. ... Can I be sure Nero is gone?"

For an instant the look of despair on his face evoked pity from me. The feeling passed as quickly as the thunder I heard rumbling in the distance.

"I don't think there's anything to worry about, my lord," I said. "It's unlikely he would stay in hiding for fifteen years and suddenly reappear. Even if he did, the army would never support him. No one would welcome Nero back. We were well rid of him."

"Is that what you'll be saying about me in a few years? 'We were well rid of him'."

I took a deep breath to ease the tightness in my chest. Why is it that anything one says in Rome can be twisted to mean the very opposite? "No, my lord. Of course not. Your administration is winning praise on all sides. It's well attested that Nero was erratic, even incompetent."

"But, my dear Pliny, he was the last of Augustus' direct descendants, the last man who could claim Julius Caesar's blood. If he's still alive, then my family's claim on the title of *princeps* could be contested. My opponents would have someone of Caesar's blood to rally around."

"My lord," Tacitus said, "the rumor of a resurrected Nero has been floating around practically since the day after he died."

Domitian looked at him in surprise. "What do you mean, son-in-law of Agricola?"

Tacitus gritted his teeth but answered civilly. "As Josephus mentioned last night, a few months after Nero's death an impostor appeared in the province of Asia. He gained quite a following before he was captured and executed. And in the fall after Vesuvius erupted another impostor appeared, also in Asia. He caused hardly a stir before he was apprehended."

Domitian mulled over that information for a moment. "But, even if Nero stays dead, what if some genuine, living member of his family were to appear, someone with Caesar's blood?"

His dilemma was real. Vespasian, his father, had assumed the name 'Caesar' when he came to power and passed it on to his sons, but he could not infuse their veins with the blood that ought to go with the name. To that extent, they would be pretenders as long as the memory of Augustus and his family lasted. Fifteen years after the death of Nero, the public's love for Augustus' family had not abated, if grafitti and crowd reactions in the theater were any gauge. The appearance of an actual descendant of Caesar—even the rumor of his existence—could prove troublesome to a ruler from any other family, and disastrous to one as unpopular as Domitian.

"Nero had no children, my lord," Tacitus said. I was again grateful for his acquaintance with history. Since our return from Syria he had spent hours in my library, reading my uncle's finished works as well as his copious notes. "Well, there was a daughter, but she died in infancy. His mother, Agrippina, died almost twenty-five years ago. Nero was her only child."

"Her only child, *as far as we know*," Domitian said, emphasizing the words by punching the air with his finger. "What if there is someone else?"

"Do you have some reason to think there is?" I asked.

"Possibly. And that's why I need your help, Gaius Pliny. I've read the report from Florus, the governor of Asia, about your handling of a very serious matter in Smyrna. That's why I invited you to dinner. He praises your keen perception, your ability to conduct an inquiry, and your discretion. You—and Tacitus here, even if he is Agricola's son-in-law—seem the sort of men I might rely on. You acquitted yourselves admirably in the archives last night."

I was wondering if I dared to ask the question that had been gnawing at me all night. What would it cost me to accuse the *princeps* of murder?

"And I did not have that man killed," Domitian said. "I will eliminate anyone who threatens me"—he glared at Tacitus as Agricola's surrogate—

"but I don't murder people in cold blood."

Rumors to the contrary had abounded since the day Titus died. Many people suspected Domitian had a hand—possibly both hands—in his brother's death.

"My lord, I never would have dreamed ..."

Domitian stood and leaned over my table. "You've been wondering about it all night, Gaius the necromancer. 'Did Domitian kill that poor man just to test me?' As I told you last night, I can sense what people are thinking, just from the expressions on their faces. So, don't deny it. That's what you've been asking yourself."

"No, Caesar, I assure you ..." I wanted to run, to crawl under the table, anything so I wasn't standing in front of this man right now. He seemed to be growing larger as he spoke, like some ogre from a nursemaid's story.

"You think too highly of yourself, Gaius Pliny, if you believe I would waste a skilled mason just to pose a conundrum for you. Of course, your uncle always thought too highly of himself, so I guess you come by it honestly."

Domitian sat back down, returning to his normal size, and I managed to draw a breath.

"My lord, may I ... may I ask what did happen to him?"

Domitian examined his fingernails. "He was killed yesterday morning, about the second hour, by a falling brick. He was a workman on my new house. Regulus and I were observing the progress of the work when the accident happened. I had been trying to devise some way to verify what Florus said about you ever since I read his report. This opportunity just seemed to present itself, like a gift from the gods. Perhaps even from my deified father." He chuckled at his own joke. "I'm satisfied that you do have some remarkable skills. I want you to put them to my service."

"We will assist you in any way we can, my lord," I said. Tacitus nodded beside me. What other answer could we give? How can a trapped animal resist the collar closing around its neck?

"Good." Domitian leaned forward and folded his hands over my papers. "I want to know as much about the demise of Nero and his family as possible. I'm particularly interested in one item—his mother's memoirs."

"But, my lord, you can buy a copy of Agrippina's memoirs in any bookstore. I have one here in my library. My uncle referred to it in several of his books."

"Send someone to fetch it," Domitian said.

"Could we just go to the library?"

"No," Domitian snapped. "I don't want to be seen by any more people than necessary. You'll understand why in a few moments."

I stuck my head out the tablinum door and sent Aurora to retrieve the book.

While we waited, Domitian pulled a leather pouch from under his tunic and dropped it on my table. "This is a letter which Agrippina wrote to Nero. Josephus and his assistants came across it a couple of days ago. At the end, apparently as a taunt to Nero, she says she has recorded a certain incident in her memoirs. But that incident is not in my copy of the book."

"Are you sure yours is complete, my lord?" Tacitus asked.

"It goes up to the last week of her life. The incident I'm referring to happened several months before that."

Aurora knocked on the tablinum door and stuck her head in. "Here's the book you wanted, my lord."

Domitian grabbed the box of scrolls from me before I even had a good grip on it. It fell on the table and one of the scrolls began to unroll. "Just as well," he said with a laugh. "We need to get toward the end." He found the scroll he wanted, scanned the last few pages and shook his head. "It's not here either."

"What is the incident, my lord?" I asked.

"You'll see when you read the letter. Then I want you to find out if this is a true version of Agrippina's memoirs. Could she have written something else and hidden it away? Could her memoirs have been censored by Nero to remove anything embarrassing to him?"

"But, my lord, don't you have more resources for that than we do?" I said.

Domitian shook his head quickly. "Josephus will continue to search the archives. But I don't believe any other copies of the memoirs are there. If I set my men looking for them elsewhere, everybody will become aware of it and want to know why I'm interested in them. I've already told Josephus and his assistants to tell no one about this letter or any other references to the memoirs, under penalty of death. And this is the original, not a copy. I don't want anyone else to see it."

"I'll be sure it's locked away, Caesar." Since my return from Syria I had become more careful about keeping important documents out of sight, where only my two or three most trusted slaves could get to them. I had been given reason to believe that Regulus' network of spies reached even into my household.

"Good. And then you'll look for a fuller version of Agrippina's memoirs?"

"But, my lord, where would we even begin?"

Tacitus spoke up. "It seems likely that she would have entrusted an unedited copy to someone especially close to her. Perhaps one of us could look in the archives for the names of such people. They might be mentioned in letters or in reports to Nero."

"Then Josephus will find them, I suppose," Domitian said.

"Josephus might not recognize their importance, my lord."

"And you think you would?"

"My search would be more specific, my lord, more limited. It might yield better results."

Domitian gave him a grudging smile. "You sometimes make good sense, Cornelius Tacitus. Come by later today and my secretary will have a letter giving you permission to use the archives. Just be careful you don't trip over Josephus. He practically lives there."

"But," I said, "if we can't admit we're looking for these other memoirs, what reason would Tacitus have to be in the archives? Other people will be there. They'll strike up conversations." I had accompanied my uncle on trips to libraries around Naples, so I know how the pale-skinned denizens of those places seek out others like themselves, mostly to show off their own work or some curious old document they've run across.

"I've contemplated writing a biography of my father-in-law," Tacitus said. "He began his career under Nero."

"Hmmph!" Domitian drummed his fingers on my table. "What has Julius Agricola done to merit a biography?"

Let's see, I thought. *Besides conquering more of Britain than any other Roman governor—not much, I suppose.* Tacitus' mention of a possible biography was almost a challenge to Domitian. He'd never said anything about the project to me before.

"Well, no matter," the *princeps* said. "As a pretext it'll do as well as any. If word of it gets out, people might even applaud my generosity." He stood and we snapped to attention like soldiers. "Thank you for seeing me, Gaius Pliny. Keep me informed of how your search is going. You'll have to communicate with me, and I with you, through Josephus. I can't risk anyone finding out that I'm interested in this document."

As Domitian made his exit Tacitus and I collapsed into chairs. The room itself seemed to exhale in relief.

48

IV

WHEN WE COULD BREATHE normally again I looked at Tacitus in disbelief. "He wants us to find a book no one has seen for twenty-five years? A book that may not even exist? Who does he think we are?"

"Apparently your reputation has preceded us all the way to the top of the Palatine."

"I don't suppose we have any choice but to try, do we?"

"Not when we've been asked to do a favor for the *princeps*. And asked in person. You know he doesn't like to exert himself. He always rides in a litter when he goes out. Since he walked over here in the rain, he must consider this extremely important."

I picked up the pouch Domitian had left on my table and opened it. It contained a single rolled-up sheet of papyrus. Part of the broken wax seal still clung to the top edge. Before reading it, I examined it carefully.

"I don't think it's a new piece of papyrus," I said.

Tacitus nodded. "It is drier and yellower than a fresh piece. Is there any way to tell how old it is?"

"We could compare it to pieces in my library. Dymas would know when various things were copied or purchased."

"But do you want him to be able to read it?"

I flipped the papyrus over. "I'll let him look at just the back. There's nothing on it but some scribbling."

"What is it?"

"Greek letters. But badly formed, like a child was learning to write. I don't recognize the word."

"Perhaps it's a message in code."

"Let's not be so dramatic," I cautioned. "More likely, someone was testing a pen."

Tacitus turned the letter back over. "What does it say?"

"We'll get to that. At the moment I'm more concerned about whether it's genuine." I moved an oil lamp closer to the document. "I wonder if we can find anything else with Agrippina's seal on it."

"Do you think the *princeps* himself would hand you a forged document?"

"Let's just say that at times I appreciate the Skeptic position: Can we ever know anything for certain? It strikes me as a little too convenient that this letter was 'found' just two days ago."

"If the letter was actually just discovered then, it might explain why Domitian spent so much time discussing Nero at dinner last night."

"Or, if Domitian wants me to think the letter is genuine, the conversation about Nero could have been staged."

"Why would he go to such lengths to get you interested?"

"That I don't know, but I think there's more to his request than just finding Agrippina's unedited memoirs. And I suspect Regulus has some role to play, to settle a score against me if for no other reason."

Tacitus chuckled and shook his head, as though hearing something he considered ridiculous. "Regulus would be amused, I'm sure, to know how much credit you give him for being the guiding force behind all that is evil in Rome. Considering how evil Rome is, that role would be a tall order for any man."

"But Regulus was there, at Domitian's invitation, and he heard the same conversation we did. I don't think Domitian—or any ruler—does anything without design."

"Friend Pliny, your childhood nurse must have told you some memorable tales about monsters under your bed. You're still seeing them, even in daylight."

"I'll try to warn you before one of them bites your backside off."

I turned my attention to the text of the letter. The handwriting was amateurish, of a quality I would never accept from a scribe of mine, even in a short note, but it was easily legible. I read aloud:

> *Agrippina, mother of Nero Caesar, sends greetings to Nero Caesar, son of Agrippina.*

"That's a strange way for a mother to begin a letter to her son." Tacitus held out his hand and I let him take the letter.

"Unless she's reminding him of who put him in power. From the stories I've heard, she wanted to be queen of Rome."

"She put her face all over Nero's coins at the beginning of his reign," Tacitus said. "And she sat beside him to receive foreign dignitaries."

I took the letter back and read a bit more.

Dearest son, I'm sure you will be concerned to know that I have been having some distress with my stomach the last few days. But I am blessed with a strong constitution, fortified by some medications I've been taking. By the way, thank you for the pastries you sent me for the Saturnalia. They were quite tasty. What was that extra ingredient your cook used?

"Hmmph!" Tacitus said. "Imperial correspondence sounds just as insipid as what the rest of us write."

"You're missing the whole point." I tried to remain patient. "He tried to poison her. And she knows it and wants him to know that she knows."

"How do you get that out of what you just read?" Tacitus snatched the letter out of my hand. A corner of the papyrus sheet tore off between my fingers.

"It's so obvious, my dear Tacitus." I tapped the papyrus with my index finger. "Look at the juxtaposition of the items. 'I have a stomachache after eating something you sent me.' The sarcasm of the bit about the extra ingredient in the pastries is patent. She must have been taking antidotes for the poisons in advance. That would be the 'medications'."

Tacitus eyed me like a schoolboy chastised by his teacher for missing the subtlety of some passage in Virgil. His reputation as an orator, I've come to realize, rests on his technical brilliance and his fine voice, not on his reasoning ability. I took the papyrus back from him and resumed reading.

I shall record your act of kindness in my memoirs, along with all your other signs of filial devotion, so that posterity may know just what kind of son you are.

"So that sentence isn't really a compliment?" Tacitus asked.

"Exactly. This woman was vicious. No wonder Nero turned out to be such a monster. But at least she's telling us that she wrote about this in her memoirs. And it's not in my copy or Domitian's."

Tacitus furrowed his brow and rubbed a hand across it, as though following my line of reasoning was painful for him. "But if she doesn't mean what she appears to be saying in the rest of the letter, why do you take that part seriously? If you're going to explain away some passages, why not all?"

His questions stopped me for a moment. "Your point is well taken. Perhaps she used the fiction of putting things in her memoirs to threaten Nero."

"So we may be looking for a non-existent document. On the basis of a letter that might have been forged."

My shoulders slumped. "We can't dismiss that possibility."

"Why would the *princeps* put us in such a position?" Tacitus asked.

"I don't think Domitian would. Regulus might."

"Gaius Pliny! Do you really think Regulus could manipulate the *princeps* himself?"

"Domitian is still relatively young. He relies on advisors more than his brother or father did. Regulus has been waiting for years to worm his way back into the emperor's good graces. His presence at dinner last night makes me uneasy about this whole matter. I wish we didn't have to be involved."

"Do we have any choice?"

"No more than gladiators who are told to enter the arena and fight."

Tacitus raised his arm like a gladiator saluting the crowd. "Well, read the rest of the letter as we march to our deaths."

"There's no need for melodrama." At least I hoped there wasn't. I turned back to the letter.

> *I am enjoying some quiet moments here. Your cousin, Rubellius Plautus, stopped by to visit me yesterday. As you'll recall, he and his family spend most of their time at their villa near here. His son is such a bright little boy. Rubellius himself is a handsome man. I told him if he weren't already married, he would make a good match for me.*

"Nero had a cousin?" Tacitus turned my hand so he could see the letter for himself.

"And the cousin had a son. That's what Domitian is so worried about. She calls him a little boy. If Agrippina died twenty-five years ago, the son would be ... about thirty by now."

"He could certainly lay a claim to the principate. Domitian's right about that."

"What happened to him, I wonder? And to Rubellius?"

"Rubellius must be dead," Tacitus said with his customary eagerness to leap to a conclusion. "Otherwise someone would have put him forward when Nero died. Galba and the other generals who fought for power then could hardly have had a claim as strong as someone of Caesar's blood."

I nodded in agreement. "Let's see if Agrippina tells us any more about the son."

> *If—may the gods forbid—your union with Octavia should prove childless, perhaps you could adopt Rubellius' son, as*

Claudius adopted you. With the boy's ancestry, he could prove a strong support for your position, as you did for Claudius.

"Do you see the threat there?"

Tacitus looked at me blankly.

"Remember Britannicus, Claudius' son?"

Awareness spread over Tacitus' face. "That's right. When Agrippina married her uncle Claudius, she already had a son from a previous marriage."

"And Claudius adopted that son and renamed him Nero. Then Agrippina pushed Britannicus out of the nest. The stepson became the heir."

"So you think she was threatening to shift her support to Rubellius and his son?"

I read the lines again. "It sounds that way to me. If she put Nero into power, perhaps she thought she could maneuver another of Augustus' descendants into the same position."

"Slow down," Tacitus said. "This is becoming complicated. She says Rubellius was Nero's cousin. But that word can mean anyone who's related to you in any degree."

"That's true. And the relationship could be through Nero's father. Who was his father?"

Tacitus rubbed his chin for a moment. "Before he was adopted his name was Domitius. I forget the full name, but I know the family name was Domitius."

"That's no help. The Domitii are almost as numerous as you Cornelii."

"True. My own mother-in-law comes from a branch of the Domitii. No imperial connections, though, thank the gods."

"It seems we'll need some expert help to sort this out. Rubellius and his son must have had some connection to Caesar's family. Otherwise Agrippina couldn't have contemplated putting him in Nero's place."

"Do you think that's what she had in mind?"

"Listen to this next bit." I resumed reading the letter.

The senate is less likely to think of opposing you—or any ruler—when they know a successor is being groomed. Rubellius could even be a regent if—may the gods forbid—something should happen to you. He is widely admired in his own right, in spite of his preference for philosophy over real life. He brought along his mentor, Musonius Rufus, a tiresome Stoic, if that isn't redundant. The man presented me with a copy of a treatise he's written on why women should study philosophy. Even with all the leisure time you've given me now, I won't get around to that.

"How could she find Musonius 'tiresome'?" Tacitus asked. "From everything I've heard—from you as well as from others—he's a remarkable man."

"You know how much I've come to admire him in the short time I've known him. But when this was written, he would have been young. That incident of walking onto the battlefield between the two armies didn't happen until the civil wars after Nero's death. That was when his reputation began to grow."

"Pity he's out of town at the moment."

"I'll talk to him as soon as possible and see what he remembers about this incident."

"Does Agrippina say any more?"

"Just a closing line."

I do hope to return to Rome in the spring.
    Given at Antium, on the fourth day before the kalends of January, by my own hand.

"She wrote it herself?" Tacitus said.

"That would account for the poor handwriting." Though anyone of Agrippina's class, or mine, could read and write, we rarely pick up a pen ourselves.

"You're hardly one to criticize anyone else's handwriting," Tacitus said. "I've heard your scribes ask you to dictate to them, rather than write something out and ask them to copy it."

I ignored the jibe. "I wonder if she had no scribe, or if she just didn't trust anyone to take this down." I put the letter back in its pouch. "Do you, from your historical reading, know anything about Rubellius Plautus?"

"I can't recall that I've ever run across the name. You have one of the largest libraries in Rome, and your uncle wrote a history that covered Nero's reign. If you want to know something about Rubellius, there could be no better place to start."

"You're right. And I want Dymas and Glaucon to examine this letter, to see if they can assure me of its authenticity."

"Let me know what they tell you. I have to finish working on my speech. Mucius' case will be tried in a couple of days. I just hope the rain lets up so we can hold court outdoors."

I nodded. Any skilled orator dislikes speaking inside. The heavy curtains which partition a basilica muffle sound and prevent the movement of air. The courtroom begins to feel like the over-heated *caldarium* of a public bath. One's best speech becomes limp and soggy. "I'll be there to cheer you on. And I'll bring some of my clients with me."

"I would appreciate the support. Julius Agricola offered to have some of his veterans there, but I'm not sure it would help Mucius' case to be identified with Agricola's supporters, especially ex-soldiers. A couple of dozen of your clients, though, could make a very favorable impression."

"You shall have them."

"Could I also presume on your friendship and ask you to bring along that scribe of yours who knows Tironian notation? I'd like to have a record of my opponent's speech and I hate to pay the going rate to hire a scribe."

"He'll be there, pen in hand."

We walked to the door. Moschus brought Tacitus' hat and cloak. The rain was heavier now than when he arrived. His slaves got on their rain gear.

"Shall I have my litter-bearers take you home?" I offered.

"That's generous of you, but no. I like to experience Rome in the rain. It washes away the crowds and the smell. I can almost imagine what it must have been like to live here in the early days of the republic, when Rome was just a small town and a successful general like Agricola didn't have to fear the jealousy of a *princeps*."

I closed the door behind Tacitus and started back across the atrium. The floor under the impluvium was now thoroughly wet, so I had to watch my step on the slick marble. I returned to the tablinum and savored another bite of Domitian's bread as I mulled over Agrippina's letter and the fate of Rubellius Plautus and his son. Could they somehow be linked to Agrippina's unedited memoirs? Was Domitian giving me a hint? Or leading me on some fool's errand?

In either case, why?

* * * *

With another bite of cheese and one more swallow of wine I left the tablinum and turned into the passageway leading to my library. My uncle bought property next to this house, at an exorbitant price—as if there is any other kind in Rome—to add a wing for his voluminous library. He acquired books as avidly as he read them. He kept his

scribe, Dymas, busy taking notes on passages that were read to him as well as things he observed himself.

Among the numerous works he composed was the history Tacitus had mentioned, in thirty-one volumes, beginning in Caligula's time and coming up to Vespasian's reign. If my uncle had known anything about Rubellius Plautus, that was where I would find it.

"Gaius!" My mother's voice and the patter of feet sounded behind me at the same time. "Gaius!"

I stopped and waited for her to catch up with me. At least I could assure her I had eaten something.

"Is it true?" she asked breathlessly. Her most trusted slave, an older woman named Niobe, a heavy-set midwife, shadowed her. "Was the *princeps* here in our house?"

"Where did you hear such a thing?" I knew the answer to my question, but I wanted to avoid a lie or a direct admission.

"It's all the slaves are talking about."

And, of course, there was only one slave who could have started the story on its merry rounds—my garrulous doorkeeper. His first owner had castrated him, years ago. He should have cut out his tongue instead.

"Moschus should pay attention to his duties and not spread gossip like some old crone at the village well." I glared at Niobe.

"But the seal," my mother insisted. "He saw the *princeps'* seal."

"Just because a messenger bears the seal of the *princeps*, Mother, doesn't mean he's the man himself. Surely you know—"

"Aristides saw him too, dear, as he was leaving. It's his job to know people."

Like a fire spreading out of control, this story had already grown too large for me to extinguish it, short of killing every slave I owned, the way the vigiles sometimes knock down buildings ahead of a fire. The best I could hope for was to contain it before it got out of my house. It would do Domitian no good to don a disguise and slog through the rain to enlist my help if my slaves immediately blabbed the secret all over Rome. What might the *princeps* do when he learned I couldn't keep the news of his visit to myself?

The only hope for dousing a large fire in Rome is rain. And the rain might help me now. In this weather there was no reason for any of my slaves to leave the house.

"Mother, no one else must know about this."

Her face turned pale. "What's wrong? Has someone informed on us?"

"No. That's absurd. Why would you even ask that?" But her question knotted my stomach. Did she know something I didn't? Did someone have reason to inform on us?

She glanced nervously at Niobe. "It's nothing, dear, just ... Well, what was the *princeps* doing here?"

"He wanted to ask me about something we discussed at dinner last night. But my conversation with him cannot be spoken of outside these walls. None of the slaves is to leave the house today. And if I hear any more talk about this, I'll send every one of them to work in the fields on one of my estates." For the soft, well-fed slaves of an urban household, that was the ultimate threat. I shook my finger at Niobe. "Make that clear to them."

The two women turned and scurried off. Niobe held my mother's arm in a way that seemed much too familiar for a slave. A stranger would have taken them for sisters.

Before turning back toward the library I stood still and closed my eyes to dispel the wave of anxiety my mother had caused me. I couldn't deal with my scribes unless I was calm myself. I tried to focus my thoughts again on Agrippina's letter. Determining whether it was genuine was the first hurdle I faced.

As soon as I stepped into the library I was soothed by the sounds of pens scratching against papyrus and pumice stones smoothing new rolls. Slaves are sometimes surprised when their owner appears in their work space, but not my scribes. They know I love books and find a library a comforting place. If the world were ever turned upside down and I were to find myself a slave, I pray—to gods in whom I do not believe—that I would be put to work as a scribe. Spending my life among books would be a large measure of consolation for falling into servitude.

Against one wall of the library tables were set up for the scribes who are recopying the 160 unpublished scrolls, with writing on the front and back in a very small hand, which my uncle left me. They're copying them in a more legible script and putting the material in some kind of order, instead of the haphazard way it was recorded. In the new scrolls passages will be arranged by broad subjects: plants, animals, laws, noteworthy people, oddities of nature, and so on, in the manner of his *Natural History*.

These scrolls epitomize my uncle more accurately, I feel, than his published works. He collected information the way some men collect Corinthian bronzes, fascinated by each individual piece but never seeing any kind of unity among them. Whatever order there is in his published works was imposed on it by his scribes, especially Dymas, who worked with him for almost thirty years. Most of the snippets in these unpublished scrolls never found their way into works like his *Natural History* because they contradicted the standard opinions of our day.

The scrolls also epitomize my uncle's dislike of waste, whether of materials or time. A few months before he died, he and I attended a dinner party. When the slave who was reading mispronounced a word, the host made him stop and go back over the entire line. My uncle asked, "Could you understand what he said?" When the man admitted he could, my uncle replied, "Then why make him go back? You've cost us at least ten lines." The small handwriting and the use of the backs of these scrolls allowed my uncle's scribes to pack in as much as would normally be written on two and a half scrolls.

Three scribes were busy copying the scrolls, and I stopped to look over their shoulders. It is tedious work, I admit. A scribe reads through one of the original scrolls, copying passages onto whatever new scroll they belong on. It requires a lot of shifting back and forth to the new scrolls, but I believe it will make my uncle's work more useful to me. At present I have to browse through scroll after scroll, often getting frustrated by the minute handwriting, or rely on Dymas' memory about what is recorded where.

"How many have you finished?" I asked one of the scribes.

"Fifty, my lord." He pointed to the book box where the original scrolls were placed after the copying was done. "The work would go more quickly if we could read the writing more easily. We can hardly finish a page without putting it under the glass. Look at this bit."

I picked up the scroll and peered at the passage he had pointed to. My eyes, though sensitive to light, are keen, but I could not be sure what the tiny letters said. I stepped over to the table where the reading glass, a ball filled with water, was mounted in a frame with four legs. Anything placed under it appears to be larger.

"Dymas," I said, "why did you ever write this small?"

"I was merely doing as your uncle requested, my lord," Dymas said from the table where he was working. "He said he wanted to save space and discourage casual readers who might get their hands on the scrolls."

Dymas is sixty now, stoop-shouldered and bald except for a fringe of gray hair. His eyes are starting to fail him. He squints badly and must rely on the glass to enlarge anything he reads. Everything he writes in his own hand is done in large letters. But, even if his vision is growing dim, his memory, a kind of inner vision, is amazing. Like the blind prophet Teiresias in the myths, as he loses one type of sight, the other seems to grow stronger.

I expected to see his son, Glaucon, by Dymas' side. Glaucon serves as my chief scribe. At thirty-five he is gradually assuming the responsibilities his father has carried for many years. His fingers are as permanently ink-stained as the old man's. Although I took Glaucon to Syria with me, he and I have an uneasy relationship. The day after my uncle's funeral he asked me to manumit him and his father. He said my uncle promised to do that in his will. There was no such clause in my uncle's will, and the man's audacity offended me. His ill-timed request upset my mother so badly she wanted me to sell both father and son. I wouldn't do that, but I resolved not to consider manumitting them any time soon.

Glaucon was nowhere to be seen, though. Dymas has told me that he fears his son does not have the soul of a scribe. He writes well, but he has no curiosity about the documents, no love of deciphering a poorly written passage in a scroll he's copying, no ability to deduce what an earlier scribe might have intended. To my surprise, he had volunteered to go to Syria with me, and I had taken him in hopes of inspiring him by entrusting him with greater responsibility. That hope proved vain. He did his job and nothing more.

Dymas was huddled over a scroll with another scribe, Peleus, a red-haired fellow who is three years older than I am and shorter by that many fingers. Dymas tells me that, unlike Glaucon, he has a wonderful gift for words and an encyclopedic memory. He has even mastered the complicated system of Tironian note-taking. A shy young man who stuttered as a boy, he overcame the problem, like Demosthenes, but it occasionally gets the better of him if he is nervous.

"Isn't Glaucon here?" I asked.

"My son has gone out on an errand, my lord."

So much for my order that no slaves leave the house today. "What sort of errand on a morning like this?"

"He heard of a shipment of scrolls arriving today, my lord. He wanted to purchase as many of them as he could. Recopying your uncle's notebooks has depleted our supply. At our present rate, I estimate we will need over 300 scrolls to complete the task. Is there something I could help you with?"

I opened Domitian's pouch and extracted the letter. Laying it on the table face down, I said, "Please tell me all you can about the age of this papyrus."

Peleus started to turn the letter over, but I pressed it down on the table. I wished the remaining fragment of Agrippina's seal—if it was Agrippina's—weren't so prominently displayed.

"The content isn't important," I said, trying to appear nonchalant. "I'm merely interested in the age of the papyrus."

Dymas felt the papyrus, raising it off the table slightly and sniffing at it, then rubbing it between his fingers. I wondered if he could feel the writing on the other side. The ink was thick, as though inexpertly mixed. The letters were raised enough that someone might identify them by feel. He ran his hand slowly over the seal, then examined it under the water-filled globe.

"These letters are badly formed, my lord. Do you know why someone wrote them on the back?"

"The letters don't matter right now. The age of the papyrus is the only question."

I felt better when he put the document down in front of me again. "What do you think, boy?" he asked Peleus. If he called someone older than I am 'boy,' I wondered what he thought of me.

Peleus bent over and peered closely at it. "This torn corner is recent."

"Very recent, in fact," I said.

"That's one indication that it's not a fresh piece of papyrus, my lord," Dymas said. "I would estimate it's older than yourself."

"I'm twenty-one," I snapped. "Do you mean it's twenty-five years old, or a hundred?"

"Much closer to twenty-five, my lord," Dymas said. "It has some moisture left in it. Is that helpful?"

"Yes, it is." I rolled the letter up and put it back in its pouch. The fact that the papyrus was about the right age didn't prove Agrippina had written this letter, but if the papyrus had been only a few years old ...

"May I ask a question, my lord?" Dymas said.

I hesitated and hated myself for it. In the four years since my uncle died the most difficult thing I've had to learn about dealing with the slaves I inherited from him is to assert my authority over the older ones. It feels too much like giving orders to one's grandparents.

"Yes, Dymas, go ahead."

"How, my lord, do you come to have a document bearing the seal of the lady Agrippina, mother of Nero?" He was asking a question he knew he had no right to ask, but elderly slaves often lose their fear of punishment and become impertinent.

"Is that what this is? How can you be sure?"

"I recognize the seal, my lord. I was a younger man in your uncle's service when Agrippina and Nero came to power. Your uncle commanded a cavalry squadron on the Rhine. Communications that our legion received from Rome carried this seal as often as Nero's own."

"But this seal has been broken and part is missing. How can you tell what it looked like?"

"Will you look at it under the glass while I describe it, my lord?"

"All right." I removed the letter from the pouch again, placed it under the glass, and concentrated on the remaining fragment of the seal. It showed the upper part of a woman's body and some sort of structure behind her.

"Agrippina's seal," Dymas said, "showed a woman—her mother— standing in front of a bridge. Isn't that what you see, my lord?"

Was that what I was seeing? Or was he planting the idea in my mind? "I suppose it is. It's difficult to say, the way it's broken. Why would she have chosen that image for her seal?"

"She regarded that as an auspicious moment in her own life, my lord. Germanicus' troops—he was her father—were in revolt and threatening to tear down a bridge across the Rhine. Germanicus and some of his loyal troops were on the German side of the river. If the bridge had been destroyed, he would have been trapped there and slaughtered by the barbarians. The elder Agrippina stood on the bridge, the story goes, and shamed the troops into backing down. At the time she was pregnant with her daughter, the younger Agrippina. The daughter liked to claim it was her mother's pregnancy—thus her unborn self—that brought the soldiers to their senses."

"You know a great deal about her life then? The younger Agrippina's, I mean."

"Only as it relates to events in Germany, my lord. Your uncle dictated his history of the German Wars to me. My memory soaks things up, the way papyrus absorbs ink."

"I wonder what other information about Agrippina has been soaked up in here." I glanced around at the shelves heavy with papyrus rolls, like lumps of dough on the shelves of a baker's shop early in the morning.

Peleus answered. "I'm sure there's much to be learned about her in here, my lord. Is there something in particular you're interested in?"

I could hardly tell him the *princeps* had asked me to find an unexpurgated copy of Agrippina's memoirs. How was I going to find something when I couldn't admit I was looking for it? And wasn't even sure it existed.

"No, nothing in particular." I tried my best to sound indifferent. "She and Nero were discussed at a dinner I attended recently. That conversation piqued my interest."

Dymas glanced at the pouch containing Agrippina's letter. I knew he wanted to ask what connection it had with my conversation. I felt my motives were as obvious as the letters magnified under our glass. I wanted to escape his scrutiny. The best way to do that was to put him to work.

"I'd like for you to assemble whatever information you can find about Agrippina and Nero. A sketch of their lives, if you will, especially hers."

Dymas and Peleus both bowed their heads. Dymas spoke. "It would be easier for us to find whatever you're interested in, my lord, if you could tell us what we're looking for."

His simple statement was as close to a challenge as a slave dared come. I looked at him more intently than I ever had. He and Glaucon have always been here, like pieces of furniture. They've lived in 'my' house longer than I have. No one, except my steward, knows more about my affairs than Dymas and Glaucon. They are privy to all my correspondence and come and go as they please, as Glaucon had this morning ... For all I knew, he could have gone to report to Regulus.

"I probably won't know until I see it." I used to hate it when my uncle said anything like that to me. It's dismaying how quickly we become our elders. "Just find me as much information on Agrippina as you can by tomorrow morning."

"Yes, my lord," Dymas said. "Your uncle wrote a lot about her. In fact, it seems to me that he recorded some odd characteristic of hers in his *Natural History*. Something to do with her face or her mouth."

"An odd wart perhaps? A third nostril?" My uncle, as erudite as he was, did become overly interested in people's quirks and physical deformities.

"I can't recall the passage at the moment, my lord. I will check on it."

"If it's nothing more significant than that, don't bother me with it."

* * * *

As I left the library I decided to hide Agrippina's letter in my bedroom, which is in the back of the house, off the peristyle garden. It's unusual for me to venture into that part of the house during the day. Once I'm up and about my business, the garden and the rooms around it become the women's part of the house, my mother's realm. There she supervises preparation of our meals and insists on working wool with the slave women, in the manner of noble women of the Republic, a hundred years ago and more. Every tunic or toga I wear is made by her own hands, right down to the equestrian stripe. Tacitus adores her antiquated virtue.

Turning into the passageway leading to the back of the house, I heard the laughter of two little girls, the daughters of my steward, Demetrius, and his Egyptian wife, Siwa. Demetrius gave the girls perfectly good Greek names, but their mother calls them Hashep and Dakla, after her mother and sister, and that's how they're known in the household. She converses with them in Egyptian, but they use Greek with their father and the rest of us. I suppose it's time they learn Latin. They are seven and five. Their company never fails to delight me, like listening to the chattering of birds.

A light, warm rain was still falling when I emerged into the garden. The slave women were working under the cover of the portico that runs around it. The first one who spotted me greeted me more loudly than she needed to.

"Good morning, my lord." That alerted the rest of them.

Demetrius' daughters were standing on the edge of our fishpond. At least, a fishpond was what the builder of the house had intended it to be. My uncle found it more trouble to raise fish than to send a servant to the market to buy them. I played in this pool with the children of our servants when I was a boy, as long ago as that now seemed. My uncle's death propelled me, at seventeen, into adulthood, like a rock being pushed down a slope. Spending time with the children of my servants allows me to escape my responsibilities and sneak back into my youth now and then.

The girls were nude, just as Aurora and I used to be when we played here at that age. Hashep, the older one, looked at me in surprise—like

Artemis must have looked at Actaeon when he stumbled upon her bathing. I think she was about to cover herself with her hands, when Dakla said, "Uncle Gaius! Watch!" She pushed Hashep into the water and jumped in after her.

They surfaced, spluttering and wiping water off their faces. Hashep stayed crouched down, with only her neck and head above the water. Apparently she had grown modest during my year in Syria. Dakla had no such inhibitions. The water was deep enough that she could swim a few strokes toward the end of the pool where I was standing.

"Would you get your lyre and play a song for us?" she asked.

"One of the ones you made up," Hashep said from her end of the pool.

I have never admitted to anyone outside my household that I play the lyre. A Roman man of my class who plays any musical instrument is considered foppish, but I find plucking the strings very soothing. One of our servants taught me when I was a boy. I've even found that I have a certain facility for devising new melodies.

"All right," I said. "I'll play you something, but I am out of practice. I didn't take my lyre with me to Syria, you know." I had left it behind because I knew a military tribune playing his lyre would not be well received in a legionary camp.

"Will you teach us how to play a song?" Dakla asked. She boosted herself up and sat on the edge of the pool.

"You said you would," Hashep reminded me.

"I can't sit out there in the rain and play," I said. "Why don't you get out of the water and put on your tunics while I get the lyre? Then we'll sit under the portico ..."

"Girls! Don't bother master," their mother said in her halting Greek as she emerged from one of the workrooms off the garden. She's only a year older than I am, and now carrying another child. Niobe's midwifing skills would soon be needed. One look at Siwa revealed the source of her daughters' sleek black hair and lustrous dark eyes. Their lighter skin was their father's main contribution.

"It's not a bother, Siwa," I said. "And I did promise them."

Siwa shooed the girls out of the fishpond as I hurried to my bedroom. I keep a strongbox under the bed and hide the key in a location that only Demetrius and I know. But I did not want to risk even Demetrius seeing Agrippina's letter, so I resorted to a trick from my childhood. Lying face-down on my bed, I reached behind and under it and slipped the pouch containing the letter into the webbing of rope that supported the mattress.

I was just pushing myself up off the bed when I heard Hashep's voice behind me.

"What's taking you so long, Uncle Gaius?" She was standing in my door. Her light, bleached tunic made her hair and eyes seem even darker. How long had she been standing there? Had she seen what I was doing?

"I just needed to put something away. Now, let's play some music."

Hashep stepped into my room and took the lyre from the peg in the wall over my bed where I hang it. The wall is decorated with a fresco of Orpheus playing his lyre to soothe the monsters of the Underworld. I've placed the peg so that my lyre covers the one in the picture. "I'll carry it for you," Hashep said.

* * * *

Sitting in the far corner of the garden, the girls and I played and sang until their mother called them to help her at some task. Hashep sang with confidence and an ability to follow—even anticipate—the nuances of a melody that surprised me in a girl of her age. She learned quickly the two or three strokes on the lyre that I was able to teach her in spite of her younger sister's jealous interference. I decided she should be given more training in music. Having such a skill could help her rise above the status of a kitchen drudge, her most likely fate. As soon as she had mastered a song or two, I would have her sing at a small dinner.

When the girls were gone, with my assurances that we would sing again soon, I picked up the lyre. After a year away from it, I hadn't been sure I would be able to resume playing with any fluency. The tips of my fingers had softened. They would be sore for several days, but before I put the instrument away I strummed a few more chords and picked out one of my favorite melodies. I had almost forgotten how soothing this could be.

And I needed to be soothed. Finding myself the guest of honor at the *princeps'* house, being forced to examine a corpse in his library, then having Domitian himself show up at my door this morning with a demand that would probably be impossible to meet—any of that could unnerve even the stoutest heart. All of it together was enough to leave my heart near panic.

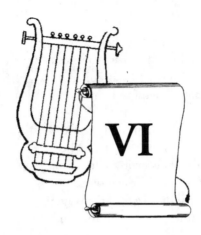

I HAD JUST FINISHED a song and was about to put away my lyre when my mother came into the garden, accompanied by Niobe, whom she seemed to be comforting. Peleus, Niobe's son, walked on the other side of his mother. They were among the slaves awarded to my uncle for his service in Titus' campaign against Jerusalem. Their Greek names had been given them to replace their unpronounceable Hebrew ones. Like her mythical namesake, Niobe had obviously been crying, although she showed no sign of turning to stone.

My mother, with tears in her own eyes, spotted me. "Oh, Gaius, Niobe and Peleus need to ask you something. Something important."

"Are they their advocate, Mother? Can't they speak for themselves?"

My mother put her arm around Niobe. "I'm sure they can, but Niobe came to me when she heard the news, and I just thought I would— "

"News? What news?" Why were slaves hearing news before the master of the house?

Niobe started to speak, but the tears erupted again. Mother looked at Peleus, who stepped forward.

"It's my uncle, my lord. My mother's brother. He's been killed."

"I'm sorry. When did this happen?" Even as fast as news travels across Rome's far-flung empire, the man could have been dead for weeks.

"Two days ago, my lord."

"Then he lived close by?"

"Here in Rome, my lord. He was brought here, as we were, after Jerusalem was destroyed." He didn't add the words 'by you Roman dogs,' but the sentiment lurked in his tone.

"What happened to him?"

"He was killed while he was working, my lord. Hit by a falling brick, or so we're told."

By the gods! Could there be two? Trying not to show my surprise,

66

I straightened up and stood directly in front of Peleus. "What is ... was your uncle's name?"

Niobe cried out something that sounded like a violent sneeze.

"His name was Menachem," my mother said, squeezing Niobe's shoulder. The slave buried her face in my mother's stola and sobbed. "She's very upset because it's their tradition that the ... person who has died not be left alone between death and burial and that he be buried as quickly as possible." Her own eyes were teary, recalling the deaths of her own brother and her husband, no doubt.

"And none of this was done?" I asked Peleus. He at least seemed to have his emotions under control.

"No, my lord. We just learned of his death an hour ago."

"He lived in Rome, you say. Did you see him often?"

He nodded. "He was a freedman, my lord, emancipated a few years ago after his work on the Amphitheater. He continued in Caesar's household, though. He was a mason. His Roman name was Maxentius."

Unable to suppress a gasp, I motioned for Peleus to follow me across the garden. When I was sure we were out of the women's hearing, I said, "This is an amazing coincidence. I saw your uncle's body yesterday, a few hours after he died." I didn't tell him the entire story, just that the man had been killed by a brick falling from a great height and hitting him on the head.

"Forgive me, my lord, for doubting you, but that's what I find so hard to believe."

"Why is that?" His refusal to believe me didn't really come as a surprise. I'd always found him obstinate, one of those young men who refuses to accept his status as a slave and, because of that attitude, probably fated always to be a slave.

"My uncle had great skill at plastering walls, my lord. He told us just a few days ago that he was working on the cryptoporticus of Domitian's new house. It would take him several more days to finish it, he said."

"What difference does it make where he was working?"

"The cryptoporticus, my lord."

Of course. The underground walkway. It was completely covered. Nothing could have fallen on Maxentius from any height, great or otherwise.

* * * *

No amount of lyre playing could settle my nerves after my mother left, arm-in-arm with two of my slaves, to attend the funeral of a freedman, a Jew, a man she'd never known, a man she never would have known, no matter how long he might have lived. I couldn't stop her. To avoid having my authority in the house undermined even further, I had to send a small troop of slaves to escort her, as though I approved of the whole business.

While awaiting their return, I tried to work on my accounts in the tablinum. Although Demetrius had kept good records while I was away, I couldn't concentrate on the documents he was showing me. Too much had happened since Tacitus and I started up the steps of the Palatine yesterday. It seemed his wife's fortune-teller had proved to be prescient—my life would never be the same.

I finally gave up and sent Demetrius to do something more useful with his time. Then I sent a slave to tell Josephus that I was on my way to see him. I needed to know more about where and how he found Agrippina's letter.

As my litter-bearers worked their way through the crowded streets I tried to make sense of a rapid, bewildering series of events. What disturbed me most was that Domitian had lied to me, not just once but twice. First in the archives, where he staged what was supposed to look like an accident, then right there in my own house. If Maxentius' death was an accident, it didn't happen the way Domitian told me. Based on what Peleus told me, I had to assume that Maxentius had been murdered.

I drew a deep breath, unwilling to accept my own conclusion, in spite of all the evidence carrying me to it, just as surely as the Tiber carries a boat to the sea. The man had been working in an underground passageway, out of sight of other workmen. From my examination of his body, I concluded that he'd been hit on the head by a brick, and hit hard. If it hadn't fallen from a great height, as Domitian claimed, then someone struck him with considerable force.

And if that was true, I saw some frightening questions confronting me: Had Domitian killed the man, perhaps with his own hands? Why? Could I trust anything Domitian said? About the memoirs? About not killing his brother?

A slave from the archives met me at the foot of the Palatine and escorted me past the Praetorians there. Even though I had made the journey up these steps once before and returned safely, I felt my breathing growing more labored as I ascended, and not just from the steepness of the hill.

Josephus was waiting for me under the stoa next to the temple of Apollo. He did not invite me into the archives, but took me to a bench near a fountain.

"We can talk more freely out here," he said, "where there are no bookcases or convenient little nooks to conceal eavesdroppers."

Our backs were against a solid wall, painted with a scene from one of Caesar's battles in Gaul, and the bubbling of the fountain would make our conversation impossible to hear unless someone was sitting next to us. A servant left a jar of wine, a jar of water, and two cups on a three-legged table in front of the bench.

I waited until the servant withdrew. Pulling out the pouch, which I had tied to a leather strap around my neck, I showed Josephus the letter. "This is what I need to ask you about."

"How did you get that?" His voice was steady, but he couldn't keep his face from betraying his surprise.

"Domitian brought it to me this morning. He said you found it in the archives."

"Yes, I did. Three days ago." He poured wine and water in the two cups and moved one toward me.

"Where exactly did you find it?" As illogical as it seemed, I hoped Agrippina's original diary might be close to where this letter had been kept. Josephus quickly disabused me of that notion.

"Oddly enough, it was in some boxes of Titus' papers. Domitian sent them over. He said I might find something useful in there pertaining to the war or the fall of Jerusalem."

I returned the letter to its pouch and slipped it back under my tunic. "But what would a letter from Agrippina to Nero be doing among Titus' effects?"

"I wondered that myself," Josephus said, speaking softly and darting his eyes around, even though there was no one near us. "Given the subject matter, I suspect someone found it when Vespasian took power. Nero's fall was so sudden he had no time to clean out his records. And the three short-lived rulers who came after him weren't in power long enough even to learn where the archives are."

I sipped the wine. It was Chian, very rich. "Do you think Vespasian and Titus kept this letter because it worried them?"

Josephus nodded and stroked his beard. "The existence of a rival is the constant worry of any ... tyrant. And if that rival has a stronger claim to power, the worry becomes a nightmare."

"Were Vespasian and Titus hunting for blood relatives of Nero?"

"I never heard them express such a concern, but I imagine they were ... always vigilant."

"So it's likely this letter is genuine." I touched it like some sort of amulet.

"Funny you should raise that question. It occurred to me immediately when I found it among Titus' effects. If it had been anywhere else, I don't think a doubt would have crossed my mind, but Titus had a remarkable skill with a pen. He could copy exactly the way another person shaped his letters. Once, while we were at dinner outside the walls of Jerusalem, he told me to write something in Hebrew. Then, writing in a language he didn't even know, he copied it so precisely that, had I not seen him do it, I could not have told which was my copy and which was his. He laughed and said, 'If I don't follow Vespasian to power, I'll become the most celebrated forger of all time'."

"Are you suggesting that Titus might have forged this letter?"

Josephus raised his hands and shrugged. "I'm merely saying he had the skill to do it."

"But why forge a letter that could undermine his family's claim to power?"

"He wouldn't do it for that reason, of course. But he might do it and leave it where Domitian would find it, just to annoy his brother. There was no love lost between them, you know."

I nodded. Everyone in Rome knew how much Domitian resented his older brother because of the preferential treatment Vespasian bestowed on him. During Titus' brief reign Domitian conspired against him and talked openly about encouraging the army to revolt. Titus had displayed remarkable restraint toward his troublesome brother. Perhaps too much, if there was any truth to the rumors about Domitian's role in his death.

"But the seal on the letter is authentic," I said.

"How do you know that?"

"My chief scribe knows Agrippina's seal. He has verified this one."

"Does that necessarily mean she sealed the letter herself?"

The question caught me off-guard, like a throw from an unexpected angle in a game of *trigon*. "Who else could have?"

"Anyone who had her seal." Josephus sipped his wine. "Agrippina was murdered at night by a squad of Nero's guards. In the accounts of her death that I've read, I've never seen any mention of her seal being destroyed. Someone could have kept it in order to forge documents that would incriminate her friends. That has been known to happen."

"You make me wonder if we can trust the genuineness of any document."

"A little skepticism about written documents is always healthy, Gaius Pliny. Some knowledge of history is also useful, as your uncle knew and as your friend Tacitus seems to appreciate. Do you read much history?"

I shook my head. "It doesn't interest me."

"Would it interest you to know about the relationship between Titus and Nero's family."

"What relationship?"

"Because Vespasian was such a successful general, Titus was raised in Claudius' house. It was supposed to be an honor for Vespasian's family, but it also gave Claudius a hostage to insure Vespasian would not turn his army on Rome. Titus was educated alongside Nero and Britannicus, who became his close friend. When Nero poisoned Britannicus, Titus picked up the fatal cup as it fell from Britannicus' hand and swallowed the last few drops. He hoped by dying with Britannicus he would free his father to overthrow Nero. All he got for his noble sacrifice was two days of indigestion."

"By the gods! I had never heard that story."

"I heard it from Titus himself, and I read it in your uncle's history, the one that continues Aufidius Bassus' work. There's a copy in this library, but I'm sure you have one of your own."

I had the information I'd come for, and I was in no mood for a snide lecture on the deficiencies of my education, so I stood to leave. "You've given me a great deal to think about, Flavius Josephus. Thank you for taking the time to see me."

Josephus remained seated and refilled his cup, with much more wine than water. "I enjoy talking with you, Gaius Pliny. By the way, what do you make of the scribbling on the back of that letter?"

"It looks to me like someone was practicing writing Greek."

"But not doing it very well, was he?"

"No." I touched the pouch hanging around my neck again. It felt heavier than when I had climbed to the top of this hill. "Could you make any sense of it?"

"I could not. I suspect it's not actually Greek. Perhaps some kind of code using Greek letters."

"But why would Agrippina have written such a thing on the back of a letter she was sending to her son?"

Josephus stroked his beard. "Do we know she wrote it? It could have been written before or after she wrote the letter. Nero had her confined to a house near Naples at that time. Writing material might have been scarce. Perhaps she picked up a scrap."

"So it could mean nothing."

Josephus raised his cup in a toast. "Or everything."

* * * *

As I reached the bottom of the steps a light rain started to fall, making me glad I had come in a litter. I closed the curtains on the side the rain was coming from. My bearers made good time until we reached the Flavian Amphitheater. The rain had brought the shows there to an early end, and the crowd was streaming out like ants from a hill into which a boy has thrust a stick. I felt like a scrap of food being carried along in that swarm as the litter was turned toward the nearby baths of Titus.

"We can't get through, my lord," Aeolus, the chief of my bearers, said. "What do you want us to do?"

71

"Let's just follow the crowd until we get to that fork ahead. It isn't the best route, but it will take us home."

I was about to draw the other curtains when I recognized a man walking past my litter.

"Greetings, Valerius Martial!" I called.

Martial is a young poet whose reputation has risen dramatically in the last few years. I count him among my friends rather than my clients, though not among my closest friends. The linch-pin of our relationship is a woman, but we have mutually pledged to say nothing about her in public. She now lives on a small farm near Nomentum, a few miles northeast of Rome, a farm which I gave Martial two years ago, out of my affection for the woman, not for Martial.

Martial turned toward me in surprise. "Good day, Gaius Pliny, if there can be anything good about such a sodden day."

"Are you going far? Would you like to ride with me?"

"That's a welcome offer, if you're going home. I have business atop the Esquiline myself." He climbed into the litter and we arranged ourselves at opposite ends and closed the curtains.

"How is everyone at Nomentum?" I asked.

"They are well. I've just returned from spending several days out there. It's wonderful to be able to escape the heat of the city at this time of year. Your generosity is still appreciated."

"You don't need to make any further mention of it. Where may I take you?"

"To the house of Marcus Aquilius Regulus, if you'll pardon me for speaking that name. I've been invited to—"

I shook my head. "No explanation is necessary. You're under no obligation to me."

The surging crowd brought the litter to a halt. "Brace yourself," Martial said.

"For what?"

"With this rig you might as well hang out a sign, 'RICHEST MAN IN THE CROWD.' Just wait."

I heard the arguing voices of a man and a woman drawing closer to my litter.

"Off with you!" the man cried. "One like this has no need of a bag of bones like you. He's got much better at home."

"Bugger yourself!" a raspy woman's voice replied. "He wouldn't feed his dogs with them clumps of scraps you call sausages."

Martial and I jerked back as the woman shoved her head and shoulders through the curtains. She wore a blonde wig and enough make-up for all the women, slave and free, in my house. The rain was threatening to turn it into a paste. As she bent over to talk to us, her loose gown revealed—deliberately, I was sure—a pair of wrinkled, aging breasts.

"Good afternoon, my lord. What can I do for ... Oh, two of you! Not that I mind, but that'll be a bit extra."

As the blood drained from my face, Martial put his hand on the woman's head to push her away. "Perhaps another time, Grandmother. I'd rather talk to the sausage man."

The woman stiffened her neck and wouldn't let Martial dismiss her. "Please, my lord. I'll do anything you like. With this weather the gents ain't been hangin' around long enough to have a little fun. I've lost my spot under the arches, and I've not ate in near two days."

"That's one of the perils of your occupation," Martial said. "Now step aside and let me talk to this other flesh peddler."

The drops that started from the woman's eyes weren't rain. I reached into my money pouch and pulled out a denarius. "Here," I said, "get yourself something to eat."

She snatched the coin so rapaciously I feared she might take one of my fingers with it. "Oh, thank you, my lord! Thank you! I'd be happy to earn it. You just tell me what you'd like."

"We'd like for you to go away." Martial gave her another push, this time with his foot.

As the litter began to move again the sausage man stuck his head in and Martial completed his transaction. We resumed our trip, with the litter filled by the aroma of greasy, grilled animal scraps and some spicy sauce. My own diet tends toward vegetables and fish, lighter fare. The combination of the smell and the swaying of the litter as we started uphill soon affected me as though I were on a boat.

"You look a bit green," Martial said around a mouthful of sausage.

I opened one of the curtains and stuck my head out. "I just need some air."

"You'd have been a lot sicker if that old whore had climbed all over you."

When we neared my house I directed my bearers to go on to Regulus' house, which is nearer the top of the Esquiline than mine. He has bought properties on either side of his and expanded his house so his wife, Sempronia, can have her own wing, giving her the privacy to indulge some of her rather peculiar interests. Everyone in Rome knows their marriage is an arrangement of financial convenience between two greedy, power-mad individuals. Every day prayers and sacrifices are offered that they will not have a son. The city survived Caligula and Nero; no one believes we could survive the monster that would be the son of Regulus and Sempronia.

"You can stop here," Martial said. "I know you don't want to risk an encounter with Regulus."

We were still a block away from Regulus' front door but in sight of one of his servants' entrances. As Martial said his farewell, a man stepped out of Regulus' door and threw the hood of his cloak over his head against the rain. I caught only a quick glimpse of him before he walked away in the opposite direction. Something about him seemed familiar, but I dismissed the notion. Men in hooded cloaks in the rain all tend to look alike.

"Isn't that your man Glaucon?" Martial asked.

* * * *

When my litter-bearers deposited me back at home I retreated to the garden, the place where I go when I need to collect myself. Much of my early childhood was spent on my uncle's country estates, where I could walk in the fields and woods. In my teens, when my mother and I began to spend more time in Rome, I found this garden a refuge from the responsibilities for which my uncle was training me. Since his death I had had several more trees planted here, to create as much of the feel of the woods as I could.

The garden had suffered from neglect while I was in Syria. Even the best gardener needs close supervision, and the two slaves Demetrius assigned to the task proved to be unequal to it. I had brought the best *topiarius* from my Laurentian villa to oversee the recovery of this garden. Thanks to his skill and the ample rain this summer, it was convalescing nicely. Compared to those in my villas at Laurentium or Tuscany, it was small—only twenty paces by thirty—but childhood memories made this a special place.

Paths paved with tufa stone wound their way diagonally across the peristyle, skirting the piscina where Hashep and Dakla liked to play. I followed the one that led to my bedroom at the opposite corner. Apple and pear trees stood in the center of the four sections created by the paths. Boxwoods, carefully pruned into the shapes of mythical creatures, outlined the four sides of the garden. The rose bushes on my right were heavy with blossoms. On my left beds of violets and poppies glistened with rain.

Several of my female slaves were crossing the garden, carrying baskets. They nodded their heads and wished me a good afternoon. I wondered if they were actually working or merely trying to give the appearance. My uncle would occasionally stop one of his slaves and ask just what he or she was doing. He sometimes discovered they were merely walking from one place where they had been unoccupied to another place where they planned to continue in idleness.

After making a circuit of the garden I sat on a marble bench under a trellis with grape vines running over it. Above the bench, in a niche in the rear wall of the house, stood a marble bust of my uncle. A similar memorial of my father sits on a pedestal at the other end of the garden, outside my mother's bedroom. The right cheek of that bust shows a dark, smooth spot where my mother caresses it each time she walks by. I have no recollection of my father at all. Four years after my uncle's death, I can still visualize  him, although the memory is dimming, the way images in even the most vivid dream fade after we wake.

I studied my uncle's bust, wishing he could advise me. He had to live for fourteen years under that madman Nero and virtually withdrew from public life during that time, but then he got to enjoy the last years of his life under Vespasian and Titus, two very reasonable men. What made the third member of this family so different? Domitian was worried about Nero returning when he himself acted like a reincarnation of the very man he feared.

There were so many questions I needed answered. In addition to all the questions Domitian had forced on me, I now had to wonder why a slave of mine was leaving Regulus' house when I had not sent him there. Was my scribe, a man who saw all of my correspondence and private papers, one of Regulus' spies?

Images—of Domitian in my tablinum, of Domitian and Regulus standing over Maxentius' body, and of Glaucon leaving Regulus' house—raced through my mind until they blurred together like the spokes of a fast-moving chariot wheel. Closing my eyes, I tried to hear my uncle's voice, deep and a little raspy because of his persistent breathing problems. But all I heard was the rustle of the leaves on the trellis above my head. Perhaps I should take that as the voice of a god. Shrines have been built around just such ethereal phenomena.

I needed someone to talk to, not just a mute marble muse but someone who could actually respond to me, so I sent a slave to invite Tacitus to dinner.

VII

WHILE WAITING FOR Tacitus' reply, I went to my bedroom and retrieved the writing box I keep there. Sometimes when I wake up early I work on a draft of a speech or a poem before going out to meet my clients. The box contains pens, a vial of ink, and some pieces of papyrus. Held on my lap, it serves as a writing table.

Returning to my seat in the garden, I pulled out Agrippina's letter and made two copies. One I intended to place in my library, the other in a secure place in my tablinum. The original would go back in its hiding place under my bed. I was putting things back in the writing box when a young girl's voice split the air.

"Give me that!" Hashep cried.

"You can't make me!" Dakla said. When she squealed I could tell the sound was moving from the atrium in my direction. I stood and took a few steps toward the piscina.

In another moment Dakla ran into the garden, with Hashep only a few strides behind her. The younger girl almost knocked me down as she put me between her and her sister, clinging to my tunic.

"Uncle Gaius," Hashep said, "please make her give me that."

"What is it?" I asked.

Hashep hesitated. "Just ... something I was writing."

I reached behind me, pulled Dakla off of my tunic, and lifted her into my arms. She waved a piece of papyrus over her head. My arm was too long for her, though, and I took it away from her and handed it to Hashep without looking at it.

"Thank you, my lord," she said. It was the first time she had called me that. Suddenly seeming too mature, she bowed her head and left the garden.

I put Dakla down and knelt in front of her. "Dakla, why do you annoy your sister so much?"

"She wouldn't play with me." The little girl's lower lip stuck out. "She wanted to practice her stupid writing."

"Now, writing is very important. It's how we tell our ideas to people who are far away from us, too far away to talk to. And it's how we learn what people thought many years ago."

"Hashep was writing a stupid song. She thinks she can write them like you do."

I could see I wasn't impressing her. "Would you like for me to teach you how to write some letters?"

She nodded her head eagerly. I stood up and took her hand.

"I just happen to have my writing box here. Come sit with me."

We sat side by side on the bench, sharing the writing box. "Your name is actually easy to write," I said. "The first letter, delta, is three straight lines, two down and one across, like this." I formed the Δ. "Then an alpha. It's also three lines, but the line that goes across is in the middle." A "Then a kappa." K

"They're all three lines," Dakhla said.

"That's true. The lambda is only two lines, though." Λ

"It looks like the alpha."

"There's no line across the middle."

"Oh, that's right." She didn't sound entirely convinced.

"Then another alpha at the end. Now you try it." I dipped the pen and handed it to her. She bent her head over the writing box and diligently copied over and over the letters I had written at the top of the page.

Watching her, I wondered how my life had gone from the simplicity of learning to form letters to the complexity of trying to figure out if a letter from a long-dead woman was what it purported to be and, if it was, what significance it held. Could I have kept my life simpler, and safer? Some men of my class chose not to pursue a public career. They lived quietly on their country estates, undisturbed by surprise visits from the *princeps*. My uncle had been harsh in his criticism of such men. They wanted to enjoy the benefits of Roman prosperity, he said, without doing anything to contribute to it. But even he had held no offices for ten years while Nero was in power.

"Look, Uncle Gaius! I did it!" Dakla startled me as she held up the papyrus proudly. Her letters wobbled and she had ink all over her hands, but she had indeed spelled out her name: ΔΑΚΛΑ

"That's very good, sweetheart. Do you want to show Hashep?"

"Not yet. Can you teach me to write my name in Egyptian letters? Hashep can't do that."

"I'm afraid I don't know Egyptian letters. They're pictures, aren't they?" The only ones I'd ever seen were on the obelisks brought from Egypt and set up in Rome.

"Yes. Like this." Dakla pulled out a necklace from under her tunic and held up the pendant so I could see it. "My papa got it for me. It's my name in Egyptian letters. On the other side it's in Greek. Hashep has one, too."

I peered closely at the piece of lapis lazuli on the silver chain. It had obviously cost a great deal. How had my steward been able to save enough out of his own money to afford two of them? I'd better pay closer attention to those account ledgers he showed me.

Three Egyptian symbols had been cut into the rich blue stone in a vertical row. The top one looked like a man's hand with the fingers extended and the thumb sticking up slightly. The second was simply a cup with a small handle on one side, and the bottom one a crouching lion. But why only three symbols when the child's name in Greek required five letters?

Odd, I thought, how a word from one language can be written with the letters from another. I turned the locket from front to back a few times. An Egyptian could look at Dakla's name in Greek and never recognize it. But isn't that what we Romans do all the time with Greek words and names? Plato wouldn't know his own name in Latin letters, nor would he recognize the Latin word 'philosophia,' even though he spoke it and wrote it many times in his own language.

"There's Hashep!" Dakla said. "I'm going to show her this. Thank you, uncle Gaius."

Waving the piece of papyrus, she ran off after her sister. As I put my writing materials back in the box, I noticed the copies of Agrippina's letter that I had made. They were fair copies, with the same number of lines as the original, but I hadn't written the odd Greek letters on the back. I pulled the original out of the pouch I was still wearing around my neck and unrolled it once more.

There were six Greek letters on the back. Or Greek-looking letters. Perhaps they were just written by someone who didn't know the language very well. If I were to draw the Egyptian characters in Dakla's name, I'm sure an Egyptian would think they looked barbaric. These letters did not spell any Greek word with which I was familiar.

But what if they were intended to spell out a Latin word?

Even that didn't work. I tried them backwards in both languages. They still made no sense. Somewhere in my uncle's notes I had read that Julius Caesar used to write in a code, substituting D for A, E for B, and so on. Applying that principle first in Greek, then in Latin, I still could not turn these letters into any recognizable word.

My failure raised two possibilities. First, I had not guessed the correct substitution pattern. Second, the Greek letters were being used to write a language which I did not know.

I was relieved to put the problem aside when a familiar voice said, "If I'm going to spend so much time over here, perhaps I should rent a room from you." Tacitus strode into the garden.

"You could have waited and come in time for dinner. You didn't have to return with the slave." But I was glad he had, rather than waiting a couple of hours to come along.

"I appreciate the invitation. Any excuse to get away from my wife is welcome, but none more than an invitation from you."

I closed the writing box and we settled onto couches in the exhedra, the outdoor eating area at the far end of the garden. The women's work was done for the day, so it was safe for men to enter this part of the house again. Aurora brought wine, cheese and bread. I instructed her to wait by the piscina instead of standing behind my couch. The flute and lyre players I had summoned were placed halfway between us and the piscina. This conversation, I suspected, was not going to be one I wanted to be overheard by even my most trusted slave.

"How is your speech for that court case coming?" I asked, to give Aurora time to get out of earshot.

"I believe I'm ready," Tacitus said. "It's not a very complex case and I've still got a few days to work on it. Do you want to hear a bit of it?"

"Later, perhaps. I doubt I could concentrate on it right now."

"What's troubling you? Your brow hasn't unfurrowed since I got here."

I told him first about Maxentius working in the cryptoporticus and my conclusion—the only possible conclusion—that he couldn't have been killed by a falling brick. My words seemed to hang in the warm, muggy air, with the flies darting in among them.

"Are you suggesting Domitian killed him or had him killed?" The shadows cast by the late afternoon sun partially obscured Tacitus' face, but I couldn't miss the anxiety in his voice.

"I'm convinced he was murdered. By whom, or on whose orders, I don't know. And I'm sure Domitian lied to me about what he knew about Maxentius' death."

"Why? What purpose of his would it serve to do that? You might as well suggest there's some connection between the mason's death and Agrippina's memoirs."

"What if there is?"

"Oh, Gaius Pliny, where did you come up with that centaur of a speculation?"

"I didn't. You did, just now."

"I was joking and you know it. Any connection between those two things would be as unlikely as a creature half-human, half-equine. Maxentius would have been a very young man living in the East when

Agrippina died. What possible connection ... No, it simply isn't worth wasting any more time on."

"You're right, I know. Anyway, I'm more concerned about the question of his murder."

"'Murder' is a strong word. Every *princeps* since Augustus has had people killed, if they haven't done it themselves. It's inevitable when you have the type of government we now have."

"Your beloved Republic had its share of assassinations and bloodbaths. Don't forget Sulla's proscriptions, Caesar's twenty-three wounds, and Cicero's head on a pole in the Forum."

Tacitus raised his cup. "That point I'll have to concede. Perhaps Rome can't be governed under any guise without the need to eliminate the enemies of those who govern. But in the past they've been people who seemed to pose a threat—members of their own families, members of the senate, rebellious generals. Why would someone as powerful as Domitian kill an insignificant workman?"

"That's just it. I can't think of any reason."

"Maybe he did it for sport. Nero used to disguise himself and lurk around the streets of the city at night, attacking people."

"Nero was a madman. Domitian is colder, more calculating. If he killed this man, there had to be a reason."

"I thought you believed it was to test Pliny the necromancer."

I grimaced at the reminder of the scene in the archives. "But why kill this particular man? Was he actually inspecting the work on his new house when he just happened on Maxentius and decided to kill him on a whim? I find that hard to believe."

"If you don't believe it, you have to assume that the ruler of the Roman world set his sights on one insignificant man, someone who would be no more important to him than one of these flies would be to you or me." Tacitus waved a hand over the table.

I liked his analogy. "But what if one of these flies lands in my wine or on the food I'm about to eat. Then that particular fly draws my attention to itself." An obliging fly landed on the table right in front of me. I put my hand slightly behind it and when it tried to fly again, I caught it and crushed it.

"How do you do that?" Tacitus asked with a laugh. "I've never been able to catch one of the accursed things."

"Someday I'll tell you." I raised my hands and rubbed them together to signal Aurora to bring me a bowl of water and a towel. "It's a little trick I learned from my uncle's scrolls."

"Ah, yes. Those infamous, oracular 160 scrolls." He waited until Aurora was far enough away again. "But how would Domitian's attention ever have been drawn to the fly that was Maxentius? How could Maxentius have landed in a position where the *princeps* would notice him and want to crush him before he could fly away?"

"That's what I intend to ask Peleus, if he ever gets back from his uncle's funeral. But there is one more thing I need to catch you up on." I told him about my visit to Josephus and what I had learned about Titus' relationship with Nero's family and his cleverness with a pen.

"He wanted to be known as the world's most celebrated forger? Where's the logic in that? To be celebrated, a forger's work would have to be recognized as forgeries, and that would mean they weren't good enough to fool anyone."

"I don't believe this letter is a forgery," I said, wiping my hands on the towel and reclining again on my couch. "And I suspect those markings on the back of the letter have a significance we haven't understood yet."

"Perhaps you should have Peleus look at them. If he can master Tironian notation, he might recognize some other kind of code or secret writing."

"Good idea. Now, let's put this business aside. It's making my head ache. Why don't you divert us with a piece of your speech?"

Tacitus would be speaking for the plaintiff in a case of a disputed inheritance, to be heard before the Centumviral Court in the Basilica Julia. His introduction, like most of his oratory, was more notable for its style than its content. But, after I made a few suggestions, I felt he stood a good chance of carrying the day. My clients and I would applaud him vigorously in hopes of swaying the members of the court.

It was growing dark and slaves were lighting torches in the garden when Demetrius approached us. "My lord, you wanted me to inform you when your mother returned."

"Ask her to come out here and bring Niobe and Peleus with her."

Tacitus and I stood as my mother crossed the garden. She sat on the third couch and, much to my surprise, invited Niobe to sit beside her. Peleus understood his place well enough to remain standing as Tacitus and I sat on the edges of our couches. The clothing of both slaves was torn in front. I would inquire about that after I'd assured myself of my mother's well-being.

Kissing her on the cheek, I said, "I'm glad to see you home safely, Mother. I was worried about you."

"Why? I was never in any danger."

"You look ... tired." It wasn't exactly the right word, but I had never

81

seen this expression on her face before. She appeared less anxious, almost younger.

"Tired? Why, no, dear. I feel exhilarated."

"Where have you been all this time?"

"We went first to their synagogue." She held Niobe's hand.

"What's a synagogue?" Although it was Greek, the unfamiliar word stumbled off my tongue.

"A sort of temple. Could you explain it?" my mother said, turning to Peleus.

"Actually, my lady, my lord," Peleus said, "it's a place of study and worship, but not a temple. For us there is—or was—only one temple."

Again, he didn't say 'until you Roman dogs destroyed it,' but his tone certainly implied that.

"Where is this synagogue?" I asked.

"In the Subura," my mother said, as calmly as she might have said 'in the Forum.'

I jumped up. "The Subura?" Rome's most disreputable neighborhood, home of thieves, beggars, cut-throats and whores. And Jews, it seemed. I turned on Peleus. "You took my mother into the most dangerous part of Rome? How dare you!"

"Calm yourself, Gaius. Phineas didn't take me. I went along with him."

"Phineas? Who is Phineas?" Confusion deflected my anger.

"The young man you're berating. That's his true name. And this dear woman is Naomi. That's what we shall call them from now on."

New names, my mother strolling in the Subura—this was too much to take in at once. "We'll discuss that later, Mother. In private. Right now I want to talk with ... Peleus. Perhaps you could see how preparations for dinner are coming. I'd like to eat out here."

"Very well, dear." She and Niobe stood. "But don't chastise Phineas too severely. He and his mother have suffered a terrible loss, just as we did four years ago. Keep that in mind. Come, Naomi."

Peleus didn't turn around, but Tacitus and I watched the two women until they entered the kitchen. My mother's step seemed more confident than it had since my uncle's death, her back straighter. And she had ventured out of the house for longer than she had at any time since the eruption of Vesuvius. I wanted to talk to her apart from Niobe, to see if I could determine what influence the slave woman was exercising over her. Even if their relationship seemed helpful to my mother at the moment, there was no predicting what effect it might ultimately have. I would do whatever it took to protect her, even if it meant sending Niobe to one of my country estates or selling her.

But first I had to deal with Peleus. I stood in front of him and looked him up and down, like a centurion inspecting a legionary. I consider myself a kind and reasonable master, but I wanted to show Peleus—and Tacitus, for that matter—just how stern I could be.

I tugged at the front of his tunic. "How did this get torn?"

"In our funerals the clothing of family members is torn in this way, my lord. It's a sign of mourning."

"And a waste of perfectly good garments. Which are my property, I must point out." I paced around him. Tacitus leaned against his couch, arms folded across his chest.

Peleus seemed cowed, exactly as I intended. He kept his eyes down. "They ... they can be mended, my lord. My mother will do it when the period of mourning is over."

"How long is that?"

"Seven days."

I shook my head. "I'll not have servants of mine going out in mended clothing. People will think we've fallen on hard times. Just cut them up and use them for cleaning. And you can pay for them out of any money you have saved up."

"Yes, my lord. I'm sorry, but it is part of our custom—"

I cut him off, stopping right in front of him. "I'm sure I'll be hearing about this funeral from my mother for days to come. It seems to have had a strange effect on her. As for you, I'm very angry that you abused the privilege I gave you."

"My lord, I only did what you gave me permission to do. I escorted my mother to her brother's funeral. We returned by dark, as you told us to."

"But I did not give you permission to take my mother into the Subura." I noticed Tacitus straightening up, as though he was about to join me in a two-pronged assault.

"We didn't ask her to go with us, my lord. She joined us just as we were leaving."

I moved behind Peleus now, to his left, where he couldn't quite see me without turning his head. As a military tribune in Syria I had seen officers question men from this position. It seemed to unsettle them, like being attacked by an enemy they couldn't see. "When she told me she was going, I assumed it was at your mother's invitation."

"My mother would never presume to ask such a thing, my lord, especially considering how long a walk it was."

That surprised me. "It's not that far from here to the Subura and back."

"But my uncle was buried along the Appian Way, my lord, near the tomb of Caecilia Metella."

Tacitus gasped. "What? That's almost ... two miles south of the city!"

I stormed around in front of Peleus, my face just a few fingers width from his. I drew myself up to emphasize my slight advantage in height. "Do you mean you forced my mother to walk all that distance, as frail as she is?"

"No one forced her, my lord. I told her she ought to go home after we finished our prayers in the synagogue. But she wouldn't hear of it."

I could hardly think of what to ask next. Tacitus stepped in. "Did you at least find a chair for her to ride in?" His resonant voice was still in good form after his earlier practice with his speech.

Peleus flinched at this attack from his flank. "No, my lord. In our funerals it's forbidden for anyone but the deceased to be carried, unless it's just impossible for them to walk. The lady Plinia made the trip without any difficulty that I could see. It was comforting to my mother to have her there, but awkward as well."

"Awkward?" Tacitus said. "How could it be awkward to have a member of such a noble family at your uncle's funeral? I should think the lady Plinia's presence lent great prestige to the whole affair."

"Our funerals are quite simple, my lord. Our holy books teach that the first man was made from the earth. When we die we return to it, bearing nothing, just as we came from it. Displays of wealth and social standing are forbidden. We had to ask the lady Plinia to remove her jewelry."

Now that he mentioned it, that was something else different about my mother. I don't think I had ever seen her without earrings, a couple of rings, and especially the gold bracelet my father gave her. I wondered why she hadn't put them back on after the funeral was over.

"That's enough about this funeral," I said, sitting on the edge of my couch. "I'll get my mother's side of the story later. Now I want to know more about your uncle and about his death."

The change of topic and the softening of my tone caught Peleus off balance. "What do you want to know, my lord?"

"Just give me a brief account of his life. I'll stop you or ask questions as I see the need. He was a mason, wasn't he?"

"Yes, my lord." He took a deep breath. "Well, he worked in all kinds of masonry, but he was especially skilled at plastering."

"And he was a freedman?"

"Yes, my lord. He and my mother came from a family in Pergamum in Asia. When my father died, my uncle—who was a widower—took my mother and me in. We lived there until two years before the war broke out. That year we went to Jerusalem for the Passover, our holiest feast. My uncle and my mother decided to move there. My uncle opened his own shop and employed several other men. But then the war came."

"How old were you by then?"

"I was eleven when Jerusalem fell. We almost starved during the siege."

"Yes, I understand it was horrible." I hoped I sounded sympathetic.

"I've heard my uncle talk about it, and I've read Josephus' account."

"Josephus!" Peleus turned his head and spat. "That self-serving traitor was safe outside the walls, growing fat at Titus' table, while his own people were eating rats and shoe leather to stay alive." With his face contorting in rage and his fists clenched, he took a step toward me. "If you ever have to choose between them, my lord, take the shoe leather."

I pulled myself up to my full height and put my hand on his chest to stop his advance. "How dare you threaten me!"

Tacitus grabbed Peleus' arm and twisted it behind his back, forcing the slave to one knee. His face, twisted in anguish like some Pergamene sculpture, showed his realization of the seriousness of what he'd just done. "For - for - forgive me, my lord. I d - d - didn't mean ..."

I looked down at him until he dropped his gaze. When I signaled to Tacitus to release him, Tacitus pushed him to the ground, face down. As his master I would have been within my rights to hit him, even to have him whipped. But what would that accomplish? It would further confirm his opinion of Romans in general—and his master in particular—as cruel tyrants. Flogging him might make my other slaves fear me a bit more. Or perhaps they would only hate me. The hardest part of the life of someone of my class is knowing he is surrounded in his own house by all these people who resent him and who would welcome his death if they could only be sure what would happen to them afterward.

"Just remember," I said, "that none of us—slave or free—controls our fate. Things often work out in our lives due to events which we do not set into motion and cannot stop. Now, get up and go on with your story,"

"Yes, my lord." He pulled himself together, stood up, and continued his tale. "My mother and I happened to be among the slaves allotted to your uncle after the fall of the city. Because of his skill as a mason, Menachem was taken by Titus along with other workmen. At least we all ended up in Rome."

"And you've had no reason to complain of your treatment in this house, have you?"

Peleus said nothing, just stared at the wall over my shoulder.

"Have you?" I repeated. "Have you ever felt the whip across your back or shackles chafing your wrists?"

He shook his head. "No, my lord. You, and your uncle before you, have been ... as kind as any slave could hope."

"Your uncle didn't fare as well, did he? I saw the whip marks on his back."

I thought I saw tears in Peleus' eyes. "He could not accept his status as a slave, my lord."

"I think he imparted some of that spirit to you," Tacitus said.

85

"I admired him very much, my lord," Peleus replied without looking at Tacitus.

"Your uncle was working on Domitian's new house when he died. What other projects had he worked on?"

"The Flavian Amphitheater and Titus' baths, my lord."

"Do you know of any reason why someone would have killed him?"

"No, my lord. Why would you ask that?"

"Because I think he was murdered, and I want to know if it was just a random crime or if someone killed him for a particular reason." The someone, of course, being Domitian. The particular reason ... that was still to be determined.

"Did he ever mention arguments he'd had?" Tacitus asked. "Anyone he'd antagonized?"

"No, my lord. But I imagine that could happen. Menachem was something of a braggart."

"What did he brag about?" I asked.

"About the baths of Titus, my lord."

"He was proud of his work there?"

"Yes, my lord, and he liked to talk about what he saw beneath the baths."

"Beneath the baths?" I turned to Tacitus, who raised an eyebrow.

"The baths were built on top of part of Nero's Golden House," Tacitus said. "But I don't know what's beneath them. I thought Nero's house had been obliterated."

"Not entirely, my lord," Peleus said. "The work was done in such a hurry that the foundations for the baths were built right through Nero's house. If you know how to get there, you can still see parts of the house."

"And your uncle knew how to get there?" Tacitus asked.

"Yes, my lord."

"Did he take you there?" I asked.

"Yes, my lord, a couple of times."

"What did you see?"

His face grew animated. "The most amazing wall paintings, incredible designs worked into the plaster. Some of them still had gold leaf on them, although most of that had been stripped off."

I turned to Tacitus. "There's our connection, as tenuous as it may be."

"What do you mean?"

"A connection from Nero to Domitian through this mason. Maxentius saw Nero's house. Domitian is worried about Nero coming back to life, and now Maxentius is dead."

Tacitus scoffed. "That 'connection' wouldn't support a spider. Next you'll be telling me Regulus had something to do with it."

"Didn't Domitian say he and Regulus were inspecting the work on his new house when Maxentius was killed?" I turned to Peleus. "Did your uncle ever do any work for Marcus Aquilius Regulus?"

"Yes, my lord, he did. Last year."

"There you are," I said to Tacitus. "Regulus knew Maxentius. Do you still think his death was random?"

"But why would Regulus want to kill some man who had plastered his walls?"

"Forgive me, my lords," Peleus said, "but there's more to it than just plaster."

Tacitus and I turned back to him.

"I guess I can admit it, now," he said, "since my uncle is dead . ... He was one of Regulus' spies."

VIII

AFTER I DISMISSED Peleus, Tacitus and I sat on our couches and looked at one another in disbelief.

"Could it be a coincidence?" Tacitus finally said.

"You know I don't believe in coincidences," I said. "And, if I did, this would never qualify. The man who's killed so Domitian can test my deductive abilities just happens to be a man Regulus knows. And the two of them just happen to be there when this poor fellow has an 'accident.' I'll never believe it was a coincidence."

"But why would Regulus sacrifice one of his spies?" Tacitus asked. "And a spy who had connections in the imperial household, at that."

"It must have something to do with Nero."

"Why 'must'?"

"Because Maxentius went into the Golden House. He must have said something about what he saw there. Something that upset Domitian."

"But you heard Peleus. He saw wall decorations. How could that have upset Domitian?"

Before I could answer, my mother appeared in the garden. Tacitus and I both stood quickly.

She had bathed and put on a clean stola, bleached but undyed. She rarely wore much make-up; tonight her face was entirely natural, her hair pulled back into a bun on her neck. She wore no jewelry, not even my father's bracelet. She could have been a middle-aged slave as easily as a noble Roman matron.

"May I join you?" she asked.

"It would be an honor, my lady," Tacitus said. He offered her his place on the middle couch, but she refused and reclined on the low couch.

"I can see my Gaius better from here."

Even in the dim light I caught Tacitus' slight smirk. Both of his parents are dead, and I doubt his in-laws dote on him the way my mother does on me.

"Well, lady Plinia," he said as we resumed our places, "it sounds as though you had an eventful day."

Mother took his comment as an invitation. "It was one of the three most memorable days of my life, along with Gaius' birth and the eruption of Vesuvius."

"That's impressive company." Tacitus glanced at me with undisguised amusement. "What made this day so remarkable?"

"The austerity and simplicity of Menachem's funeral. The Jews don't allow any display of the deceased's wealth. There's no eulogy that goes on for hours—"

"You mean, like the one I gave for my uncle?" I said. I still considered that speech my best to date, especially since I was only seventeen at the time and had not expected to have to make it for several more years.

"Now, dear, I know you meant well and until this afternoon I thought your speech was splendid. But, now that I've seen how meaningful a simple funeral can be, I wonder why we go to all the trouble and expense that we do."

"How simple was it?" Tacitus asked.

"They recited some prayers and read passages from their holy books in the synagogue, and the man who led them was singing as much as reading."

"How is *that* impressive?" I asked. "There's no effort required to chant words no one understands out of some crumbling old book. The Arval Brethren do that." I jerked a piece of bread off the loaf, almost knocking over my cup of wine.

"Don't be petulant, Gaius," Mother said. "Your eulogy was impressive. This was more than that. Or different. It was ... spellbinding. I can still hear it."

I snorted. Women and slaves seem to share a susceptibility to religion. Various cults are thickly populated with them. My uncle thought it was because religion offers them a chance to feel powerful, something they don't find in their daily lives. As a rule, such a feeling is harmless, but it can't be allowed to fester until it disturbs the natural order of society.

"Your slave said you walked almost to the tomb of Caecilia Metella for some sort of burial ceremony," Tacitus said.

"Yes. They've carved out an underground burial place. A catacomb they call it."

"Not a mausoleum or a regular necropolis?" I asked.

"No, it's a cave. As you walk along the road, you would never know it's there. You don't see the entrance until you're right in front of it. Steps lead down to a series of chambers. The bodies are placed in niches in the walls."

"So, you not only walked over four miles, but you climbed up and down steps as well?" I was amazed that my mother, as frail as she seems, had stood up under all that exertion. In a few hours she had seen parts of Rome that, in all her forty years, she'd hardly even imagined existed. For that matter, she'd seen parts of it I had never seen, and never wanted to.

"I'm tired now, dear. I'll admit. But I was carried along by some kind of energy I'd never felt before."

"What exactly do they do to the body?" Tacitus asked. "Is it anything like the mummifying that the Egyptians do? That takes a couple of months."

Mother took a sip of her wine. "They don't do anything. The body is wrapped in a plain linen sheet and left in the cave for a year. Then the bones are gathered up and placed in a stone box."

"How grotesque!" I muttered.

"That's what I thought at first," my mother said. "But as I looked at the inscriptions on the wall—many of them in Greek—I saw how much it meant to these people to have a place not only to remember their dead but to be in their presence. It made me realize I have nothing to connect me to my husband or my brother in that way."

"Why do you say that? Their portrait busts stand in this very garden," I pointed out. "My father gave you a gold bracelet which you've never taken off until today."

She touched her bare wrist. "I'm joining Naomi in her mourning for seven days. I'll wear the bracelet again after that. But it's not really a part of your father. Neither is that bust. Everything that was him and my brother was consumed by the flames. Why do we want to obliterate our loved ones like that?"

"It's what we've always done," I said. "You'd have to ask our ancestors the reason."

"If they even had one," Tacitus added. "People don't often know the true origins of these ancient traditions. That's why they make up myths. I doubt the Jews know why they have such fanatical opposition to burning the bodies of their dead that they have to dig these caves."

"Naomi says they believe their bodies are given to them by their god. They should be returned to him as whole as possible, with nothing added or taken away. That's what their holy books teach."

Having Naomi—I might as well get used to the name—and her holy books cited as authorities was getting tiresome. I wanted to talk about something else.

"Mother, you said you want to change Niobe's and Peleus' names, to go back to their Jewish names."

"Yes, I do."

"But their names sound barbaric."

"No more barbaric than Hashep and Dakla. We tried to impose Greek names on them, but we all call them by the names their mother gave them."

"No one calls me by the name you gave me. I'm no longer Caecilius; I'm Pliny."

"I didn't give you either of those names. You were named after your father, as custom dictates, and when you were adopted, your name was changed, as the law requires."

"And I've accepted that change. Why can't Niobe and Peleus?"

"But the change of your name wasn't imposed on you against your will. You could have refused the adoption and the estate."

"And how would I have cared for you if I did?"

"Was that your only reason for accepting your legacy?"

She was broaching an uncomfortable topic. "Mother, why do these people matter so much to you?"

"Because I matter to them." Her voice seemed stronger, more alive, than it had since my uncle's death. "Naomi was a great comfort to me while you were in Syria. We discovered we have so much in common. She has only the one son, but she lost a daughter when the girl was an infant, just as I did. We've calculated that both of our little girls would have been eighteen now. Then Naomi lost her husband and was taken in by her brother, just as I was. Now she's lost her brother, as I did, violently and unexpectedly. You may not have thought about it, but you and Phineas have lived very similar lives as well."

I drew back in shock. "How can you compare my life to a slave's?"

"It's true," she insisted. "Phineas lost his father when he was three, the same age you were when your father died. He was raised by his uncle, as you were, like a son. Now his uncle has died tragically, just as yours did."

"Mother, people die and families take care of one another. The law expects them to. This story must be repeated a thousand times over every year. Why should an imaginary parallel arouse any sympathy in me for this ... Phineas?" I forced the crude sound through my lips.

She fixed her eyes on me. "Because I know you have a good heart, Gaius. You are your father's son, and you were raised by my brother. Two finer men never lived. Your uncle died trying to save people from Mt. Vesuvius. You've told me he is your exemplar."

I looked to Tacitus for help, but he was focusing all his attention on opening a mussel with a knife. "What do you expect me to do, Mother?" I finally said.

"Find out who killed Menachem." Her voice was soft and all the more compelling. "Naomi and Phineas are powerless to do anything. Does that mean they can't know what happened to someone they loved? They're slaves, yes, but they're also human beings. Don't they have the right to know?"

When did she become a Stoic philosopher? I wondered. But she was only urging me to do something I wanted to do for my own reasons.

"All right, I'll do whatever I can."

"Thank you, dear. And, Cornelius Tacitus, will you help him? I know this could be a dangerous business."

"I promise I'll do my best, lady Plinia, to keep your Gaius out of trouble."

I almost threw a piece of bread at him.

"Thank you," my mother said. "Thank you both."

We talked for a bit longer about the events of the last few days. My mother pressed me to explain why Domitian had come to our house. Even as I evaded her questions, I wondered again if there was any connection between that visit and Menachem's death, especially in light of what I now knew about the mason's relationship with Regulus and his visits to Nero's Golden House, but I did not voice my concern.

The day's exertion finally did overtake my mother. With her head cradled on her arm, she dropped off to sleep. If she hadn't been snoring gently, I might have worried about her.

"Get Ni ... Naomi," I told Aurora. "Tell her to come to my mother's room to prepare her for bed."

"Yes, my lord." She seemed to know whom I meant. I wondered how long this change of names had already been in effect in the women's part of the house. The transition would be easy to make. Someone who had a cold would pronounce both names about the same.

When I picked up my mother to carry her to her bedroom, she felt as light as a child in my arms.

Naomi was waiting for me in my mother's room. She didn't say anything until I had laid my mother on the bed. Then she dropped to her knees. "My lord," she said in a hushed voice, "thank you for your kindness to my son earlier this evening. You had every right to punish him. He has a rebellious spirit, I know. I've tried to teach him to appreciate how kind you and your uncle have been to us, but—"

I took her hands and pulled her to her feet. I don't like people kneeling in front of me as though I were some sort of god. "This isn't necessary. Just take good care of my mother. I do want to talk with you some more about today's events. For now, you tend to my mother. And, again, I am sorry for the loss of your brother."

"Thank you, my lord. Thank you."

I leaned over and kissed my mother on her forehead.

* * * *

Tacitus was ready to leave when I returned to the garden.

"Would you be willing to join me on a trip tomorrow?" I asked. "Just for the day."

"Certainly, as long as it gets me out of the house. As the old poet Semonides said, 'You cannot enjoy any day when you must spend it, from beginning to end, with your wife.' Where are we going?"

"Out to Musonius' villa."

"All that way? Why?"

"He's the only person named in Agrippina's letter that we know is still alive. And he's the only person we know who met Agrippina and had some connection to a relative of hers. I want to ask him some questions in confidence."

After Tacitus left I sat under the trellis in the garden a while longer, sipping some wine, looking at the bust of my uncle, and trying to find any pattern that would make sense out of all that had happened over the past couple of days. My slaves came out to clear the table. Not wanting to be disturbed, I told them to leave it until morning, so they extinguished the torches and lamps and wished me a good night.

Because of the heavy clouds that still hung over the city, there was no light from the moon or stars. The darkness that surrounded me in my garden was as dense as the darkness engulfing me in this search for a missing, possibly non-existent, book. There was one difference, though. I could walk across my garden in the dark without bumping into anything because I knew it so well. But everywhere I turned in the search for Agrippina's unedited memoir, I seemed to trip over some problem or question, like a hidden tree root. Had Titus forged the letter Domitian showed me? Did the letters on the back of it mean anything? What had Maxentius—or Menachem—seen in Nero's Golden House that made him a threat to Domitian? Had Domitian arbitrarily killed him? And why was my own scribe coming out of Regulus' house?

The only theme I could find emerged from the mocking words of the seer Tacitus' wife had consulted: *If you go up the Palatine Hill, your life will never be the same.*

It was late, but I knew I wouldn't be able to sleep if I went to bed, so I sat under the trellis, quiet and still, for so long that I lost track of time. Eventually I heard the voices of people going home from a dinner party. Then two nightwatchmen, the *vigiles*, passed on their rounds, chatting quietly, marking the end of the first watch of the night.

As soon as the watchmen's voices had faded, a figure in a hooded cloak emerged from the front of the house and hurried across the garden. I had my mouth open to call him to a halt, if it was a man. Then I decided it was more important to know where this person was going. Servants do sneak out. Every master knows it. Even if we post guards, we can't stop them, since the guards are likely to turn a blind eye, if they aren't the ones sneaking out themselves. It's usually harmless, resulting in nothing more serious than an inconvenient pregnancy somewhere in the neighborhood. But, given my present state of anxiety, if one of my servants was sneaking out, I wanted to know who, and I wanted to know where he was going and why.

The figure kept to the edge of the garden, where the shrubbery was thicker, and crouched down, moving with the assurance of someone who knew the path well. He opened the door in the back wall of the garden, paused as he checked to make sure the street was empty, then went out and eased the door shut.

I climbed the trellis and boosted myself up so I could see over the back wall, which is almost twice my height. The figure was walking up the hill, toward Regulus' house.

Dropping to the ground and picking up the knife Tacitus had used to open the mussels, I let myself out the rear door. For a moment I feared I had already lost sight of the figure. The way his cloak and hood blended into the walls, and with everything turning gray due to the lack of moonlight, I had to peer intently to pick him out.

As I took the first few steps, something felt odd. Then I realized this was the first time I had ever been out of my house in Rome without an escort of my slaves or clients. In some districts I would have been dead by now. Once the sun goes down the streets of Rome belong to people who have no regard for law, no respect for life or property. Traveling in a group is the only way to guarantee one's safety.

But I was alone, absolutely alone. I gripped the knife tightly.

The hooded figure paused near one of the servants' doors at the back of Regulus' house. Someone, also wearing a cloak and hood, came out, kissed him, and took his hand. Judging by the blonde hair peeking out from under the hood, I assumed the second figure was a woman.

So that was all it was—a clandestine flirtation with a servant from another house. I might as well go home. The risk of being out on the streets alone at night wasn't worth spying on one of my servants and his paramour. I could roust someone at home and put him on guard at the back door so I could learn the identity of the man in the hood. Tomorrow morning I would chastise him soundly and that would be the end of it, until he sneaked out again. I almost laughed at myself for being worried about something so insignificant in the midst of all the other questions confronting me.

But a voice inside me said, *This isn't just any other house. Someone in your house is involved with someone from Regulus' house.*

As the two figures climbed farther up the hill I followed them, pressing myself so close to the walls of the houses that I felt like I was part of the graffiti I was rubbing against. I kept them in sight until they reached an entrance to the Gardens of Maecenas. The woman kissed the man again, put her hand on his crotch, and laughed—a low, hungry noise. Then I lost sight of them as they entered the Gardens.

Maecenas, the friend of Augustus, established these Gardens over a century ago. Occupying about half of the top of the Esquiline and open to everyone, they provide a cool, pleasant spot where even the poorest citizens can find some relief from the heat and crowding of the city. When I entered the Gardens I was immediately aware that the hooded couple weren't the only people there. I gripped my knife more tightly as I heard rustling and whispering in the bushes around me.

The couple found a relatively private spot near the old city wall, which runs through the Gardens. I crouched behind a statue of Priapus—appropriately enough—and watched.

The woman kept her back to the man. He put his arms around her, almost as though he was taking her captive, then removed her cloak. Underneath it she was nude. With one hand he cupped her breasts while the other hand ran down her stomach. He kissed her neck, and I could hear her moaning. He pushed her to the ground. Breathing heavily, she fell on her knees and elbows. Because of the shrubbery, the lower part of her body was all I could see. The pale skin of her slender hips and legs stood out against the dark wall behind her. The man threw off his own cloak and I saw my scribe, Glaucon, ready to mount the woman.

The women in my own household consider Glaucon quite handsome. He does not appear to be as old as he is, and he wears his hair foppishly long on his neck and just over his ears. Apparently his admirers formed an even wider circle. This might account for some of the arrogance the man displays, a characteristic which seems to make him even more appealing to women. If he were not Dymas' son, I would have little patience with him.

I was relieved to see that he was involved in nothing more sinister than some surreptitious coupling. But was this all there was to it? If he had this kind of connection—I immediately regretted my own choice of words—how could I be sure he wasn't involved with Regulus' household in some other way? Could he be one of Regulus' spies?

Those were questions I would rather consider in the safety of my own home. The furtive noises I heard around me seemed to be passing the word, *He's alone. He can't defend himself.*

I walked back down the hill as quickly as I could. I would have run, but someone running on pavement makes too much noise. When I reached my house I pulled on the door, but it held fast. I yanked it again. It was barred!

Demetrius, faithful steward that he is, must have made a final check of the doors before going to bed. What could I do now? I couldn't pound on the door and waken someone. To do that would be to admit I had been out spying on one of my slaves. I would never have any authority in my household once they heard about that. My only consolation was that Glaucon was going to be surprised, too. He must have been counting on everyone being asleep so no one would notice the door being left unbarred for a short while.

Or he knew some other way in.

As I considered how I might gain entry to my own house I heard a noise behind me. Before I could react, something collided with me. A heavy, hairy arm grabbed me around the chest, pinning my arms, and a filthy hand clamped over my mouth. "If you squawk," a man's deep voice snarled, "I'll snap your scrawny neck."

The strength in the hand made me believe he could do it. I tightened my grip on my knife and struggled briefly. The man almost lifted me off the ground.

"So, you sneak out of the master's house and they lock the door on you." He laughed viciously in my ear and tightened his grip, almost squeezing the breath out of me. "They'll miss you tomorrow, but nobody'll know where you went, 'cause you didn't tell anybody you was goin', did you? You'll fetch a nice price. Pretty young one like you. Did you have fun watchin' them two?" He moved his left arm lower, reaching for my crotch. "I hope you enjoyed it, lad, 'cause they'll take a knife to you and before long you'll be spreadin' your cheeks just like her ladyship back there. And your voice will be as high as hers."

The man was taller than me. I could feel his chin on the back of my head. As the arm around my chest moved lower, he had to relax his grip on my right arm. The hand stopped when it ran across the equestrian stripe sewed onto my tunic. He gripped it and pulled it up to where he could see it over my shoulder. That let me glimpse his face out of the corner of my eye. It was a brutal face, made even uglier by the patch he wore over his right eye.

"May the gods help me!" he gasped. "I thought you was a slave. What's a lord doin' runnin' around in the streets by himself at night?"

I wanted to make him an offer. If he would let me go and help me get into my house, I would forget the whole incident. But his hand clamped tighter over my mouth.

"No choice now, though. I have to kill you."

He started to twist my neck, but, in his instant of hesitation, I threw my arm over my shoulder, plunging the knife into him with all the force I could gather. I didn't care where it struck him. He made a gurgling noise and pulled me down to the pavement with him as he collapsed.

For a moment his arms locked more tightly around me, then began to loosen. When I pushed him off of me I could feel my tunic sticking to me. I pulled it off and found it soaked in my urine and the villain's blood, spurting from the wound in his neck. He twitched a few more times, then went limp. I wiped the blood off my arm and off the knife and dropped my tunic beside him. I would have dropped the knife, too, but it had my initials carved in the handle.

By the gods! What was I to do now? Locked out of my own house, standing naked in the street, with a man dead by my own hand at my feet.

I ran my hands over the wall of my house. If some of my servants were in the habit of sneaking out at night, they must have a way of getting back in. They couldn't always rely on the door being unbarred.

At the point where my house joined my neighbor's, I found it. My neighbor's house protruded beyond mine about the span of a hand. The surface of his wall and mine at that point was rough enough to offer a few toeholds, and one of the vines in my garden had grown over the wall. With the knife in my teeth I managed to scale the wall, work my way over to the trellis and climb down it into my garden.

I dropped the knife back on the table with the other dirty dishes, alarmed at how much clatter it made. Suddenly I knew I had to wash myself. I could feel that bastard's hands all over me, and his blood. At this hour the bath was out of the question. I was sure to wake somebody if I went in there, so I ran to the piscina, plunged in and submerged myself several times.

Then I grabbed what was left of the wine from dinner, went to bed and lay there shivering uncontrollably until the wine ...

* * * *

"My lord." Demetrius' voice was loud, almost as loud as the pounding in my head. "My lord, forgive me, but you're needed in the garden."

Still naked, I opened the door only far enough to peer around it. The sun wasn't fully up yet. "What is it?"

"There's been some trouble in the street behind the house, my lord. The Urban Cohorts are here to talk to you about it."

"To me? Why do they want to talk to me?" I'd better start playing innocent from the first moment.

"I don't know, my lord. But they insist on seeing you."

"All right, just a moment." I closed the door and fumbled in the dark to find a tunic. *This will be the end of me,* I thought. *Arrested for murder. What will happen to my mother?* I used the chamberpot. I didn't want to soil another garment.

The captain of the Cohort for our region of the city stood at my back door, accompanied by four other members of the guard. Over his arm he had draped a bloody, urine-stained equestrian's tunic. My tunic. I willed myself to stay calm.

"Good morning, sir," the captain said. "I'm sorry to bother you so early, but I need to ask if anyone in your household knows anything about the murder of this ruffian." He stood aside so I could see the body lying in the street. I forced myself to glance at it with as much surprise and disgust as I could muster. The size of the pool of blood surrounding him did genuinely amaze me.

"Who is he?" I asked.

"He called himself the Cyclops," the captain said, "because of his size and that patch over his eye. He was one of the worst villains in Rome, capable of anything."

As I could testify. "Do you know when this happened?"

"The vigiles said he wasn't here when they made their first rounds. They found him a short while ago and came to get us. We need to know if anyone in your house knows anything about the matter."

My mother, her shadow Naomi, and a number of my other slaves and freedmen were gathered in the garden by now. I turned to them. "Did anyone see or hear anything last night? Any sounds of a struggle? If you heard anything at all, it's important to let the Cohorts know. Don't be embarrassed if you were doing something you shouldn't have been. No one will be punished."

For my own sake I needed to know if any of them had an inkling of what I'd done.

They all shook their heads and looked at one another. Glaucon stood at the back of the crowd. *How odd,* I thought. *He had to step over the body to climb up that wall, and yet he isn't betraying a thing. I hope I look that calm.* And I knew I would never be able to trust him again. If he could conceal this, he could conceal anything.

I turned back to the captain. "I'm afraid we can't help you. Is there anything else?"

"Well, sir, there is the matter of this tunic." He held up the garment. "It's got the equestrian stripe on it, and you are equestrian, aren't you, sir?"

"Yes, and so is someone in every house on this street." I wondered if there was anything about my blood or my urine that might enable him to identify it as mine. But that was ridiculous. Blood is blood, and urine is urine. I couldn't let myself panic. If I could remain calm for a few more minutes, the Cohorts would be gone.

"I was just wondering, sir, if the owner of this garment might be missing. It appears to belong to a smaller man. I don't think the man who wore this could have killed the Cyclops by himself. There must have been others involved in whatever happened out here last night."

Some of my anxiety eased when I heard him drawing such an erroneous conclusion. I wasn't even tempted to brag that I'd done it alone. "That makes sense. And the tunic could have been stolen out of a bath house." As long as he was on the wrong path, why not urge him to go a little farther along it, a little farther away from me?

He nodded. "Well, that's certainly true. Happens a lot, doesn't it? Still, sir, do you mind if I ...?" He stretched out the putrid garment, holding it by the shoulders and almost touching me with it. "That gives me some idea of the size of at least one of the fellows involved. But we don't know if all the blood on this came from the Cyclops."

"I'm the only one in my house who wears the stripe, and I'm fine, as you can see." I held out my arms. "No scratches, no injuries of any kind." As long as he didn't look at my upper leg, which I had scraped badly in my scramble over the wall.

"Yes, sir. I see that. As soon as we search the house, we'll be on our way."

"Search the house? Why ...?"

"We have our orders, sir. We're to search all the houses on this street." He raised his voice to everyone in the garden. "All of you, go to your rooms now. Leave your doors open and stay there until we tell you you can leave. Sir, if you'll just take a seat over there"—he pointed to the *exhedra*—"we'll be done and out of your way as quick as we can."

I stumbled to a couch. What could they be looking for, except the murder weapon? And that was right here on my table. Could I move it before anyone noticed it? I ran an eye over the table, then gasped in disbelief.

The knife was gone!

No, it couldn't be. I dropped it right on top of the dirty dishes last night. Everything else was still there, right down to the mussel shells. But the knife was gone.

I wanted to get down on my knees and look under the table and the couches, but that would just attract the Cohorts' attention. When none of them were looking at me, I scanned the ground under the table and the other couches. The knife simply wasn't here. But it had to be here!

One of the Cohorts approached the exhedra, saluted me, and did a perfunctory search "I'll need you to stand up, sir, so I can look under your couch."

I wasn't sure my legs would hold me, but I managed to move to another of the couches while the soldier ran his hand over and under the one I'd been sitting on. He lifted the pillow, patted it, and dropped it back in place.

"Thank you, sir," he said.

All I could hear was a voice in my head screaming, *Where is that accursed knife?*

Looking in bushes, the Cohort worked his way across the back of the garden toward my mother's room.

"My lady," he said, "please step out here."

My mother complied and the soldier began tossing the blankets on her bed and pawing his way through her chest.

Running over to my mother's side, I said, "Must you do that?"

"It's orders, sir," the soldier said without stopping. "Other squads are doing the same to every house on this street."

Next came Naomi's room. While I was in Syria Mother had given the slave woman the unusual privilege of a room next to her own. The soldier stood at the door and motioned for Naomi to come out, but she remained sitting on her bed.

"Forgive me for not getting up," she said, placing a hand on her stomach, "but I am in my monthly."

What happens to women each month is as much a mystery to me as the changing appearance of the moon. Roman men are taught to avoid contact with them at that time, and our women are taught to seclude themselves for a few days until the business is over.

The soldier hesitated. "I've at least got to ... look around in here," he said. "Those are our orders: search every room."

That was what he proceeded to do, looking in the small chest and in a box Naomi kept near the door. The whole time he kept himself as far away from her bed as he could.

It took almost an hour for the Cohorts to search the entire place. It would take my servants the rest of the day to clean up. Finally the captain gathered his men at my back gate. "I'm sorry to have disturbed you, sir. If anyone in your house does recall anything pertinent, please let me know. We're eager to reward the person who rid the city of this vermin." He and his men turned to leave.

I didn't believe he really meant to offer a reward, but I knew this was my last chance to confess what I had done. And what had I done, except defend myself against a vicious criminal? I had no choice. If I had hesitated for an instant, the man would have killed me. How could any court find me guilty? I'm no cold-blooded killer. I've never even had the heart to order one of my slaves whipped.

But in a Roman court, anything might happen. I would have to admit why I was out in the streets alone at night. As soon as Regulus heard that I suspected my scribe of having some sinister connection with him, he would probably prosecute me. For that matter, the Cyclops might have been one of Regulus' men. Could that be why they were searching? Had Regulus used his influence with Domitian?

If Regulus got involved, he could twist the whole situation around until I became the assailant and the Cyclops an innocent victim of my murderous rage. I once heard Regulus boast that his technique in court was to grab his opponent by the throat, like a hunting dog, and not let go until he brought him down.

No, I would not take that risk. There were no witnesses, no evidence—except for a missing knife—that I had done anything. The Cohorts were on their way out the door, satisfied that I knew nothing about the incident. If I could maintain my composure until they were gone, I would leave it at that.

Demetrius closed and bolted the door. I let out a slow breath and said, loudly enough for everyone in the garden to hear, "When you put the gardeners to work today, have them prune that vine over in the corner."

"How far back do you want it cut, my lord?"

"All the way to the ground."

WHEN TACITUS ARRIVED for our trip out to Musonius' villa the whole house was still buzzing with the news of the dead man found in the street. By then the story had him spurting blood the way Vesuvius spewed molten rock. The Urban Cohorts had carted the body away and I had set some of my slaves to scrubbing the street. I just wished I could wash the incident out of my memory that easily. But Tacitus wouldn't let me.

"Why would they search your whole house?" he asked again as he watched my servants restoring order.

"They said they were searching all the houses on this street."

"For someone who rid Rome of a villain like that? It doesn't make sense."

"No, it doesn't," I said. *But neither does anything else that has happened to me in the last few days.*

As we got a bite to eat before setting out, I scanned the exhedra for the missing knife. Even as addled as I was last night, I knew I had put it right on this table, on top of the other dishes.

"You seem distracted this morning," Tacitus said.

"It's all the uproar about that man being killed."

"That's understandable. In this part of town a dead body on your doorstep is unusual. I imagine in the Subura it would be a rare morning when you didn't find one. And can you picture some fellow, stripped of his tunic, running from the scene? That story will be all over town by midday. I wonder if it's anyone we know. Don't you find that amusing?"

The horses I had rented arrived later than promised, so it wasn't until mid-morning that Tacitus and I, accompanied by half a dozen of our slaves, were riding along the Via Flaminia. The road, one of Rome's oldest, follows the Tiber north toward the Apennines. With the rain of the last few days the river glistened and the fields of wheat and other grains on either side of the road looked fat and well-watered.

But I hardly noticed the scenery. Not even helping Tacitus compose his speech—his first in a Roman court in over a year—could take my mind off of the man I killed last night, and the missing knife with my monogram on it. If there was anyone I ought to be able to talk to about what I'd done, it should be Tacitus. The jokes he'd made earlier, though, seemed to seal my lips. Would I ever be able to tell anyone what had happened? Did someone—the person who took the knife—already know?

Like a schoolboy memorizing a passage from Virgil, I kept going over the incident, hearing every word the Cyclops said. Most of it still chilled me. One thing puzzled me. Why had he referred to the slave woman Glaucon was servicing as 'her ladyship'? I doubted a thug like that was capable of sarcasm.

"My lord, we're approaching the tenth milestone," one of my slaves observed.

That reminded me that I had to put aside my worries about last night and concentrate on my reason for this trip. Musonius never talked much about this villa, but he had once mentioned it was near the tenth milestone. What he had failed to mention was the two other villas within sight of that milestone. The inhabitants of the first house where we stopped directed us to Musonius'. His wasn't actually on the Flaminia but about a mile west of it on a side road.

We turned off the side road onto a smaller sandy road, little more than a path, which wound for another half a mile or so through carefully tended olive groves. Unlike the other homes around it, Musonius' appeared to be a true villa rustica, a working farm, not a pampered escape from a luxurious domus in Rome. Servants looked up from their tasks. I couldn't understand the puzzlement, almost apprehension, I read in their faces. Several of them turned and ran as soon as they laid eyes on us.

"They don't look pleased to see us," Tacitus said.

I nodded. The servants on my estates are always happy to see visitors from the city. Their arrival promises a break in routine, more festive meals, a chance to catch up on gossip.

"They act like we're invading the place," I said.

"I wonder where they'll set up their defenses," Tacitus said.

We met the defenders when we came around a bend. A dozen men stood across the road, armed with swords and spears. As soon as we drew our horses to a halt, more men rushed out of the olive groves and blocked the way behind us.

"What's the meaning of this?" I demanded. "I'm a friend of Gaius Musonius."

The oldest man in the group facing us stepped forward. Though not particularly large, he had the stance of a former centurion. His hair, black with some gray salted in, was cut in the short legionary style. "Friend or not, sir, you were not invited to come out here."

"Yes, I'm sorry to intrude, but I need to talk to Gaius Musonius."

"He'll be returning to Rome on the kalends of August. He'll be happy to entertain you at his house in the city."

"This matter can't wait that long."

"I have my instructions, sir. Gaius Musonius does not wish to have visitors on this estate."

"Could you at least take a message to him, to see if he will talk to us? If I may ask him a few questions, then we'll be on our way back to Rome."

"I'm sorry, sir. He does not wish to have visitors here, for any reason. Now, I must ask you and your party to leave."

He took my horse's reins and tried to turn him around. The animal reared. I grabbed his mane and squeezed my knees against his sides, holding on for dear life. The other horses nickered, on the verge of bolting. None of my slaves are skilled riders.

Tacitus, the best rider among us, reached over, took my horse's reins, and said something to calm him. When I had him under control again, I said to the centurion, "If you do not take a message to Gaius Musonius, I will tell him in August that you turned me away. When he hears what I wanted to ask him about, he will probably come out here the very next day and have you flogged for your incompetence."

"I am a free man and a citizen, sir. But Gaius Musonius does not treat even his slaves that harshly."

"If you turn me away, I promise you, you'll feel his wrath, however he may express it."

The man turned to the fellow next to him, hoping for guidance, I guess. Finding none in that blank round face, he searched for it on the ground, with his head down. Finally he looked back up at me and said, "Who are you, sir, and what is your message?"

"I am Gaius Pliny. My message is for Musonius only." I signaled for the slave who was leading the horse that carried our supplies to come closer to me. Drawing a wax tablet from the bag, I wrote two words: Rubellius Plautus. Then I tied the cover over the tablet and sealed the knot with a bit of the wax and my ring.

The centurion took the tablet from me and gave it to one of the younger men behind him. "Maccius, carry this message to the house." Maccius, a wiry boy in his late teens with sweat already running from his curly black hair, nodded and set off running.

"He's the fastest among us," the centurion said. "He'll be back shortly."

While we waited, the centurion withdrew far enough from us to make it clear he had no intention of entering into a conversation. I wanted to dismount, but, with no mounting stone in sight, getting back on my horse would prove difficult, so I stayed put.

Tacitus guided his horse close to mine and leaned over to me. "We had an easier time getting into Domitian's house," he said.

"Then we had an invitation," I reminded him.

"But I've never known a Roman of our class to be so hostile to guests. There is a certain degree of hospitality expected, even when a stranger shows up at your door." He glanced around, jerking his head toward the men blocking the road behind us. "I don't like this at all."

"I agree. If it were anyone but Musonius, I'd be afraid we weren't getting out of here."

"I'm wondering why the Musonius you claim to know in Rome is so different from Musonius on his country estate. Why go to all this trouble unless you have something to hide? Something big."

We heard Maccius' footsteps pounding on the road before we saw him. He caught his breath and reported something to the centurion, who glanced at us in surprise, then stepped toward us and drew himself up straight.

"Gaius Musonius will allow you to come to his house. You must stay with us as we escort you. Your slaves will be taken to the servants' quarters."

I nodded my assent, not that our house slaves would likely resist, but Archidamos, the biggest and boldest of them, might. I made sure I caught his eye and nodded my head.

The two dozen or so men on foot surrounded us, cutting Tacitus and me off from our servants. We advanced about a quarter of a mile. When we came in sight of a house, the slaves were turned aside by the men walking with them. Tacitus and I proceeded to the house and drew our horses to a halt in front of it.

The place gave an impression of venerable age. If it were mine, I would have had the plaster patched and whitewashed several years ago. Sitting on a slight rise, it was a typical two-story Roman house, four sides enclosing a courtyard, but on each end of the house a two-story wing projected forward about ten paces with a portico joining them. Four steps led from the portico down to our level.

Musonius stood in the center of the portico, with a look on his face that betrayed uncertainty and displeasure. I'd never known him to be anything but affable. He wore a rough, unbleached tunic with no equestrian stripe or other decoration on it. Against the tan cloth his white hair and philosopher's beard stood out much more than they did against the bleached garments he wore in Rome.

As I dismounted, Musonius stepped forward. His gait seemed slow, like that of a man in pain. "Gaius Pliny! This is most ... unexpected." He might as well have said 'unwelcome.' His voice, usually so mellifluous and warm, conveyed that message clearly in its tightness.

"I'm sorry if we've inconvenienced you, Gaius Musonius," I said as we embraced. "There is something I need to ask you about. I didn't feel it could wait until you returned to Rome."

"So I gathered from your message. Before we engage in such a serious conversation, though, may I know the identity of your companion?"

I introduced Tacitus.

"Agricola's son-in-law?" Musonius said in my ear. "Have you brought him here to hide him from Domitian?" I gasped at his candor. "He's welcome if you have. Now, let's eat in the courtyard while we talk."

Musonius gave instructions for the slaves and horses to be taken care of, then showed us through the portico and one wing of the house into the central courtyard. He slipped his arm through mine, but it felt more like he was leaning on me than guiding me. He kept glancing from side to side, for all the world like a man whose wife has returned home before he's gotten his mistress out of the house.

The courtyard was as shabby as the rest of the house. It was simply a bare, open space, without the shrubs or a fountain that would grace the garden of a house in Rome. We reclined on couches with worn covers in a corner of the courtyard under an awning that had too many holes in it to offer much protection against rain. As my gaze swept over the scene, I thought I glimpsed a figure in one of the windows opposite us. But the apparition vanished too quickly for me to be sure.

Two slaves brought wine and plates of fruit—apples and figs—and bread and cheese. We made small talk while they served.

"Please forgive me if I'm not as courteous as I should be," Musonius said. "I've been having a lot of pain in my back and when I urinate."

"Are you being treated by a doctor?" I asked.

"No, it's something I've experienced before. It will pass, but until it does, it is torture of the worst kind."

When the slaves withdrew, Musonius said, "Now, Gaius Pliny, you've brought up a name I have not heard or spoken in many years. Why are you interested in Rubellius?"

"I just recently became aware that he was a cousin of Nero's, possibly even a rival."

"That's all distant history, as dead as the men themselves. Why does it matter to you?"

"It doesn't to me, but others in Rome have become curious about what happened to Rubellius and his family."

From the way his eyes narrowed I knew he understood who those 'others' were but wasn't going to say anything aloud. "You have a splendid library, my dear Pliny," Musonius said as he sliced an apple and offered us pieces. "Surely you could find the answers to your questions there. You didn't have to ride all this way and pester an old man who just wants to be alone with his thoughts and his pain."

"Forgive me, Gaius Musonius, but none of the scrolls in my library knew Rubellius personally. None of them accompanied him on a visit to Agrippina shortly before her death. Did she actually propose to marry him and overthrow Nero?"

Musonius jerked upright so quickly he winced. "By the gods! How did you learn of that?"

"You're better off not knowing, I assure you. But you were an intimate friend of Rubellius', weren't you?" I had him on the defensive, like a gladiator who has knocked away his opponent's shield. I wanted to press my advantage, to back him into a corner.

"Yes, I was his mentor. He was a promising, thoughtful young man. If he could have purged himself of the blood that connected him to Nero, he might have won great renown as a philosopher."

"Did you give Agrippina anything on that visit?"

"Why do you ask that? How do you know so much?"

"Please allow me to impose on your friendship a bit more, sir. It's vital that I have an answer to that question."

"I presented her with a copy of one of my first treatises, on why women should study philosophy. She accepted it graciously, but she probably erased it and used the scroll to write something else."

I felt a weight lifted from my shoulders. There were only three people who could have known a detail like that. The letter Domitian had shown me must be from Agrippina's hand.

"Did Agrippina give you anything?"

"Why would she have given me anything? She had virtually nothing. Nero had her closely under guard."

Musonius, not being a duplicitous man, seemed to be having difficulty telling a lie.

"You mentioned Rubellius' connection to Nero," Tacitus said. "What exactly was that connection?"

Seeming relieved by the change of topic, Musonius reclined again on his couch. His gaze darted around the courtyard, as though he was checking for eavesdropping slaves before sharing a delicious bit of gossip. He kept his voice low. "Rubellius' mother was Julia, the daughter of Livia Julia. She, in turn, was the daughter of the younger Antonia, who was the daughter of Augustus' sister, Octavia."

"Nero was descended from Octavia's other daughter, the elder Antonia, wasn't he?" Tacitus asked, helping himself to some more wine.

"You know your history well. Nero and Rubellius, each being descended from one of Augustus' nieces, had the same degree of relationship to Augustus and thus to Julius Caesar."

Movement in a window opposite us again registered in the corner of my eye. I tried to glance in that direction without attracting Musonius' attention, but I couldn't see anyone. "So Rubellius could have challenged Nero's right to rule," I said.

"That's what Nero was afraid of. That's why he had Rubellius killed."

"What about Rubellius' son?"

"His son was killed with him."

It saddened me to think of the life of that 'bright' child Agrippina had mentioned being snuffed out. "How did that happen?"

"A couple of years after Agrippina's death Nero sent Rubellius into exile in Asia. I accompanied him and his wife and son. We lived there for two years. Even before Piso's conspiracy nearly toppled him, Nero was imagining plots on all sides. Rubellius and his son were the closest living male descendants in the Augustan line, so Nero accused Rubellius of complicity in a plot and ordered him executed."

"Was Rubellius plotting against Nero?" Tacitus asked.

"No, but he was always a focal point for those who detested Nero. And his reputation grew even as he tried to stay in seclusion. There were those, including Rubellius' father-in-law, who hoped to stir up a revolt against Nero. They needed a figure to rally around."

"Who was his father-in-law?" I asked.

For an instant Musonius looked like a man who had said something he hadn't intended. "Lucius Antistius Vetus," he finally admitted. "He was Nero's colleague in his second consulship and some years later was proconsul of Asia."

"And his daughter was called Antistia?" I had to ask because, in our modern times, women are sometimes given two names, the traditional one from their father and another from a grandfather or honored ancestor.

"Yes," Musonius said.

Tacitus reached for a pear. "You said 'they needed a figure to rally around.' Did you not want Rubellius to rule?"

"As a Stoic, I believe the world is ordered as it must be. It is not anyone's place to overthrow a ruler. He is in his destined place."

"Even if he is a bad ruler?"

"Then we must try to teach him to be better."

"But perhaps someone is destined to overthrow the bad ruler," Tacitus said.

Musonius pursed his lips and nodded. "There is that possibility. I would have supported Rubellius if he had chosen to claim the power. My concern was that he might have been too good a man to be a ruler. He was a truly good man, well-versed in Stoic philosophy—if his teacher may be so immodest as to say so. He was blessed with a temperate nature, the very embodiment of Plato's philosopher-king. People could sense his virtue, his nobility, as soon as they met him. But such men often find it difficult to make the hard decisions a ruler must make. They want to deliberate and look at things from all sides. Sometimes a ruler doesn't have that luxury."

"Why didn't he oppose Nero, if, as you say, he was so popular and had as good a claim to power as Nero did?" I asked.

"Rubellius was afraid for his family. He knew he would be risking his life if he took up arms against Nero, especially after Agrippina was murdered. Without her support, no revolt against Nero had much chance of success. Rubellius was willing to take the risk himself, but he would not jeopardize his wife and son."

"And yet his son was killed," I said. "What happened to his wife?"

Musonius' face grew dark. "You came out here, you said, to ask about Rubellius, not his wife."

"Did something happen to her, too?" I persisted. "It was her husband, not her, who was descended from Augustus. What did she have to fear?"

"Friend Pliny, I am in a great deal of pain and you have taxed my hospitality to its limit. I'm sure your horses have been watered and fed by now and your slaves offered some refreshment." He glanced at the sun's position. "If you keep up a steady pace, you should make it back to Rome before dark."

Musonius stood, although he could not straighten up, and slipped his feet into his sandals. I couldn't understand why he was dismissing us so summarily. He had not invited us out here, it's true, but he had never told me this place was an inviolable retreat with armed guards. I felt like he was just waiting for us to leave so he could perform some cleansing ritual and remove all trace of our intrusion.

With our unwilling host nudging us toward the exit, Tacitus and I had no choice but to stand and retrieve our own shoes.

"May I relieve myself before we go?" I asked.

"If you must," Musonius said. "Through that door and to your left." He pointed to a door at the rear of the courtyard.

"I suppose I should as well," Tacitus said.

The door to which Musonius directed us creaked on its hinges as it gave access to the lower floor of the house's rear wing. The paint on the interior walls was not only faded but long outdated in style, showing nothing but colored geometric patterns. To our right we saw a set of stairs going up to a landing and turning, to our left the door to the *latrina*.

"He doesn't spend a lot on upkeep for this place," Tacitus said as we entered the latrina, which could accommodate three people at a time.

"He maintains his house in Rome much better. It's not elegant, but at least the paint's not flaking off the walls."

"Do you suppose he doesn't have the money to keep up two places?" Tacitus asked. "Maybe he doesn't want visitors out here just so he won't be embarrassed by his poverty."

"But for a poor man he has a lot of servants on this estate. Whether they're slaves or freedmen, he has to feed and clothe them. That takes money."

"About that you would know more than I." Tacitus has only one piece of property outside of Rome. His father left him a farm in Gallia Belgica, with an overseer and some slaves to tend the place and to take care of Tacitus' brother, who is deformed and incapable of living on his own.

"I admit Musonius' behavior is odd," I said, "but I don't think there's anything sinister about it."

"Speaking of sinister," Tacitus said in a low voice, "were you aware someone was watching us from a window while we were eating?"

"I thought I saw something, but I couldn't make it out."

"I'm almost certain it was a woman. Could Musonius be hiding a mistress out here?"

"Why would anyone in Rome hide a mistress?" I asked. "The customary practice is to flaunt them."

"But most people don't set themselves up as great moral teachers the way Musonius does. Maybe that's why the old hypocrite needs all this secrecy. Keep her out of sight, but close enough to Rome that he can get to her whenever he wants. Or perhaps Musonius has some truly perverted sexual tastes and keeps her out here for those purposes."

"I refuse to believe Musonius capable of anything so despicable. Perhaps this girl is some slow-witted child or relative of his. As you know, Rome is no place for someone like that. She would be a laughing-stock."

"The kindest thing in that case is to dispose of the child at birth," Tacitus said, "as my father should have done with my poor brother."

"Musonius has unusual ideas about many things. I've heard him argue that women ought to be educated alongside men. Perhaps he believes even an imperfect child should be raised and protected from the outside world."

Tacitus shook his head. "Doing that saps a man's resources, with no hope of a return on his investment. No marriage, no alliance with a wealthy family. You know what a burden my brother is to me. Maybe that explains the condition this place is in."

When we returned to the courtyard Musonius was waiting for us at the other end, leaning against a door into the house. He straightened up as best he could when he saw us and led us through to the portico. Our slaves were already mounted and the burly centurion was holding the reins of my horse and Tacitus'. Musonius waved for us to hurry up.

"He takes Catullus too literally," Tacitus said. "'Hail and farewell'."

We had just stepped into the portico when a young woman appeared from a door to our left. "Why, cousin Gaius," she said brightly, "you didn't tell me we had guests."

I stopped, but Musonius took me by the elbow. "They're just leaving. They have to get back to Rome by tonight."

"You're come all the way from Rome?" the young woman said. "I should think we owe you a meal and a night's hospitality. I'm Cornelia, by the way, but everyone calls me Nelia."

She was almost as tall as I am, with a square face and brown hair parted in the middle and pulled back into a bun on her neck, a somewhat old-fashioned style. I would have called her striking, rather than pretty. She wore no make-up, and her skin, tanned by the sun, would make her look like a servant among Rome's refined ladies, who pride themselves on the paleness of their complexions. She seemed younger than I am, but I couldn't guess her age.

I thought Musonius might introduce us, but he just stood there with a look of disgust on his face. I freed my elbow from his grip and said, "My lady, this is Cornelius Tacitus, and I am Gaius Pliny."

"Pliny?" Delight and puzzlement mixed on Nelia's face. "How can you be Pliny? You're too young. You couldn't have written all—"

"You're confusing me with my uncle. He adopted me in his will."

"His will? Is he dead?"

"He died trying to rescue people during the eruption of Vesuvius."

"I'm so sorry." She reached out and touched my hand. "I hadn't heard. We're only ten miles from Rome, but sometimes I think news gets to Britain more quickly than it reaches us." She glanced accusingly at Musonius.

"Nelia," Musonius said, "you're delaying their departure."

"Why are you being so rude, cousin Gaius? Why can't we offer them our hospitality?"

"You're not going to be satisfied until I do, are you?" Musonius said.

"No, I'm not." She crossed her arms over her chest, like a man letting you know he has made up his mind about something.

Musonius turned to us with a sigh. "Do you gentlemen have time to stay with us tonight?"

With a nod from Tacitus I said, "We will accept your gracious invitation."

"Wonderful!" Nelia said, clapping her hands together but not smiling. As happy as she seemed, she appeared reluctant to smile.

"We'll see how wonderful you think it is," Musonius said. "You must tell cook we have two guests and six more servants to feed. And you'll have to see that rooms are ready for all of them. Now get to it."

"Yes, cousin Gaius. Cornelius Tacitus, Gaius Pliny, I look forward to talking with you later." She turned and ran off toward the back of the house, lifting her stola enough to expose the lower part of a lovely pair of legs. If a woman in Rome had done that, it would have seemed flirtatious, but it seemed a perfectly natural thing when Nelia did it.

"You never told me you had a cousin out here," I said to Musonius. "Why haven't you brought her to Rome?"

"Friend Pliny, I will not answer any more questions. You have intruded where you are not welcome and have caused me great distress."

"I deeply regret that, sir. I hold you and your family in the highest regard. Perhaps it would be better if we left."

Musonius shook his head ruefully. "It's too late for that."

* * * *

After we dispatched Archidamos and another slave to tell my mother and Tacitus' wife we were staying the night, Musonius turned us over to his steward Marcus Laberius, the former centurion, and excused himself. We were given a tour of the estate. I tried to strike up a conversation with Laberius, but all I learned was that he had served in Illyricum and had been hired by Musonius five years ago, after his retirement from the legions. He ignored any questions or comments about Nelia.

Our tour ended in the bath, which was as rustic as the rest of the villa, with cold and warm pools in one poorly painted, dimly lit room. The slaves did not allow us to linger in the warm pool, when it would have felt good to soak muscles sore from bouncing around on our horses and then being led on a tour that sometimes felt like a forced march, especially if Laberius didn't like a question I asked. When we dried off they gave us unbleached tunics with no stripe on them.

"Where are our tunics?" Tacitus asked.

"They're being laundered and will be ready for you in the morning," one of the servants informed us.

"I didn't think they were particularly dirty."

Nudging Tacitus toward the door, I said, "This may be Musonius' way of teaching us a lesson in humility. Take away our striped tunics, and what is the difference between one man and another?"

"I could think of a few ways to settle that question," Tacitus said.

After our bath Tacitus and I stood in the portico, looking out over a vista of wheat fields, with a row of trees beyond suggesting a stream, no doubt flowing toward the Tiber.

"Who do you suppose this Nelia is?" Tacitus asked.

"You heard Musonius. She's a cousin of his."

"Is that 'cousin,' as in a blood relative, or 'cousin' in the sense of Alexandrian poetry, a lover?"

"I doubt she's either. She might be an unacknowledged daughter."

"Why work so hard to keep something so trivial a secret? Who in Rome would care if he had a bastard daughter by one of his slaves? That would make him a member of a very large club."

I motioned for him to keep his voice down. "That puzzles me, too. And it's what makes me think there must be a bigger secret he's trying to keep."

* * * *

Whatever that secret was, I had no chance of discovering it during dinner. Musonius reclined on the high couch, with Nelia opposite him on the low couch, while Tacitus and I shared the middle couch. The simple meal began with a dish of melons cooked in honey with parsley, pepper, and liquamen and passum. The main course was chicken fried in oil and liquamen, flavored with dill and leeks. With that came a dish of beans cooked with leeks, coriander leaves and cumin seeds. The final course was dates stuffed with ground nuts and stewed in red wine with honey.

Although he did not say much himself, Musonius kept the conversation on my uncle's works. The old philosopher seemed tired, withdrawn. Whatever was giving him such pain was wearing him down. At first I had the sensation he was watching me, gauging how Nelia and I got along. Nelia, though, was such a lively conversationalist I soon turned my attention to her. She had read my uncle's books more thoroughly than I had.

"It's so amazing that I'm talking to the son of the great Pliny," she said.

And would that, I thought, make me the less-than-great Pliny?

"Was he your teacher?"

113

"He supervised my lessons, but I had tutors because my uncle was so busy with his government work."

"And yet he still found time to write so much."

"He never wasted a moment. If he was resting or bathing or eating, someone was reading to him and a scribe was taking notes on things that interested him."

"His books cover so many topics."

"Do you have a favorite?" I asked.

"I think his best is the *German Wars*. That scene with Agrippina standing on the bridge to stop the soldiers from destroying it while Germanicus and his troops are trapped on the other side of the Rhine—it's just spellbinding."

As she recited a few lines I glanced at Tacitus and could tell he was thinking the same thing I was. I had told him what Dymas told me about the seal on the letter Domitian brought us. Now here was another reference to the same scene. For one who, like myself, refused to believe in coincidence, it was uncanny, to say the least.

"How did he come to write that?" Nelia asked.

I took a sip of wine to collect myself before I answered. "He told me he started on it while he was serving in Germany. He dreamed Drusus, the father of Germanicus, was standing over him, asking my uncle to preserve the memory of his family's conquests in Germany. My uncle stood on that bridge himself."

"That's why his description is so vivid! What a wonderful story. It's just the sort of thing I can never pick up, being stuck out here. Cousin Gaius treats me like a character in a myth who carries a curse that will ruin anyone she comes into contact with." She meant it in jest, I could tell, but Musonius did not take it kindly.

I could sympathize with her. I had been raised largely by myself on my uncle's estates, although my mother had been with me. Now I spend my days surrounded by people, but they're all dependent on me or want some favor from me. Tacitus is the first real friend—as distinct from a social obligation—I've ever made.

"It's a lovely estate," I said. "You must enjoy living out here."

Nelia laughed, putting her hand over her mouth. "You didn't have much time to look at anything. From my window I saw Laberius marching you two around like recruits."

"Old soldiers find some habits hard to break, I guess. But some of my happiest days were spent on my uncle's estates, reading and writing. And you've had an education few men in Rome could rival. Do you read Greek as well as Latin?"

"How could I study philosophy if I couldn't read Greek? Cousin Gaius' own writings are in Greek. I can also speak Celtic. One of our slaves is a Celt. I asked her to teach me the language. It gave me something to do, and she was happy to have someone with whom she could converse in her native tongue. And I've made a start at deciphering Etruscan."

"Etruscan? Why bother with a dead language?"

"There are markings on some old stones around our place that I'm sure are Etruscan. The letters are a form of the Greek alphabet, but the language is quite different."

"The emperor Claudius wrote a history of the Etruscans," Tacitus said in that way he has of dropping historical tidbits into a conversation, often with the effect of stopping it cold.

"Yes, I've read it," Nelia said. "He provided me with some clues to reading the language. He quotes a few documents and even writes a few lines in Etruscan. He says at one point that he knows of only one other living person who can read it."

"Who was that?" Tacitus asked.

"He never gives the name. I wish I had something longer written in the language so I could see if I really can read it."

I **SLEPT WELL,** tired out from my ride and the forced march around Musonius' estate. The next morning the sky was overcast, but it looked like the rain might hold off. Our laundered tunics were brought to our rooms along with a bit of food. Musonius met us in the portico while our horses were brought from the stable. His omnipresent centurion waited by the mounting stone. Musonius carried a sealed document in one hand.

"We'll be on our way as quickly as possible," I said. "And, again, I apologize for intruding on your privacy. I hope you can forgive me."

"It's already forgotten, my dear Pliny. In fact, it may all work for the best. Things have a way of doing that. It's ironic. I've spent my life training myself and others to make the best decisions, to think through their actions and try to foresee the outcome. Yesterday, when I read your message—that dear name, Rubellius Plautus—I knew at once what my answer should have been. For years I've had one simple rule: do not let *any* outsider onto this estate. Yesterday I threw it away like a worn-out tunic. I spent a restless night mulling over some things, and I've come to a decision. I need to ask an enormous favor of you, one that will put me in your debt for the rest of my life."

"You know I'll do anything for you, sir, and you need never consider yourself obligated to me." Even as I spoke those words, I could recall too many stories in which someone had made such a promise, only to regret it.

Musonius put a hand on my shoulder, whether to steady himself or to keep me from running away, I couldn't tell. He was not so old a man that his age should be wearing him down. I hoped he was not seriously ill. But his question drove all such concerns from my mind.

"Will you take Nelia to Rome?" he asked.

I would have been less surprised if he had hit me in the face. "Take Nelia ... to Rome? Why?"

"To keep her safe. I have raised and protected her practically her entire life, but I'm not up to the task right now. I need help, and I think you're the man to provide it."

"Why have you raised her in secret?" Tacitus asked. "What happened to her parents?"

Motioning us to benches in the shade of the portico, Musonius sat down heavily. "The story is longer and more complicated than I can tell right now. The gist of it is that her father was murdered before she was born. Her mother died when she was three. She has no other family. Nelia will be eighteen next month. Over the past couple of years she has become more and more restless, the way young women do at this time of their lives. I hoped my tutelage of her might produce a different sort of woman, but, as you heard at dinner, she sees herself as a captive and doesn't understand what I'm trying to do for her."

"Against whom are you protecting her?" Tacitus asked.

"I'm not ready to tell you that yet," Musonius said. "I haven't even told her because I don't want to alarm her. But there are powerful people who would try to kill her if they knew she was alive. I need to move her to some safer place until I can decide what is best for her."

"Why can't she just stay here until you're ready to move her?" Tacitus asked, and it seemed to me an eminently sensible suggestion.

Musonius shook his head wearily. "She has met a young man from the next estate and thinks she's in love with him. She's given up reading philosophy and taken to amorous poetry. Ovid and Propertius and worse stuff. She's even writing it. No matter how closely we watch her, she finds ways to be with him. As bad as I feel right now, I can't deal with this problem. I need someone to take her away for a short time, until I'm strong enough again to cope with her and she's gotten over this infatuation."

"She's of marriageable age," I said. "If this young man's family is prosperous enough to own an estate out here, don't you consider him a suitable match?"

"No, I do not." He shook his head as though wearied by its weight but certain of his answer. "Not at all. The man who marries Nelia will need to be strong enough to protect her, as I have for all these years."

"But how can he protect her if he doesn't know who might harm her?" I asked. "How can I protect her if I don't know where the danger might come from?"

"I know I'm asking too much, Gaius Pliny, but you have position and influence in Rome, quite beyond your years. There are other powerful men in the city, it's true, but you also are a decent man. Of those there is a perennial shortage."

Just like a character in a myth, I had walked into a trap set by my own good intentions. "I'll do as you ask, sir, but only until you return to Rome in August. At that point, I will hand her back into your care."

"And I'll repay the favor by giving you this." He held out the sealed document he had been holding. "It tells you all I know about Nelia and why I am so concerned for her safety. I only ask that you read it after you've left here and that you not reveal its contents to her."

"Very well." I accepted the document from his hand, feeling like one of those messengers who bears a letter telling the recipient to kill the messenger.

"Thank you." Musonius called to the centurion. "Laberius, bring Nelia here."

"How does she feel about this decision?" Tacitus asked.

"We'll soon find out," Musonius said.

"You haven't told her?" I jumped up.

"I couldn't until I knew whether you would accede to my request."

I turned away from Musonius and walked to the edge of the portico, giving myself a moment to settle my anger. I felt duped. As I had gotten to know him over the past three months, I had come to respect the old philosopher as straightforward, guileless, perhaps the only man in Rome who could be described by those terms. Now he was manipulating me and moving his cousin—or whoever she was—around like a pawn in some game.

We all turned as the door on the south end of the portico opened and Nelia came out, with Laberius on her heels. She hadn't quite finished dressing for the day. Her long hair, still unpinned, flowed down onto her shoulders, softening her face.

"Good morning, Cornelius Tacitus, Gaius Pliny. I planned to see you off, but Laberius said I should come right away. Is there something wrong?" She turned to Musonius. "Are you ill again, cousin?"

Musonius took her hand and pulled her down next to him on the bench. "No, child, the pain is not so bad this morning. But I have something important to tell you."

Concern clouded Nelia's face. "What is it?"

"Nelia, I want you to go to Rome with Gaius Pliny. He has agreed to take you."

As quickly as a summer storm flares up out of soft clouds, her concern for Musonius turned to anger at him. "To Rome? Am I to be passed from one jailer to another?" She stood and flashed a lightning bolt at me with her eyes.

"Oh, come, child. It's not like that—"

"You don't want me to be with Marcianus, do you? He's not good enough for you. Well, I love him!"

"Please calm down, Nelia. This is for your own good. You've always wanted to see Rome. You've begged me many times to take you there."

"But now I want to stay here with Marcianus. You can't make me go to Rome." She clenched her fists and stamped her foot.

"Please don't make this difficult," Musonius said. "It's already been decided. Take Laberius with you, and two of the servants who usually take care of you. You'll stay in Pliny's house and behave yourself until I arrive in August. Now, go pack some things while Laberius hitches up the wagon."

"I won't go!" Nelia cried.

Musonius cringed and put a hand on his lower back, as though he had been stabbed. "You will go," he said, gritting his teeth, "if Laberius has to tie you up and toss you into the wagon like a sack of grain."

The sight of the old man's obvious pain seemed to deflate Nelia's anger. She knelt in front of him, her hands on his knees. "Cousin Gaius, are you all right?"

"I will be, child. This will pass, as it has before. Until it does, I need to know you're in safe hands. It will make things much easier for me if you go to Rome with Pliny. It will only be for a short time, I promise you."

Nelia lowered her head, like someone who's received an oracle from a god. "All right, cousin. I'll do whatever you ask. Give me time to pack some things."

I walked beside Nelia to the door. "I'm sorry, my lady. This is as big a surprise to me as it is to you."

Nelia turned so Musonius could see her face. She smiled at me, but she said, "I hate you, Gaius Pliny. Why did you have to come out here and ruin my life?"

* * * *

It took another hour to get Nelia and her servants ready to travel. Laberius showed a soldier's impatience with civilians who don't know how to pack. He finally had to give in and use two wagons, the second one with seats and a cover for shade. That meant finding two more servants who could drive the second team and return the wagons to the estate.

Tacitus and I could do little but sit under the portico and watch. As we did, he said, "You came out here to get a little information, and you're going back with ... what? A prisoner? A hostage?"

"She's a guest," I snapped.

"A most unwilling one, with an equally unwilling host. That could make for some amusing moments."

"My friend, I'm in no mood for humor right now."

"So I see. But there could be some advantage in this for us." He eyed Nelia's companions, all of them freedwomen, as he spoke.

"What possible advantage can you find in this fiasco?" I hoped he wasn't just setting me up for another joke.

"If Nelia has lived around Musonius all her life, she might know something more about Rubellius Plautus. Get her away from here, give her time to get over her resentment, let my wife entertain her for a few days, and she might divulge something."

"How could she know anything? She wasn't even born until after Rubellius was murdered."

"But who knows what Musonius might have mentioned over the years? He's been her teacher. He also doted on Rubellius. Perhaps he held him up to her as an *exemplum*. At the worst, you've got that note and his promise to tell you more when he returns to Rome."

The sun was at about the third hour when we finally said goodbye to Musonius and started up the winding track that would take us to the side road by which we had come in. Tacitus and I rode in front with two of my slaves. The other two slaves formed a rear guard behind the wagons, at Laberius' insistence, even though they couldn't really guard anything. The centurion rode in the second wagon with the baggage, keeping his distance from Nelia and her maids. Nelia made no more protest. In fact, she said nothing until we reached the side road.

"Gaius Pliny," she called with a smile, "may I ask a favor of you?"

I had already granted one favor too many that morning, so I looked over my shoulder at her with skepticism. This time I would make no promises in advance. "What do you want?"

"I'd like to ride a horse instead of bouncing around on this dreadful wagon."

My eyebrows went up in surprise. "Do you know how to ride?"

"Laberius taught me."

The centurion stood in the wagon, as surprised as if a German had sneaked up behind him and rattled his helmet with a club.

"My lady, you promised you wouldn't say anything or let anyone else see you riding."

"What's the point in being able to ride if I'm just going to trot around the barnyard?" Nelia asked. "Gaius Pliny, may I ride one of your horses?"

I was inclined to do anything within reason that might mollify her. "Well, I suppose—"

"Sir," Laberius cut in, "I think that would be most unwise. Horses can be so unpredictable. My lady could be thrown and injured."

"Nonsense," Nelia said with a snort. "You were a good teacher, Laberius. And these horses are gentle old nags. I can handle any of them."

"Let's try it," I said. "If I don't feel it's safe, you'll have to go back into the wagon. And it will be my decision, not yours."

"Of course," Nelia said with a sarcastic bow. "The jailer always has the last word."

Instead of letting her provoke me into an argument, I brought our caravan to a halt and told the slave riding in front of me to switch places with her.

"I'd rather ride that one," Nelia said, pointing to one of the horses behind the wagons.

I called the slave she had pointed to and had him change places with her. That was accomplished more easily because Nelia was mounting from the wagon, not from the ground. She did look like she knew what she was doing as she patted the horse's neck and grasped the reins confidently. She didn't seem to mind that when she straddled the animal, her stola rode up, revealing more of her shapely legs than would be considered proper, even in decadent Rome.

"Are you comfortable now?" I asked.

"Yes, thank you. I like the feeling of having my legs wrapped around a stallion."

Tacitus chortled. "That one's a gelding. Of course, most males are by the time a woman gets through with them."

Laberius admitted defeat and sat down in the baggage wagon. "Please keep a close eye on her, sir."

"Why don't you ride between Tacitus and me?" I suggested.

"Whatever the jailer says." As we resumed our journey she expertly maneuvered her horse between mine and Tacitus'.

"I hope we make it to Rome before the rain starts again," I said. I didn't know what else to talk to her about.

"Let's not waste time on trivial chatter," she said. "I'm sorry I was rude to you earlier, Gaius Pliny. In the past whenever I asked about going to Rome, cousin Gaius told me it was dangerous for me to go there, but he wouldn't tell me why. Now, with no warning, he sends me to Rome when I want to stay on the estate."

"Is the danger connected with your father?" Tacitus asked. "Who was he? Who killed him?"

"His name was Lucius Cornelius Catulus. Cousin Gaius says that's all I need to know. I don't know who killed him or why."

"When did that happen?"

"Eighteen years ago, a few months before I was born."

"What happened to your mother?"

"She died when I was three. From a fever, cousin Gaius says. He has been my guardian since then."

"Are you related to Musonius through your mother or your father?"

"My mother was his cousin, he said."

121

Tacitus and I exchanged a glance. In what sense had Nelia's mother been Musonius' 'cousin'? The physical sense or the way that poets use the word to mean a lover?

Conversation died down as we turned onto the Via Flaminia. After a quarter mile or so we passed over a bridge.

"This stream is the boundary of cousin Gaius' estate," Nelia said. "I guess I'm now off of his property for the first time in fifteen years. I hope I never have to go back."

I didn't like the sound of that. I had every intention of handing her back over to Musonius in August. "Why do you resent him so much?" I asked. "He seems to have provided for you most generously."

"He is a kind, wonderful man," Nelia said. "But I'm a grown woman. Whatever reason he had for keeping me in hiding all these years, surely the danger has passed by now. I want to live a normal life. I want to be with the man I love."

"That would be Marcianus, the boy on the next estate?"

"Yes, and this is his family's property ... so I will be leaving you!"

She dug her heels into her horse's sides and slapped him with the reins. As he bolted ahead of us, our horses reared in surprise. Tacitus slid off his. I managed to keep my seat. Laberius' bellowing nearly made all the animals panic. As soon as I got my horse under control I took off after Nelia.

She had gained a good lead and turned off onto a road that I assumed led to Marcianus' house. My horse broke stride when I made the turn because the side road was packed sand, quite different from the stone of the Via Flaminia. But he recovered quickly.

I could see Nelia ahead of me, her stola flapping wildly. Something caused her horse to shy. He reared, and I was afraid Nelia was going to be thrown off. By the time she got him back under control, I was right on her heels.

Drawing alongside her, I tried to grab her reins. She kicked at me and used the ends of the reins like a whip on my arm.

"Leave me alone! I don't want to go to Rome!" Tears were streaming down her face.

I managed to get enough of a grip on her arm that I thought I could pull her off the horse. Whether I could get her onto my horse I didn't know, but I had to stop her. Clamping my knees on my horse's sides as tightly as I could, I pulled on her arm and drew back on my horse's reins at the same time. Nelia came off her horse, but her weight brought me crashing to the ground with her. Our horses stumbled, then recovered and ran on without us, their reins trailing in the dust.

Still lying on the ground, Nelia kicked out at me. "Damn you! Now look what you've done."

I had had more than enough. Struggling to get my breath back, I grabbed her leg and pulled her toward me. Then I threw my weight on top of her. "Shut up!" I said, clamping my right hand over her mouth. "Shut up, you silly girl. I'm not going to hurt you, but I am going to take you to Rome, just like Musonius—"

Then she bit me. Hard.

"Ow! By the gods!" I rolled off of her, clasping my hand in pain. I knew she was getting up to run, but then I heard horses' hoofs and voices.

"Stop right there, my lady!" Laberius ordered. I looked up to see him, Tacitus, and a couple of my slaves on horseback. Laberius waved the two slaves on ahead. "Round up those horses. And be quick about it."

* * * *

Nelia fell silent as we resumed travel. She sat between Laberius and one of her female companions, her eyes down. I think, if Laberius had had a set of manacles, he would have clapped them on her. Glancing over my shoulder from time to time to check on her, I noticed her leaning on the woman and wincing as though she was in pain. I slowed my horse and dropped back beside the wagon, afraid she might have been injured.

"Are you all right, Nelia?"

No answer, eyes still down.

I addressed the other woman. "Is she all right? Does she seem feverish?"

Before the woman could say anything, Nelia snapped, "Tell him I'm fine, Chloe. As fine as I can be when I've been yanked off my horse and slammed to the ground."

I could play the game too. "Tell your mistress that, when we get home, I'll have my midwife check on her."

Nelia raised her head enough to glare at me with what might have been fear in her eyes. "Tell him that won't be necessary. I'll not have some stranger examining me."

"My lady," Laberius said, "this is not how Gaius Musonius taught you to behave. You're being incredibly rude. What happened wasn't Gaius Pliny's fault."

"It's all right, Laberius," I said. "Little girls sometimes have these moods."

Nelia's back stiffened and her lip curled, but she didn't rise to my bait.

"There's an inn at the next milestone," I said. "We'll stop there, since it's going to take us a couple of more hours to reach Rome at the pace we're keeping."

"The rest will do us good, sir," Laberius said.

"I'm placing Nelia completely in your hands," I told the centurion. "It's your responsibility to get her to Rome in one piece."

"That will be easier to do, sir, if nobody lets her ride a horse."

I rode on ahead without comment.

The inn looked to be one of the better sort, which is like saying a woman of the streets is one of the higher sort of prostitutes. The floors were clean and a door at the rear opened onto a terrace overlooking a stream that fed the Tiber. I gave instructions to the innkeeper for food and drink for our party and showed him enough money to make him eager to serve us. Laberius sat Nelia down at a table in a corner, as far from a door as possible. She would not look up at him.

When everyone had been seated and was eating, Tacitus asked, "Wouldn't this be a good time to read that note from Musonius?"

"I was going to wait until we reached Rome."

"Great Jupiter, man! If you have no curiosity, at least take pity on a friend who's consumed by it."

"Very well." I retrieved the document from the bag where one of my slaves was carrying it. Tacitus and I took our food and sat on a bench overlooking the stream behind the inn. The recent rains had it running full, barely a pace away from us. Tacitus picked up a handful of pebbles and tossed one into the water. I broke the seal on the papyrus to find that Musonius had written me a letter:

> *Gaius Musonius Rufus to his dear Gaius Pliny, greetings and thanks.*
>
> *You have put me forever in your debt by taking Nelia to Rome. Until I am well again, I cannot care for her as I should. To fulfil my promise, I will now tell you all I know about her family, as little as it is.*
>
> *Nelia's father, L. Cornelius Catulus, came from Cisalpine Gaul. His family and mine have known one another for several generations. Over his parents' objections he married a cousin of mine, Fulvia, a girl from one of the less prosperous branches of our family. His father disowned him, so he and Fulvia left Italy and settled in the province of Asia.*
>
> *While he was in Asia, Catulus seems to have run afoul of some very unsavory men. I believe he involved himself in some underhanded schemes to make money. As you know, I came to Asia accompanying Rubellius Plautus in his exile. Catulus somehow learned I was there and sent his wife to ask for my help.*
>
> *While Fulvia was in my home, a messenger arrived with news that Catulus and his young son had been killed by people to whom he owed large sums of money. I, of course, felt obligated to take Fulvia in. Only then did she tell me she was carrying a*

child. She had not even had a chance to tell her husband.

That child was Nelia. She and Fulvia lived with me for three years. Then Fulvia discovered she had a tumor in her breast, as sometimes happens to women. The Greek physician who examined her called it a karkinos. He could not tell her a cause or a cure, only that such tumors always portend a slow and lingering death as the karkinos spreads from the breast to other parts of the body. Fulvia chose to end her life quickly and with dignity, with the assurance that I would provide for Nelia and protect her from the vengeance of her father's enemies.

Another pebble plopped into the stream "My mother died two years after she found tumors in her breasts," Tacitus said. "It would have been better if she'd done what Nelia's mother did. But she was afraid no one would take care of my poor brother."

Tacitus rarely talks about his family. I waited silently for a moment, to see if he would say any more. But all he did was throw another pebble into the water, so I resumed reading:

I chose to keep Nelia in hiding because the men who killed her father also killed her brother. If they would murder one child, I thought, they would not hesitate to kill another. I did not send anyone to inquire into Catulus' death because I did not want to give his enemies a clue as to where Fulvia had gone.

That is all I can tell you about Nelia's family. It is more than she knows, and I must trust you not to tell her any of this. Knowledge of it would cast a cloud over her life. I have dedicated myself to keeping her safe and happy.

"Well, there we have it, I guess," Tacitus said.

"It's all very neat, isn't it?" I rolled up the letter. "Almost too neat."

"What do you mean?"

"He tells the story as though he's anticipating our questions. We might ask, 'Why didn't you send someone to inquire about Catulus' death?' But he's already answered that question."

"Then why aren't you satisfied?" Tacitus tossed another stone into the stream, trying to hit a branch as it floated by.

"Because he raises other questions that he doesn't answer. He's vague about some things. Exactly *where* in Cisalpine Gaul was this Catulus from? I was born there, but I tell people I'm 'from Comum in Cisalpine Gaul,' not just 'from Cisalpine Gaul.' Where in Asia did Catulus settle? Asia's a big province."

"You're a master of understatement. It took us most of April to bounce across it in those dreadful wagons."

"Exactly." I took one of his pebbles and threw it in the water. "So how did Catulus find out Musonius was there? And why doesn't Musonius want Nelia to know all of this?"

"That's what I'd like to know," Nelia said from behind us. Tacitus and I sprang to our feet and turned to face her. The woman Chloe stood close to her.

"My lady," I said, "I didn't know you were there. Where's Laberius?"

"He gave me permission to go to the latrina. For the moment Chloe is my jailer. May I see that letter?" She held out her hand as though expecting me to obey a command.

"As pleased as I am to have you speaking to me again, I must say no." I rolled up the letter and held it close to my chest. "As you must have heard, Musonius told me not to reveal any of it to you."

"But you already have. Now I want to know the rest of it."

She stepped toward me and grabbed the hand holding the letter. Before she could pull the piece of papyrus away, I took it in my other hand and threw it into the stream. We watched it bob and spin as the swift current carried it off.

Nelia reddened, her face so close to mine I could feel her hot breath. "Damn you, Gaius Pliny!"

I pushed her away. "Young lady, that's the second time today you've cursed me. All I'm doing is trying to follow the request of a friend. It would make my life a lot easier if I threw you into that stream."

"I wish you would!" She swung at me. I blocked the blow—a solid one—and Tacitus grabbed her arm from behind.

"Let go of me!" Nelia twisted away from us, but she lost her balance and tumbled into the stream. Chloe screamed and ran back into the inn.

Slipping my sandals off, I jumped in after her, grateful once again that my uncle had insisted I learn to swim. The water was only chest deep, but the current was strong, the footing difficult. Nelia must have swallowed a lot of water when she fell in. She was gasping and struggling to keep her head up. I caught up with her as we came to a bridge. The stream was so full I had to duck to get under it. Ahead I could see the spot where the stream joined the Tiber. If I didn't get Nelia out of the water quickly, we would be in real trouble.

Her hair was the first thing I could grab hold of. Pulling her head above water, I gripped her arm. "Relax! I've got you. Just lie back on the water. Let me pull you in."

But, gasping for breath in her panic, she threw her arms around my neck. We were both starting to sink when a rope landed in front of me.

"Grab on, sir!" Laberius yelled.

I got a good grip on the rope with one hand and wrapped my other arm tightly around Nelia. I was relieved to feel myself no longer carried by the current but being pulled against it, back toward the bridge. With a quick glance I saw Laberius, Tacitus, and several of my slaves hauling us in. Finally I found enough footing to be able to push us toward the bank of the stream.

"Almost there, sir!" Laberius shouted in encouragement.

Once I was sure we were going to get out of the water, I became aware of Nelia's body pressed against mine, with only our wet garments between us. She had such a tight grip on my neck that her breasts were thrust against my chest. When I had my feet under me and could stand, I let go of the rope, picked her up, and carried her onto dry land. We collapsed in a heap, but Nelia wouldn't let go of me.

"Well done, sir," Laberius said as he and Nelia's women crowded around us. "Are you all right?"

"I think so," I said.

The women pried Nelia off of me. She was coughing and crying as they helped her back to the inn. I sat still for a moment, to catch my breath and to shake off—no, to savor—the impression of Nelia's body against mine.

I was only vaguely aware of some of my slaves standing near me, probably wondering what they could do to help. Tacitus reached out a hand to help me up. "You're quite the hero, my friend. Let's get you cleaned up."

Nelia had a change of clothes in her trunks. I had to borrow a dry tunic from Laberius. As we piled into the wagons and mounted our horses to resume traveling, I stopped alongside their wagon.

"Are you all right?" I asked Nelia.

"Yes," was all she would say before she turned her face away from me.

"You owe Gaius Pliny sincere thanks, my lady," Laberius said sternly. "He saved your life."

"If he had let me see the letter in the first place," Nelia snapped, "none of that would have happened."

"Sir," Laberius said, "I must apologize for—"

"Don't apologize for me," Nelia said, turning on him so fast her wet hair sprayed water in all directions. "Don't *ever* apologize for me."

"Never mind, Laberius. Next time I'll just let her drown." I kicked my horse with my heels and moved to the head of our line.

* * * *

About an hour later I slowed my horse and dropped back to Nelia's wagon, but I addressed Chloe. "Have you ever been to Rome?"

"No, my lord."

"Well, we're coming to the Milvian Bridge."

"Is that in Rome, my lord?"

"No, but it's near it. When I was a boy and we traveled to Rome from my uncle's estate outside Comum, I always knew that crossing this bridge meant we were almost there."

"When he was a boy?" Nelia said with a snort. "Let's see, that was last year, wasn't it?" She still wouldn't look directly at me, but she did start looking around. After all, this was what she had wanted for years to see: Rome, the capital of the world.

We were crossing the Milvian Bridge when the clouds parted and the sun broke through as though celebrating its release from prison. As sensitive as my eyes are to bright light, I was momentarily blinded. Glowing shapes seemed to dance in front of me. I put up a hand to shade my eyes until they could adjust.

From the Milvian Bridge the Via Flaminia runs as straight as a road can into the city while the Tiber snakes alongside it on the west. The low-lying ground between the road and the river is prone to flooding. The city hasn't grown this far north yet, so the houses on the east side of the road still have a rustic feel to them. The outskirts of the city are marked by the Pincian Hill, rising on our left, with a wall running along its base. As we reached it Tacitus dropped back and rode on the other side of the carriage.

"We're entering the Campus Martius," I said. "On that hill are the Gardens of the Domitii."

"Where Nero killed himself," Tacitus added.

Damn Tacitus and his love of history! I hadn't made any connection between Nero and this spot as we rode by it on our way out of town. Now I had to recall that Domitian was waiting to know what I had found out about any surviving relatives of the dead emperor. Did he know we had gone out to see Musonius? Should I report to him that the trip was a waste of time?

"Chloe, ask him what that is." Nelia pointed to a large circular structure looming on our right.

"Tell her it's the mausoleum of Augustus," I said.

"It's awfully big just to bury one person, isn't it, Chloe?"

"Other members of his family are buried there, too—his wife, a nephew, some grandchildren, maybe others. I'm not sure."

"Why are there ... I mean, ask him why there are trees growing on top of it."

"There's a park around it." I was getting tired of the game.

"This field used to be open for military training and assemblies of the people," Tacitus said. "But Pompey, Caesar, then Augustus, started build-

ing on it when there was no longer any need for the people to assemble or train. I suppose someday it will be just as thickly populated as the rest of the city."

I snorted. "Preposterous. It's too far from the Forum. It wouldn't be practical for people to live out here. They would spend all day just getting to and from the center of town."

With the sun emerging completely from behind the clouds, I was finally beginning to feel dried out from my dunking in the stream. The sensation of Nelia's breasts against me wasn't fading, though.

About a stadium's length south of the Mausoleum we passed Augustus' Altar of Peace. Just beyond that, where another road intersected from the left, we came to the Porticus Vipsania, built by Augustus' general and son-in-law, Vipsanius Agrippa, the grandfather of our memoir-writing Agrippina. For almost a hundred years the porticus has been a popular gathering place for people who live on the north side of the city. I pulled my horse to a stop. Food vendors, prostitutes, and beggars turned our way, like predators in the forest who've all spotted the same prey. I knew we couldn't stand still for long.

"My slaves and I can take this road and reach my house without going through the main part of the city," I said. Since Julius Caesar's time vehicular traffic has been banned in the center of Rome during the day. If it hadn't been banned by law, the crowds of people in the streets would effectively bring it to a halt.

"Take my horse," Tacitus said. "You need to return him. I'll hire one of those litters to carry me home." He slid off his mount and handed the reins to one of my slaves.

Guiding my horse to the side of the road, I leaned down and said to Tacitus, "Did you get your letter allowing you access to the imperial archives?"

129

"Yes. I just haven't gotten back there yet."

"Please go as soon as possible. Look in those boxes we saw that were marked 'Letters of Nero.' Look for anything that mentions Antistius Vetus or his daughter, or Rubellius."

* * * *

We skirted the worst of Rome's congestion, going through the Porta Quirinalis in the old wall, across the Quirinal and Viminal Hills, and finally up the Esquiline to my house. Nelia did not get to see any of the city's famous buildings, but there would be time for that. Seeing her wince in pain, I wanted to get her into Naomi's hands as soon as possible.

Our arrival at the door of the house threw everyone into an uproar. In spite of my repeated explanations, my mother didn't quite understand why I had come back with more people, goods, and wagons than I set out with.

"And this girl looks sick," she said.

"She fell," I told her. "I want Naomi to take a look at her."

"All right," Mother said. "Take her to the Ariadne room. I'll send Naomi."

Two of my slaves brought a small chair. Nelia sat in it and they carried her into the house.

While Demetrius made other rooms off the garden ready for Nelia's servants, Laberius told Musonius' drivers to start back right away, since storing the horses and wagons overnight would be difficult. But it might have been easier than turning the wagons around in the narrow street. Several of my slaves and some bystanders finally had to be enlisted to push the wagons until they were headed in the right direction. Considering what I had to pay everyone for their help, it would have been cheaper to find a stable.

As the wagons lumbered away, I entered the house, hoping for a degree of normalcy. But there was Laberius, talking with my steward Demetrius. Not just talking with him but giving him orders about how Nelia had to be quartered between him and the two female servants she had brought with her. But that, Demetrius told him, would mean moving some of our servants into different rooms.

"Then do it," Laberius said.

Demetrius looked past him at me. I nodded. It was only for a short while, I reminded myself.

When I found a shady spot in the garden Aurora brought me some wine. I asked her to send Dymas, Moschus, and Aristides to me. Among them, surely, my chief scribe, doorkeeper and nomenclator could tell me what I needed to know. They knew, or knew the names of, anyone in Rome of any significance for the past twenty-five years.

But they didn't know this man.

"Lucius Cornelius Catulus?" Aristides said, repeating the name slowly, like a man tasting a new, somewhat suspicious, wine. "I've never heard of him, my lord."

"He's no one your uncle ever knew, my lord," Moschus added.

"And I've never run across the name in anything your uncle and I read, my lord," Dymas said. "The cognomen Catulus is more common among the Lutatius family than among the Cornelii, I believe. And it hasn't been used for several generations at least."

I sent them back to their work and sat musing about the mysteries of Nelia. There were big questions, such as who her father was and who killed him, and small questions, such as the odd lumps I felt with my thumb when I had my hand clamped over her mouth. When I put my hand over my own mouth, I felt nothing like that.

"Would you like some more wine, my lord?" Aurora asked. I hadn't even been aware of her approach.

"Yes, thank you." As she filled my cup, I studied her mouth.

"Is something the matter, my lord?"

I stood beside her and, almost apologetically, raised my hand. She was my slave; I could do anything I wanted to with her body, but her status as the daughter of my uncle's mistress separated her from the rest of my slaves and made me hesitate even to touch her.

"This may seem strange, Aurora, but I'm going to put my hand over your mouth. Just bear with me for a moment."

I laid my hand over her delicate mouth, with my thumb as close to where it had been on Nelia's face as I could recall. "I'm going to press a bit, but I'm not going to hurt you."

"I know you won't, my lord," she mumbled through my hand.

No matter how I moved my thumb, I could not detect any lumps like those I had felt in Nelia's mouth. And Aurora didn't bite me. Instead, lifting her eyes to mine, she gave my palm the barest kiss.

"You've been hurt, my lord," she said, taking my hand in hers. "Let me tend to that." She had me sit down and, dipping a cloth in the undiluted wine, knelt beside me and began to clean the place where Nelia had bitten me.

She had just finished when my mother and Naomi approached us. "Have you looked after Nelia?" I asked.

"I have, my lord," Naomi said. "She has no broken bones or serious injuries, only some bruises. What I'm concerned about is whether she's going to lose her baby."

131

My cup clattered to the pavement and broke. Aurora jumped back from me.

"Baby? What ... what baby?"

"She's about three months pregnant, my lord."

"How could that be?"

Naomi blushed and looked at my mother in amusement. "Well, my lord ..."

"That's not what I meant. I know *how*. I think I even know *who*. You say you're concerned about whether she's going to lose the baby?"

"Yes, my lord." Naomi recovered her composure, folding her hands in front of her. "A hard fall can cause a woman to miscarry. But she's a strong, healthy girl, and there's no bleeding. That's a good sign. I've given her something to relax her. She should rest for a few days and let nature take its course."

"Is she still awake?"

"Yes, my lord."

"Then I want to talk to her."

My mother stepped in front of me. "But, Gaius, the poor girl needs to rest. You treated her very roughly."

"I ...?"

How did I become the villain? I wasn't the one who bolted or the one who struck the first blow beside the stream. But there's no sense arguing with women once they decide to band together, so I didn't even attempt to correct her view of the incidents.

"I don't think it will tax her to answer a few questions, Mother. She won't even have to get out of bed."

Mother looked at Naomi, who nodded. "Very well, dear. But I'm going to be there, and if I feel you should stop, I'll tell you."

I had to acquiesce. This was a new side of my mother, or rather a side I only remembered from the days before Vesuvius erupted. She looks frail and speaks softly. Over the past four years I had forgotten how determined she could be once she made up her mind things would be done a certain way. Something about her had been different since she returned from the funeral of Naomi's brother. She seemed to have found a new vitality, like a flower that's been watered after a long dry spell.

"Let's go then," I said, and I followed her and Naomi across the garden to Nelia's room.

"I'll see if she feels like talking to you," Mother said. She and Naomi entered the room, leaving the door open to admit more light. That allowed me to hear the conversation.

"Are you feeling any better, dear?" Mother asked.

"A little. The medicine Naomi gave me is starting to work."

"Good. My son would like to talk with you." Her tone was so apologetic she might have been asking the *princeps* for a favor. "Do you feel up to that?"

"Couldn't it wait until later?"

"It might be better to go ahead and let him ask a few questions now, to take the edge off his curiosity. He is inordinately curious. Then you can talk with him at greater length when you're feeling better."

"All right. The jailer always has the last word."

"I beg your pardon," Mother said.

"He'll know what I mean."

"I certainly do," I said, stepping into the room. "And I'm tired of hearing you talk about me that way. I was asked to do a favor for a friend. At considerable inconvenience to myself and my family I have agreed to let you stay here for a while. You will get to see Rome, which you claim you've always wanted to do. But all I've heard from you is complaints. I don't expect you to appreciate what I'm doing or to like me, but I do expect you to be civil."

Nelia started to cry. I wonder if men will ever develop a defense against women's tears. Naomi sat on the bed and took Nelia's hand. How fitting that the fresco over Nelia's bed showed Ariadne, abandoned by Theseus on the isle of Naxos, her hands outstretched, her tears flowing.

"Now look what you've done," Mother said, rushing to the defense of a weeping member of her own kind. "You've upset her. I think you should leave."

"No. No, let him stay," Nelia said, sniffing and rubbing her eyes. "Gaius Pliny is right. He deserves better treatment from me than he's been getting." She looked up at me and I knew she had just wrested control of the situation away from me in my own house, and she knew it, too. How long until she would be ordering my slaves around?

"I suppose they told you I'm carrying a child," she said.

133

I nodded. "About three months along, I gather."

She looked down, in shame, I hoped. "So now you understand why I wanted to stay on cousin Gaius' estate, to be near my child's father."

"Just to be absolutely clear," I said, "Marcianus, the boy on the next estate, is the father, isn't he?"

"Why, yes. He's the only one who could be. What do you think of me?" She brushed away a tear, drawing another of my mother's harsh glances in my direction.

"I'm uncertain about too many things," I said, "to know what to think of you."

"I've told you everything cousin Gaius has told me. What else do you need to know?"

"Who your father was, to start with."

"Didn't cousin Gaius tell you in his letter?"

"I want to know what Musonius told *you*."

"He told me that my father was Lucius Cornelius—"

"Not just his name. Who *was* he? None of my slaves who are knowledgeable about such things has ever heard the name, not even my nomenclator. And he served with my uncle in Cisalpine Gaul, where this Cornelius Catulus supposedly came from."

"Is that what Musonius told you?" When I didn't answer, Nelia stuck out her lower lip and said, "If you had just let me see his letter, you wouldn't have to worry about what to tell me and what to conceal from me."

My mother looked from one of us to the other. "Letter? Why did Musonius write you a letter?"

"Because there's something about my parents he doesn't want me to know," Nelia said before I could explain.

"Where is the letter?" my mother asked.

"Gaius Pliny destroyed it rather than let me read it," Nelia replied, folding her arms over her chest and pulling the blanket up over her.

"Gaius! Why would you do such a thing?"

"Musonius instructed me not to reveal the contents of the letter to Nelia."

"That's entirely unreasonable. And unkind. Don't you think a child deserves to know who her parents were and what happened to them?"

"I don't know Musonius' reasons, Mother. All I can do is what he asked of me."

"So her father was named Lucius Cornelius Catulus?"

"That's the name Musonius gave me, but it isn't a proper Roman name, and yet it's not some half-Roman, half-Greek concoction from the provinces either."

"Well, you'll just have to ask cousin Gaius about it," Nelia said. "Perhaps he'll write you another letter."

"That's another problem I'm having. I'm not sure I can trust anything Musonius has told me about you, or anything he's told you about yourself."

My mother gasped. "Now, dear, that's very harsh. I don't know Musonius, but I do know his reputation. His integrity is unquestioned. Why would you doubt him?"

"Because he has raised Nelia in complete isolation and won't tell anyone why."

Mother turned to Nelia. "What reason does Musonius give for raising you that way?"

"He says it's my best—my only—hope of safety." Nelia's voice softened, as though she was making herself afraid.

"Why would you need to worry about your safety any more than anyone else in Rome?"

"I'm not really sure. Cousin Gaius won't tell me anything specific. He says it would only worry me. He says my father got into trouble—what sort, I don't know—and was killed shortly before I was born. My mother died when I was three. I don't remember her."

"And you know nothing about your father except his name?" Mother raised an eyebrow.

"Cousin Gaius won't tell me anything else about him, or about what he did. He says it's better that I not know. After my mother died cousin Gaius brought me to his estate here, and I haven't set foot off the place until today."

"He has your interests at heart, I'm sure," Mother said, patting Nelia's hand. "He wants to protect you."

"I think he's just a mean old man." Nelia's lower lip jutted out.

I jumped back into the conversation. "That's not the impression I have of him. He's a most gracious host in his house in Rome. He welcomed me warmly there."

Nelia met my eyes as though I was a slave who had interrupted his mistress. "There seem to be two Musoniuses. I hope I'll get to meet the Roman one someday. How did you come to know him?"

"While I was in Syria I met his son-in-law, Artemidorus—"

"Son-in-law?" Nelia's surprise seemed genuine. "But that means he has a daughter. He's never mentioned her—or any children—to me."

I had no reply to that. How could a man divorce his life in Rome so completely from his life in the country? My esteem for Musonius was crumbling. What was he hiding? From whom was he hiding it?

"What is she like?" Nelia's voice dripped with jealousy. "This ... daughter?"

I suppose, in a way, she had considered herself Musonius' child all these years. Now to learn that there was a legitimate daughter—she must feel betrayed, like a woman finding out her lover is married.

"Well ... she's a ... a lovely girl." Why did I suddenly feel like I was on trial?

"How old?"

"About fifteen, I think."

Nelia sat up in bed and continued to fire questions at me. "Musonius isn't married ... is he? Who was her mother?"

"Musonius' wife died ... in childbirth." A fact I hated to mention, since Nelia would be undergoing that perilous experience in a few months. She was too angry to make the connection.

"How long has this girl been married?"

"A year. I was at the party celebrating their first anniversary."

"She's well educated, I suppose."

"I couldn't judge. I met her only twice, on social occasions."

"So, he gives his daughter in marriage when she's fourteen. I'm eighteen and he won't let me even talk to a boy."

Like someone inexperienced in speaking in court, she had exposed a weakness in her own case. I seized on it. "But obviously you have talked to one. In fact, you've done a good deal more than talk."

"Gaius!" my mother said.

"You can't make me ashamed of what I did." Nelia placed a protective hand on her belly and glared defiantly at me.

"Now, now," my mother said, laying her hand over Nelia's. "Don't upset yourself. How did you meet this boy?"

Nelia turned to her and smiled, like a little girl sharing a secret with her mother. "There's an old bridge over the stream that's the boundary between our estates. It's Etruscan, I think. I like to study the writing on it. Marcianus saw me there one day. At first I wanted to run from him. I thought he was one of those people cousin Gaius had warned me about."

"The ones who would want to kill you?"

"Yes, but he's so sweet. He brought me books. Not philosophy and history, like cousin Gaius wanted me to read, but poetry. Catullus, Ovid, Cornelius Gallus. Wonderful poems."

"Seductive poems," I said.

Nelia blushed. "Well, yes."

Mother silenced me with a look, then turned back to Nelia. "Oh, child, you have nothing to be ashamed of. If Musonius had let you meet people in a normal way, you wouldn't have been swept off your feet by the first boy who spoke to you."

What's happening here? I wondered. Now Musonius was at fault for something Nelia did. My mother should be pleading cases in court. She was proving adept at turning everything in her client's favor.

"What is Marcianus like?" Mother asked.

Nelia's face lit up. "He has the darkest eyes and a voice I could listen to all day ... and all night. The first time he kissed me ... I felt like a tree must feel when it's hit by a bolt of lightning."

Mother, Naomi, and Nelia laughed softly together, like members of a mystery cult who share a secret reserved only for the initiates. Had my mother actually known such feelings for my father? I felt a shudder of revulsion.

This was too much to bear. "I hope you rest well, my lady," I said. "Perhaps we can talk again when you're feeling better."

* * * *

I don't think the women even knew when I left the room. Since I was in the garden, I decided to make one more effort to find the knife I used to kill the Cyclops. It had disappeared from the table before the dishes were cleared. That told me someone deliberately picked it up. Had they noticed something about it? As dark as it was that night and as frightened as I'd been, I couldn't be sure I'd gotten all the blood off. If someone took it to possibly use it against me—Glaucon came immediately to mind—I would have to turn the whole house inside out to find it.

Like Domitian searching for Agrippina's memoirs, I didn't want to draw that much attention to the thing. But what if someone noticed it while the Praetorians were at the gate, made a few quick deductions, and dropped it into the bushes to get it out of sight?

I was on my knees looking in the bushes around the exhedra when I heard sandals on the paving stones behind me.

"Can I help you find something, my lord?" Phineas said.

Scrambling to my feet, I brushed the dirt off my tunic. "No. It's ... it's of no consequence. Do you want something?" From the way he was twisting his hands I knew he wanted to say something difficult.

He stopped a few paces away from me, looking down at his feet or over my shoulder—anywhere but at my face. "I want to thank you profusely, my lord, for overlooking my outburst here in the garden the other day. I never meant to threaten you. Please believe me. I would never do anything to harm you. You've been most kind to me and to my mother ..."

I suppressed a smile. "And you've recited the speech she wrote for you quite nicely. You need not finish it."

His face reddened. "But, my lord—"

"I know you suffered horribly when Jerusalem was under siege, and I know I'll never understand just how much you suffered. Some things we're never able to put entirely out of our minds. To this day, whenever I see dark clouds on the horizon, I feel like I'm watching the eruption of Vesuvius again. You'll never know how close my mother and I came to dying then and what scars that experience has left on both of us. She loved her brother and I loved my uncle as much as you and your mother loved yours."

"I've no doubt of that, my lord."

"You're a clever man, Phineas. An accident of fate has made you a slave. Like the Stoics, I believe we should all work as hard as we can, in whatever place we find ourselves, and take advantage of whatever opportunities befall us. It may be your fate to be a slave now. That doesn't mean it is your fate to be a slave for the rest of your life."

"My lord, I was not going to ask for my freedom."

"Nor was I going to offer it ... at this time. As far as I'm concerned, the incident in the garden is forgotten. I'm tired from my journey, and all I want at the moment is a bath." A bath that would let me loosen muscles tight from riding and soak the bruises I had incurred in my struggle with Nelia. No one else seemed to appreciate that she wasn't the only one who'd taken a hard fall off a horse and been dunked in a stream.

But that was not to be. I had just reached the door of the bath when Moschus caught up with me. "My lord, there is someone here to see you."

"At this time of day? Tell him to come back tomorrow morning."

"But, my lord, it's Marcus Aquilius Regulus."

Regulus? At my door? At this hour? What had I done to deserve that? Moschus kept his head down as though he was somehow to blame for Regulus' appearance.

I sighed in resignation. "Tell him I'll be there right away. I'd at least like to put on one of my own tunics. Offer him something to drink." *Something poisonous*, I was tempted to add.

"Yes, my lord."

A fresh tunic was the least of my concerns, but changing into one gave me a few moments to brace myself for a confrontation with Regulus. What could he possibly want? Had he discovered Glaucon's liaison with one of his slaves? Was the woman pregnant? That would be easy enough to settle. Under Roman law the child of a slave woman belongs to her master, regardless of who the father is. Regulus would not have to trouble himself—or me—to discuss that. So what did he want?

When I entered the atrium Regulus was sitting on a bench in the shade of the west side of the impluvium, sipping a cup of wine. "Good day, Marcus Regulus," I said, seating myself on the bench on the south side of the pool. "To what do I owe the honor of this visit?"

"Good day, Gaius Pliny. Thank you for receiving me at this hour. I haven't been here in many years, since you were a child. You're certainly leaving your mark on your uncle's house." From the way he was looking at my new frescoes and wrinkling his nose, I knew he meant that comment in the sense of a dog leaving its mark on a street corner.

"What can I do for you, Marcus Regulus?" The edge in my voice was intentional.

He gave a short laugh. "You're right. No point in pretending we can be friends, or even courteous to one another. Very well, then, right to business. I wanted to ask you if you knew anything about the murder of that cut-throat the other night."

My heart raced almost as fast as it had when the brute grabbed me. Why was Regulus asking me about this? Did he have the knife? I took a deep breath. "The one who ... called himself the Cyclops?" As if there were so many murders in our district I needed to specify one.

"Yes. Have you heard anything more about it?"

"Nothing. I left the city the next morning and just returned barely an hour ago."

"Oh, where did you go?"

"To visit a friend."

He sat silent for a moment, apparently hoping I would, as nervous people often do, start chattering to fill the void. Finishing his wine, he looked around as if he expected more. "This is an excellent vintage," he hinted. In the face of my silence, he continued. "It troubles me a great deal to have a man killed in the shadow of your house and in sight of mine. We can't let that sort of thing become a regular occurrence right outside our homes."

"One incident—the first in years—hardly seems to me to be a cause for great concern."

"But we must act to prevent a second."

"That's the duty of the Urban Cohorts and the vigiles."

Regulus slapped his knees. "The Cohorts and the vigiles can't keep our district under constant watch. The best they can do is pass through a couple of times during the night. What we need is watchmen of our own to guarantee our safety. There are retired legionaries in the city who would be ideal for the job."

I shook my head in disbelief. The man had enough gall to be divided into three parts. He wanted me to pay for watchmen who would be his chosen men, I was sure, so he could keep himself informed about the movements of everyone around him. I could never have foreseen that, by defending myself, I would give Regulus an excuse to establish his own private army on my doorstep. But what else could I have done? And how could I refuse to participate in what would, if left in his hands, amount to an extortion scheme?

"Well, what do you think, Gaius Pliny? I've already spoken to others around us. They like the idea. It would be a small price to pay for the safety of our wives and mothers, to spare them the shame of being accosted—or worse—outside their own homes."

Since Regulus' wife had no shame and his mother had long since died from the shame of bearing a child like him, that last sentence must have been inspired by the sound of women's voices coming toward us. I turned to see my mother, Nelia, and several slave women enter the atrium. My mother was saying, "And you must see ... Oh, Gaius, dear. I didn't realize you were talking with someone. Good day, Marcus Regulus."

Regulus and I stood. "Good day, lady Plinia," he said. "Please excuse my untimely visit. I tried to see your son yesterday, but he was away."

"Yes," my mother said with all the innocence of a mouse playing between a cat's paws. "He went to visit Musonius Rufus at his villa on the Via Flaminia."

I had to stop this conversation. If I dared, I would have rushed over and put my hand over my mother's mouth and escorted her out of the atrium. I tried to get her attention, to warn her with my eyes not to say any more. But Regulus had picked up the scent of a prey that could be brought down easily.

"So that's where the old greybeard has been," he said, taking a step toward my mother and Nelia. "I haven't seen him for some time. How is he?"

"He's been ill," my mother said.

"I'm sorry to hear that." Regulus shook his head so slowly and sincerely that I almost believed him.

I stepped between Regulus and my mother. "Do we have anything else to discuss, Marcus Regulus?"

"I suppose not." He turned to the women. "We've been talking about that ghastly murder that took place behind your house two nights ago."

Mother shook her head. She doesn't get out into society enough to recognize the people who are dangerous, who can loosen your tongue without plying you with wine. "Oh, yes, it was horrid."

"I understand the killer left a blood-soaked toga at the scene."

"A tunic, actually. And I would call it blood-*stained*, not soaked."

"So you saw it?"

Something was finally making my mother uneasy, but not enough to silence her. "The captain of the Cohorts showed it to us ... when he came to our door the next morning."

"I see. Rumor does make things grow, like water on a thirsty field. So I suppose the axe with which the fellow was beheaded is also an exaggeration."

I had to step in. "That's a gross exaggeration. He was stabbed in the neck with a knife." Then I stopped to think. Did the captain actually tell me that? Or was I revealing something that only the killer would know?

My comment seemed to upset my mother. "How did you feel about having your house searched?" she suddenly asked Regulus.

He drew himself up in surprise. "Your house was searched? By whom?"

"By the Cohorts. They said they were searching all the houses on this street."

"My house isn't on this street, to be precise."

"One of your servants' entrances is," I said, "to be precise."

"Oh, that. I'd almost forgotten. It's in my wife's wing of the house. So your house was searched." He could hardly suppress his glee. "What were they looking for?"

"They never told us," Mother said. "They just pawed through everything. It took the servants the rest of the day to put things right."

Regulus nodded and pursed his lips, as though weighing her answer. "It is odd that they would search the homes of people like yourselves when this violent act was undoubtedly perpetrated by some other criminal, someone just as dangerous as the Cyclops himself. That's why, Gaius Pliny, I believe we should do something to defend ourselves. Rome is becoming a more dangerous city every day. We wouldn't want anything to happen to your mother or to this lovely young woman"—he turned to Nelia—"whom I don't believe I've met."

'Lovely' was being generous to Nelia at the moment. She had not fully repaired the damage to her appearance from our fall and struggle. Her hair was loose, her face still dirty in spots.

"This is the lady Cornelia," my mother said, in evident relief at getting away from the subject of murder. "Musonius' cousin. She's visiting with us for a while."

"Musonius' ... cousin? I didn't know he had a cousin." Regulus' eyes narrowed. "Where has he been keeping you, my lady?"

"I've lived most of my life on his estate," Nelia said. Something in the tilt of her head and the tone of her voice made it clear that topic was not to be pursued.

"Oh, I see," was all Regulus could say.

My battle to keep Regulus from extracting any information from my mother or Nelia had been lost. Now all I could hope for was to limit my losses and make an orderly withdrawal. "I'm surprised to see you up, lady Cornelia. I thought you were ... exhausted from your trip."

"I'm feeling better, thank you. We're on our way to have a bath before dinner."

"And Nelia asked to see the rest of the house," Mother put in.

Surveying her newly conquered domain? I wondered.

"Well, I'll get out of your way," Regulus said, turning for the door.

"I would invite you to dine with us, Marcus Regulus," my mother said, "but by this hour I'm sure you already have plans."

Regulus' face showed that he was as surprised by the hint of an invitation as I was. "That would be delightful, lady Plinia," he said when he recovered. "But tonight I'm dining with Caesar Domitian. And I must go or I'll be late. Let me know what you decide about my offer, Gaius Pliny."

When the door was safely shut behind Regulus I turned to the women. "Mother, you said entirely too much. I've told you that Regulus cannot be trusted."

"That's what your uncle used to say, too. He even claimed Regulus had spies in other people's houses." She waved her hand to dismiss the thought.

"Spies?" Nelia said. "Whatever for?"

"He wants to know anything and everything that's going on in Rome," I told her. "And he'll report even the smallest bit of gossip to Domitian."

"But, Gaius," Mother said, "surely you don't believe any of our people could be disloyal."

"I told you what I learned on my way back from Syria."

"Oh, that. Why would that make you mistrust everyone in our house?"

I ran my eyes over the slave women accompanying my mother. "I don't mistrust everyone, just the one who's spying for Regulus."

"Are you sure there's only one?" Nelia asked.

THE NEXT MORNING brought clear skies and sunshine, which brought out the biggest crowd of my clients since my return from Syria. Their problems seemed to spring up like mushrooms after the rain: a sick child, a dying mother-in-law, new living quarters needed before their present building collapsed around them.

As I listened to their litany of troubles and requests I wished I had someone on whom I could lay my worries. Did Regulus suspect anything about my involvement in the death of the Cyclops? What had he told Domitian about his visit to my house yesterday? The sudden appearance of an unknown relative of Musonius'—if that's who she actually was—would surely arouse interest up on the Palatine.

I shook my head to drive out such thoughts and tried to focus on my clients.

"No, my lord?" the man standing in front of me said. "But I hadn't finished ..."

"Oh, I wasn't denying your request, Marius. I was just trying to ... to clear my head. Please, go on."

Before my year in Syria I had handled my clients' problems in much the same way my uncle had, the way most men of my class deal with their clients—by throwing money to them and hoping they will go away as quickly as possible. But my experience in Syria, especially on the return journey, caused me to realize that plebeians' joys and sorrows—in fact, all aspects of their lives—mean as much to them as mine do to me. That's not how aristocratic Romans are taught to think as we grow up.

I now try to get to know something about my clients in the hope that my help to them can be more effective. Some of them seem to appreciate my interest; others seem puzzled, even offended, if I ask to know more than they volunteer. They just want to get their daily dole and be on their way.

But today two of them hung back as the rest left. One, Publius Torquatus, was accompanied by his daughter, dressed in what was clearly her

143

finest gown and a few pieces of cheap jewelry. The name of the other, older, man escaped me at the moment. I did remember the nervous young man with him as his son. Both were tall, lean, with the stained hands of men who worked with some sort of dye. Then I remembered: this was Mercator, a fuller. He had a small shop on the edge of the Subura where he dyed and bleached cloth.

I pulled Demetrius aside. "Is there something I need to do with these people?"

"You are to help them arrange the marriage of Torquatus' daughter to Mercator's son, my lord. You were supposed to talk to them yesterday morning. When you did not return from Musonius' villa, I told them to come back today. I trust that was the right thing to do."

"Yes, of course. Bring them here. We'll sit by the *impluvium* and get this settled as quickly as possible."

Demetrius bowed his head and herded the two fathers and their children toward where I had taken a seat by the impluvium. Demetrius stood beside me. Some of the arrangements had been agreed to by both parties in advance. This marriage would be sine manu, as most marriages are today, a less formal arrangement than in the old Republic. What remained to be settled was the size of the dowry. Torquatus had a small sum of money saved up, but not enough to satisfy Mercator. As patron of both men, it was my responsibility to negotiate the amount of the dowry and then to make up the difference between what Mercator would accept and what Torquatus had on hand.

I was in no mood to haggle, so I let Mercator have more than I probably should have. Then I entered on the contract the total amount of the dowry. "Demetrius will give you my share when we're finished here," I told Torquatus, a short, round man with hair everywhere but on top of his head.

"Thank you, my lord."

"How old is your daughter?"

"Thirteen, my lord. Fourteen in October."

"Is she nubile?" While Roman girls marry young, I have told my clients I would never consent to the marriage of a girl who had not begun her monthlies.

"Oh, definitely, my lord. Just see for yourself." He gathered up some of the girl's gown and pulled it tight so that it outlined her breasts and her round hips. She blushed scarlet. "And she's a virgin. You can check for yourself."

"That won't be necessary," I said quickly. "When will the betrothal party take place?"

"Two days before the ides of August, my lord," Mercator said. "And the wedding will be ten days after that."

I turned to the girl, who looked very young, in spite of all the paint and powder she was wearing. Her features were well-defined, almost sharp, presumably like her mother. For her soon-to-be husband's sake, I hoped so. I could not imagine a worse fate for a man than to wake up some morning in bed next to a female version of Torquatus.

"Is this acceptable to you? Do you want to marry Mercator's son?" The bride's consent to a marriage is not required, but I think, if she's to be handed over like so much property, someone should ask her how she feels about it. Women aren't farm animals, after all, even if some men treat them like they are.

"Yes, my lord. I'm happy to be marrying him." She looked at the young man with a glint of pleasure in her eye, which he returned.

"Very well, then." I held out the document so Demetrius could drop some wax on it. Letting the wax cool for a moment, I pressed my seal into it. "I hope you will be happy and prosperous in this marriage."

"And you, my lord?" Torquatus asked. "Will you be married any time soon? That would be a grand celebration for us all."

I laughed. "There's no immediate danger of my marrying, though I'm sure it will happen in good time."

As I watched them leave, though, I wondered if I ever would take a wife. My uncle never married. He was one of those Roman men who found a mistress among his slaves, a woman named Monica. They were devoted to one another and lived together as though they were husband and wife for fifteen years, in spite of my mother's constant, head-shaking disapproval. Monica died only two years before Vesuvius erupted, and my uncle remained alone after her death.

The only real reason Roman men have to marry is to beget legitimate children to whom they can leave their property. My uncle could fall back on me. I have inherited two estates—from my natural and adopted fathers—and have already begun to increase my holdings. But to whom would I leave my property if I died childless? Would Domitian, or someone like him, seize it? Is the desire to protect my property sufficient reason to marry, when Tacitus reminds me almost daily what a burden marriage can be?

* * * *

Having satisfied my obligations to my clients, I headed for the library with some misgivings. Dymas had told me he'd gathered a number of scrolls containing information about Agrippina and Nero. Since I could not tell him exactly what I wanted to know, he asked if I would be willing to look over the scrolls myself. History has never been my favorite type of reading, perhaps because my uncle tried so hard to make me like it. While Vesuvius was erupting, I sat in the garden of our house, copying passages from Livy which my uncle had assigned me. I haven't picked up a scroll of the Paduan's work, or any other historian's, since. But I might see something in these scrolls which Dymas would not recognize as important.

One table had been cleared and there Dymas and Phineas had assembled the scrolls we were to look over this morning. Glaucon was out on another 'errand,' Dymas informed me. He seemed surprised that I didn't ask the nature of it, but I merely wondered where Glaucon and his lover from Regulus' house would go to couple during the day.

Dymas did the best he could to read the scrolls under the water glass. He had called on two young scribes to assist us, but they were inexperienced and I soon saw that Phineas and I would bear the brunt of the work. Relying on Phineas' skill with Tironian notation, I did most of the reading, dictating anything useful that I found to Phineas, who could take down my words as fast as I spoke them.

By mid-morning I had sent the other two scribes back to copying my uncle's 160 scrolls. They were actually slowing Phineas and me down. Toward midday Glaucon strolled in. He and I exchanged the sort of glances that people give one another when they share a secret neither can acknowledge.

"Is there anything I can help you with, my lord?" Glaucon asked.

Phineas and I were working so smoothly together I didn't want Glaucon to intrude and disturb us. "See what your father is doing and assist him," I said, looking down to dismiss him.

As Glaucon turned away I pulled out the sheet of papyrus on which Phineas had been keeping track, in regular Latin script, of important events in Agrippina's life as far as we could deduce them from the scrolls assembled in front of us.

"This would be much easier," I said, glancing from one piece of papyrus to a note on another piece, "if we had some reasonable way to determine exactly how many years ago something happened. We Romans build bridges, roads, and aqueducts that amaze the world and last for hundreds of years, but we can't keep track of dates without using clumsy terms like 'in the eighth year of Augustus' or 'in the tenth year of Tiberius.' What is the connection between those dates?"

"We Jews," Phineas said, "count from the beginning of the world, my lord. Don't some of your historians date things *ab urbe condita*, 'from the founding of the city'?"

"A few do, but it isn't accurate, since we don't know exactly when Rome was established. How do you Jews know how long ago the world began?"

"Our teachers—the rabbis—have knowledge of such things, my lord."

"Knowledge not to be revealed to outsiders, I take it."

"I would rather not, my lord."

"Were you studying to be a ... rabbi?" I asked on a hunch, my tongue stumbling over the strange word.

He lowered his head and then looked back up at me. "My ability with languages and my love of our Law had been noted by the elders, my lord. I was eleven when Jerusalem fell. In another year I would have begun serious study."

"Your skills have certainly proved useful to me."

"Thank you, my lord. Shall we see what we know about Agrippina so far?"

His question re-established the proper relationship between us, something I was finding hard to do. Phineas was a likeable young man and my mother's reminder of the similarities between my life and his had made me regard him in a different light. Under other circumstances, we probably would have been friends.

I shuffled a few pieces of papyrus. "The easiest date to establish is that she died twenty-four years ago, in the fifth year of Nero."

"Yes, my lord, in March of that year."

"But we found some disagreement about the date of her birth."

"Yes, my lord. She seems to have been born about sixty-eight or sixty-nine years ago, just after Tiberius came to power."

"And you think sixty-eight years ago is more likely," I said, "even though my uncle's account makes it sixty-nine?"

"With all due respect to your uncle, my lord, he was careless about numbers. Our other sources show greater precision in that regard."

Phineas was displaying the insight into documents which Glaucon would never achieve. It came close to the sort of mystical vision that initiates into a religious cult claim to experience. Suddenly they understand things on a deeper level than ever before.

"All right, sixty-eight it is," I said. "She married when she was thirteen, and Nero was born nine years later, or ..." I started calculating in my head.

"Forty-six years ago, my lord."

"Exactly." I put my finger on the next item on Phineas' list. "When Nero was two, Agrippina was exiled, along with her sister, to the island of Pandateria, where she spent about two years. Her brother, Caligula, sent her there, and her uncle, Claudius, recalled her as soon as he came to power."

Phineas put his pen down. "I hesitate to say anything, my lord, because I've heard you say you don't believe in coincidences, but ... my mother and my uncle have some connection to Pandateria. I've heard her mention the place."

I was as surprised as I was when he threatened me in the garden. "Bring her here at once. Don't tell her what it's about, just get her in here."

Phineas ran from the library, sandals slapping the mosaic floor.

I couldn't let myself get too excited. Whatever connection Naomi might have to Pandateria, she would have been an infant when Agrippina was there. She couldn't know anything directly, only what others had told her.

"Dymas, how old is Naomi?"

"Let me check, my lord." My chief scribe retrieved a scroll containing the names and origins of all my slaves, roughly in alphabetical order. Holding it under the water glass, he scanned it and counted on his fingers until he said, "She appears to be ... forty-three years old, my lord."

"By the gods! She was born while Agrippina was on Pandateria."

"So it would seem, my lord."

Rubbing my hand over my eyes, I tried to absorb all the information flooding over me. If Naomi had some connection with Pandateria, that meant her older brother, Menachem, was also there. Could that be one more unlikely connection between Menachem the mason and Nero the *princeps*, or would Tacitus say I was grasping at straws? I wished fervently that Tacitus was here, to help me sort all of this out, but he was going to the imperial archives this morning to search through Nero's letters for anything that mentioned Agrippina or Rubellius Plautus.

Phineas returned in a few moments with his mother, accompanied by my mother and Nelia. Aurora and two other female slaves trailed them, bearing trays of food and wine. Naomi hung back, almost hiding behind Nelia.

"Phineas said you wanted to talk to Naomi," my mother said. "What's the matter?"

"Nothing is the matter. I just want to ask Naomi about something. Why did all of you come with her?" I knew I was doing a poor job of concealing my irritation.

"We were about to eat," Nelia said, "and we thought you needed something, too. Phineas said you've worked all morning without taking anything."

Now that I'd stopped poring over the scrolls I did feel the need for something to eat and drink. "Put it down on that end of the table," I said. "Be careful of the scrolls. Phineas, get some ink and fresh papyrus and take notes."

When we were settled, with the women at the end of the table and Naomi sitting across from Phineas and me, I turned to her. "I need to ask you some things about your family."

"My family, my lord?"

"What do you need to know about her family?" my mother asked.

"Mother, please let me talk to Naomi. This will take forever if you keep interfering. I am not angry at her. I just need some information."

"Very well, dear." She folded her hands in her lap. "I'll be quiet."

Somehow I doubted that. "Now, Naomi, Phineas says you have some connection to the island of Pandateria."

She glanced at her son as if to ask why he hadn't warned her that question was coming. He kept his head down, absorbed in his writing. "I was born there, my lord," she said.

"What were your parents doing there?"

"They were freedmen in the service of Lucius Antistius Vetus. He was the emperor's procurator on the island. He made sure people who were sent there in exile stayed there."

"So he was their jailer," Nelia muttered from the end of the table.

"I thought we agreed there would be no more of that kind of talk," I said, glaring at her. She picked up a piece of cheese but would not lower her head or appear the least bit intimidated. I turned back to Naomi.

"How did your parents come to be enslaved?"

"They were taken captive, my lord, in an uprising led by Judas the Galilean."

I realized then that her family's fortunes had been reversed enough times to shake any Stoic's confidence in fate. The parents went from being free people to slaves to freedmen, then the children and their grandchild fell from freedom back into slavery. Whether they would be freed again was now entirely up to me. "But you lived in Asia, didn't you, when Phineas was born? How did you get there?"

"When Antistius left the island, my lord, he released my parents from any further obligation to him and gave them money to set themselves up. They didn't want to go back to Judaea because there was so much trouble there, so they went to Ephesus, where they had relatives. My father was a stone mason and plasterer, and he taught my brother that craft, just as my mother trained me to be a midwife."

I heard Dymas shuffling through scrolls. "Do you know anything about Antistius Vetus?" I asked over my shoulder.

"According to the *Fasti,* my lord, he was consul with Nero in Nero's second year. Then he held some other posts and finally was proconsul of Asia. Your uncle used some of his writings as a source in the early volumes of his *Natural History.*"

So the man had a rather distinguished career. Sharing a consulship with the *princeps* was a privilege reserved for very few. "Were you still living in Asia when Antistius was governor?" I asked Naomi.

"Yes, my lord, but we didn't have anything to do with him. My parents were both dead by then and he would not have known me or my brother."

The scratching of Phineas' pen was the only sound in the room as I pondered my next question.

"Back to Pandateria. Do you know who was exiled there when you were a child?"

Anxiety clouded Naomi's face. "We were told never to talk about that, my lord."

"It's all right," I said. "She's been dead for twenty-five years. It was Nero's mother, Agrippina, wasn't it?"

"Yes, my lord."

"But everybody knows she and her sister were sent there." I laid my hand on the scrolls in front of me. "It's in these books we've been reading. Why were you told not to talk about her?"

"Not about her, my lord." She glanced at my mother for reassurance. "About her baby."

* * * *

Phineas' pen stopped scratching and a heavy silence fell over the room.

By the gods! I thought. *A sibling of Nero's. Domitian was right to be afraid.*

"Agrippina had a baby?" I was suddenly finding it difficult to breathe. "While she was on Pandateria?"

"Yes, my lord."

"A boy or a girl?"

"A girl, my lord."

That made things slightly easier. A girl could not challenge Domitian directly, but girls can have other babies. The line of Julius Caesar and Augustus could continue through her. I waved my hand over the scrolls Phineas and I had been reading. "Not one of these books says anything about Agrippina having a baby on Pandateria, or having any other child than Nero. Why are you the only one who knows this?"

"Nobody knew she was pregnant when she came there, my lord."

Phineas pointed to a scroll of Aufidius Bassus' history. "She was sent there, my lord, because she'd been having an affair with a man who tried to overthrow her brother, Caligula."

I picked up the scroll and rolled it back to the passage we'd read. "Oh, yes. Lentulus Gaetulicus was her lover. And her sister's." My mother blushed; Nelia did not. "So I guess he would have been the father, assuming what your mother is saying is true."

"It is the truth, my lord," Naomi said, with a hint of pleading in her voice. "I swear it. Agrippina must have been about two months along when she came to the island."

Out of the corner of my eye I saw Nelia rest a hand on her belly.

"How do you know all this?" my mother asked before I could. "You were just an infant."

"My mother was the midwife who delivered her, my lady."

"And no one suspected Agrippina was pregnant?" I asked, glancing at Nelia.

"My mother said she stayed in a part of the house away from everyone else, my lord. My mother was the only servant who waited on her during the whole time."

"What became of the child?" I asked.

"Agrippina left her with Antistius and his wife, my lord, to raise as theirs. Antistius' wife wore something under her gown to make herself look pregnant and stayed to herself a great deal during those months."

The implications of what I was hearing stunned me into silence. One of my slaves harbored a secret that could shake Rome's government to its foundations and probably destroy me and my household. Now, thanks to my lack of foresight, a dozen other people knew it: my mother, Nelia, and all the scribes and serving women who had been listening to this conversation because I didn't send them away before it started.

I stood and raised my voice.

"What you've all just heard must never be mentioned outside this room. Phineas, make a list of everyone who is here now." The young scribe's pen scratched rapidly. "If I ever hear that even a word of this has been whispered to anyone else, all of you will be punished more severely than you can possibly imagine." I paused to let my words sink in. "Now I want everyone but Naomi and Phineas to leave."

The slaves scurried out, as though they were escaping a punishment, but my mother and Nelia remained seated. "You cannot order us to leave, Gaius," my mother said. "Surely you don't believe we would ever reveal any of this."

"Mother, you know any secret can be divulged by a slip of the tongue. I trust you, but there is too much at stake here. I know how women are." I turned to Nelia. "Forgive me for being frank, but I've known you only three days, and there is so much about you that I don't know. I must insist that you leave."

Nelia stood, facing me across the table. "Gaius Pliny, I know we both still bear bruises from the last time I asked you to trust me, but I swear to you I will cut out my tongue before I betray your confidence in this."

My mother took Nelia's hand and pulled her back down to her seat. "Besides, Gaius, we'll just get Naomi to tell us everything once we get back to our rooms. You know how we women are. Wouldn't it be better for us to hear it now, when you can know what's being said?"

The edge in her voice made me yield to the inevitable. I sat down heavily, wishing I could stop the whole interrogation and go soak in a bath or play my lyre. But there was only one direction to go, and that was forward.

"So, Naomi, you and your parents and your brother knew Agrippina had a child other than Nero."

"Yes, my lord, but I've never told anyone." She put her hand over her heart. "My mother didn't tell us until after Agrippina was dead. Antistius gave my parents a lot of money to be sure we would never tell. My mother said Agrippina wanted to have the four of us killed to silence us, but Antistius wouldn't allow it. When they settled in Ephesus, my parents changed their names because they were afraid Agrippina would have them tracked down and killed."

"The money must have come from Antistius himself," I said. "Caligula stripped Agrippina of everything when he exiled her."

"All I know, my lord, is that my parents never wanted for anything but they always lived under a cloud of fear after Claudius brought Agrippina back from exile and restored her estate to her."

"Do you know if Menachem ever told anyone about this?"

She didn't answer for a moment. "I can't say for sure, my lord. He was given to boasting, puffing himself up, and he got all excited about those pictures he saw down there in Nero's house, especially the one with the dog."

"Did he take you down to see them?"

"He offered to, my lord, but I didn't want to go. He showed me the pictures he drew, the copies he made of the pictures in Nero's house."

I gasped audibly. "He drew pictures?"

"Yes, my lord. Four of them, but the one with the dog was the one he was most excited about. He said we knew what it meant and nobody else did."

"What was in that picture?"

"It was strange, my lord, and gruesome. It showed a woman hanging from a tree. Off to one side there was a mother dog, snarling and nursing two pups. It was pretty—I mean the colors and all—but I didn't like it."

"What did your brother think it meant?"

"Well, my lord, he said the lady hanging from the tree was Nero's wife, Octavia."

"What made him think that?"

"The tree had eight branches, my lord, and the woman only had eight toes."

Phineas moved a couple of scrolls aside to find one he wanted. "Here it is, my lord. Nero sent Octavia into exile and then had her executed ..." He stopped, as though unwilling to read what came next.

"What's the matter?" I asked.

"She died on the island of Pandateria, my lord."

I shook my head slowly. If I didn't believe in coincidence, how could I explain all I was hearing?

"What about the dog?" I asked Naomi, almost dreading her answer. "What did Menachem think the dog represented?"

"He said the dog was Agrippina, my lord, suckling her two pups, one a boy and the other a girl."

"But that means Nero eventually learned about Agrippina's other child."

"I suppose so, my lord."

She may have told him herself, just to taunt him, I thought, recalling her jibes about poison and about Rubellius' son as a possible heir in the letter Domitian had given me. "Why was Menachem so sure the dog represented Agrippina?"

"It was her teeth, my lord."

"Her teeth?" I said.

"Yes, my lord. Agrippina had several extra teeth on the upper right side of her mouth, my mother told us, just where the dog in the picture had some extra ones."

Those words were barely out of Naomi's own mouth when my mother looked at Nelia in astonishment. Nelia jumped up so quickly she knocked her chair over and ran out of the library.

"We'd better go see about her," Mother said. Without waiting for me to dismiss her, Naomi followed my mother.

* * * *

"I want to see those pictures," I said to Phineas. "Do you know where they are?"

"Probably in my uncle's room, my lord. We haven't had a chance to clean it out yet."

"Where did your uncle live?"

"In an *insula* on the edge of the Subura."

"Tell Demetrius to get six or eight of my slaves together, and make sure there are some big fellows in the group, Archidamos in particular. We're going to your uncle's room."

Archidamos is my largest slave. A former gladiator, he is blind in one eye and bears a scar on his face that makes people move out of his way, even though he is one of the gentlest souls I've ever known. I make certain he carries my money pouch when we are out in the streets on foot.

Today we were about halfway down the Esquiline when we ran into Tacitus and a few of his slaves.

"Sounds like an interesting way to spend the morning," he said when I told him where I was headed. "More profitable than mine."

"You didn't find anything?"

He shook his head. "I'm going back tomorrow."

Phineas led us to the apartment house, the insula, where his uncle had lived. Though large, it was not enormous as such places go, only four stories high. They're called insulae because they are not connected to any neighboring buildings but are surrounded on all sides by the street, like an island surrounded by water. Hot in the summer and cold in the winter, they are wretched places, some housing as many as four thousand people. My uncle had owned two insulae, but I sold them soon after I came into my inheritance. In my opinion, they are simply too much trouble for the money they earn the owner.

Like most of these buildings, the first floor of this one was taken up with shops. I noticed a wine shop, a sandal maker's and a brothel on our way in. While Tacitus and our slaves waited on the street, Phineas took me up the stairs leading to the second floor and knocked on a door. It was opened by the landlady, a woman about my mother's age and height but at least twice as wide as my mother.

"Phineas, my boy!" she said. "So nice to see you. Oh, and you've brought company. Forgive me, my lord." She bowed her head to me and I returned the gesture.

"Dorothea," Phineas said, "this is Gaius Pliny, my master. We would like to see my uncle's room."

The landlady looked puzzled. "Certainly. Just go on up. You needn't ask me."

"Don't you know? He was killed four days ago."

"Killed? Oh, no! What happened?"

Phineas glanced at me. "Something fell on him while he was working."

Dorothea's hand flew to her mouth. "Oh, how dreadful! Your mother must be heartbroken. Please tell her how sorry I am to hear about this. I knew I hadn't seen Maxentius for several days, but I had no idea ..."

"It has been a great shock for us."

The landlady shook her head sadly. "Have you come for his things then?"

"I have some other slaves downstairs," I said. "We'll remove as much as we can. I'm sure you'd like to rent the room."

"Well, not to be unkind, my lord, but the owners do expect me to keep the place full. His was one of the ones with a key. Let me get it for you."

Maxentius' room was on the fourth floor, so we would have to go back down to the street and around the corner to a stairway that led to rooms opening on the north end of that floor. Dorothea entrusted the key to Phineas. "Just return it to me when you're ready to leave."

The stairs were steep and narrow, as they usually are in these places, but these didn't smell as bad as the stairs in the two buildings my uncle had owned. Dorothea must have hired someone to clean up the vomit and human waste which the inhabitants of a typical insula left on the stairs as a matter of course.

When we reached the fourth floor my slaves had to stand on the steps while Phineas, Tacitus and I stepped up to the small landing. Phineas turned to the first door on the left and started to put the key in the lock. But the door swung open at his touch, the lock broken. The room looked like someone had picked it up and turned it over several times. A bed and a small chest lay on their sides. Anything the chest might have contained was strewn around the room. A table was overturned, two chairs smashed.

"Who could have done this?" Phineas cried.

"Let's see if we can find out." I knocked on the door of the next room. The door was opened slowly by a small man with almost no hair and, to judge from his sunken cheeks, no more teeth than hair. Behind him cowered a woman whose oily gray hair hung loose over her shoulders. I doubted if the two of them together could have broken an egg, much less the lock on Maxentius' door.

"Do you know who broke into the room next door?" I asked.

"No, my lord," the old man said. "We ... we didn't see nothing."

"We couldn't see," the woman said. "They told us to stay in here and keep our door closed. That's what we done."

"Shut up, woman!" the man said. He turned back to me. "She ain't quite right." He touched his head.

"How many were there?" I asked, looking past him and directly at the woman.

"Three, I think," the woman said, her voice quavering.

"Why didn't you tell Dorothea what happened?"

The two of them remained silent.

"Did they pay you to keep quiet?" I motioned for Archidamos to give me my money bag and drew an aureus out of it. "I need to know what happened next door."

The man took the gold coin and rubbed it on his tunic. "There was three of them, my lord, like my woman said. Big fellas. They broke the lock and we could hear them tossing stuff around, like they was looking for something."

"Were they carrying anything when they left?" Tacitus asked.

"Couldn't say, my lord. We didn't open the door again until we was sure they'd gone."

"Why didn't you report this to the Praetorians?" I said.

"I think these fellas was Praetorians, my lord."

Tacitus and I exchanged a worried glance. "You think?" I asked. "Were they wearing Praetorian uniforms?"

"No, my lord, but they was big, like your fella there, and they carried themselves like Praetorians, with their chins up and looking at everybody else like they wanted to crush us."

"How long ago were they here?"

"Four days ago, my lord, early in the morning, while Maxentius was working."

That was the day he was killed. "Thank you," I said. "You've been very helpful."

"Please don't tell anyone we talked to you, my lord," the man begged.

"I won't, and you don't need to tell anyone you talked to us." I tossed him a couple of sesterces and he closed his door.

Tacitus stayed by the door while Phineas and I entered his uncle's room, pushing some of the mess aside to give us a place to stand.

"There's nothing left," Phineas said. "This was all he had, and they've torn it to shreds."

"What about the pictures?"

"I don't see them, my lord. There were four of them, done on pieces of parchment, about this big." He showed me with his hands, measuring about a cubit in each direction. "He kept them rolled up and wrapped in a piece of leather."

We walked around the room, picking up anything big enough to conceal something, but there was no sign of a rolled up piece of leather or any torn pieces of parchment. Running my hands over the walls, I checked for hiding places with no success.

"This makes no sense, my lord," Phineas said. "Why would someone ransack his room and take the pictures?"

"How would anyone know he had them?" Tacitus asked from the doorway.

Phineas could only shrug and shake his head.

We made our way back to Dorothea's apartment and told her what had happened.

"You can throw out anything in his room," Phineas said. "There's nothing left worth having."

"I think I've already got the only thing he had that was worth anything," the landlady said.

"What do you mean?" I asked.

She waddled into her apartment and returned with a rolled-up piece of leather. "About six months ago he couldn't make the rent, so he gave me these. They're pictures of some kind. I thought they were really pretty and colorful, so I told him I would take them instead of the rent." She unrolled the pictures.

"There are only three here," Phineas said. "Where's the fourth one? The one with the dog."

"Oh, that was the best one. I bartered it for some wine, some really fine Chian."

"How long ago was that?" I asked.

"Eight days ago, my lord, maybe ten." Her jowls shook as she laughed. "Like I said, it was some really fine Chian."

"To whom did you trade it?" I asked.

"Diogenes, my lord. His shop is right downstairs."

"How much rent did Maxentius owe you?" She told me the amount. "Can I give you that and a bit more and get the pictures?"

"By all means, my lord."

The deal was struck and we went down to Diogenes' shop, but the wine merchant didn't have the fourth picture any more.

"I sold it, my lord," he informed us.

"To whom?"

"I had it pinned up on the wall, right over there, my lord. Maxentius came in and saw it one night. He bragged to the other customers about it being his work and how he'd copied it from something he saw down in Nero's house. Next day a fellow comes in and offers me a handsome price."

"Did you know the man?"

"Never seen him before, my lord."

"What did the picture look like?" I asked.

"It was real colorful, my lord. It showed somebody hanging from a tree and off to one side there was a dog nursing two pups. One looked like a male, the other female. But the mother dog was what I thought was so unusual. She was snarling and her teeth looked funny."

"Funny in what way?"

"There was too many of them on one side."

* * * *

"It looks like the trail goes cold here," Tacitus said as we emerged back onto the street. "At least we got two independent descriptions of the picture, and they agree."

"Three, actually, my lord," Phineas said. "I saw the picture, and my mother and the wine merchant have described it quite accurately."

"But I want to see it myself," I said. "My uncle used to stress the importance of autopsis. To understand something you need to see it for yourself."

"But you can't," Tacitus pointed out. "The picture is gone."

"I can't see Maxentius' picture, but the one he was copying from is still there, isn't it?"

"You mean the one in Nero's house?"

"Exactly."

"But that's buried under the Baths of Titus now."

"Not really buried, my lord," Phineas said. "The bath was built over it, but you can still go down under the bath and see the picture."

"And that's exactly what we're going to do," I said. "Right now."

"You're going to the Baths of Titus?" Tacitus asked in disbelief.

"Yes, I'm going to the baths of Titus."

Phineas' eyebrows arched to Apennine heights. "The baths of Titus, my lord? Are you sure?"

"Yes, I'm sure. And you're going to take me down to see whatever your uncle showed you in Nero's house."

"Will you come with us?" I asked Tacitus.

"I can't. Julia wants me at home to prepare for the dinner party we're giving tomorrow. You and Nelia are invited."

"I didn't know about this."

"I'll bring your invitation—whenever Julia determines which of our slaves can most accurately copy the script of Domitian's scribe. But today she insists I be at home to tell her what things looked like at Domitian's dinner. Even how the slaves were dressed."

"Aren't you afraid of being accused of treason if you copy Domitian's triclinium?" I asked him. "People have been arrested for much less."

Tacitus nodded. "That's why I've given her a description of a triclinium that looks as little like his as possible. Please don't spoil things when you see it."

I assured him I wouldn't. "Are you planning to supply a dead body in your library?"

"It might be mine if I don't get home soon."

158

AS **STRANGE AS A TRIP** to the Baths of Titus might sound to my friend and my slaves, I was sure it would put me back on the right path to solving the problem Domitian had dumped in my lap. I had hoped that talking to Musonius Rufus would lead to some information about Agrippina's memoirs and any possible relatives of Nero and Caesar, but that trip proved an utter waste of my time and had left me burdened with an ungrateful—and pregnant—houseguest. Let Mother and my slaves deal with her.

A slave in my own house had told me that Agrippina had a second child, a daughter, raised under the name of Antistia. The only proof of that claim—and it would never stand up before a court—was a picture in the ruins of Nero's Golden House. Maxentius, the man who had seen that picture and made a copy of it, had been murdered. I was reasonably certain Domitian had something to do with that murder. I would not be surprised to learn he had the picture.

Like the middle term of a syllogism, Nero seemed to be the connection between Maxentius and Domitian. I couldn't talk to Maxentius or see his picture, and I couldn't trust anything Domitian told me. My best course of action seemed to be a visit to the baths which now sat on top of the Golden House. If Maxentius had learned something from Nero's house, perhaps I could too, if I could get into the bowels of the place.

We left the Subura and passed the Flavian Amphitheater and the Ludus Magnus behind it, where the gladiators trained. The Baths of Titus sat on a ledge jutting out from the lower part of the Esquiline and overlooking the Amphitheater. Steps led up from the floor of the valley to the level of the baths. Hastily built to be ready for the opening of the Amphitheater, they had quickly acquired a reputation as little more than a gigantic brothel.

But that did not mean the regulars were necessarily from the lowest social ranks. Tunics with both the broad and the narrow stripe could be found in the dressing rooms of this bath. Their wearers did not go there to bathe so much as to gamble and arrange unsavory liaisons. The worst

159

condemnation I had heard of the place was that even Tacitus found himself uncomfortable during the one visit he made there.

It was not altogether ironic that baths bearing Titus' name had gained such an unsavory reputation. I remembered my uncle expressing his reservations when Titus became *princeps*. As a young man, Titus lived an extravagant, licentious life—perhaps the result of those years growing up in Nero's company—but my uncle hoped he had inherited from his father a basic decency which would emerge as he matured. And he had quickly proved a more fit ruler than his brother and successor, Domitian.

Standing in the shadow of the Amphitheater and Titus' Baths, it was hard to imagine when Rome did not look like this. I had never seen it otherwise.

"In one of his poems," I said, "my friend Martial says 'only one house stood in the whole city.' Archidamos, you were in Rome then. What did that house look like?"

Archidamos scratched his nose, a nervous habit of his that annoys me no end. "Well, it wasn't really one house, my lord, more of a series of buildings, none of them very tall. It stretched from the house where Nero actually lived on the Palatine over here to the Esquiline. Down in this valley there were lakes and patches of woods and lawns. Where we're standing now was a huge lake. It had small buildings along the sides of it, to make it look even bigger than it was, not that it wasn't plenty big enough. What made everybody so mad at Nero was how big his house was and where he put it. If he could have torn down the Forum, I think he would have done it."

"But when Vespasian took over," I said, "didn't he immediately begin tearing down the Golden House and building things like the Amphitheater?" I was only seven and living on one of my uncle's estates when Vespasian became *princeps*, so I had no real memory of that time.

"Well, my lord, the Golden House wasn't torn down so much as it was covered over. When they were excavating for Vespasian's projects, they just dumped the dirt and rocks on Nero's house. The back half of Titus' Baths are built on that sort of fill material. The roofs of most of Nero's buildings collapsed. They filled in his lakes, cut down his trees. Some of Nero's material was torn out and re-used in other buildings. It was like watching ants eat up a carcass. The whole place disappeared in about a year."

I turned to Phineas, who was standing on my right. "How many times did your uncle take you into the Golden House?"

"Twice, my lord."

"Since he did plastering, I assume the walls and roof of the baths were completed when he started to work."

"Yes, my lord. The work was in its last stage."

"How did you get into Nero's house?"

"He took me down the stairs into the furnace room, my lord. One wall of the furnace room was part of Nero's house. In that wall there was a door that led to another of Nero's rooms. The roof had been covered over, but it hadn't collapsed. It was like going into a cave."

"Where are those stairs?"

"They open off of the caldarium, my lord," Phineas said. "There's a set of stairs on each side of the baths."

"They put them there, my lord," Archidamos said, "because the furnaces need to be close to the hottest room in the building. And the stairs let people working down below get out, in case of a fire."

That made sense. "Can we just walk down those stairs?" I asked. On my previous trips to a public bath, I had never noticed any stairs, and it certainly had never occurred to me to contemplate going into the nether reaches of the place. I'd never been in the furnace room of my bath at home. "I don't want to attract any more attention than necessary."

"We ought to find the man in charge, my lord, and get his permission." Archidamos rubbed his thumb against his first two fingers. He was right. Everything, and everyone, in Rome has a price. "If we start down there and somebody stops us, everybody will notice."

"Right. That will be our plan, then. Archidamos, you will find that man. The rest of us will meet you at the stairs."

* * * *

There were no games scheduled in the arena today, so I thought the crowd in the baths might be small.

I was wrong.

Since there were no games, everyone who would have been in the Amphitheater seemed to have gone to the baths instead. Scores of people lounged in front of the building, some playing on the game boards which are scratched into the steps of almost every public building in Rome, while others watched and bet on the outcome.

Phineas touched my elbow and pointed to my left. "My lord, look there."

I looked in that direction and recognized one of the spectators—my slave Aurora. Because of the large crowd, she was not aware of me. She seemed to be engaged in conversation with a man standing next to her. Their heads were close together, and they did not appear to be paying much attention to the game, glancing at it only cursorily. Then the man slipped some money into Aurora's hand and left. The game wasn't over, so I wondered if the man was paying off a bet. Aurora waited, as though she was counting to a certain number in her head, then turned in the other direction, toward my house, and vanished into the crowd.

"Did you know that man who was talking to Aurora?" I asked Phineas.

"No, my lord."

I would have liked to send someone to follow the man she had been talking to, but I had already lost sight of him.

I paid the entry fee for me and my slaves and we elbowed our way into the apodyterium, the dressing room. In a large public bath there are normally two dressing rooms, one for each gender. This bath offered two rooms, but men and women were using both indiscriminately.

Finding a couple of empty niches, we left our garments there with a slave to guard them. Archidamos set off to find the man in charge of the baths. I tied a towel around my waist, as did Phineas, but the other slaves who accompanied me didn't bother to cover themselves.

We were almost out of the dressing room when I noticed Phineas' bare feet. "Put your sandals on," I said.

"Why, my lord?"

"By the time we get to the caldarium the floor will be so hot you won't be able to walk on it in your bare feet. Surely you know that."

"This is my first visit to a public bath, my lord."

I looked at him in disbelief. "You've *never* been in one before?"

"No, my lord, never. We Jews don't approve of such immodesty." But he couldn't turn his eyes away from the two nude young women who brushed past him at that moment.

One of my other slaves chortled. "And they don't like to show off their chopped off pricks. His is going to be popping out from under that towel pretty soon, though."

"No more of that," I said quickly. "The rest of you, be sure he knows what to do and how to act. Remember, we don't want to draw attention to ourselves. Now, let's go."

This bath was laid out like any public bath. From the dressing room we passed into the *frigidarium*. While I went to one of the large basins of cold water in the center of the room, my slaves gathered around one of the basins along the walls which custom dictated they use. As I washed off a bit I noticed that Phineas stood apart from my other slaves, studying the decorations on the wall intently. Jews have a reputation for keeping to themselves, but I had never thought of Phineas as being different from the other slaves in my household.

I was puzzled when Phineas approached me, bowing and acting more servile than I had ever seen him.

"My lord, may I show you something?"

I followed him to the edge of the room. He ran his hand along a tendril design worked vertically in plaster which divided the huge wall into sections. Painted green, the plaster leaves gave an uncanny impression of life. When I looked closer I could even see the nodes where the leaves joined the stem.

"I watched my uncle do this," Phineas said with pride.

I could see that he was close to tears, but I did not want to acknowledge his emotion in such a public place. "It's remarkable work. Did he paint them as well?"

"No, my lord. Someone else did that. But all this plaster work is his."

"He was clearly an artisan of great skill."

"Thank you, my lord." He placed a hand on one of the leaves, looked up, and began mumbling something in what I took to be Hebrew, from all the guttural sounds.

I left Phineas to his admiration of his uncle's work and his incantations. I had barely gotten back to my place at the cold-water basin when I heard a familiar voice.

"Gaius Pliny, is that really you? What brings you to this sink of degradation?"

I turned to see Martial approaching me.

"Good afternoon, Valerius Martial. So this is where you find your inspiration." Martial's epigrams are witty, often salacious, reflecting rather than criticizing the morals of our day. Whether he'll ever be reckoned among Rome's great poets, I cannot judge, but for now he is quite popular, and that seems to suffice for him.

Martial looked around him, as though reluctant to admit what his eyes were telling him. "My Muse dwells not on the heights of Mt. Helicon, I'm afraid. She's more inclined to wallow in the city's sewers."

"She has plenty of company."

"May I buy you a drink, Gaius Pliny?" He edged unsteadily closer to me, his breath reeking of cheap wine. He was still wearing his tunic, so he wasn't here to bathe but to recite his poetry and cadge a dinner invitation. He occasionally entertains at one of my dinners and I give him money whenever he asks.

I doubted that the wine in this place would be Falernian, but I didn't want to offend Martial. He frequently lampoons individuals by name. Some regard it as a mark of distinction to be mentioned—even ridiculed—in his verses. That's an honor I can forgo, so I accepted his offer. The wine merchant had just gotten to us when a hissing, rumbling noise, a sort of murmur of excitement, began behind us. I could make out a rhythmic chant: 'Spatale, Spatale.'

The noise grew to a swell as a woman walked into the frigidarium. Or perhaps I should say two breasts followed by a woman. I could never have imagined a woman's breasts could be that large and the rest of her body so slender. How could she stand up straight? It defied all the rules of architecture and engineering. But she did and even kept her shoulders thrown back like a legionary. She was wearing nothing but sandals and a towel draped over one shoulder.

Every man's head turned, even those men who seemed more interested in other men. Someone shouted, "Martial, your verse!" Other voices picked up the cry.

"Excuse me, Gaius Pliny," Martial said. "My Muse has arrived and our public calls."

He set his cup on the edge of the cold-water basin and fell in step beside the woman. Her blonde hair and fair skin stood out all the more against his dark hair and olive complexion. She smiled provocatively at him as she stopped by another of the large basins of cold water. Martial cupped his hands and began ladling water onto her enormous breasts. A raucous male sound filled the room as the woman cupped her breasts and rubbed them together. I could tell I was watching an act she and Martial had played before. An audience formed in a circle around them.

As Martial continued his lustrations he began to recite:
"Dasius the doorman keeps careful count.
No one bathes here for free.
But Spatale the divinely endowed?
He makes her pay for three."

Spatale turned toward Martial and he spluttered as he rubbed his face between her breasts. The onlookers broke into applause and shouts of approval. Martial grabbed the towel off Spatale's shoulder, wiped his face, then carefully dried her breasts, playfully pinching both nipples when he finished. Spatale gave a high-pitched squeal. That seemed to be the signal for the spectators to unleash a shower of coins. Spatale scooped up her share and handed them to a couple of young women whom I hadn't noticed until then. Servants of hers, I assumed. Throwing her towel back over her shoulder, she headed for the next room in the bath. Martial tucked his coins into a bag inside his tunic.

When he returned to my side Martial said, "I can offer you something better now." In a long swallow he drained the cheap wine he had first bought—which I hadn't even tasted yet—and signaled to the wine merchant. "Some Setine!"

"Who ... who was that woman?" was all I could say.

"Spatale lives in the rooms below mine. Unlike me, she has lots of regular visitors."

"So she's a courtesan."

"No, she's a whore. And isn't that a pity?" He lifted his cup in a toast. "A whore. The same as I am. Only difference is, she makes her living on her back while I have to hustle around places like this, trying to wheedle money out of people."

"But you have a talent, a keen wit."

Martial snorted. "And Spatale has big tits. All we do with our 'talents' is entertain people for a while. We do things they can't bring themselves to do but want to see done. I'm a buffoon, Gaius Pliny, just like she is. But I know it." He hit himself on the chest and looked at me with his intense, dark eyes. I thought I caught a glimpse of his anguish.

"Don't be discouraged. This kind of humor has an honorable tradition in Rome, all the way back to Fescennine verses and Plautus' plays. Even Cicero wrote bawdy poems."

"None of which were performed in a public bath."

"But what you just did was as funny as anything Plautus wrote."

Martial waved his hand in disgust. "Spatale and I came up with that routine three days ago. We've got a couple of more days before the mob tires of it." He jingled the coins under his tunic. "We'll get what we can out of it. Notice, I didn't say we would milk it for all it's worth. I wouldn't subject a man of your refined tastes to such an atrocious joke."

A change of subject seemed like a good idea. "If you're so unhappy, you could leave Rome, go live on your farm in Nomentum."

"Ah, yes, 'my' farm."

But it is yours."

"No, it's a reminder of your generosity." He called the wine merchant over again. "And not even your generosity to me, but to her."

"What difference does it make how you got it?" I said, a bit offended. This particular farm was a very desirable piece of property. "We've all accepted favors from our friends at one time or another. There's nothing shameful in that."

He glared at me over his cup and took a long drink.

I was ready to move to the *tepidarium* and then to the stairs down to the furnace room, but I wasn't sure how to disentangle myself from this self-pitying drunkard.

A woman, running up to Martial, provided the means of my escape. She was older than my mother and nude. Her wrinkled skin and sagging breasts validated Plato's arguments in the *Republic* about why older women should not exercise with men. She pressed a coin into the poet's hand and pulled him away from the cold-water basin.

"Here he comes," the woman said excitedly. "You promised me you'd recite it the next time we saw the bastard."

Stepping away from the basin and signaling to my slaves to follow me, I looked back in the direction where Martial was now trying to focus his attention. The man he seemed to be drawing a bead on was someone I recognized from my appearances before the Centumviral Court, although I did not know his name. His face wore a perpetual sneer and he was too old to have hair that black. I slowed down to see what sort of barb Martial had crafted to pierce his hide.

Martial's voice rang out over the buzz and chatter of the other bathers:
"Zoilus, you foul the bath
  by sticking your butt in it.
We're all thankful, though,
  that you don't make it any dirtier
  by dunking your head!"

Amid the ensuing storm of laughter I passed from the frigidarium into the tepidarium. The warmth felt good. I hadn't intended to stay in the cold room so long. This warm room contained two sizeable soaking pools, with a bench carved around the edge so people could sit in the water up to their necks. On tables around the pools men and women were getting massages, which were being given by both men and women. I've never cared much for massages, because I just don't like being touched, especially by strangers and on parts of my body where many of these people were being 'massaged.'

I was questioning my own wisdom in coming into this gigantic brothel when Archidamos found me. He had in tow a short, solid, dark-complected man with a shaved head. The man wore his tunic pulled up above his knees and belted. He had removed the sleeves, revealing a tattoo on his upper right arm which probably concealed a mark from his days as a troublesome slave. I took him to be from North Africa, with some Punic ancestry.

"My lord, this is Cyrenius, the overseer of the bath."

Cyrenius nodded his head enough to acknowledge my rank but not enough to appear servile. I suppose it is difficult to keep social distinctions in mind when you work in a place where everyone around you is naked.

"I understand you have a request to make, sir," Cyrenius said.

"Yes. It may seem a bit strange, but I would like to go down into the furnace room. I'm interested in seeing—"

Cyrenius held up a hand to stop me. "No explanations necessary, sir. None wanted, really. People ask to do this every day."

"They do?"

"Yes, sir. Some of my bathers like to watch the slaves work. Bunch of burly fellows down there. They have to be. I'm told that the golden-red light given off by the furnaces falls on the men's muscles glistening with sweat and creates the effect of a highly polished bronze statue. Some people find it quite … arousing. For myself, I go down there only when I have to. The heat and the smell are appalling."

"So you don't mind if we go down there?" I was amazed at how uncomplicated this was turning out to be.

"Well, sir, entry to the furnace room is a privilege, and, like any privilege, it must be paid for." He sounded as apologetic as a man selling his only child into slavery. He hated to do it, his voice said, but what choice did he have?

As the only fully-clothed member of my party, Archidamos pulled my money bag from under his tunic and dropped several denarii into Cyrenius' outstretched hand. The bathman counted the coins, counted the number of people with me, and stuck out his hand again.

"There's an aureus in there," I told Archidamos. "Give it to him and be done with it." I didn't want to stand here all afternoon dickering. And I didn't want to mention that the bag actually contained several gold pieces.

"Very kind of you, sir," Cyrenius said, holding up the aureus as if he could determine the purity of the gold with his eye. "Let me escort you to the steps."

He led us into the caldarium and into one of the apses built off of either side of the room. The apse was much wider than the archway leading into it. Behind the wall of the archway, not visible from the main part of the caldarium, was a door with a guard seated in front of it. The guard, a tall Nubian who easily outweighed any two of the slaves with me, stood as soon as he saw Cyrenius.

"More gawkers?" the Nubian said. "It's been a busy day." He patted a bulging money bag tied around his waist.

"Enjoy yourselves," Cyrenius said over his shoulder as he left. "Stay as long as you like. Just don't get in anybody's way. If you run into trouble, don't bother calling for help. We can't hear you up here."

XIV

"**TROUBLE, MY LORD?**" Phineas said. "What kind of tr-tr-trouble could we m-m-meet down there?" The return of his stutter emphasized how nervous he was. And he was the only one among us who had been down here before. Perhaps we should all be stuttering.

The Nubian swung the heavy bronze door open but did not step aside for us. "Don't mind him, lad. There's only been a couple of folk went down there that didn't come back."

"Wait a minute!" I said. "Do you mean people have been killed down there?"

"Did I say anything about killing, my lord? I just said they haven't come back. There's dark corners down there. And the furnaces are so hot they'll burn up anything in no time. Nothing left but soft, fluffy ashes. All I'm saying is, be careful." His smile struck me as sinister, or it may just have masked a joke, the sort local people often like to play on strangers.

When he still did not move out of the open doorway, I motioned for Archidamos to give him some money. At least the man wasn't greedy. A couple of denarii satisfied him. He stepped aside and waved us through. We huddled together on a landing as the door closed behind us. I wondered if it would cost as much to get out as it had to get in.

The elegance and finery of the baths ended abruptly at the door. The walls on this side of it were bare stone. No craftsmen like Phineas' uncle had wasted their skills here. No musicians, poets, or wine-merchants strolled in the gloom. It took a moment for my eyes to adjust to the eerie half-light. I didn't think my ears would ever adjust to the roar of the furnaces. It was louder than the worst storm I've ever heard at sea. And yet it couldn't drown out the yelling of the slaves stoking the furnaces or the crack of whips urging them to their work.

Cyrenius' description of the sweat glistening in the flickering light was true. The men who worked down here—as nude as the bathers above them—looked like some alien race, with polished bronze for skin. They were not as large as the Nubian guarding the door, but they seemed to be made of pure muscle. Near the back wall a squad of them were splitting wood from a pile that looked like the palisade of an army camp waiting to be assembled. Others tossed the large split pieces to the men at the furnaces. How could we mere Romans have conquered and enslaved such powerful creatures? I felt I had fallen into a nightmare from which I could not awaken.

The only thing that wasn't as dreadful as I'd feared was the smoke. There was a hint of it in the air, like the acrid smell that hangs over a town after a fire, but most of the smoke went into the ducts in the walls and floors along with the heat. The smell Cyrenius mentioned was made up of the sweat of fifty or more slaves and the stench from the open pit where they relieved themselves.

In the gloom I could tell that the stairway ran along a wall on our right and was open on our left. It was wide enough for two people, but if anyone got jostled, the fall would be the same as from the top of a two-story building.

"This must be the outer wall of the building, my lord," Archidamos said, squinting down the steps. "I'm afraid my one old eye can't make out much down there."

My eyes were more comfortable in the dim light than in the bright light of day. "There's a landing halfway down. I see two men on it, one standing behind the other ..." Then I realized what the men were doing and hoped they were finished before we got that far.

"Let's go," I said. "Single file, and slowly."

As we descended into this man-made underworld, I thought of Odysseus and Aeneas and their journeys to the land of the dead. But neither Homer nor Virgil—nor any other poet with whom I was familiar—pictured the underworld as a place of fire and stench. Even the poets' descriptions of Vulcan's forge were heroic compared to this. The closest I could come to a description of a place like this was what Plato says in the *Phaedo* about the Pyriphlegethon, the river of fire which rises out of Tartarus and flows around the world underground, erupting in volcanoes like Etna and Vesuvius.

If I could walk into the bowels of Vesuvius, would I find something like this—fire, gloom, horrible smells and unearthly noises? What of the men consigned to labor down here? Plato says some people will be tossed into the river of fire to atone for wrongs they've done to others. But after a year they can plead with the souls of their victims to release them from punishment. What crimes did these poor wretches commit to justify their confinement in this place? Would any of them ever walk out of here?

As we neared the landing I began to appreciate how large the three furnaces were. Each one stood about half again as high as a man. Squeezed between the pillars supporting the floor of the bath, they were circular, perhaps ten paces in diameter, with openings, about two cubits square, on opposite sides. They appeared to be made of two layers of stone. Large tile ducts led out of the top of each furnace and branched off into smaller ducts running under the floors and into the walls of the bath.

Standing so close to these monsters, more heinous than anything Heracles or Perseus fought in a Greek myth, questions rolled over me like the heat from the furnaces. How long could a man—even a strong man—survive working down here? As difficult as it was for me just to breathe, how long would I survive? What happened to slaves who died down here? How quickly could these furnaces consume a body? People killed in the arena were used as food for the big cats in the shows. Were bathers upstairs being kept warm by more than just the labor of these slaves?

As we descended the stairs the heat and smoke became more oppressive. I found it difficult to draw a breath. If I tried to breathe deeply, my lungs burned. If I took shallow breaths, my body demanded more air. It was as though I was suffocating without anything over my face. Was this what my uncle felt like when he lay dying in the midst of Vesuvius' eruption? Cyrenius' words came back to me: 'Don't call for help. You can't be heard on the other side of the door.' Panic threatened to surge over me.

"Are you all right, my lord?" Phineas asked. He didn't seem to be having any trouble breathing.

"Yes. Just a little trouble ... getting my breath." His voice steadied me.

By the time we reached the landing I was getting the knack of forcing my body to breathe against its will. I tried to ignore the two men, who, in their coupling, seemed as oblivious to us as a pair of rutting animals.

Phineas leaned over to me as we started down the lower section of the stairs. "My lord," he said loudly, "this reminds me of a p-p-place outside Jerusalem. It was a huge trash pit in a valley called G-G-Gehenna, below the city walls. It caught fire years ago and no one could put it out. People just kept throwing g-g-garbage in, and it kept burning and smoking and stinking. From up on the walls it looked like a lake of fire. They even threw the bodies of executed criminals in there."

"At least they waited until they were dead."

We came to the floor of the furnace room and huddled near the wall. Only the faintest traces of the decorations from Nero's time could still be seen. Whatever of the marble floor had survived the construction of the bath had been ruined by the daily routine of the furnaces. The remaining wall decorations were now so smoke-stained I could not make out any details.

"We're not going to be able to tell anything from this," I said to Phineas.

"The picture we want to see is in the other room," he replied, pointing to an archway a dozen paces away from us.

A man carrying a whip approached us. I jumped when he cracked it to get our attention. He had the build and disposition of a gladiator. "Cyrenius don't usually let such a large group come down at one time," he said. "Just stay over here and keep out of our way."

"But we'd like to go through that door," I said.

"That's where the men sleep. It's off-limits."

Archidamos anticipated my signal and pulled out the money bag. I fished out the first coin my hand landed on—an aureus, as luck would have it—and gave it to the whip-wielder. He bit it, nodded, and turned back to his business.

"Phineas, you come with me," I said. "The rest of you wait on the steps." Phineas and I edged our way along the wall until we reached the doorway. The other room was pitch dark. The gloomy glow of the furnaces did not penetrate more than a few steps beyond the door.

"We can't see anything," I said to the man with the whip.

"Oh, do you want a torch?" he asked, but he made no move to give us one until Archidamos came back down and gave him a few denarii. Then he picked up a torch and lit it by simply touching it to the side of a furnace. "The men won't be happy if their sleep is disturbed."

The room we entered was circular, at least fifty paces in diameter, with a domed roof that I could barely see when I held the flickering torch as high as I could reach. Hardly anything was left of what must have been an ornately painted plaster ceiling. The green and white marble tiles on the floor were laid in a complex pattern that was difficult to discern with all the dirt and slaves' trappings on it. Around the edge of the room I could make out fifteen or twenty sleeping men. I doubted that anything short of an earthquake would wake the wretches.

"What do you suppose they dream about, my lord?" Phineas asked.

"Something pleasant, I hope." *Probably about tossing a lot of Romans into the furnace,* I thought. "Now, what did your uncle seem particularly interested in?"

"I believe it's over here, my lord." He glanced back at the door, getting his bearings. "I'm sorry, but it has been two years and we had more light then."

Stepping over a couple of sleeping forms, he led me to a spot about a quarter of the way around the circuit of the room. He motioned for me to hold the torch closer to the wall as he examined the frescoes. Their style was heavy and garish, separate scenes framed by a dark painted border, using strongly contrasting dark and light colors. Within each border there was a large central panel with related scenes or designs in

171

smaller panels around it.

"This is it, my lord," Phineas finally said, tapping one of the small panels.

I stepped closer to the wall. Big chunks of the fresco had been chiseled out. "Was it this badly damaged two years ago?" I asked.

"Not nearly as bad, my lord, but some of it was already gone. Some of the details of the fresco, my uncle told me, were actually overlaid with gold leaf. Looters cut out all the gold and anything that looked like gold."

So pieces of the Golden House ended up back in the hands of the people. There was a certain justice in that, but I wasn't going to admit it in front of a slave.

The central panel before me depicted a figure that I could recognize as Nero in the guise of Dionysus, with maenads and satyrs playing around him. Nero was so hated that, after his death, most images of him were destroyed or discretely stored away. But his coins still circulate, and one need see him only once to recognize his face forever afterwards. With his heavy jowls, languid eyes and curly blonde hair, this figure was definitely Nero.

The smaller panels showed various scenes from the Dionysian myths. Only three could still be made out. One had his mother, Semele, being destroyed when she asked to see Zeus in all his Olympian glory. Another showed the women of Thebes tearing king Pentheus apart under the ecstatic influence of Dionysus. The only other one I could make out depicted a lesser known story of Dionysus. It showed the Athenian girl Erigone searching for her father, Icarius, who had been killed by shepherds and buried under a tree.

"That's the one my uncle was most interested in," Phineas said, pointing to the Erigone panel.

"This one? How odd." Even as a boy I had thought this particular story supported Plato's argument that all myths ought to be banned from the ideal state.

"What is the story, my lord? My uncle didn't know it."

"According to the tale, Dionysus showed Icarius, king of Athens, how to make wine and Icarius shared it with shepherds from a nearby village. When they began to feel the effects, they feared they'd been poisoned and they clubbed Icarius to death. Erigone found her father only with the help of his dog, Maera. In her despair she hanged herself. The dog jumped down a well and drowned. To punish the Athenians, Dionysus drove the women of the city mad. He rewarded Icarius by turning him into the constellation Bootes. Erigone became the constellation Virgo, and Maera became the Dog Star."

In the picture before us Erigone was hanging from a tree, under which her father could be seen. I could make out eight branches, but Erigone's toes were no longer discernible. A dog lay off to one side, nursing two pups.

"I've never seen or heard of that detail in this myth," I said.

"The d-d-dog seemed to be what attracted my uncle also, my lord," Phineas said. From his heavy breathing I could tell he was working hard to control his stutter.

"It does look as though the dog is snarling, but I can't make out any teeth." I took the torch and held it as close to the picture as I dared. "I wish it weren't so damaged."

"It was in much better condition two years ago, my lord," Phineas said. "My uncle's picture showed that."

"Well, we're not going to learn anything here. Let's get out of this— what did you call that pit in Jerusalem?"

"G-G-Gehenna, my lord, the lake of f-f-fire that was never quenched. If we wanted to curse someone, we would say, 'May you be thrown into G-G-Gehenna'."

* * * *

Upon my emergence from the underworld I really did need a bath. And I thought it would strike everyone as odd if I came out the baths dirtier than when I went in. My slaves and I did not linger at any stage of the process, though. They were as eager, I think, as I was to put the whole ghastly vision of the furnaces behind them. I hoped it would have the salutary effect of making them see that their service in my house was light compared to what some had to endure. I knew it would make me investigate the conditions under which my slaves worked when they tended the furnace for my bath at home.

* * * *

Demetrius and Moschus, both highly agitated, were waiting for me in the atrium when I returned home. As much as I wanted to examine Menachem's pictures closely under the waterglass, I could see that I would first have to deal with whatever was bothering them. I sent Phineas on to the library with his uncle's pictures and turned to my steward and doorkeeper.

"What's the matter?" I asked.

"We have a visitor, my lord."

Saying even that made Demetrius so uncomfortable I had visions of Domitian in my house again. The terrors of the baths seemed to pale in comparison. "Is it ... anyone important?"

"It's a man named Marcianus," Demetrius said. "He came to see the lady Cornelia."

"And you let him in?"

"Moschus did, my lord."

"I didn't want to," Moschus said, "but my lady Plinia said I must. And Demetrius said it was all right as well."

Demetrius glared at Moschus. "What could I say, my lord, once your mother had invited him in?"

"All right. Quiet, both of you. He's in the house. There's nothing we can do about that now. Where is Laberius?"

"Your mother told him not to interfere, my lord," Moschus said. "She sent him to the library."

I hoped the retired centurion didn't rearrange all of my books into a testudo. "And where is Marcianus?"

"He and the lady Cornelia are talking in the garden, my lord," Demetrius said. "Your mother and Naomi are with them."

It's a bit late to be chaperoning them, I thought.

"Get Laberius and Archidamos and a couple of other men and come to the garden," I told him. "Stay in the shadows until I call for you."

I paused when I walked into the garden and took in the sight of Nelia and a young man sitting at the far end, under the trellis shading my uncle's bust. Even sitting down, the young man appeared to be rather tall, with light hair, not quite blond, and the tan skin of a farmer. He held Nelia tightly in his arms. Her breasts were pressing against him the way they had pressed against me when I pulled her from the stream. Her eyes locked onto his.

"Leave them alone, Gaius," my mother's voice said softly. I turned to my right to find her sitting on a bench alongside Naomi, the two of them carding wool.

"Why did you let him in the house?" I knelt and kept my voice down to match hers.

She didn't even look at me. "They're in love. He's the father of her child. We have no right to keep them apart."

"It's not a matter of rights, Mother. Musonius sent her here to keep her away from him. We have an obligation to keep them apart."

"Gaius, the boy walked ten miles to get here."

"I don't care if he crawled over the Alps. I'll not have him courting her in my house."

My mother looked up at me with that maddening half-smile that women use when they think they know exactly what a man is thinking. And what's even more maddening is that they're usually right. "Why, dear Gaius, are you jealous?"

Behind her I could see Naomi trying to hide a smirk. She turned her attention to a knot in the clump of wool in her hands.

"Jealous of what? Nelia's nothing but a burden cast on me by a friend, and she's carrying another man's child. What would I have to be jealous of?"

"Then leave them alone."

"No. Musonius wanted to keep them apart." I stepped out where they could see me.

"Gaius, wait!" my mother called.

Nelia and Marcianus turned toward me. He stood as I strode past the piscina.

"Good afternoon, sir," he said when I came to a stop in front of him.

Still seated and holding his hand in both of hers, Nelia said, "Gaius Pliny, this is Marcianus."

"I know who he is. What I don't know is why he's here."

"He came to see me."

"He's done that. Now it's time for him to leave."

"Ah, yes, the jailer speaks. Well, this time the prisoner has something to say." Nelia stood and slipped her arm through his. "I'm leaving with Marcianus."

"No, you're not. You're going to stay here until Musonius comes for you. And that can't happen soon enough to suit me."

"Sir," Marcianus said, "meaning no disrespect, but you cannot hold Nelia here against her will. If she wants to leave with me, she's free to do so."

"Demetrius!" I called. My steward, Archidamos, Laberius and two other servants stepped out of the shadows under the peristyle. The sight of them had the desired effect on Marcianus. His eyes widened and he gasped. Nelia threw her arms around him.

"The only one leaving, young man, is you," I said. "Do not come back and do not attempt to contact Nelia. When Musonius returns to Rome, the two of you can talk with him about your future. But I can tell you right now what his answer will be."

My slaves surrounded Marcianus, pulling him away from Nelia's tightening grip. Laberius grabbed Nelia by the arm and held her back as she struggled to reach Marcianus.

"Don't worry, my love," the young man said over his shoulder. "I'll never be far away."

When the door at the back of the garden had closed behind her lover and the bar was slipped into place, Nelia looked at me with tears in her eyes. "I hate you, Gaius Pliny. I hate you!" She jerked away from Laberius and ran toward her room, meeting my mother and Naomi at the piscina.

As my mother gathered Nelia into her arms, she glanced back at me with almost as much anger in her eyes as Nelia had displayed.

* * * *

Since none of the women in my house would speak to me, I had Aurora bring my dinner—a simple meal of chicken with some beans and bread—into the library, even though that meant eating upright instead of in the more natural, more healthful reclining position. Feeling sorry for myself, I decided not to water the wine too much.

"Will you need anything else, my lord?" Aurora asked.

"Not now. Just wait outside." I still did not know how I would ask her about what I'd seen at the baths. What was she taking money for? Was she betraying me? Selling herself?

She did not move. "My lord, may I speak to you about something?"

"Of course."

"I know you saw me at the baths earlier today, my lord. I want to explain what I was doing there."

"All right."

"When my mother died, my lord, your uncle provided a small tomb for her ashes, on the Via Nomentana."

This was something I hadn't known about.

"He paid for the upkeep of the tomb as long he lived. After he died, your mother refused to pay any more."

"Why would she do that?" I suspected I knew the answer already.

"She hated my mother, my lord. She wouldn't let your uncle keep her ashes in the house. I have paid the fee for the tomb the last few years, but I don't have enough money left. The *collegium* that owns the site says they will empty her ashes and sell the tomb to someone else if I can't keep paying. I've had to sell the jewelry my mother left me to get the money. Today I sold the last piece. I don't know what I'm going to do now."

She began to cry. Even that she did quietly. I took her in my arms.

"You should have come to me long before now, Aurora. I'll be glad to pay for the tomb. I'll reimburse what you've paid, and I'll do what I can to get your mother's jewelry back."

"Thank you, my lord. Thank you. I knew you would be kind, but I didn't want to cause trouble between you and your mother."

I wiped her tears with the napkin she'd brought me. She threw her arms around my neck. That's when I noticed Phineas standing in the library door, his mouth hanging open. I gently, and reluctantly, unwrapped Aurora's arms and pushed her back to a respectable distance.

"Come on in, Phineas," I called as he turned around. "It's all right."

"Oh ... I can ... I can come back later, my lord." Aurora slipped out of the room.

"It's all right. Sit down. Have something to eat."

Phineas stood motionless. "But, my lord ..."

"Phineas, this afternoon we went to the Underworld and back together. It's just the two of us here. It would be ridiculous to insist on formality. Sit down."

"Very well, my lord." He sat across the table from me, his back stiff.

I pushed the plate toward him and he tore off some bread, which he began to eat in small bites. "Were you coming in here for something in particular?" I asked.

"I wanted to work some more on the question you raised, my lord, of Rubellius' position in Augustus' family."

"Some more? So you have been working on it?"

"Glaucon and I were putting together something to show you, my lord."

"Where is Glaucon? I rarely see him these days."

"He does seem to ... go out frequently, my lord."

"Do you know the woman he's coupling with?"

Phineas' ears burned. "I didn't realize you knew about her, my lord."

"I know she's someone from Regulus' household. Has he said anything to you about her?" I took a bite of the chicken, one of my favorite dishes, fried in wine with coriander, dill, and pepper.

"No, my lord. Glaucon has very little to say to me."

I heard Aurora talking to someone outside the door and started to get up, when Tacitus poked his head in the door. "Dinner in the library? What's the occasion?"

Phineas jumped to his feet. Since my mouth was full, I waved him back down and motioned for Tacitus to join us. When I could speak, I said, "What brings you over at this hour?"

"I had to get out of the house. Julia is dithering over plans for that dinner tomorrow. I don't think the servants are going to get much sleep tonight. Here's your invitation. Nelia's invited, too." He laid a piece of papyrus on the table.

"I doubt she'll come. In fact, I doubt she'll ever speak to me again." While Aurora brought in more plates and cups I told him how I had evicted Marcianus from the house.

He shook his head slowly. "That wasn't a smart thing to do."

"What do you mean?"

"Women don't like to see a man exercising his power over a rival. It makes them sympathetic to the rival."

"'Rival'? You sound like my mother." I slammed my cup down, making Phineas jump. "Marcianus and I are not rivals for Nelia. To be his rival I would have to be attracted to her. I assure you I'm not, not in the least. Now, that's all I want to hear about Nelia. Phineas, show us what you've learned about Rubellius."

"That was a deft bit of subject-changing," Tacitus said with a laugh.

Phineas went to the cabinets on the far wall of the library and pulled out several scrolls. I moved plates so he could lay them in front of us. He remained standing on the other side of the table.

"Sit down," I said.

"Yes, my lord. Thank you."

I wasn't being a generous master. I just don't like having people standing over me while I'm sitting.

"What is this?" I pointed to a large piece of papyrus, made from several pieces glued together, which he kept rolled up.

"Tracing the connections among Augustus' descendants, my lord, makes finding one's way out of the labyrinth seem like a child's game. I've tried to illustrate what we've found." He unrolled the over-sized piece of papyrus and turned it toward us. Names and lines ran all over it.

"By the gods!" Tacitus muttered. "A map of the streets of Rome would be less complicated than this."

Phineas ran his finger over a line starting from Augustus. "The blood of Julius Caesar is the thread, my lord. Except for Tiberius, everyone who ruled Rome, or had any hope of ruling it before Vespasian, was related to Caesar in some way, through either Augustus or his sister Octavia. They were Caesar's grand-nephew and grand-niece, his only blood relatives."

"Let's start from Augustus," I said. "He had a daughter, Julia." I pointed to her on Phineas' chart.

"Yes, my lord. And, as you can see, Julia bore several children to Vipsanius Agrippa."

"One of them was Agrippina the Elder."

"Yes, my lord. She married Germanicus, son of Drusus. With Germanicus the blood of the Claudian family begins to mingle with that of the Julians."

I followed a line from Germanicus back to his mother. "He was the son of Antonia, the daughter of Augustus' sister, Octavia. So he had Julian blood of his own, apart from his wife."

"That's right, my lord. And he had Marc Antony's blood as well."

"By the gods, so he did," Tacitus said. "Antony was married to Octavia for a time as a way of cementing friendship with Augustus, or Octavian as he was then. He fathered two daughters by her."

"And because of that, my lord, every *princeps* of the family—Caligula, Claudius, and Nero—had Antony's blood along with Caesar's."

"Antony? That explains a lot," Tacitus said. "Do you have a pen and some red ink?" he asked Phineas.

"Of course, my lord." The scribe brought the materials from another table.

"What are you going to do?" I asked Tacitus.

"If we're going to following a bloodline, let's make it look like a bit of blood."

He dipped the pen in the red ink and drew a line over Phineas' original line, beginning with Augustus and going through Julia down to the elder Agrippina. Phineas hovered over him, obviously unhappy Tacitus was defacing something he had put so much work into.

The red line did stand out like one colored thread woven into a white garment. It was all I could see now. "Don't you want to run a line from Octavia down to Agrippina, too?"

"Good idea," Tacitus said. "There's Julian blood there as well."

When I saw the two lines converge, a realization hit me. "Agrippina's maternal grandfather and her paternal grandmother were ... brother and sister," I said slowly, reluctant to believe my own deduction.

"That sounds positively incestuous," Tacitus said, curling his lip. I was surprised he could sound repulsed by anything of that sort.

"It looks like the elder Agrippina and Germanicus—who were both descendants of Julius Caesar—had several children."

"Yes, my lord, three sons and three daughters, one of them the younger Agrippina. Two of the sons were executed by Tiberius on suspicion of treason. The other, Caligula, succeeded Tiberius."

"And the younger Agrippina married Gnaeus Domitius Ahenobarbus. Who was he?"

Tacitus ran his finger back up the line from Domitius' name. "It appears he was the son of the elder Antonia, the *other* daughter of Antony and Octavia."

"So, another dollop of Caesar's blood for Agrippina's children," I said. "It sounds like Augustus regarded his family as some sort of herd he was trying to breed."

Tacitus extended a branch of his red line through Domitius and the elder Antonia back up to Octavia. "Don't breeders of herds usually rent a stud from a neighboring farm, to avoid becoming too inbred?"

"I guess Augustus was working on the model of the Ptolemies in Egypt. They married their sisters and nieces. I never realized how 'close-knit' his family was."

"Nor did I," Tacitus said. "I've read some of their history, but I've never seen the story laid out like this before."

"But, wait ... Claudius was the ... brother of Germanicus, the father of the younger Agrippina. He married his own niece?"

"He forced the Senate to approve the marriage, my lord," Phineas said.

"But Agrippina had only one child, or two, if Naomi is to be believed. And yet her mother had six children."

179

"And her grandmother had ... at least six," Tacitus said, pointing to a line on the chart.

"So, might one expect this younger Agrippina to have had more children?"

"That would be a reasonable expectation, my lord. But, of course, there are ways of preventing or ending a pregnancy."

"We all know," Tacitus put in, "that a woman of Agrippina's class would not have to face the dangers of giving birth if she did not want to."

I nodded my head sadly. Everyone in Rome's senatorial class knows that many of our women are reluctant to bear children. Since the time of Augustus the emperors have decreed that a man must be the father of three children to qualify for high office, the *ius liberorum trium*. Then they have to grant exemptions so enough men are eligible to fill the positions. My uncle had no children; my father had only me. My mother would gladly have had more children, but she lost one child before birth and another only days after she was born.

I wondered if Agrippina, on the other hand, had been one of those women who take extraordinary measures to insure that they don't have children. And when she got pregnant in spite of her precautions, she gave the child away, to Antistius and his wife.

"You were interested in Rubellius Plautus, my lord?" Phineas said.

His question brought my attention back to the chart. "Yes, by all means. Where is he?" Tacitus pointed him out at the very bottom of the oversized page.

"He was such an insignificant figure in the family," Phineas said, "that we had trouble finding much at all about him. What we know is this: Tiberius and Vipsania, Agrippa's daughter, had a son, Drusus Julius Caesar, who married Livia Julia, a daughter of the younger Antonia by Tiberius' brother Drusus. They produced a daughter, who married Rubellius Blandus. The child of that union was Rubellius Plautus."

I ran a finger along the lines on the chart. "That makes him the great-grandson of Tiberius and great-great-grandson of Octavia, Augustus' sister."

"So he had Caesar's blood," Tacitus said, extending his red line.

"A rather generous dollop of it," I said. And that, I thought, would give him a legitimate claim to the title of *princeps*, if Agrippina decided to abandon her son and support someone else as his rival.

"And notice his wife, my lord." Phineas pointed to the name beside Rubellius'.

ANTISTIA.

THE NEXT DAY, after a morning salutation that seemed interminable, I returned to the library to see if I could learn any more about Agrippina's time on the island of Pandateria. Could she have kept the secret of a baby so well hidden that neither her closest friends nor her worst enemies knew of it?

With the help of Dymas, I plowed through any books I owned which would have covered that period. But not even my uncle's history or his notes on the works he had consulted shed any light on the matter. No one seemed to know that Antistia was anything but the daughter of Lucius Antistius Vetus and his wife.

Did Agrippina ever admit to anyone that she had had another child? But she must have, if Nero knew it and portrayed it in the picture in his Golden House. Did he learn it from her unexpurgated memoir? If that document fell into his hands, it probably no longer existed.

"We need another set of eyes," I said. "Where is Glaucon?"

Dymas hesitated. "He ... he didn't come home last night, my lord."

"Didn't come home? Do you know where he was?"

"I'm sure he went to see a woman, my lord."

"The one in Regulus' house?"

"I believe so, my lord. He doesn't tell me anything about his activities any more."

"Perhaps I should restrict him to the house, or send him to one of my other houses."

"It might be best to send him somewhere else, my lord." The old man's bleary eyes clouded with tears. "I deeply regret the trouble he has become to you."

I put a hand on his shoulder. "You've been a good father, Dymas, and loyal to my family. You have nothing to be ashamed of."

"A son is a reflection of the father, my lord. If I may say so, you are a son to whom any father could point with pride. But Glaucon ..." He shook his head.

"Tell Demetrius to send some men out to look for him."

"Thank you, my lord. I'll send Phineas to assist you." He left the library with his shoulders straighter than they had been all morning.

I was back in a corner of the library when I heard someone enter. I thought it was Phineas, but one of Mother's slave girls found me and said, "My lord, your mother would like to speak with you. She's in the garden, at the back."

That made me suspicious. The back of the garden is the most secluded place in the house. It's where I would ask to talk to someone if I wanted to be certain the conversation would not be overheard. What could my mother have to say that would require that much privacy? Had she heard already about my paying for Monica's tomb? I had resolved just to do it and not tell her about it.

She was sitting under the trellis shadowing my uncle's bust, with Nelia beside her. She patted the cool stone bench on the other side of her but I remained standing.

"I'm sorry to interrupt your work, dear," she began, "but I think we need to talk."

I sighed heavily and rolled my eyes. "About what?"

"That's a very petulant sigh, Gaius. I've heard that a lot since you returned from Syria."

"I'm busy right now, Mother. Please say what you have to say."

"There's no need for you to be rude, dear. I just want to talk about Nelia."

I looked at Nelia, who kept her eyes down as modestly as a Vestal Virgin, then back at my mother. "I have nothing more to say about, or to, the lady Cornelia. She is welcome to stay here, because of my promise to Musonius, but she need have no further dealings with me."

As I turned away my mother said, "Gaius, you come back here!"

I was determined not to give in to her until I heard Nelia say, "It's all right, Mother Plinia. We can't expect him to listen to what I have to say."

Mother Plinia! By the gods, where would this end? She was ensconced in one of the nicest rooms in my house and had rearranged the furniture to suit herself. She was already ordering my servants around as though they were hers. I could overlook such rudeness in a guest, but I would not let her steal my mother from me.

I stopped and turned back to see Nelia slip her arm through my mother's. Mother patted her hand and smiled.

"What do have to say to me?" I asked, clenching my fists as my anger rose.

"You treated Nelia shamefully yesterday," Mother said, "throwing Marcianus out of the house like that."

"I was only trying to honor my obligation to Musonius."

"There's that petulant tone again, dear."

"Mother, what do want from me?"

"I want you to apologize to Nelia. She is our guest and you—"

"Apologize? I'll do no such thing. I have nothing to apologize for."

"Then," Nelia said softly, "will you let *me* apologize to *you?*"

I blinked like a mule that's been whacked to get his attention. When I recovered from the shock, I asked, "For what? For everything or for one particular thing?"

"You're right, Gaius Pliny." She nodded slowly, as though yielding to my superior wisdom. "There are several things I should apologize for. Your hand, for instance. Is it healing?"

I glanced at my palm, which was still sore. "It's been tended to."

"I'm glad. Perhaps I can cover everything by saying I'm sorry for acting like such a foolish little country girl the last few days. I hope you can understand that I've experienced so much that's new and different since I left Musonius' villa, things I could never have imagined. It's been hard for me to make sense of it all."

"You've been to strange and different places, dear," Mother said to me. "And you went there willingly, not because someone suddenly decided to send you away from the only home you'd ever known. Surely you can sympathize."

If I could get as much emotion into my voice as my mother just did, I would win every case I tried in court. "All right. I accept your apology. Is that all you wanted?"

"Now, just a moment," Mother said. "We want to clear up any possible misunderstandings. Go ahead, dear." She nudged Nelia.

Nelia looked up at me and I met her eyes for the first time. I could not look away. "Yesterday afternoon," she began, "I saw Marcianus again—"

"With my permission," Mother said.

"Yes, with Mother Plinia's permission. I met him in the Gardens of Maecenas and we spent several hours together."

"I'm sure you enjoyed that." Mother didn't say anything, but her eyes scolded me. *Don't be petulant, dear.*

Nelia shook her head. "I did not enjoy it, I'm sorry to say. With all I've seen of the world beyond the Via Flaminia now, I felt I was not with the same person I knew a few days ago. I realize that's because I'm not the same person I was then. I thought I loved Marcianus, but it was just because he was the only boy I'd ever known. Now that I can compare him to other men, I see he's not the one I want to be with. He hasn't changed. He wants me to go back to the estate and marry him. I could never be happy there, with him."

"Did you tell him that?"

"I haven't yet, but I will."

"What about your baby?"

She laid a hand on her stomach. "I haven't told him about that either."

"You said he was the father. The law says the baby is his, not yours."

"I realize that. Mother Plinia and I talked about it for a long time last night. I still haven't decided—"

"My lord!" Dymas called from the other end of the garden. "My lord, it's urgent. Please come quickly." He began running toward us.

I couldn't imagine what my elderly scribe would find so pressing, but I didn't care, as long as it gave me an excuse to get away from this unwelcome conversation. Nelia's voice was as alluring as that of the Sirens, whose song drew sailors to their destruction on the rocks. She had obviously seduced my mother. Naomi, I was sure, had fallen under her spell, too. Somebody in the house had to keep a clear head.

Dymas panted as he reached us. "In the … atrium, my lord. It's … Glaucon."

With Dymas, my mother, and Nelia on my heels I hurried toward the atrium. I could hear the murmur of a crowd, indicating that many of my servants were already there.

In the center of the crowd stood Regulus and several of his servants. That was surprising enough. What stopped me in my tracks was the sight of Glaucon, on his knees next to Regulus, who held a rope tied around Glaucon's neck, like a triumphant general with his prize captive. My slave's hands were tied behind his back. His left eye was swollen shut, and blood trickled from the corner of his mouth.

"What is the meaning of this, Marcus Regulus?"

"I should be the one asking that question, Gaius Pliny."

"Have you beaten my slave? You know you have no right to do that."

Regulus boomed in his best courtroom voice, "When I find a man coupling with my wife, I have the right to kill him." He jerked on the rope, and Glaucon staggered forward on his knees.

"With your *wife?*" I stood over Glaucon, cupped his chin in my hand, and lifted his head. "With Regulus' wife?"

"I didn't know … who she was, my lord," Glaucon croaked. "I thought she … was a servant."

The image of a woman stepping out of the servants' entrance of Regulus' house came into my mind. Because of the hooded cloak she was wearing that night, I hadn't been able to make out her features. The hair sticking out beneath the hood had been blond. I didn't know Regulus' wife, Sempronia, except for having seen her a few times. She wasn't blond, but wigs are easy to come by. Everyone in Rome knew she and Regulus were married in name only. Each of them indulged in whatever activities took their fancy, with whoever took their fancy.

"Is that what she told you, that she was a servant?"

Glaucon nodded and winced at the pain the movement caused him.

I turned to face Regulus. "A man cannot be found at fault when a woman has deliberately deceived him."

Regulus snorted. "Even at your tender age, Gaius Pliny, you must know enough Roman law to realize a woman cannot be culpable. As Cicero said, 'Before the law, women are children because of their weakness of mind.' The only fact that matters here is that your servant was coupling with my wife. I could have killed him on the spot. The law allows me to do it. Because of my regard for you, I have brought him back here, but I demand that you punish him severely."

"What do you mean by 'severely'?"

"I don't think death would be too harsh a penalty." He paused to let a gasp pass through the crowd of my servants. "My honor would be satisfied, though, if you had him castrated." He gave a signal to one of his servants, who pushed Glaucon, sending him tumbling face first toward me. Regulus dropped the rope. "I'll leave him for you to deal with as you see fit. If I ever find him near my house or speaking to anyone in my household, I will kill him."

As Regulus and his entourage filed out my front door and Dymas rushed to his injured son's side, I thought to myself, *At least now I know Glaucon isn't spying for Regulus.*

* * * *

"So you think he'll be all right?" I asked Demetrius as we, at long last, settled down to work in the tablinum. The uproar caused by Regulus' visit had finally subsided to a low hum of conversation among my servants.

My steward nodded. "Dymas says he has only minor injuries. The worst seems to be a broken rib. Glaucon told him he wasn't tortured, just cuffed around, tied up and held overnight. Three of Regulus' men apparently followed him and Sempronia when they left the house."

"What do you think I should do with him?"

"Well, my lord, Marcus Regulus was very insistent and named the punishment he thought would satisfy him."

"I would never castrate any slave of mine," I said, to Demetrius' obvious relief, "especially not to gratify Regulus and his whore of a wife. Glaucon needs some time to recover from his injuries. When he's on his feet again, I'll decide what to do with him."

A sharp knock sounded on the partly opened door and, without waiting for a response, Nelia stepped into the room, carrying a scroll. Demetrius and I stood.

Before I could ask what she wanted, she said, "Sinon." With that she laid the scroll on the table in front of me and left the room.

Demetrius and I looked after her, open-mouthed, until he said, "'Sinon,' my lord? Is that what she said?"

"Yes." I didn't have to look at the scroll to know it was the second book of Virgil's *Aeneid*. The Trojans come out of their walls one morning to find the Greek fleet gone and the great wooden horse standing on the plain before the city. They're unsure what to make of it until they find a Greek soldier named Sinon, tied up and abused, who tells them the Greeks planned to sacrifice him to insure a safe voyage home, but he escaped. Priam takes pity on him, orders him to be untied and cared for. Sinon then tells a pathetic story which convinces the Trojans to take the horse—with its belly full of Greek soldiers—inside their walls.

That evening the sun set on Priam's house for the last time.

* * * *

I did not see Nelia or my mother for the rest of the day, although I was aware of a great deal of activity in the women's part of the house. Mother sent a servant to ask me to use the bath early in the afternoon so she and Naomi could have the time they needed to get Nelia ready for the dinner at Tacitus' house.

I wished there was some way I could persuade her not to go. There was so much I didn't know about her, and I would prefer not to expose her to any more people until I had answered some of my questions. Musonius asked me to protect her, not set her out where everyone could see her. Julia and her friends would be spreading gossip about her all over the city by tomorrow morning, I was sure. But Nelia had apologized, so we were back to being polite to one another.

About the tenth hour of the day I was entering the garden, on my way to my room, when I heard the voices of a group of women coming toward me. I stopped to make way for Nelia and her attendants, led by my mother and Naomi, like nymphs flocking around Artemis.

"By the gods!" I muttered.

The woman approaching me was barely recognizable as the girl who'd been dragged into my house three days before. Her hair was done up in what I assumed was the latest style, and she wore make-up, not slapped on with a trowel, as most Roman women do, but applied sparingly in exactly the right places so that all I saw was her exquisite face, not a coat of paint. She wore a light green stola complemented by a necklace and earrings and bracelets of gold and jade, none of which I had ever seen before. One of my clients is a jeweler. I suspected he had been rousted out of his afternoon's rest to open his shop. My mother's worry about our finances seemed to have been allayed.

"Good evening, Gaius Pliny," Nelia said with a slight smile. She gave me the distinct feeling she was welcoming *me* into *her* house. Even on Musonius' estate she would never have been mistaken for a simple country girl. Now she looked regal, like a character in a myth who has been disguised until a divinity reveals her true nature.

"What? Oh, yes," I stuttered. "Thank you."

"Are you all right, Gaius?" my mother asked.

There's nothing like a mother's voice to douse a man's amorous feelings. But was that what I had just experienced? "Yes, I'm fine, Mother. What about you, Nelia? Do you feel like going out?" I turned to Naomi. "I thought she was supposed to rest."

"She should be all right, my lord," Naomi said. "She'll be carried in a litter and will be reclining on a couch at dinner. Just don't let her exert herself too much."

"And how do you propose I stop her if she does?"

"You won't have to drag me off a horse or pull me out of a river," Nelia said, reddening. "Your mother and Naomi have talked some sense into me, and I've promised them I will cooperate with you until cousin Gaius returns to Rome."

"I would appreciate that." Even though I didn't entirely believe it. If she did cooperate, it would only be to throw me off guard until she was ready to do whatever she had in mind. But I had to appease my mother. "I assure you, lady Cornelia, you will receive nothing but the most courteous treatment from me and my household. Now, Demetrius probably has the litter waiting in the atrium. I'll meet you there in a moment."

I stood aside to let Nelia and her *clientela* pass. My mother fell out of the pack and stayed by my side as I started for my room.

"She's such a lovely girl, Gaius."

"After all the work you and your women put into her, how could she be anything else?"

"Oh, I'm not talking about her looks. I mean her personality. She's sweet, intelligent, charming."

I could have added 'conniving,' but I thought better of it.

"Did you know she's the same age—almost to the day—that your sister would have been if she had lived?"

I stopped and turned to face her. The aching welled up in her eyes. So that's what I was up against. Mother had found her long-lost daughter, the one who died only a few days after her birth. It might even have been her idea to have Nelia call her 'Mother.' Naomi, too, as I recalled, had lost a daughter of the same age as my mother's. That was the beginning of the bond between two grieving mothers. Now they'd found their little girl, and Nelia had found not just one mother, but two to replace the mother she lost when she was a child.

"Mother, please remember, she'll be here only a short time." I took a few steps toward my room. "When Musonius returns to Rome, we'll send her to him."

"We'll see about that when the time comes, dear."

That stopped me in my tracks. "What do you mean, 'we'll see about that'?"

"Nelia's old enough to make up her own mind about what she does and where she goes. But she has no experience of the world."

"She has enough to be pregnant."

Mother lowered her eyes. "Yes, there is that. But she's never been to a dinner like the one she's going to now. She's never even ridden in a litter. She grew up ten miles outside of Rome, but she knows no more about life here than if she were from ... India. A girl that naïve needs someone to protect and guide her. We tried this afternoon to give her some idea of what to expect, but you'll need to be her teacher as well as her escort this evening."

"Well, silly me. I thought I was going to have a pleasant dinner with a friend." I put my hands on my hips.

"Gaius, this petulance you've been displaying lately is most unbecoming and most uncharacteristic. Since you got back from Syria, something has been different about you."

How could I begin to explain to her all I had experienced during that year, but especially during those fateful few days in Smyrna on the trip home?

"I will keep a close eye on her, Mother. I promise." I turned toward my room.

"Thank you, dear. Now, one last thing."

I must have sighed more loudly than I realized.

"That was a most petulant sigh," Mother said.

"Everyone is waiting on me," I said over my shoulder.

"They can wait long enough for me to tell you something important." I stopped and half-turned back toward her. "What is it?"

She lowered her voice. "I haven't had a chance to tell you about ... the knife."

I felt the blood drain from my face. "'The knife'? What ... what are you talking about?"

"Gaius, you don't need to keep your guard up against me. I'm your mother. I'm not going to inform on you. My only concern is whether you're all right."

"Yes, Mother. I'm fine. Now, tell me about this knife."

"Your knife, dear. The one you killed that dreadful man with."

I sighed, in relief this time, not petulance. "All right. Yes, I admit it. I killed him, but I had to or he would have killed me. Do you have the knife?"

She nodded. "Naomi noticed it on the table in the exhedra that morning the Cohorts came to the house. She was standing with me when we recognized the tunic they were carrying as one of yours—"

"How could you?" Suddenly I was having trouble breathing. If a couple of women could identify it, who else might?

"We made it, dear."Mother put her hand on my arm. "We sewed the stripe on it. How could we *not* know it? When Naomi saw a bloodstained knife on the table, she feared the worst. She's a much more clever woman than you realize. She slipped the knife under her clothing and, when the soldier came to search her room, she pretended to be in her monthly. You saw that."

"Yes. It was clever. No man would touch her in that condition."

"She got the idea, she told me, from a story in one of the Jewish holy books."

"They must be strange holy books, indeed, that tell stories about women and their monthlies."

"They're different from anything I've ever read, but quite charming in their own way."

"You've read them, too?"

"Yes, dear. I'm sure Naomi would be happy to have you read them as well."

"You know what I think of gods and myths, Mother. Where is that knife now?"

"We scrubbed it completely clean and put it back in the kitchen. No one will ever know."

As grateful as I was, I wished they had buried the accursed thing or dropped it into a sewer. Now every time I cut a piece of bread or cheese, I would wonder if I was using the knife I had plunged into the Cyclops' throat.

MY UNCLE ALWAYS chided me for preferring to walk rather than ride in a litter. He rode everywhere he went, with a reader constantly at his side so he could make good use of time spent in travel. His excessive girth and his breathing problems made walking difficult for him, but I've sometimes wondered whether his health might have been better if he had walked more. I always feel invigorated when I walk. But, if my uncle had walked, he might not have accomplished as much in his studies and his writing.

For our trip to Tacitus' house Demetrius had prepared my largest litter and picked out a few extra slaves to carry it and clear a path for us. Naomi and Chloe were chosen to attend to Nelia. I told them to walk right behind the litter, in its wake, so to speak.

"Can't Naomi ride with us?" Nelia asked. "She is old enough that I worry about her walking."

"She was quite capable of walking to her brother's grave a few days ago, and that was a round trip of four miles."

"Cousin Gaius says it's not fair to the servants to make them walk when we ride."

"Would it be fair to the slaves carrying the litter to add the weight of another person?" She had no answer to that, so we set out.

The advantage to walking, accompanied by just a few slaves or clients, is that you can, like an experienced legion, shift your formation to meet conditions on the battlefields which Rome's streets often become. You can slip through a narrow opening in the crowd or detour at the last moment down a side street. Riding in a large litter, carried and surrounded by a dozen or more slaves, is like being on a lumbering trireme. Your maneuverability is limited and you have to stay in deep water.

Still, given our concerns about Nelia's condition and given how crowded the streets would be in the late afternoon and taking into account the threat of rain, the litter was our best choice. Laberius and a couple of my burlier slaves would provide extra protection. I didn't particularly want Laberius along, but he was determined not to let Nelia out of his sight.

As we settled into our places in the litter, facing one another, a dirty-faced boy of about ten ran up to us, his outstretched hand holding a wax tablet. "For the lady Cornelia," he said.

Nelia took the tablet and I gave the boy a denarius. He stepped away from the litter but did not leave, in case there was a reply to be delivered.

Breaking the seal, Nelia opened the tablet and read it silently. Then she turned to the boy and shook her head. "There will be no reply."

Disappointed, the boy turned and ran away.

Nelia turned back to me. "It's from Marcianus. He wants to see me again."

"I didn't ask," I said.

"But I want you to know. He says if there is no reply to the message, he will know that we have no future together."

"Are you sure that's what you want?"

"Yes, I am." She tossed the tablet into the corner of the litter. "Can we leave the curtains open? I want to see everything." The girlish enthusiasm in her voice sounded genuine, and I recalled my mother's description of her as a naïve stranger from far away. But I still didn't trust her.

"Does 'everything' include the beggars and prostitutes and the garbage in the streets?"

"My, you are a cynic, aren't you, Gaius Pliny? Rome is the biggest city in the world. When people say 'The City' they mean only one place. I want to see it, to feel it. All of it."

"So you shall then." I signaled for the servants to tie the curtains back. That meant the scented cloths we hung inside the litter to mask the odors of the street would be of no use. But Nelia wanted to see and feel all of it.

"Thank you." Nelia's expression of gratitude turned to a shriek as the litter-carriers lifted us. I had heard Aeolus, their leader, give the command and was bracing myself, but Nelia hadn't known what was about to happen. Out of a childish sort of spite, I hadn't warned her.

Being lifted in a litter can be a shock. The motion is sudden and rarely smooth. The litter tilts and sways until the carriers get it settled and get in step with one another. They sometimes stagger under the weight, especially of a litter as large as this one. People have been known to topple out if they're not ready and if the carriers are particularly clumsy.

Our route took us past the Temple of Minerva, the public building closest to my house. Like most Roman temples, it reminds me of a box in which the divinity is sealed up, whether for her protection or ours I'm never quite sure. To avoid a treacherous descent straight down the hill, Aeolus made several turns, first right, then left, as though we were going down a staircase.

"These are all homes," I pointed out to Nelia, "mostly apartment houses."

"They're huge!" She leaned out of the litter and gawked at the four- and five-story buildings which covered an entire block and kept the narrower streets in shadow except at midday.

On the lower part of the Esquiline the streets became crowded and the beggars aggressive. My slaves were pushed up against the sides of the litter as they defended us against the onslaught. Even the battle-hardened Laberius had trouble keeping his feet under him.

"Can't we give them something?" Nelia asked. "Wouldn't that make them go away?"

"Just the opposite. It would be like cutting your leg and holding it out in front of a pack of ravenous wolves. We would be mobbed and devoured."

"But they're poor and hungry, and you have so much. Cousin Gaius says it's immoral for a few people to be so wealthy and the rest so poor."

"Oh, has Musonius sold his house in the city and the estate where you grew up? Has he given up his equestrian stripe?"

She pouted. "Are you saying he's a hypocrite?"

"My dealings with him the last few days have made me re-evaluate Musonius' teachings about a number of things. Let's just leave it at that."

We turned right on the Via Tusculana. As we turned, Nelia caught her first glimpse of the Flavian Amphitheater looming over and dwarfing everything around it.

"Great Jupiter!" she muttered. "Cousin Gaius said it was gigantic, but I could never have imagined ..."

"Some people have nicknamed it the Colosseum," I said, "because it's so ... well, colossal. Domitian isn't happy about that. He wants his family's name attached to it."

As we drew nearer the Amphitheater Nelia shook her head. "It's unbelievable, incomprehensible. Almost frightening."

"You said you wanted to see everything."

"How do you live here? How do you breathe?"

"You sound like the country mouse in Horace's fable."

"That's how I feel. Everything here is so overwhelming. Part of me wants to run away."

"You have to get used to it. Some part of you has to go numb. The Amphitheater is still new to all of us, remember. It was completed only two years ago."

"What's it like inside?"

"I've never been in it."

She looked at me in disbelief. "I thought everyone in Rome except cousin Gaius attended the games."

"It feels that way. Tacitus adores the games. I don't like the bloodshed, the frenzy of the crowd. I'm sure I'll have to attend something there some day, as a favor to a friend, but I'm in no hurry. Now, over here is the Temple of the Deified Claudius." I pointed to the structure—large enough in its own right—on the other side of the street.

"Oh, yes," Nelia said. "Agrippina marries her uncle, poisons him, then has him declared a god. She's the most heartless women I've ever read about."

"But you admired her mother, the elder Agrippina. Defending the bridge and all that."

"Saving your husband is heroic. Marrying your uncle and poisoning him is despicable."

We made another turn and passed by the southeast end of the Palatine. "Some people think it's worth any price," I said, "to live on top of this hill."

"Would you want to be *princeps*, Gaius Pl—?"

I clapped my hand over her mouth. "Don't ever say such a thing in Rome!" I whispered. "People have been condemned for treason for even hinting at it. Do you understand?"

Her eyes bulged in fright. I was afraid she was going to bite me again, but she nodded and I removed my hand, though not before I once again felt something odd on the upper right side of her mouth.

As we passed the Circus Maximus the rain started, a dozen drops and suddenly a downpour. My litter-carriers found the footing treacherous because of the mud washing down from Domitian's building site atop the Palatine. Much of the western side of the hill was being cut away to allow for the foundations of the *princeps'* grandiose house. I closed the curtains on the litter.

"You'll have to see the rest of everything some other time," I said.

"Thank you for your patience with me. I know I've been difficult, but since I became pregnant I hardly know myself. My moods seem to change—"

She broke off as a couple of my carriers slipped in the mud. With Laberius yelling, "Watch it, you clumsy oafs!" the litter pitched to one side, rolling Nelia toward me. Instinctively I threw my arms around her. She came to rest against me. Her breasts were pressed to my chest, her face so close to mine I could feel the sweet warmth of her breath.

* * * *

Tacitus' house sits on the southwestern side of the Aventine, near the Porta Naevia. A previous owner closed off the two front rooms of the house from the interior and rented them out as shops—to a sandalmaker and a jeweler—an arrangement Tacitus has maintained, although he says his wife spends more in those shops than he takes in as rent. Being over the crest of the hill, he isn't much bothered by the noise from the Circus Maximus. From his upper story he has a nice view of the road to Ostia and a bit of the Tiber. At least on days when the rain isn't coming down in a torrent.

When we arrived at the door it opened immediately and one of Tacitus' servants motioned for my carriers to bring the litter into the vestibulum. The operation was carried out so smoothly we were barely jostled when the litter was set down.

"If it rains much harder," a deep voice said, "you'll find out if that thing floats." The curtain was pulled back and I found myself face-to-face with a beaming Gnaeus Julius Agricola.

I had met Agricola only once, shortly after Tacitus and I returned from Syria and Agricola had been recalled from Britain. Much of his career had been spent on government service in one province or another. During his consulship, six years ago, I was still too young to take part in public life.

"Welcome, Gaius Pliny. It's good to see you again." He took my hand and helped me out of the litter. The firmness of his grip, his frank, open countenance, even the gray around his temples, all exuded confidence and command. I could understand why men would embrace him as their leader and prefer him to someone like Domitian. Out of the corner of my eye I saw Laberius snap to attention.

"It's a pleasure to see you, sir," I said. "I hope your time in Baiae was relaxing."

"If boring is relaxing, then I suppose it was relaxing." He looked over my shoulder. "Oh, you did bring her. Excellent! Tacitus wasn't sure she'd be up to it."

"Yes, forgive me." I turned around and helped Nelia out of the litter. "This is the lady Cornelia, cousin of Musonius Rufus. Nelia, this is Tacitus' father-in-law, Gnaeus Julius Agricola."

"Welcome, lady," Agricola said with a quick bow of his head. "Did I hear Gaius Pliny call you ... Nelia? Is that how you're known?"

"Yes, sir. When I was a child, one of my playmates had an awful time pronouncing my name. It was easier for him just to say 'Nelia' and everyone else picked it up. Perhaps now that I'm in Rome, though, I should go by Cornelia."

"No, it's charming. And it distinguishes you from the five thousand other Cornelias in the city. Who was your father?"

"Lucius Cornelius Catulus." She looked at me, as though wondering whether I was going to express my doubts about what Musonius had told her.

"Don't know of him," Agricola said, scratching his chin. "Did he hold any offices? Provincial posts?"

"I don't believe so. Cousin Gaius told me that my family lived in Asia. My father was killed just before I was born there, and my mother died a few years later."

"My father died just after I was born," Agricola said, nodding his head slowly. "Caligula forced him to commit suicide."

"How awful!" Nelia laid a gentle hand on Agricola's arm. I could swear the old general's eyes got misty.

Agricola regained his composure. "Born in Asia, you say? I was a quaestor in Asia. One of my first posts. That's where my daughter was born, eighteen years ago."

"What a remarkable coincidence that is," Nelia said. "I'm eighteen."

"Remarkable indeed," Agricola said. "Well, I shouldn't keep you standing here. Julia is eager to meet you. She's in the triclinium, overseeing last-minute details. I offered to help, but the invasion of Britain was a minor undertaking compared to this dinner."

Laberius took charge of my slaves and the litter. By the time Nelia, Agricola and I had crossed the atrium we could hear a young woman's voice coming from the dining room. "No, that's not right! Why can't you understand what I want? Maybe a few lashes would improve your hearing. The lampstands go over *there*. Isn't that right, Tacitus?"

"Yes, dear," my friend's weary voice replied. "I believe that's the way they were arranged that night. I just didn't pay any attention to lampstands."

"Why not? Were you too busy ogling some pretty slave boy?"

Before Tacitus could respond, Agricola called out, "Julia, your guests are starting to arrive." He stopped us at the door, like a commander wary of leading his troops into an ambush.

Julia turned and forced a smile. Her face was covered with a layer of white powder, her lips painted a bright red. She wore a rose-colored gown, belted high under her breasts, and several silver bracelets on each arm. Her reddish-brown hair had been done up in one of those high styles that made her look like she was wearing a siege tower on her head.

"Gaius Pliny! How *nice* to see you." She approached me, took my hands, and brushed her cheeks against mine, making a kissing sound but never touching me with her lips. "And this must be Cornelia. I'm so glad you could come."

"Thank you for inviting me," Nelia said, stiffening when Julia embraced her.

"What a *lovely* gown." Julia stepped back and held Nelia's hands. "And that *necklace* is *spectacular*."

"For that I have to thank Gaius Pliny. He and his mother have been very generous to me."

"I'm not surprised. They're *wonderful* people. Now, I want you to feel perfectly at home here. You've met my father. This is my mother, Domitia." Julia put her arm around a small, gray-haired woman who was straightening a coverlet draped over one of the couches.

"Welcome," Domitia said. I had never met her before, but I knew from Tacitus' comments that she was not the sort of meddling mother-in-law one sees in comedies. With hardly any makeup on, her features seemed sharp, birdlike. She was about five years older than my mother and had accompanied her husband on his various military postings. The hard life on Rome's frontiers had made her wiry, unlike the soft, pampered Roman matrons I was accustomed to.

Domitia took Nelia's arm and turned her back toward the door of the triclinium. "While my daughter is finishing the preparations for dinner, may I show you the rest of the house?"

"I would *enjoy* that," Nelia said.

"And I have something to show you in the library," Tacitus said, almost bolting for the door.

"But who'll help me get ready for *dinner*?" Julia wailed. "There's still so much to *do*."

"Everything looks fine," her mother assured her. "None of your other guests has ever been in Caesar's triclinium, so they won't know if some little detail isn't right. And I'm sure Gaius Pliny is too much of a gentleman to point out anything you might have gotten wrong. Not that you have gotten anything wrong," she added quickly.

I looked around the room. "If I didn't know better, I would swear I was back on the Palatine."

"Really?" Julia beamed.

"You see, dear?" Domitia said. "Everything will be fine. Your father can help you. We'll be back shortly."

We all let out a sigh of relief when we left Agricola fulminating and escaped from the triclinium, but none of us sighed louder than Tacitus.

"Well, Julia's quite ... charming," Nelia said.

Domitia waved her hand. "You don't have to pretend on my account. I know how shallow my daughter is. If she were a stream, you could ford her without getting your ankles wet. Agricola and I did all we could do to encourage her to read when she was a child. But every time we put a book in her hands, she would pretend to get sick, sneezing and wiping her eyes. All she's ever been interested in was clothes and gossip. I don't know how dear Tacitus endures her. I suppose being gone on various postings makes marriage to her bearable. Either that or she's quite remarkable in the bedroom."

Even in the gloom of a cloudy evening I could see Tacitus redden. "Your library is this way, isn't it?" I said in an effort to extricate him.

"May I see it?" Nelia asked.

"Why don't we let the men do their business first," Domitia suggested, "while we see the rest of the house?"

Tacitus' library is much smaller than mine, housed in two rooms with a connecting door off his garden. As we crossed to it, slaves were lighting torches and fixing them in brackets under the shelter of the peristyle. The light made the garden glisten in the rain. His house is older than mine, his trees taller. Instead of a piscina he has a fountain, spurting futile drops back up at the rain.

When we entered the library Tacitus went straight to a strongbox, which he unlocked and opened. Drawing out two pieces of papyrus, he laid them on a table.

"These are precise copies of two letters I found in the archives this morning. I made them myself."

"What's in them?"

"In this one Agrippina recommends to Nero that he take Antistius Vetus as his colleague in the consulship. It would be a fitting reward, she says, for a man who was so kind to her when she was in exile, a man she could trust absolutely."

"So absolutely, it seems, she trusted him to raise her daughter as his own."

"And that leads to the second letter, in which she tells Nero she has arranged a marriage between his cousin, Rubellius Plautus, and Antistia, daughter of Antistius Vetus."

I glanced over the second letter. "She's not even asking Nero's permission. She's telling him what she's done."

"Josephus says that in Nero's early years as *princeps* she virtually ran the empire. I don't think she asked his permission for much of anything."

I shook my head in admiration. "She hides her daughter in plain sight for all those years, then marries her to the man who has the best claim, after Nero, to be *princeps*."

"Any sons Rubellius and Antistia might produce would have Caesar's blood from both parents. No one could have a stronger claim. ..."

"A stronger claim to what?" Domitia asked as she and Nelia entered the library.

"Oh, a stronger claim ... to an inheritance," I said, turning the letters over.

"Yes, in that case I have to try tomorrow," Tacitus added.

Nelia looked at me, then down at the letters. When her eyes widened, I followed her gaze. Only then did I notice the writing on the backs of the papyri. It was the same Greek-looking script I had seen on Agrippina's first letter. Tacitus had indeed made precise copies.

"Why is someone wanting someone else to die?" Nelia asked, pointing to the letters.

"What are you talking about?"

"That's what that word says. 'May you die,' or perhaps 'you will die'."

"How do you know that?" I asked.

"Because the optative form and the future tense are virtually the same."

"But I've never seen that word in Greek."

"It's not Greek. It's Etruscan. They borrowed the Greek alphabet and adapted it to their language, just as we Romans did."

The wind picked up and rain began to blow into the library. As Tacitus stepped over to the door and closed it, I recalled what Nelia had told us when we were on Musonius' estate, about how she had learned to read Etruscan through her study of some books by Claudius.

"Etruscan?" Domitia said. "They died out hundreds of years ago, didn't they? Who would be writing in Etruscan now?"

"I don't know," Nelia said. "Will you let me see the documents, Gaius Pliny, or do we have to fight over them again?"

I handed her the letters, feeling like a schoolboy summoned to the front of the class by the master. "They're letters written by Agrippina to her son, Nero, the *princeps*."

"I can read Latin also," Nelia said, turning the letters so Domitia could follow as she read.

"This Antistius Vetus," Domitia said. "Is he Lucius Antistius Vetus?"

Tacitus and I nodded.

"We lived in Asia when Antistius was governor there. It was the year after Agricola's quaestorship. We stayed on for a while because I was carrying a child and did not want to travel."

"Did you know Antistius?" I asked.

"Quite well. His house was across the street from ours. His daughter, Antistia, and I both had babies that year. Both of us had daughters."

"Julius Agricola told me," Nelia said, "Julia was born eighteen years ago. So was I. That means the two of us are the same age as Antistia's daughter."

"Yes, that would be right," Domitia said.

"What happened to Antistia?" I asked.

"It was tragic," Domitia said. "Her husband, Rubellius Plautus, was in exile because Nero feared he was plotting to take power. Before Antistia's daughter was born, Nero sent men to kill Rubellius and his son, who was only five or six. They butchered the poor man, cut off his head and sent it to Rome to reassure Nero. The servants said they looked for

Antistia, to kill her as well, but she wasn't in the house and no one knew where to find her. It turned out Rubellius' friend, Musonius Rufus, had hidden her."

I looked at Tacitus and knew he was remembering Musonius' letter, just as I was. *While my cousin Fulvia was staying at my house, word arrived that her husband and young son had been killed.*

I dreaded asking the next question, but Nelia jumped in ahead of me. "Did they ever find Antistia?"

Domitia sat down, as though the weight of the tale was too much to bear. "Yes. Nero wouldn't leave the family alone. Three years after Rubellius' death, Antistia and her father committed suicide because Nero thought they were plotting against him and ordered their deaths."

Logic dictated what the next question would be. I waited to see if Nelia would ask it, but she looked agitated, her breath coming in short gasps. "What happened to Antistia's daughter?" I asked.

"I don't know." Domitia shook her head. "Agricola and I had left Asia by then. I only heard of Antistia's death some months after it happened. I've never learned what became of the daughter. She would have been three when her mother died. Musonius was very close to the family. Perhaps he could tell you more."

Nelia put a hand to her head, and I was afraid she might faint.

"Are you all right, dear?" Domitia asked. "Here, sit down."

Nelia sat down heavily, looking at me with near panic in her eyes. "It can't ... It can't be, can it, Gaius Pliny?"

"The similarities are remarkable," I said, "too great to be coincidence."

Domitia looked from one of us to the other. "What are you talking about?"

"What you've just told us about Antistia and her family bears an uncanny resemblance to the history of Nelia's family which Musonius Rufus told her."

"But that would mean cousin Gaius has been lying to me all these years," Nelia said. "Why would he do that?"

"If you are the daughter of Rubellius and Antistia, he would have good reason to keep you hidden because you are a direct descendant of Augustus and Julius Caesar. Your blood is a threat to any *princeps*. That puts you in grave danger."

"By the gods!" Domitia gasped, clutching Nelia's hand. "Is this true, child?"

Why did these revelations always occur when there were too many people in the room? I looked at Tacitus, asking with my eyes if I should say any more.

He nodded. "She can be trusted."

"Trusted with what?" Domitia asked, suddenly looking afraid. Being associated with any hint of a conspiracy in Rome is perilous. She had not walked in here expecting to be exposed to such danger.

"There's more to it, my lady," I said, "and you may as well know the rest. We have other testimony suggesting that Antistia was actually the daughter of Agrippina, Nero's mother. Rubellius was also a descendant of Augustus. So their daughter has Caesar's blood from both of her parents."

"No!" Nelia snapped, pulling her hand away from Domitia and standing up. "I won't believe it. Not on the word of some garrulous slave who was just passing along gossip from her mother. For all you know, the Antistia who was Domitia's friend could be another daughter of Antistius Vetus ... born after he left Pandateria."

I could not dispute that possibility. All of a Roman man's daughters would have the same name, the feminine form of his family name.

"But this was his only daughter," Domitia said. "His only child, in fact. And he was very proud that Agrippina herself had arranged the marriage with Rubellius Plautus."

I held up the letter Tacitus had copied from the imperial archives, in which Agrippina informed Nero of the marriage. Nelia shook her head repeatedly.

"I don't see any other explanation," I said. "Everything we know suggests you are the daughter of Rubellius Plautus and Antistia."

Nelia shook her finger in my face. "My father's name was Lucius Cornelius Catulus and my mother was Fulvia, the cousin of Musonius Rufus. Just because I was born in Asia and my father died before I was born and my mother died when I was three, that doesn't prove anything. How many people have lost parents when they were children? Agricola's father was killed when Agricola was just a baby. Does that make him the long-lost daughter of this Rubellius?"

"Ridiculing the facts doesn't change them," I said.

"What 'facts,' Gaius Pliny? You have yet to discover one solid fact that links me to those people. You're putting together a web of speculation, like a spider lurking in its corner."

"Perhaps there's some physical resemblance," Tacitus said. "Children usually resemble one of their parents." He turned to his mother-in-law. "My lady, you knew Antistia and Rubellius. Does Nelia resemble either of them in any way?"

Domitia stood in front of Nelia and looked her over like someone contemplating the purchase of a slave. Nelia's eyes burned at me as she allowed Domitia to take her chin and turn her head from side to side.

After a moment Domitia shook her head and stepped away from Nelia, patting her on the shoulder. "It's been too many years since I saw

Rubellius or Antistia. I don't notice anything in this girl that brings back the memory of them."

Nelia looked at Tacitus and me in disgust. "There. Are you satisfied?"

No, I was disappointed. Domitia had appeared, as unexpected as a gift from the gods, with eyewitness knowledge of Rubellius and Antistia. If she couldn't see anything in Nelia that reminded her of them, perhaps I was on the wrong trail. Nelia made a strong case. People's parents do die or get killed, all too frequently. The story that Musonius told about Cornelius Catulus and Fulvia might be true and just coincidentally—how I hate that word!—similar to the story of Rubellius and Antistia.

As Domitia sat down again she said, "There was one unusual thing about Antistia, though, something that embarrassed her a great deal."

"What was that?" I asked.

"Her teeth. You see, she had several extra teeth—"

The door of the library flew open. "There you are!" Julia said. "Why are you looking at these moldy old *books*? My guests are arriving."

* * * *

Tacitus and his family took the high couch and the other guests the low one, leaving Nelia and me to share the middle couch. I was glad to see that the servants were given stools to sit on instead of being expected to stand behind our couches. That is my practice, but some masters seem to delight in forcing their slaves and everyone else's to stand for several hours.

Julia's party proved a dismal failure. The food was excellent—Tacitus' cook is almost as good as mine—but it was impossible to enjoy the meal, even the oysters, when I suspected I was reclining next to a descendant of Julius Caesar, a several-greats-granddaughter of Augustus. And she was carrying a child who, if male, could lay a strong claim to the title of *princeps*. All Domitian had asked me to do was find a diary. I had failed at that and instead had discovered someone who could plunge Rome into civil war.

Nelia would not look at me. She seemed to find nothing to laugh at, even to smile at, and she kept her head down all through the gustatio. Naomi and Chloe hovered over her, obviously aware of how unhappy she was.

As I pondered Nelia's identity and the fate of Rome, Julia and her friends kept up their mindless chatter. The other two couples were there because the wives were friends of Julia's. I had never met their husbands and Tacitus seemed only slightly acquainted with them. This was the longest time I had spent in Julia's company, and it seemed even longer. As inane as Julia was, though, the other two girls could not have sparked an idea if we rubbed their heads together. Their conversation never got beyond make-up and clothes, until baths were mentioned. One of the young men, Septicius Clarus, said he and his wife frequented the baths of Titus.

"That's where all the clever people go," he said. Then he launched into a description of the performance Martial and Spatale had given that afternoon. I was sorely tempted to tell him what Martial actually thought of all those 'clever' people like himself.

The servants had just brought in a pork dish with baked apples when Nelia sat up and said, "Gaius Pliny, may I have a word with you outside? Cornelius Tacitus, perhaps you will accompany us? And you too, lady Domitia, if you tear yourself away from such delightful company for a moment."

As we headed for the door, with Naomi and Chloe trailing behind us, Julia looked supremely annoyed, her guests slightly puzzled.

Nelia stopped under a torch illuminating the garden and turned on us. "The three of you have been ogling me all through dinner. You aren't going to be satisfied until you see them, are you?" She brought a hand up to the neck of her gown and took a deep breath. "Well, let's get it over with."

"My lady, no!" Naomi cried, grabbing her hand. "What are you doing? My master is a decent young man. He wouldn't want you to do this."

Nelia looked at her bosom and laughed. "It's my teeth, woman. He wants to see my teeth."

Pulling away from Naomi, Nelia grasped her upper lip between thumb and forefinger and lifted it. I saw three small teeth, like a child's first teeth, protruding from her gums on the right side.

"Go ahead! Take a closer look. It's the only one you're ever going to get."

Tacitus hung back, but Domitia and I leaned our heads closer to Nelia's face.

"They're just like Antistia's," Domitia said. "In the same place and not large enough to cause her lip to bulge, but they're definitely teeth."

Nelia let go of her lip. "They're a damn nuisance. That's what they are."

There was the proof that Nelia was Antistia's daughter. And Naomi's story—combined with Domitia's eyewitness testimony—left me no choice but to believe that Antistia was the daughter of Agrippina. The full significance of what I'd just seen was only beginning to sink in when Julia came stomping out of the house.

"Mother! Tacitus! You're neglecting my *guests*. Father's starting to tell his army stories. Everyone's going to want to *leave* soon." With each sentence the pitch of her whining rose.

"We were just clearing up something, dear," her mother said. "Please go back inside. We'll be there in a moment."

If my mother could have seen the look Julia gave us, she would have realized that my petulance is only a pale imitation of the original, the way Roman statues are poor copies of vivid Greek works of art. I could never make my lower lip quiver the way Julia's did.

"Well, I just think you're being so rude to my friends!" Turning in a huff, Julia started back into the house.

203

XVII

As soon as we rejoined the festivities Domitia took Agricola aside, to tell him what she had just learned, I assumed. Not long after that Nelia pleaded exhaustion and said she was ready to leave. I was surprised at how earnestly Julia prevailed upon her to stay longer. Tacitus excused himself to put the finishing touches on the speech he was to deliver in court the next morning. Agricola and Domitia saw us to the door and retired for the night, leaving the triclinium to a pouting Julia and her vapid friends.

As the litter left Tacitus' house Nelia closed the curtains, shutting out all but the dimmest light from the torches my slaves were carrying. Drawing her knees up to her chest, she folded her arms over them, curling up like a child desperate to hide.

"I thought you wanted to see the city," I said, hoping to lighten the mood.

"I'm frightened, Gaius Pliny." In the near-dark her soft voice seemed to come from far away. "I've never been so frightened."

I moved close enough to her that I could see her face. "That speaks well of your intelligence. You have good reason to be afraid."

"Domitian will try to kill me, won't he?" Her moist eyes begged me to tell her that wasn't true.

Damn Domitian! He used me as his hound to sniff out the prey, just as Tacitus suspected. As soon as he knew where she was, he would move in for the kill.

"I don't know how far he'll go." I was lying, of course. Domitian had already killed his brother to get to power and had killed Phineas' uncle merely because the mason knew that someone with Julius Caesar's blood existed. "His enemies would welcome a Julian heir. He will consider any descendant of Augustus a potential threat to his own power."

"Is that why Cousin Gaius lied to me?"

"I'm sure Musonius' only intention was to protect you."

"Who's going to protect me now?" She wiped a hand across her eyes.

I leaned toward Nelia and placed a hand on one of hers. "I will do everything in my power to see that no harm comes to you. I promise you that."

She did not seem reassured by the gesture. "You don't command any troops. How can you stand up against Domitian? You don't exactly look like Horatio on the bridge." She pulled away from my touch.

She was right. I couldn't play the role of one man valiantly holding off an advancing horde. The only way I could protect her would be to hide her, as Musonius had done. But too many people already knew about her. By now one of my own slaves who had been in the library might have said something careless. Those words would fly over my back wall and be in Regulus' ear with the speed of a lightning bolt. From there they would strike the Palatine.

"We can't defeat Domitian," Nelia said. "And I don't want to spend the rest of my life in hiding."

I just wanted to insure that she would have a rest of her life to spend, but I couldn't be so blunt. "Right now my only concern is to get you out of Rome until we can decide what we're going to do. For the time being you could go to my house at Comum. And Tacitus has property in southern Gaul. I'm sure you could stay there. Agricola might know some place in Britain where you would be safe." I congratulated myself for coming up with the germ of a plan so quickly.

"So your solution is to keep moving me farther and farther from Rome until I get to the edge of the world?" The fear in Nelia's voice gave way to a rising anger. "Then where? Ultima Thule? I'll bet Domitian would find me even there, if I didn't freeze to death first."

When someone of my class does something for a client or a friend, we expect them to express their gratitude, even if what we've done for them isn't all they wanted. That's how Roman society works. Being subjected to the anger and sarcasm Nelia was heaping on me in the gloom of my litter was like being spit on by some barbarian.

"By the gods! You are the most exasperating woman I have ever known. I've gone to great lengths to oblige Musonius by taking you into my home, clothing you, even buying you jewelry— "

She yanked the necklace off, breaking the clasp, and threw it at me. "I didn't ask you for any damn jewelry! I didn't ask you for anything. I just wanted to stay on Musonius' estate and be with Marcianus."

"This morning you said you didn't want to go back there with him."

"But I would if you'd never brought me to Rome. I could have been happy there, not knowing any of ... this."

"By 'this' do you mean Rome, or what you've learned about yourself tonight?"

"Both ... all of it. I wish I'd never seen or heard any of it." She wiped tears on her gown.

"I would gladly take you back tomorrow, but I'm sure Domitian already has his men watching the place."

Someone knocked on the wooden frame of the litter. "Sir," Laberius said softly, "may I speak with you?"

I stuck my head through the curtains. "What is it?"

Laberius drew back from my anger and motioned for me to keep my voice down. "There's some sort of disturbance ahead, sir, around the Amphitheater. The street's blocked."

Glancing ahead, I could see torches flaring, bobbing around in the dark as the people carrying them moved from one place to another. "We can get around them by going through the Forum and coming out beyond the Amphitheater."

"Is that safe at night, sir?"

"I think we'll be all right if we keep moving."

"Yes, sir. That's usually the safest thing to do, is to keep moving."

As I settled back in the litter Nelia drew herself up and wouldn't look at me. I was left to ponder the situation and my options. At first it seemed similar to the situation Musonius had faced fifteen years ago. But it was more complex. All he had to do was hide a small child, whose existence was known to almost no one and her true identity to no one except Musonius. In my litter, riding past Domitian's house at the moment, I had an heir of the Caesars, a grown woman, and a pregnant one at that. She knew who she was now, and so did a growing number of other people. Was it realistic to think about hiding her any longer?

In one sense she would be safer in my house here in Rome. If she were in some country villa, Domitian could send men to attack her without arousing much notice. He could hardly storm the house of someone of my status here in the city without provoking a strong reaction. Perhaps the wiser course, then, would be to keep Nelia in Rome but out of sight.

"Gaius Pliny," Nelia said from her corner, "I want to see the Forum."

"I'm not sure that's a good idea. The fewer people who see you, the better. The Forum will be very crowded in the morning."

"No, I want to see it now. If we're going through it anyway and if you're going to send me away soon, I want to see it."

She wasn't whining or pleading, the way I suspected Julia would. Her request fell on my ears like a command. Was that ability to bend people to her will something she had inherited from her imperial ancestors? Was it one more proof of who she was? All my life I've been taught that a person's true character cannot be hidden forever. Regulus might act like a kind and noble man for a time, but in the end his baseness would rise to the surface, the way a dead fish floats to the surface of a pond. Nelia might take on the guise of a country girl, but eventually her true imperial nature would assert itself.

"The Forum? At this hour? We're taking a big enough risk just dashing through it. If we stop and get out, we'll be risking our lives."

"Please. Just a quick peek. We have Laberius and the others to protect us. If you're going to bury me in Ultima Thule, I'd like to see this much of Rome before I go."

Feeling sure I would regret the decision, I poked my head out through the curtains and told Aeolus to take us on into the heart of the Forum. We were carried under the Arch of Titus and along the Via Sacra into the Forum. Nelia drew the curtains back.

"That's the house of the Vestal Virgins," I said, pointing to my left.

"I obviously don't qualify." Nelia patted her stomach. "I want to get out. How do I stop this thing?"

"You don't. I do." I put my arm out to signal Aeolus to halt. It takes a moment for the bearers to get themselves in position to put a litter down. But even before we touched the ground Nelia jumped out. The unexpected shift in the weight caused the litter to lurch to the other side, almost dumping me. I would have to give her some lessons in litter etiquette before letting her venture out in one again.

Recovering my dignity, I got to my feet, straightened my clothes, and wondered how best to protect us, but Laberius was already taking charge.

"This is foolhardy, sir," he said in a low voice.

"Tell that to your mistress," I said. "It's her idea."

"Let's make it quick then. Your man Aeolus and I are the only ones armed. He and half a dozen slaves should stay with the litter and the women. The rest can come with us."

"Laberius, you don't need to hover over me," Nelia said.

"My lady, don't you hear the vermin scurrying away from our torches? These are two-legged rats with no tails. Now, see what you want to see and be quick about it."

"What is this?" Nelia pointed to the triumphal monument in front of us.

"That's the Arch of Augustus," I said.

"It's a bit overdone, don't you think?" She turned her head to one side like an artist appraising her work.

"It's better not to say such things," I reminded her, "even when it's dark and you think there's no one around." I didn't admit that most people in Rome agreed with her. Unlike a typical triumphal arch, such as Titus', with its one opening, Augustus' was a triple arch. The central opening, a true arch, was flanked by two shorter passageways with flat ceilings. On top of those side openings stood statues of Parthians offering tribute to Augustus, shown driving a four-horse chariot on top of the taller central arch.

"Well, it is garish," Nelia whispered. Gathering up the loose folds of her stola, she passed under the arch and stopped in front of the building next to it. Laberius and I kept close to her. The slaves accompanying us huddled together behind us, hoping we would protect them, I think, rather than intending to protect us.

"That's the temple of the deified Caesar," I said. "Augustus built it where Caesar's funeral was held. That altar in front marks the very spot where Caesar was cremated."

I had never thought much about this building before, perhaps because I had always seen it as just a backdrop for the flurry of activity which is always going on in the Forum during the day. Now, standing here in the quiet, I sensed the truth of what Tacitus had said about the imperial monuments surrounding us, choking off the freedom of Rome's past.

Oddly enough, in spite of all the men honored here, Nelia carried Caesar's blood through women without whom the Dictator's bloodline would have dried up long ago. All of his 'descendants' ultimately came from his niece, Atia, the mother of Augustus and his sister Octavia. Anyone who was related to Augustus had to trace his or her ancestry back to Augustus' daughter or to his sister and her daughters. Augustus and his family ruled Rome for a hundred years, but no *princeps* in their line was succeeded by his son. And yet the only woman in the family honored by a monument was Octavia, and her portico was out on the Campus Martius.

This end of the Forum, the heart of Rome, had once been open. But, since the erection of Augustus' arch and Caesar's temple, no one could enter the Forum from this direction without walking through or around a structure that glorified Julius Caesar and the men in his family.

Just as Augustus' arch is larger than normal, Caesar's temple sits on an unusually high platform. Once you've climbed the steps to the speakers' rostrum in front of the building, there are five more steps leading up to the temple itself. Through the large double doors the statue of Caesar is always visible, as though he still presides over everything that goes on in front of him.

Nelia wasted no time climbing the steps. Her confident manner said she had a claim on these monuments which no one else in Rome could make. Or was she just too much of a country girl to feel the proper awe for the place? As she reached the rostrum and started up the steps to the temple, lightning flashed and thunder rumbled across the Forum. She stopped and raised her face to gaze at the huge statue of Caesar. A breeze sprang up, ruffling her stola and her hair.

I place no credence at all in the signs and omens which frighten the mob, and yet I couldn't help but shiver as I wondered if Caesar had recognized his own blood.

Another clap of thunder seemed to plant a question in my mind. Why did Nero drive Antistia and her father to commit suicide if their only connection to Caesar's bloodline was through her marriage to Rubellius? That was no connection to Caesar at all, or at least none that should have worried Nero once Rubellius and his son were dead. Without a male heir of Caesar's as her partner, Antistia could not produce another descendant of Caesar.

Unless she herself bore Caesar's blood!

Naomi and Domitia—a slave and a noblewoman who had no knowledge of one another—had testified that Antistia was the daughter of Agrippina. As unlikely as that seemed, I now realized that Nero himself had confirmed it. What reason would he have had for ordering the death of Antistia unless she presented a threat to him? And the only threat she—or any woman—could pose to Nero was her ability to produce a child who bore Caesar's blood.

If Nelia was Antistia's daughter, she posed that same threat for Domitian. I had no doubt Domitian would react to the threat exactly as Nero had done.

"My lady, we need to get out of here," Laberius said down below us. He took the torch from one of my slaves and thrust it out in front of him. Dim forms were creeping toward us.

"We'd better get down now," I told Nelia. Taking her hand, I could feel her reluctance to descend the steps of the temple.

Laberius drew his sword and gave the torch back to the slave. "Light that other torch, too."

"Do we want them to be able to see us?" I asked.

"A lit torch makes a better weapon than an unlit one," the centurion said. "Fire in his face will always make a man hesitate."

"Let's just call out for the Praetorians who're guarding the steps up the Palatine. Surely they'll hear us and—"

"And get here in time to count our dead, sir. This rabble has outflanked us. They've cut us off from the arch. We'll have to go around the other side of the temple. The gods only know what's waiting for us there."

Nelia clung to me as we began to work our way past the front of Caesar's temple. "Stay in a circle," Laberius exhorted my slaves, "facing out. Keep the lady and your master in the center. Stand firm and you might even win your freedom."

How dare the man offer *my* slaves their freedom? But I couldn't very well contradict him at this moment. We needed any incentive that would encourage a handful of unarmed house-servants to stand up against a gang of killers off the street.

"Something's odd here, sir," Laberius said to me over his shoulder. "They're not attacking us so much as they're herding us."

I sensed the truth of what he said, especially because the men around us were not brandishing knives or swords. They were using only clubs or their fists and seemed to be holding back, content, as Laberius said, to push us in one direction and into a tighter and tighter circle.

We had made our way to the very front of Caesar's temple when the men facing Laberius—what I thought of as the front of the line—surged toward us. At the same time the shadowy figures behind us melted away. We found ourselves giving ground, edging backwards, into the semicircle formed by the arms of the platform of Caesar's temple.

"Push!" Laberius cried. "Don't let them trap us."

But my slaves were overwhelmed by the weight of the assault. Some of the men surrounding us ran up the steps of the temple and jumped down on us. I put my arm around Nelia, pulling her down with me next to the altar in front of the temple.

Laberius fought bravely. Two men with swords emerged from the crowd attacking us, but they could not get past Laberius until someone ran up the steps of the temple and swung a club, striking Laberius on the back of the head. He crumbled to the pavement.

The two armed men, taller and stronger than any of the others attacking us, stepped over Laberius. One pulled me away from Nelia and flung me aside like an unwanted toy. My head struck the wall of the temple platform. I saw a bright flash and wasn't sure of anything for a moment until Nelia's scream cleared my head.

I looked up to see one of the men dragging Nelia away. To muffle her screaming, he put his hand over her mouth. *Fool,* I thought. In the next instant she bit him. He yelled and let go of her. Seizing her opportunity, Nelia picked up a torch that a slave had dropped. As the man advanced at her again, she thrust it into his face.

Dropping his sword, the brute screamed and grabbed at his eyes. He pulled a knife from under his tunic and lunged at Nelia, but, half-blind, he could only swing the weapon wildly. His partner and, I now realized, the leader of the attack, stepped in front of him. "Remember your orders!" he barked.

"Orders be damned! That bitch burned half my face off."

"We're here to do one thing."

The injured man tried to push past the other one. "She burned my face! I'm going to—" He gasped and doubled over as his companion plunged his sword into his belly.

Nelia took advantage of their confrontation to pick up the sword the injured man had dropped. I scrambled to my feet and grabbed Laberius' sword. My brief stint as a military tribune in Syria enabled me to look like I knew something about using it. The leader of the mob glared at us as though considering his options.

When he took a step toward us, Nelia drew the sword back over her shoulder. "I've slaughtered pigs bigger than you!" she cried.

The man gave a sharp whistle and the attack stopped. Two men picked up the dead assailant, and the crowd melted back into the shadows.

"Are you all right?" I asked Nelia. Any other woman I might have hugged for reassurance at that moment, for me as well as for her. But, with the sword in her hand and a kind of fire in her eyes, Nelia seemed unapproachable, an Amazon in the heat of battle.

"I'm fine," she said. "What about you?"

"Just a bump on the head." I turned to my slaves and quickly ascertained that one had been stabbed in the arm, but the others had suffered only bruises. Nelia knelt over Laberius, who was regaining consciousness.

"Carry him to the litter," I told the two nearest slaves. Nelia and I, swords at the ready, served as a rear guard while we quickly retreated from the Forum. When we reached the litter, Aeolus' eyes bulged in surprise. "My lord, what happened?"

"We were attacked. Why didn't you come help us? Didn't you hear the lady Cornelia scream?"

"I heard something, my lord, but you told me to stay here and guard the litter and the women."

I hate it when a slave can use my own orders as a defense. "We'll talk about it later. Let's get out of here."

"Yes, my lord." Aeolus began ordering people around, apparently glad to be back in charge with Laberius out of action.

As we placed Laberius in the litter, he mumbled, "My sword? Did I lose my sword?"

"We've got it," Nelia said, handing him the sword she was carrying.

Laberius ran his hand over the hilt and motioned for a torch-bearer to come closer. "This isn't my sword."

"Then I've got yours," I said.

"But this one—look here, sir." He pointed to the hilt. "The insignia. That's Praetorian."

211

XVIII

WHILE WE WERE MAKING Laberius and my slave comfortable in the litter my hand landed on the note Marcianus had sent to Nelia as we left the house earlier. Not even asking her permission, I found the stylus I always keep in my litter, smoothed out the wax in the tablet and wrote a brief message to Tacitus, telling him about the attack. On the facing side I made an impression of the Praetorian seal on the sword handle.

I picked out Critias, a slave whom I knew to be fast on his feet, and handed the tablet to him, wishing I could seal it properly. "Take this back to Cornelius Tacitus, as fast as you can. Tell him what happened here and that we have gone on to my house."

Critias looked up the dark street anxiously. "But, my lord ...?"

"I know there's some danger." I couldn't give him a sword. A slave running through the streets at night with a sword in his hand would be arrested by the first party of vigiles he encountered. I slipped the knife out of Laberius' belt and handed it to Critias. "Keep this out of sight, but at least you'll have it if you need it."

"Thank you, my lord."

"I don't know how Tacitus will respond, but I'm sure he'll send someone with you if he sends you back tonight with a message. And I'll see that you're rewarded for taking this risk." I patted him on the shoulder and pushed him on his way.

We proceeded home as fast as we could without causing discomfort to the injured men in the litter. Our arrival threw the house into an uproar. Nelia, finally giving in to tears, found comfort in Naomi's arms. My mother hovered over me, pressing me for the full story of the attack, while I tried to tend to the wounded.

We brought lamps into the atrium so Diocles, the freedman who had taken care of our medical needs since I was a child, could work. Two other men held the injured slave down and gave him a folded cloth to bite on while Diocles washed out the knife wound with the strongest wine we had and sewed it up with linen thread. My mother held the man's hand and comforted him the whole time. How could she be so sympathetic to his pain and yet so hard-hearted to Aurora?

When he finished, Diocles walked over to where I was sitting outside my tablinum, with my arms on my knees and my head down. "Are you all right, my lord? Were you injured?"

"No. I'm just suddenly exhausted from everything that's happened this evening." I looked up and took a deep breath. "How is he?"

"He'll be fine, my lord. It's a clean wound. There'll be a scar, of course, but I think it will heal quickly, with no lingering damage."

"What about Laberius?"

Diocles chuckled. "A head that hard isn't going to be affected by one blow, my lord. He'll be himself again by tomorrow."

"Good. Thank you, Diocles."

"Of course, my lord. I'll check on both of them early in the morning."

As he walked away that phrase, 'early in the morning,' hung in the air. Yes, Homer's 'rosy-fingered dawn' would inevitably come. Bringing with it—what? Domitian's soldiers knocking on my door? To whom would the Praetorian report about the failed attack on us in the Forum? When he noticed that a sword bearing the Praetorian insignia was missing, he was bound to realize I knew who was behind the attack.

What should I do? Would it be realistic to try to get Nelia out of the city? There wasn't any place under Roman rule that I could take her where Domitian couldn't find her. I had naively thought he might hesitate to attack her in Rome, but this evening had disabused me of that hope.

Three sharp knocks on the outer door reverberated through the atrium. Everyone looked in that direction and froze as though turned to stone by a glance at Medusa's head. The knocks were repeated.

By the gods! I thought. Are they here already?

Old Moschus, my doorkeeper, was still snoring in his bed, so Demetrius and I approached the door, as slowly and fearfully as characters in a Greek comedy. We heard a voice.

"Hello? Anyone? It's me, Critias. Let me in."

I sighed with relief as Demetrius slipped the bolt and opened the door. Critias entered, accompanied by two men. They had the hardened look of veteran soldiers, from the scars on their faces and arms down to the short legionary swords they carried, but they wore the tunics of working men.

"These are two of Agricola's veterans, my lord," Critias said. "Marcus Licinius and Publius Velleius." Each man nodded as Critias spoke his name. "They live near Cornelius Tacitus' house."

"Good evening, sir," Velleius said. "*Imperator* Agricola asked us to accompany your man and to relay his advice to you."

"I'll be happy to hear what he thinks."

"Shouldn't you offer them something to drink?" my mother said from behind me. I turned to find her, Naomi and Nelia eavesdropping on us.

"Thank you, but no, my lady," Velleius said. "We have an important matter to discuss with Gaius Pliny. Is there somewhere we could talk privately, sir?"

"Let's go in the tablinum."

When we got to the door of the tablinum, Nelia was right on our heels. Velleius placed himself in the doorway. "This is men's business, my lady. Please excuse us."

"You're going to talk about what to do with me," Nelia said. "I have a right to know what you're planning."

"Are you the lady Cornelia?"

"That's the name by which I've been known until today."

Velleius looked around at me for guidance.

"It would be just as well to let her hear what Agricola has in mind," I said. "It'll save me having to repeat it later."

Licinius closed the door of the tablinum and Nelia sat in one of the chairs facing my table. I sat behind the table, opposite her. Licinius and Velleius remained standing. The two small lamps still burning in the room left them half in shadow. When he spoke, Velleius sounded like an oracle pronouncing doom from deep within a gloomy cavern.

"I'll be brief, sir. Imperator Agricola recommends that you get the lady Cornelia out of Rome tomorrow morning."

"Tomorrow? Shouldn't we leave tonight?"

Velleius shook his head. "That's just the panic you're feeling, sir."

"Why shouldn't I feel panic?" I stood and came around to the front of the table. "Those were Praetorians who attacked us tonight. They had to be taking orders from Domitian."

"No doubt, sir. But they failed. If you give in to panic and run when an enemy's attack has failed, you give him the victory he couldn't earn."

"How can Agricola expect us to just sit here, waiting to be attacked again?"

"Moving at night is difficult, sir. If you don't use lights, you're stumbling along blind. If you do use lights, you're also marking the way for your enemy. Imperator Agricola urges you to spend the night preparing to move in the morning."

"Move? Where?"

"You usually take your household to one of your villas at this time of the summer, don't you, to escape the heat and pestilence of the city?"

"Yes. I was thinking of moving to Laurentium soon."

"That is imperator Agricola's recommendation."

"But where will I get wagons and horses and drivers on such short notice?"

"They'll be here at dawn."

"Agricola can do that?" Nelia said, sitting up straight.

"Those who've served under the imperator are always ready to answer his call, my lady. His veterans are settled all around Rome."

"But that will put us out on the open road in broad daylight," I said. "We'll be easy targets for Domitian."

"It's highly unlikely he'll attack you so openly, sir. There are no real charges he can bring against you or the lady Cornelia. That's why he tried to disguise his troops tonight and stage a kidnapping. Imperator Agricola believes he does not have any other strategy in mind. A good commander would, but Domitian's German campaign showed what kind of commander he is."

I leaned back against the table, feeling some relief at having decisions made for me, even if I wasn't entirely happy with them. "All right, then. What are we going to do? And does Agricola have an alternative plan?"

"He always does, sir, but I'm afraid you won't be terribly pleased with this one."

* * * *

I had never been happier to see the sky growing light. During the entire, sleepless night, as we packed, I kept expecting to hear Praetorians pounding on my door—or beating it down, more likely. But, as dawn approached, all we heard outside the house was the snorting of horses, the bellowing of oxen, and the creak of arriving wagons.

The loading of our gear went so smoothly I wished I could have a squad of retired soldiers on hand every time I needed to move. Even as tired as my slaves were, they responded to the veterans' efficiency by working more adroitly than I ever imagined they could. Before the first hour of the day had passed, the wagons were packed, the horses and oxen fed and watered. At this rate our caravan would be in Laurentium by late afternoon.

Our sudden departure did attract the neighbors' notice. In any other July my slaves would have gossiped with those in the houses around us for several days in advance of our leaving, saying goodbye to friends and lovers. Instead I had posted guards—a couple of more of Agricola's veterans who arrived shortly after Velleius—to make certain that no one left the house. If Regulus had planted a Sinon in my midst, the only thing I could do was contain him. In the morning I left it to Demetrius and my mother to satisfy the curiosity of those who stopped in. Our story was that a recent storm had done more damage to our crops in Laurentium than we first realized. I had already left to survey the situation.

Explaining my absence was easy. The hard part was sending my mother off in one direction while Nelia and I decamped in the other.

"Gaius, I'm frightened." Mother took my hand as we said goodbye in the atrium.

"You have nothing to worry about, Mother." That was my hope at least. "Agricola's verterans are with you, and more will join you along the way. We have to trust Agricola and be thankful he's with us."

"I suppose so, but look at you. Is this really necessary?" She stood back and shook her head as she picked at the dirty peasant's tunic I was wearing and touched the greasy spots on my face.

"If I'm going to ride in a cart with a group of workmen, I need to look like one of them. That's no place to flaunt an equestrian stripe."

"But it's so undignified, dear. It's as though you're some sort of criminal who can't even hold his head up in the streets of his own city."

I forced a laugh. "I could do the noble thing, like Cicero, and offer my neck to the executioner's sword."

She gasped and put a hand to her heart. "Oh, Gaius! Don't even joke about that."

"I can joke about it because this is such a minor inconvenience." I hugged her. "I'll get myself cleaned up when I get to Musonius'."

"But what about poor Nelia? Just cleaning up won't fix what's being done to her."

"We had no choice, Mother. And it's only temporary."

"Maybe not," Nelia said behind us. "I kind of like it this way."

We turned to see what appeared to be a peasant boy walking toward us in a dirty tunic that was a bit too large for him. Naomi had cut Nelia's hair almost as short as mine, so that it emphasized her square face. A strip of cloth wrapped around her chest had flattened her breasts. Her naturally low voice and her skin—brown from her life in the country and so unlike a Roman noblewoman's—would let her fit in with any gang of workmen. Standing next to her, I felt somewhat pasty myself.

Mother patted Nelia's hair like she was touching a dead animal. "Oh, dear. I had no idea it would be so short."

"It's all right, Mother Plinia." Nelia shook her head vigorously and ran her fingers through her hair. "In this hot weather it's actually quite comfortable. And it will grow back."

"May we all live long enough to see that," Mother said.

"On that cheerful note," I said, "it looks like we're ready to go. Here comes Velleius."

Agricola's veteran stopped a respectful distance from us and gave me a quick nod. "Sir, if you and the ladies are ready, we should be on our way."

We escorted my mother to the door, where Laberius was waiting beside one of my slave women who most closely approximated Nelia's height and build. With a scarf over her hair, the curtains on the litter partially drawn, and with my mother and Laberius to address her as Nelia now and then, she ought to convince the neighbors or any of Domitian's spies who might be watching that Caesar's heir was on her way to my estate south of Rome.

Mother patted the girl on the arm. "Just remember, dear, you must not call me 'my lady'."

"Yes, my lady ... I mean, no, I won't. I'm sorry. It's so hard, and it feels wrong. These clothes and the jewelry ..." She was close to tears.

"That's all right. We're all doing things and wearing things today that don't feel right. It might be better if you just let me do the talking."

"Yes, my lady." The girl clamped her lips together.

Laberius turned to Nelia. "My lady, I wish you would let me go with you. Gaius Musonius charged me to protect you."

"You're doing exactly what he asked of you," Nelia said. "By now I think anyone who's watching us knows you won't leave my side. If you're walking beside the litter on its way to Laurentium, they'll conclude that I must be in it. If you go with us in the cart, your very presence could defeat the whole plan."

"All right, my lady." The centurion bowed his head as though receiving an order from his commander. "But, if anything happens to you, I'll not rest until I find the man responsible."

I wasn't sure if he meant Domitian or me. I wanted to remind him it was Agricola's plan we were following.

"Now you need to go," Nelia said, turning him toward the door.

When Laberius was in position and the women were safely in the litter, Velleius jerked his thumb toward the back of the house. "This way, sir. My lady, if you please."

Outside the rear entrance of the house, behind a pair of horses, sat a cart with two large, solid wooden wheels and fence-like pickets around the sides but open at the back. It was long enough for a man to lie down in and a bit more than half that wide. On a bedding of straw it carried three plain clay jars with handles, lashed to the sides to keep them from tipping over. In spite of their covers the jars stank of the latrine. My house, like any large house in Rome, has water from an aqueduct flowing under the seats of its latrine. But not all of the waste gets flushed away, so twice a year I hire the people who clean out the public latrines to clean mine and cart the waste away. The three men on this cart were Agricola's

217

veterans, but they had cleaned enough material out of my latrine to make the show convincing.

One more jar still stood inside the rear door. Stopping us in front of it, Velleius picked up a handful of straw, dipped it in the jar and—before Nelia and I could anticipate what he was going to do—smeared it down the front of our tunics.

"Sorry, sir. My lady. You look the part, but you've also got to smell the part." Then he dipped the straw again and smeared it across his own tunic. "Now let's get this one stowed on the cart."

He placed the lid on the jar and looked at Nelia and me. "Let's go, men," he said loudly. "Master Pliny's not paying us to leave that stuff sitting around in his garden." Lowering his voice to a whisper, he said, "We do have to make it look real, sir. Some of Regulus' private guards are still out in the streets."

Nelia and I hoisted the jar, which came almost to my shoulders, and managed to get it onto the cart. It was the heaviest thing I had ever lifted. Velleius tossed me a piece of rope. "Tie her tight, boys. Let's go."

I walked around to the side of the cart and tied the stinking jar as securely as I could. Nelia gave it a tug, as though checking it. When she took hold of the side of the wagon to get in—call it instinct or stupidity—I started to take her elbow to help her up.

"Hey, don't try to hold me back, pal," she said, pushing me away with her foot. "Last one in has to sit between the jars, and it's not going to be me."

As soon as we found places to sit the driver flicked the reins and we started up the street, with the slop jars swaying precariously.

I slumped back and tried to breathe as little as possible. We had just reached the next corner, beside Regulus' house, when two of his guards stepped in front of us.

"Hold up there!" one of them ordered.

"What for?" our driver asked. "We've got a job to do."

"You'll have to wait until Marcus Regulus passes by."

* * * *

I nearly added some more stains to my tunic. "By the gods! What'll we do if he sees us?"

"Just stay down, sir," Velleius said, patting my arm. "A rig like this is all but invisible to someone of his rank."

"I'm 'of his rank'."

"No insult meant, sir, but would you even turn your head to look at us if you were walking by? Just stay down and you'll be fine."

He was right, of course. I would probably make a point of looking the other way, to avoid polluting my vision with so common and unpleasant a sight.

Nelia, who had crouched down beside me, wriggled her way to the front of the cart and peered between the two men sitting on the high driver's bench and over the backs of the horses.

"What are you doing?" I said. "Get down!"

"He'll never see me. And he wouldn't recognize me if he did ... May the gods strike me! Oh, Gaius, you must see this." She tugged on my tunic so urgently that I had to turn around and kneel beside her or have my garment ripped. My eyes widened in amazement.

Just a few paces in front of us strode Regulus, surrounded by thirty or more of his clients. A dozen of his slaves were outfitted as Scythian warriors, complete with long tunics over barbarian pants and leather boots, pointed caps with a ball on top and iron collars around their necks. They carried shields on their backs and had false beards pasted on. Forming a vanguard, they forced their way through the crowd of other men's clients like a spear point through unprotected flesh.

Toward the rear of the noisy cluster walked the great man himself, with a behemoth of an African slave behind him carrying a fan that doubled as a sun-shade, as though his master was some Egyptian deity. Roman aristocrats are no strangers to ostentation, but only a man supremely confident of his relationship with the *princeps* would risk such an audacious display.

"If imperator Agricola put on half as much of a show," one of the drivers muttered, "he'd be in prison by noon."

"And we'd have him out by dinner time," the other one said grimly.

As he turned his head to listen to a client, Regulus let his gaze wander toward the cart. I felt like he was looking straight at me. Regulus stopped and one of his clients called out an order, bringing the whole party to an instant halt. Regulus raised a hand toward the cart.

"You there!" he called.

My mouth dropped open and I wanted to scream. I heard Nelia gasp. But the driver, showing no emotion, remained slouched in his seat. "Yes, sir. What can I do for you?"

The crowd of people around Regulus fell quiet and parted like water giving way before the bow of a ship. I stayed where I was, with half of my dirty face poking up between the driver and his companion, afraid that, if I moved, I would draw more attention than if I stayed still. But, even when he was only two paces away, Regulus showed no sign that he recognized me.

Holding a scented handkerchief to his nose, Regulus asked the driver, "Have you been working in Gaius Pliny's house?"

"Yes, sir. That we have."

"Cleaning out the little turd's turds, eh?" His clients and slaves laughed like he was reciting Plautus. Nelia put her hand over her mouth to suppress a giggle.

"I suppose you could say that, sir," the driver said.

One of Regulus' clients broke wind noisily, provoking another round of laughter.

"Or you might put it that way," Regulus said, waving his hand as if to dispel the odor. "Tell me, is Gaius Pliny at home?"

"His steward said he's gone to one of his estates, sir."

"Laurentium?"

"I believe that's the one, sir." The driver pulled on the reins to steady the horses.

"Did you see a young woman in the house? Mousy brown hair, mannish features?"

Beside me, Nelia let out a squeak.

"Not down where we were working, sir."

"No, I suppose you wouldn't. All right, then. Go on about your business." Turning back to his entourage, he motioned for his steward to give the driver some money.

Regulus' steward is called Nestor, but he's a Jewish captive whose true name is Jacob. I have met him when he has come to my house to talk to Naomi and Phineas and accompany them to some sort of religious gathering. He is as noble a man as his master is base. As Nestor reached up to hand the driver a coin, his gaze fell on me and his eyes widened. I shook my head frantically, and he managed not to say anything. Although he glanced back at me again as he rejoined Regulus' entourage, I did not see him speak to anyone.

With the street clear, the guards signaled for the cart to proceed. When the driver turned and started up the street in front of Regulus' house and I could look at the back of my nemesis' head, the tightness in my chest began to ease. Lying on the straw in the bottom of the cart, I silently congratulated Agricola on the success of his plan. Nelia dropped down beside me.

"'Mousy' hair? 'Mannish' face? Who does that pompous ass think he is?"

"Well, at the moment you do look more like Cornelius than Cornelia," I said.

"But he was talking about how I looked before this." She kicked at the straw, but her foot hit the last slop jar, the one I had tied to the side of the cart.

"Watch out!" Velleius cried.

Too late. The rope was loose and the jar was sliding toward the rear of the cart as we continued uphill. I grabbed for it, but all I managed to do was tip it as it fell into the street. It was sturdy enough to roll a few paces before it shattered.

A stream of reeking waste flowed down the hill, overtaking Regulus' party. Those in the rear began to lose their footing. The black giant fell on his back, knocking Regulus' feet out from under him. The great man collapsed in a puddle of waste—my very own waste, but that gave me no satisfaction. A confused cry went up until someone turned back to see us. Then we heard Regulus, still flat on his back, bellow, "Get them!"

Our driver urged the horses on, but the hill was steep and we couldn't get much speed. The crowd was gaining on us.

Drawing his sword, Velleius cut the rope holding another of the slop jars. "Give me a hand," he ordered. Nelia and I helped him tip the jar out of the cart. It shattered on the second bounce. "Now the next one," Velleius said.

With the weight lightened, the horses began to make headway. The crowd chasing us found the footing more and more treacherous as the incline became slicker. Several of the mock Scythian warriors ended up face-down on the pavement, mopping it with their false beards. Then we crested the hill and entered the Gardens of Maecenas. The noise of the mob behind us faded. A left turn on the Via Labicana brought us to the road that runs down the other side of the Esquiline Hill.

Velleius tapped the driver on the shoulder. "We've lost them. You can slow down. No sense drawing any more attention to ourselves."

"I'm so sorry," Nelia said as we settled down in the straw. "I never meant—"

"Accidents happen, my lady," Velleius said with a shrug. "Although, if that last jar had been tied more tightly ..."

At least he didn't look directly at me when he said it.

* * * *

The road we were now on ran parallel to the old wall of Servius Tullius, with a narrow stretch of trees and open land between us and the wall on our left. We passed under two aqueducts, the Anio Vetus

221

and the Aqua Marcia. Just after we passed the Viminal Gate and crossed the old Via Tiburtina we could see, beyond a block of shops and apartment buildings, the wall of the Praetorian Camp looming on our right. Under the old Republic it had been illegal to station armed troops in Rome—anywhere in Italy, for that matter. Augustus, when he created the Praetorian Guard, first housed them in small units in the villages and towns around Rome, as though he could conceal their existence. His succcessor, Tiberius, dropped all pretense and built this fortress just outside the original walls of the city.

Inside the Colline Gate, Rome's northernmost gate, sits a small temple of Fortune—blind chance elevated to the status of divinity. That was where we were to meet Agricola. We had to pause at the gate to allow a unit of Praetorians to pass through. I crouched in the back of the cart and kept a firm hold on Nelia's arm.

"Don't go anywhere near that last jar," I said.

"I think it's securely fastened," she shot back, yanking her arm free as the cart started to move again.

A man who still stood like a legionary at attention was holding the reins of three horses outside the temple. When the cart stopped he nodded to Velleius, who told Nelia and me to enter the sanctuary.

I had to stop just inside the door to let my eyes adjust to the gloom. The temple faced southeast, but, because of its narrow doors, little sunlight penetrated to the interior, even at the height of summer. Two torches flickering near the altar only emphasized the enveloping darkness.

In the light of those torches we found Agricola and Tacitus studying the lead tablets fastened to the wall, on which people had recorded their thanks to the goddess for favors granted in response to their prayers—a safe voyage, the birth of a healthy son, a winning bet on a gladiator. In their tunics without the equestrian stripe, Agricola and Tacitus looked like shopkeepers or out-of-town visitors. But at least their tunics were clean.

"Well," Agricola said when he saw us, "it looks like we owe the goddess another tablet."

"I won't acknowledge the debt until we get to Musonius' villa," I said.

Something in my tone must have alerted him that all had not gone quite as planned. "Did you run into any problems?"

Before Nelia could reply I said, "We're here. That's enough for now. What next? I thought you were going to have some of your veterans ready to accompany us."

"They'll join us along the way. I can't gather too many of my men at one time, especially in the shadow of the Praetorian Camp, without attracting attention. And we don't want to do anything that draws attention to us right now."

Nelia rolled her eyes at me.

"I think there's a story here that needs to be told," Tacitus chuckled.

"It will have to wait until we're well away from Rome," I said.

"Then let's get started." Agricola gestured toward the door of the temple but was careful to keep some distance between himself and Nelia and me. "Velleius certainly gets credit for authenticity," he said, wrinkling his nose.

As Nelia and I climbed back into the cart Agricola looked puzzled. "Only one jar?"

"We had to ... improvise at one point, sir," Velleius said.

The Via Nomentana runs northeast, straight out of the Colline Gate. Just outside the gate the Via Salaria branches off and runs almost due north, up the valley of the Tiber. That was our route. About six miles ahead, Agricola explained, there was a side road crossing the Tiber and connecting to the Via Flaminia, the road which would take us to Musonius' villa.

Even though I was rattling along next to a stinking slop jar, it proved a pleasant journey, taking us first into the low hills surrounding Rome.

"Have you ever been along this road?" Tacitus asked me.

"My uncle took me once to see the falls on the Anio."

"Extraordinary, aren't they?"

"I've never seen anything quite like them."

When my uncle took me to see the falls where the Anio comes down out of the mountains I was only ten, so I didn't remember much about the trip. Today I felt I was seeing this area for the first time. Near Rome the road was bordered by expensive villas, their whitewash fresh and their red tile roofs in excellent repair. As the road rose into the hills, the houses became less frequent and more rustic, some even with thatch roofs.

I felt a sense of desolation around us. Then I realized that many trees along this route had been cut to fuel the furnaces of Rome's baths. Scrubby bushes were growing up in their place. The sight reminded me of my uncle's description of how the army had stripped Judaea of its forests to build the huge ramp which, after three years, enabled them to move their siege engines up to take the hilltop fortress of Masada. Would we denude the Apennines just so we could soak in hot water every day?

Here and there along the way we were joined by Agricola's veterans in twos and threes, some carrying bags of supplies across their horses. Velleius had to tell each new batch about our misadventure with the slop jars. Tacitus laughed harder every time he heard the story. In the final rendition Velleius had Regulus swimming upstream in a sewer with his mouth open.

By midday, when we reached the bridge over the Anio River, we had twenty men with us and a couple of extra horses. It had been about half an hour since we passed the last suburban villa.

"This is a good place to rest," Agricola said. "There are no curious neighbors. We'll have something to eat. Those who need to can get cleaned up. A couple of you men, get that jar out of the cart and dump it. No sense taking any more chances with it."

"Don't worry," Velleius said. "I tied that one."

To hide my burning face I turned to help Nelia out of the cart, but she ignored my offer and jumped down. I turned to Agricola.

"Are you sure we're safe here? Shouldn't we keep moving?"

"We're not being followed. I'm sure of that. I will post a couple of lookouts, though, just to be sure. You can relax, eat and bathe."

Shading her eyes against the sun, Nelia looked up at Agricola, who had not dismounted yet. "It won't do us much good to bathe, if we don't have clean tunics to put on."

"Everything will be provided," the general replied.

One of his veterans opened a sack he'd been carrying. "You requested five, sir. I brought a couple of extra as well." He tossed the garments to those of us who had been riding in the cart. They were coarse but clean.

"Who has the oil?" Agricola asked. Several of the men brought out small clay jars.

"Let's go downstream," Velleius said to the two men who had been with us in the cart, and they set off.

"I guess that means I'll go upstream," Nelia said.

"Shall I send someone to stand guard for you?" Agricola asked.

Nelia glanced around at the assembled veterans, then slipped her arm through mine. "Gaius Pliny can escort me."

"I assure you," Tacitus said, "he'll be a perfect gentleman."

"That's what I'm afraid of," Nelia quipped over her shoulder.

The headwaters of the Anio are the source for two of Rome's aqueducts, including one of its oldest, the Anio Vetus, which supplies the water for my own house. The river's waters are considered the most wholesome in the city. I dipped my hand in the stream and enjoyed a drink. "This will be a cold bath," I said.

"That's the way we bathed most of the time at Musonius' house," Nelia said. "He believes a hot bath weakens the soul."

We made our way up the riverbank for a few minutes, brushing aside foliage that was still wet and stepping over tree roots. The recent rain had left the ground spongy in spots. Nelia slipped off her sandals, obviously feeling more comfortable out here in the country where she had grown up.

"I hope I don't fall in," she said with a laugh. "I don't have enough hair for you to grab hold of and pull me out this time."

"You're assuming I would try to save you."

She looked up to reassure herself that I was joking. "No one would blame you if you didn't. I know I've been nothing but trouble for you, right up until this morning. And I'm sorry if I've been discourteous to you today. My tongue seems to have a life of its own sometimes, especially when I'm nervous."

"It's been a difficult day for all of us. But in a few hours you'll be back home."

She stopped and looked over the river, in the direction of Musonius' villa. "That's what I'm nervous about."

"What do you mean?"

"I don't want to go back to Musonius. How can I? He has lied to me for fifteen years. Can I even call him 'Cousin Gaius' any more? If I'm who you say I am, then he might as well be a stranger to me."

"You can't mean that. Whatever blood connection he has to you—or doesn't have—Musonius has been the only father you've ever known. The only reason he lied was to protect you. That attack in the Forum last night should show you how right he was to fear for your safety."

"I've been thinking about that attack. How can you be so sure it had anything to do with me being descended from Caesar and Augustus? You only figured that out yesterday. How could Domitian have learned about it so quickly?"

I looked around, wishing she would keep her voice down and avoid naming certain persons. "Remember all those servants of mine who were in the library when we were talking? Any one of them could have spilled the secret, even unintentionally, to someone who would pass it along to … an interested party. Or someone at Tacitus' house could have overheard our conversation in the garden, completely unknown to us. Rome has more ears than Argos had eyes."

"But what's so important about me? Any of Julius Caesar's blood that I might carry must be diluted by now. It would be no more his blood than the watered-down wine we give to children is real wine."

"But *both* of your parents were descended from Caesar, and your grandmother was descended from both Augustus and Octavia, so in you that blood is strengthened. You have as much of Caesar's blood as someone from two or three generations ago."

"If that means I have to spend the rest of my life hiding in shit-stained clothes, I'd rather open my veins and spill that deified blood on the ground right here."

"There's no need for anything so drastic. We just have to get to a safe place where we can consider what to do next. The very next thing we have to do is bathe and get back or we won't get anything to eat."

About fifty paces farther on we found a spot where a stream fed into the Anio. Because of all the rain we'd had over the past few days, the stream and the river were both full to their banks. Where the stream entered the river it had carved out a pool with enough shrubbery growing beside it to create a screen.

"I can bathe on the other side of these bushes, in the stream," Nelia said, "and you can bathe on this side, in the river."

Once she had stepped through the bushes I realized they did not make as solid a screen as she thought they might. Rather than disturb her, though, I slipped into the water and kept my back turned to her. I would have liked to have had a scraper, but the flowing water and the scented oil did a lot to revive my spirits.

I was trying to bathe hurriedly, but I froze when I felt a pair of hands on my shoulders. Then I heard Nelia's voice right behind me.

"I'll wash your back if you'll wash mine."

"WELL, *THERE* YOU ARE," Tacitus said when Nelia and I rejoined the group. "Finally! How far upstream did you have to go to spawn?"

I reddened, but Nelia just smiled. She didn't even lower her head to cover her embarrassment, if she felt any. When he saw our reactions I knew Tacitus—and probably everyone else around me—realized what had happened between us. Cocking his head, he raised his eyebrows at me in a silent question. I was still too pleasantly stunned by our love-making to know how to respond. Under no circumstances, though, was I going to make a joke or embarrass Nelia.

Instead I turned to the veteran in charge of dispensing the food. He bore a scar starting in the hair above what remained of his left ear and running down to his chin, a disfigurement so ugly I couldn't stop looking at it.

"Is there any lunch left?" I asked, trying to force my eyes to meet his.

"Nothing fancy, sir. Just some bread and cheese and a bit of dried fish. There's a couple of wineskins. Some of the men brought cups, if you don't mind sharing."

"How are you mixing the wine?"

"We're, each of us, just drawing water out of the river to suit our own tastes."

Tacitus raised the cup he had just filled with water. "Given the story we heard on the way here, we should make sure neither of them pissed in the river while they were upstream."

"No, of course not," I snapped.

"I did," Nelia said, "but it's so diluted by now you'd never know it was there." She gave me a hard glance.

Tacitus emptied his cup back into the river.

* * * *

Nelia and I were given horses to ride for the rest of the trip. Along with Tacitus, we rode in the middle of the procession, whose pace was set by the lumbering cart. Once we crossed the Anio we turned onto a side road of packed gravel that connected with the Via Flaminia. The land was flat now, and houses were rare on the river side of the road, because of the danger of flooding. On the other side most of the land was given over to grazing sheep.

Tacitus seemed more full of chatter than usual. He informed us that Julia, the daughter of Augustus and therefore Nelia's great-great-grandmother, had made it her practice to take a lover only when she was pregnant. "She liked to say she took on a passenger only when the hold was full."

For the first time since we met, I found myself wondering if he and his wife were as different as he liked to think. Perhaps he complained about her talking so much because he couldn't talk as much as he wanted to with her around. I was relieved when Nelia leaned toward him and said, "Cornelius Tacitus, I'd like to talk with Gaius Pliny alone for a moment. Will you excuse us?"

"Certainly, my lady. I'll go concoct some further strategy with Agricola. This whole plan was my idea, you know." He winked at her and urged his horse forward.

Nelia and I guided our horses to the side of the road and slowed down to let everyone else pass us. Then we fell in at the rear, a few paces behind the last horseman.

"Are you still anxious about seeing Musonius again?" I asked.

"Yes, but that's not what I want to discuss now. I want to talk about what happened when we were bathing."

"I think Tacitus has said more than enough about that."

"He certainly has. I want to tell you why it happened."

Since I had no idea why it happened, I was curious to hear what she had to say.

"I don't love you, Gaius Pliny," she began.

"I never thought you did." That was what I thought she wanted to hear.

"Please, don't interrupt me. I need to just say this. I don't mean to be heartless. There is something very appealing about you. You're quite handsome, especially your dark eyes. You are a gentleman, and you've been as kind to me the last few days as any man could possibly be. I admire you and respect you. When we left Rome this morning I thought that was all I felt for you. Now ..."

"There's no reason you should feel any more than that," I said, growing uneasy with the direction the conversation was taking.

"There are all kinds of reasons for any woman with good sense to fall in love with you. But so much has happened to me in the last few days that I'm not sure I have good sense any more. I don't know who I am, and

I don't know if anything I've believed until now is true. I thought I loved Marcianus, and then I thought I didn't. I thought I didn't love you, but now ... I don't know."

I didn't know what I felt either. I grew up assuming I would marry some day. It's what men of my class—with rare exceptions like my uncle—are expected to do. But I thought of it in terms of finding a suitable match, not falling in love with a woman. Since I had no male relatives older than myself, I would have to arrange my own marriage. That gave me more freedom than most men enjoy, but also left me with more responsibility. I had experienced love-making with three women before today. Nelia was not the prettiest or the most expert, but she was the only one I could remember now.

"To put it in the simplest terms, Gaius, I seduced you in the river because I wanted to know if there was anything more to making love than I experienced with Marcianus."

Irritated by her callousness, I waved a hand at the line of veterans riding ahead of us. "Why stop with just me? You could have your pick of eager volunteers. Line them up! Sample them all."

"You don't have to make me sound like a whore!" She lashed me across the leg with the end of her reins.

The last man riding ahead of us cocked an ear toward us.

"Eyes front, soldier!" Nelia ordered, then lowered her voice.

"I didn't want some brute who would come at me like a rutting animal. Marcianus taught me what that felt like. You are a gentle, sophisticated man. I wanted to know if someone like you could give me the experience in love-making that Ovid talks about when he says 'the woman should feel the act of love to her marrow'."

"I thought Marcianus introduced you to Ovid and the other erotic poets."

"He did, but I think he got most of his ideas about love-making from watching the animals on his estate. The stallion never worries about whether the mare is enjoying herself. I had to find out if I could find pleasure with a man."

I twisted my mouth in disgust. So Marcianus was a stallion. What did that make me? "Did I succeed on your test?"

"The question is not whether *you* succeeded. I did. Twice, all the way to the marrow. The problem is—and this doesn't make any more sense to me than it will to you—the problem is, you don't feel dangerous, like Marcianus. I know I would be completely safe with you. But, for some reason, I want the man I'm with to feel dangerous."

Oddly enough, I can understand that. You're the most dangerous woman I've ever known.

229

* * * *

We arrived at Musonius' villa in the late afternoon. Another dozen of Agricola's veterans—some on foot—had assembled nearby and joined us, piling into the cart, as we turned onto the narrow road leading to Musonius' house. This time his servants could not stop us and ran ahead to warn him. Musonius met us in front of the house, wearing his anger openly. He showed no sign of the illness that had him doubled up in pain a few days ago.

"Gaius Pliny! Cornelius Tacitus! What is the meaning of this invasion? I told you before that I prefer not to have guests out here."

"Why?" Nelia asked, still partially hidden behind Agricola. "Are you hiding another little 'cousin' from the world?"

"Nelia? Is that you?" Musonius stretched his neck to look around Agricola.

She urged her horse forward. "Nelia? Is that who I am, 'Cousin' Gaius? Can I still call you cousin? You see, I'm not sure any more. You're going to have to tell me the truth."

Musonius grabbed the reins of my horse, his face glowing red. "What have you told her?"

"Just what I've been able to deduce. There are still some large questions that only you can answer."

The old philosopher's shoulders sagged in an admission of defeat, and he sighed like a man on his deathbed. "Very well. May I know whom you've brought with you?"

"This is my father-in-law," Tacitus said, "Gnaeus Julius Agricola. And these men are veterans of his."

"This is an honor, sir." Musonius bowed his head.

"For me as well," Agricola replied. "I'm sorry we could not ask your permission before our arrival, but we believe Nelia is in danger and we needed to get her out of Rome quickly."

"You're welcome, of course," Musonius said. "The stables are over there. I'll see that provisions are made for your men."

We dismounted and let Agricola's veterans lead our horses away. "We brought our own supplies," Agricola said. "I would not expect anyone to feed this many guests dropped on him without warning."

"That's gracious of you." Musonius stepped forward to embrace Nelia, but she drew back from him. "Well," he said, dropping his arms to his sides, "I guess we have some things to talk about."

"Where can we be certain we won't be overheard?" Agricola asked.

"Let's go into the library."

"I'll post a few of my men, just to be sure. And a few around the edge of your estate."

With the guards in place and the door closed, we took seats around the main work table in Musonius' library. It was smaller than mine, but most private libraries are. Nelia sat next to me and would not meet Musonius' gaze. Agricola looked at me and nodded. I took that as a signal to begin.

"This all comes down to two questions," I said. "First, is Nelia the daughter of Rubellius Plautus and Antistia?"

Musonius nodded, looking at Nelia with sad eyes. "Yes, she is." Nelia gasped.

"Then, was Antistia the daughter of the younger Agrippina?"

Musonius seemed surprised by the question. "If she was, no one ever told me. I was no confidante of Agrippina's. The only time I met her was that one incident which you seem to have read about in a letter of hers."

"But didn't Agrippina arrange the marriage between Antistia and Rubellius?"

"Yes. She took an interest in the career of Antistia's father, Lucius Antistius Vetus. Rubellius told me Vetus had shown her some kindness during her exile on Pandateria, but she never discussed the matter with me."

I told him what we had learned from Naomi about Agrippina giving birth to a daughter while she was on Pandateria and entrusting that child to Antistius Vetus.

"Now that is news indeed," Musonius said. "Stunning news, but it might explain something that has puzzled me for years."

"What's that?" Agricola asked.

"When Nelia was three, Nero forced Antistia and her father to commit suicide. Vetus had been involved in a plot to overthrow Nero, so I could see why Nero would want him out of the way, but I never understood why he wanted Antistia dead, too. It seemed to be just one more example of his blood-lust. Caesar's bloodline came through Rubellius, I thought. Without him to father a child, Antistia was no threat, even though she was intelligent and energetic."

"But if Antistia was Agrippina's child," I said, "then any child of hers, no matter who the father was, would carry Caesar's blood and could become a potential rival."

"Or the mother of a rival," Nelia said, resting a hand on her stomach.

Agricola drummed his fingers on the table. "That strikes me as a compelling piece of evidence."

"And, on top of the pictures that Maxentius saw in the Golden House, also evidence that Nero knew Agrippina's secret," Tacitus said. "She must have told him, taunted him with it perhaps."

I turned back to Musonius. "And Agrippina never suggested any of this to you?"

"As I told you, Gaius Pliny, I met her only once. That's why, after

Nero murdered her, I was astonished when a woman claiming to be a servant of hers showed up at my door with a box. She said Agrippina had instructed her to see that I got it."

We all sat up. "What was in the box?" Nelia asked.

"Several documents, none of which I could read."

"Why not?"

"They were written in some barbaric form of Greek. I couldn't make anything of it."

"Etruscan!" Nelia cried. "It must be Etruscan. Do you still have it?

"Of course." Musonius got up and walked over to one of his book boxes. "Perhaps one of you young men can give me a hand." I jumped up to help him. Together we lifted the box and set it on the floor. Behind it a small niche had been carved into the thick plaster wall.

"I never knew that was there!" Nelia said. "I thought I had gone over every inch of this library."

"It wasn't intended to be easy to discover," Musonius said.

All the niche contained was a plain wooden box. Musonius set it on the table in front of Nelia. Opening it, she took out two thick scrolls. The box contained four more.

"That's Agrippina's seal," I said, pointing to the image pressed into the wax.

Nelia started to unroll one of the scrolls. "It's definitely Etruscan," she said.

"Why would Agrippina have scrolls written in Etruscan?" I asked.

"When she was a child," Tacitus offered, "she lived in her uncle Claudius' house for a time. Didn't you say, Nelia, that Claudius knew Etruscan?"

Nelia nodded, already absorbed in reading the scroll.

"What does it say?" I asked.

"I believe it's her memoirs."

"But her memoirs are written in Greek," Tacitus said.

I picked up the other scroll, which also bore Agrippina's seal, and looked at it, even though I could make no sense of it. "The version she published is in Greek. I think we've found the original, the one Domitian asked us to find. We'll have to compare it with a Greek version and see if anything has been omitted."

"Can you actually read it?" Musonius asked Nelia.

"It will take me a while. I've never had this much to read in Etruscan, but I think I can do it. What else is in there?"

Musonius lifted out a few loose pieces of papyrus, each bearing the same seal. "These look like short letters. See, the date at the bottom is in Latin."

"Let me see if I can read any of it." Nelia took one of the sheets from Musonius and studied it for a moment. Then she wiped tears from her eyes.

"What is it?" I asked softly.

"Agrippina is writing to her 'beloved daughter.' She's afraid Nero is going to kill her and she wants to say good-bye, even though she knows the girl will probably never see the letter. She says she's sorry she had to give up her daughter, but she had no choice. 'My arms have ached to hold you. Nothing has ever filled the emptiness in my heart caused by the loss of you.' But she's proud that her daughter has grown into such a beautiful, intelligent woman. She has done all she can, she says, to put her in a place where she'll be protected."

"Against a tyrant, is there any sure protection?" Agricola muttered.

Nelia put her hand over her eyes and began to weep. I took her in my arms and she let her head fall on my shoulder. "Oh, Gaius, this is a letter ... from my grandmother ... to my mother. I never knew my grandmother and I can't remember my mother."

"Can we regard this question as settled?" Tacitus asked. "Nelia is the daughter of Antistia and the granddaughter of Agrippina, thus a direct descendant of Augustus and one who bears the blood of Julius Caesar."

Agricola cleared his throat. "Forgive me for injecting a note of skepticism into a very touching moment, but aren't we still making an assumption? I would hate to undertake a military campaign based on this large a guess about what the enemy was going to do. Agrippina doesn't mention any names in that letter. Can we be certain about the identity of this daughter? Let's wait to see what she says in her memoirs, if she gives any more specific details."

"What more do you want?" Tacitus asked.

"Something indisputable."

"What about a physical resemblance?" Musonius said.

Agricola nodded. "That would help to convince me."

"Consider this," Musonius said. "Nelia has several extra teeth on the upper right side of her mouth."

"We've seen them," Tacitus said. "And we've been told that her mother had the same—"

Nelia slapped her hand on the table. "Why is everyone so obsessed about my damn *teeth*?"

"Something that distinctive can be a way of identifying a person," Musonius said. "On one occasion Agrippina herself used teeth that way. She had had one of her rivals executed. When the head was brought to her, it was so badly mutilated she couldn't be sure it was the right woman until she noticed a discolored tooth. Perhaps she was so conscious of teeth because she herself had the extra teeth which Nelia has, in the same place."

"I thought you met her only once," I said. "How would you know such an intimate detail?"

"Your uncle mentions Agrippina's teeth in his *Natural History*." He chided me with his eyes. "You really should read your uncle's work, Gaius Pliny."

I wanted to say, *But there's so much of it.* Somehow I didn't think Musonius would accept that as an excuse.

"And, what's more," he said, "Rubellius once remarked to me how peculiar it was that he knew two women who had those extra teeth—his wife and the mother of his cousin Nero. I guess we were too obtuse to imagine any connection."

I unrolled the scroll a little farther, as though I could actually read it. "There's no reason that you should have. Agrippina went to great lengths to keep the secret of her second child."

"I think that settles everything," Agricola said. "I'm going to see to my men."

"Then we'll have something to eat," Musonius offered.

Musonius was reaching to open the door of the library when one of Agricola's guards knocked and opened it from the other side.

"Begging your pardon, sir, but there are two men here who claim to come from Gaius Pliny's household. They say it's urgent that they speak to him."

Agricola looked at me and I shook my head. I knew of no reason anyone from my household would be here.

"Bring them in," Agricola said, "but keep a hand on your swords." He gripped the hilt of his own weapon.

The soldier spoke to someone behind him. "Go on in."

My mouth dropped open when I saw Phineas and Glaucon, both looking dirty and frightened.

"My lord," Phineas gasped, falling to his knees. "It's terrible. Terrible."

I let Nelia sit down, still clutching the letter, and took a step toward my servants. "What's the matter?"

"They've been arrested, my lord. We barely got away." Phineas began to cry.

I grabbed the front of his tunic and shook him. "Who's been arrested? Make sense, man!"

"Everybody, my lord," Glaucon said. "Your mother, Naomi, Laberius, Demetrius. Everyone who was going to Laurentium. They've all been arrested."

"Arrested? What on earth for? They haven't done anything."

"It's you they want, my lord," Glaucon said.

"Me?"

"Yes, my lord. You're charged with the murder of a Roman citizen, Quintus Decius."

I snorted in disbelief. "Quintus Decius? I never heard of the man. How could I have killed him?"

"He's also called the Cyclops, my lord."

* * * *

We gave them something to eat and drink and Glaucon and Phineas told us the whole story—how they had been at the end of the caravan, how a unit of Praetorians had stopped them as they were rounding the foot of the Caelian Hill, how they had heard the charge against me and mixed in with the crowd that gathered to watch.

"Then we slipped away," Phineas concluded. "We were fortunate to escape. I still don't know how they missed us."

"They didn't miss you," Agricola snapped. "You were let go so you could lead them straight to your master."

"But no one followed us, my lord!" The dismay on Phineas' face when he realized what he'd done seemed genuine. "I didn't know where to go. Glaucon said we should come here to you."

Glaucon kept his head down. I wished any other slave in my household had accompanied Phineas because there was no other slave I trusted less. "No one followed us, my lord," the scribe said softly. "I'm sure of it. I know what you think of me, but I would never betray you."

Agricola brushed aside their protests. "All it would take is two men. They would follow you to see where you went. By now one is no doubt on his way back to report, and the other is watching in case we move before Domitian's men get here."

"We have to move, don't we?" I said, my voice rising in panic. "We can't just sit here and wait to be taken. It'll be the end for all of us." My mother was in the most immediate danger, I knew, but Domitian was after Nelia and me. If Agricola was caught trying to protect us, he and Tacitus would fall along with us, and Musonius would be dragged down as well.

This time there would be no exile to a rocky island. Not for any of us.

"If we move," Agricola said calmly, "we'll be out in the open. This place can be defended. I'll send a few of my men out tonight and have twice as many here by tomorrow morning. Domitian will probably send a small force to avoid drawing attention."

"Why do you think that?" I was amazed at Agricola's ability to put himself in the mind of his opponent.

"He knows he has to get Nelia, but he doesn't want a lot of people to know why. Since we arrived before your servants did, his look-outs don't know our strength. Whoever comes to arrest you tomorrow will be expecting to face a few of Musonius' servants, not a contingent of armed, experienced men. We'll have the advantage of numbers and surprise."

* * * *

Nelia and Musonius went off to talk privately. Nelia took the box containing Agrippina's memoir. I knew I shouldn't interfere. All I wanted to do was sleep, but that wasn't possible. With torches doused, Agricola, Velleius, Tacitus, and I sat in Musonius' open courtyard and talked long into the night about how we ought to proceed. Agricola kept most of his men out of sight in the stable, except for a few whom he stationed on the edges of Musonius' property. One of them reported that they had located the hiding place of Domitian's look-out.

"Shouldn't we capture him?" I asked. "Find out what he knows?"

Agricola shook his head. "He doesn't know anything. Whoever comes tomorrow may be expecting to see some signal that everything is all right. If they miss that signal, they're likely to wait and call in a larger force. As long as we know where the look-out is, he's no danger to us. We just have to be sure he doesn't see any unusual lights or movement to alert him to how many men we actually have."

"How can I just sit here when my mother is in Domitian's hands?"

"What could you do if you went back to Rome?" Tacitus asked.

"With Agricola's men—"

"My men aren't going back to Rome." Agricola's voice was quiet but rock-hard. "It would be foolhardy to storm the Palatine and try to rescue your mother. We don't even know if that's where Domitian is holding her."

I jumped up from my chair. "Do you think she might be in the Praetorian Camp?" Imagining her a prisoner in Domtian's house was bad enough. Any other possibility was too frightening to dwell on.

"You need to calm down, Gaius Pliny." Agricola grabbed my arm and pulled me back down into my chair. "Wherever your mother is, we don't have the forces to make a direct assault. Nor would I do so, even if I had a couple of legions under me. Any success I've had is due largely to one principle: whenever possible, make the enemy fight on my terms."

"But if we kill or capture a few of Domitian's men, he'll just send more. What do we gain by holding up here?"

"What would we gain by running?"

"Our freedom."

Agricola shook his head. "If we got across the Danube—which I'm certain we could never do—would you be content to live in a German's hut? Could you leave your mother in Domitian's clutches?"

"You've already said you won't go back to Rome to rescue her."

"That would be futile."

"But so is staying here to fight. And so is running away." I saw an abyss of despair opening in front of me. "Are you saying we have no hope?"

"No, I'm not. I'm formulating a plan, but before I can put it into action, I have to see who shows up here tomorrow."

By the time we went to bed the rain had started again, slow and steady. I took some comfort from knowing that Domitian's look-out would be thoroughly soaked by morning. We were likely to be damp ourselves. Musonius' rustic house, though it had no visible leaks, seemed to absorb moisture like a sponge. I wondered how he kept his books from rotting. Even Agrippina's memoir, which couldn't be more than twenty years old, already felt like a relic from Caesar's own time. If it wasn't re-copied soon, it would start to crumble and would ultimately be lost.

A servant showed me to a room next to Nelia's. Seeing a light under her door, I decided to risk a knock. She opened the door, still holding a scroll in her other hand. She barely looked up from it to speak to me.

"Oh, Gaius Pliny. What can I do for you?"

That thing you did in the river would be nice, was the first thought that came to my mind, but I managed to keep it there. "I just wanted to say goodnight. Musonius has put me in the room next door."

"Good. That's a comfortable room." She seemed ready to end the conversation, or perhaps just uncertain where to turn it.

"Is that one of Agrippina's scrolls?" I asked.

"Yes, I brought the box up here to study them."

She stepped back, inviting me to enter the room. The box of scrolls sat on a small table beside her bed. The only other pieces of furniture were a bronze lampstand and a chest with a small vase on it. Musonius kept to his Stoic—almost Spartan—principle of simplicity in his décor.

"Is that Greek?" I asked, nodding at the vase.

"No, it's Etruscan. We found it a few years ago when we were digging a well."

"It looks like it was done by a Greek artist."

"Or by someone who studied with the Greeks."

I peered closely at the vase, noticing a chip where a shovel had hit it. It depicted a muscular figure wearing nothing but a lionskin draped over his shoulder and carrying a club. Almost certainly Heracles. If only I could read the writing. But it probably said 'stallion.'

"What about the book? Can you read any more of it?"

"I've found the place where she talks about Pandateria."

"So quickly?" I turned back to Nelia.

"She didn't translate names of people or places into Etruscan. She just wrote them in Greek letters, so they're easy to spot." She showed me a place on the scroll. "See, here's her sister Livilla's name. And here's Pandateria."

"And that's Antistius, isn't it?" I said, pointing to a spot lower on the page.

"Yes. This is where she talks about having a daughter while on Pandateria and giving the child—my mother—to Antistius Vetus and his wife."

"That's the final bit of proof then, isn't it?"

"There's also this." She held up another one of the scrolls. I could see that an earlier work had been erased so the papyrus could be reused. "As often happens when a scroll is erased," Nelia said, "the older writing eventually becomes visible again. I guess the ink was absorbed into the papyrus more deeply than the pumice stone could erase and it rises to the surface. This is the scroll that Musonius gave Agrippina when he visited her with Rubellius—with my father."

She held the scroll under the lampstand at an angle and I could see Greek letters beneath Agrippina's Etruscan.

"His treatise on why women should study philosophy?"

"Yes." She dropped the scroll back into the box without even rolling it up. The confidence and bravado seemed to drain from her face, like water drains out of a bucket with a hole punched in its bottom. "Gaius, I'm so scared. Hold me."

I never did find out whether that other room was comfortable or not.

* * * *

At dawn more of Agricola's veterans began drifting in, one or two at a time, always from a direction that kept them away from Domitian's soggy look-out. Agricola's own look-outs were posted along the Via Flaminia, the most distant two miles down the road. They would pass along a signal as soon as they saw a squad of soldiers—or any group of men who even looked like soldiers out of uniform—headed our way.

Agricola still wouldn't tell us what his plan was while we ate a bit of breakfast. All he would says was, "One piece of what I need to know is still missing, and it's the keystone of the arch."

"Whatever you have in mind," Nelia said, "I'm going to be standing beside Musonius."

"My lady, if you'll pardon me, that's insane. You need to be well hidden. You're the treasure Domitian is looking for. We can't just put it out in front of him."

"He's never seen me," Nelia insisted, "not even with my hair long and in women's clothes. He'll never recognize me looking like this."

I put my hand on her arm. "But why do you have to take this risk, now that we—"

She jerked away from me. "Gaius, nothing that happened between us last night or this morning gives you the right to tell me what to do. I will stand by Musonius or I will reveal myself to whoever comes looking for me."

About the fourth hour we got word that a Praetorian officer and six men were headed in our direction.

"Only six?" I said.

"Remember, he doesn't have any idea of our numbers," Agricola said. Then his face darkened with a second thought. "Or he's got another contingent coming from somewhere else." He quickly ordered two men to ride north and see if anyone was coming from that direction. "He could have sent a messenger during the night to gather troops from beyond here. A single man could have slipped past us without notice."

At midday the Praetorians rode up to Musonius' house, as Agricola and I watched from behind the shutters in an upper window. Like everything else here, the shutters were old and badly in need of repair. The cracks and warped places in them gave us a perfect vantage point.

The man leading the Praetorians wore the praefect's armor, glistening in the sun which was now breaking through the clouds. He paid no attention to the 'servants' he saw working around the place, who were Agricola's veterans. As the horses came to a stop I got a better look at him.

"Great Jupiter!" I said. "Is that Domitian?"

Agricola didn't seem at all surprised. "Why, I believe it is."

I STARED AT DOMITIAN through a crack in the shutter and then back at Agricola in disbelief. "You knew he would come out here himself, didn't you?"

"'Knew' is too strong a word. I didn't see that he had any other choice."

"But why?"

"This is a job he can't trust to anyone else. Rumors can hurt him as much as facts. If there's one living relative of Julius Caesar left this long after Nero's death, might there not be others? He has to make certain Nelia is dead, along with anyone who knows about her."

"That would be you, me, Tacitus, Musonius. How many more?"

Agricola clapped a hand on my shoulder. "Trying to answer that question is what may drive him mad and what makes him so predictable. He can't trust the job to underlings. You know those myths where a servant is supposed to get rid of a baby but passes the job along to someone else ..."

"Who hands it off to someone else, and it never gets done."

"And twenty years later, there's the rival—Oedipus or Cyrus—who was never supposed to have survived infancy. Domitian knows those stories, so he knows this job has to be done by his own hand, today."

"Why didn't you tell me you expected him?"

"It would have ruined your night. Nelia's too, I gather."

I hadn't gotten much sleep. Fearing I might have to confront Domitian in the morning, though, would have unmanned me completely. I turned his question back on him. "Did you get any sleep?"

"Yes. A soldier learns he can't change what's going to happen in the morning, any more than he can stop the sun from rising. The best thing he can do is to make sure he's well rested and ready to face whatever awaits him." He patted me on the back. "Now that we have the keystone in place"—he pointed to Domitian—"here's what you have to do."

As Agricola revealed my part in his plan, we watched Musonius walk out to meet Domitian. Agricola had already explained Musonius' role to him—on the assumption that Domitian would show up and that Musonius wouldn't lose any sleep—so the philosopher was bent over and hobbling as though still in pain. One servant held his arm, while two others walked behind him.

The two behind him were Agricola's men, both with short swords concealed under their tunics. The one holding his arm was Nelia in her young man's disguise. Agricola and I both held our breath, but Domitian took no notice of her.

"Caesar Domitian," Musonius said, so weakly I could barely hear him, "this is an unexpected ... honor. What can I do for you?"

Domitian was having trouble keeping his horse still. The animal seemed to sense the danger to which his rider was oblivious. "You can surrender the criminal Gaius Pliny so he can face the charge of murdering the citizen Quintus Decius."

With Nelia's help Musonius labored down his steps and took the horse's bridle, rubbing his muzzle and calming him. "But, Caesar ..."

"Don't deny that he's here, old man. He arrived yesterday and hasn't left. I know that."

"Forgive me, Caesar. Yes, Gaius Pliny came here as my guest. You know what obligations a host has to his guest under Roman law and age-old custom."

"I know a Roman citizen cannot harbor a man who's guilty of murdering another citizen."

Musonius' eyebrows shot up and his voice strengthened. "Guilty? You said he was accused. What is so important about this matter that you yourself have ridden all this way to attend to it?"

From the way the soldiers looked at one another I could see Musonius' question was one they'd been asking themselves. The old philosopher's calm amazed me. He was within striking distance of several armed soldiers, but he might as well have been talking to a group of children. Of course, he knew that some of Agricola's men, with spears ready, were hidden on the roof of the house with orders to plant their weapons just above the breastplate of any man who reached for a sword.

Domitian pushed Musonius away with his foot, sending him staggering back. Nelia barely kept him on his feet. "This is your last chance, old man," the *princeps* growled. "Shut up and bring Pliny out here before I send my men in after him."

Musonius gestured for Nelia to fetch me. I met her just inside the door, trying to remember what Agricola had told me to say. He hadn't worked out all my lines because, he said, we didn't know exactly how Domitian would respond. I would have to improvise.

241

Nelia threw her arms around me and kissed me hard. "I pray to any and all gods that nothing happens to you," she said.

This was no time for a discussion of my skeptical views. Two of Agricola's veterans, who had been stashed in the library with Tacitus, joined us. We hesitated for a moment, to make it appear they had to search for me. Nelia mussed my hair and tore the front of my tunic, then ran back out to stand beside Musonius.

"Come out, Gaius Pliny!" Domitian called. "You can't escape. My men are all around this place."

A bald-faced lie. Agricola's look-outs had not reported seeing any other troops.

Agricola's men each took one of my arms and dragged me out onto the portico that linked the two wings of Musonius' house. This would give us four armed men ready to confront Domitian.

"Musonius!" I cried out, struggling with the men on either side of me. "You can't do this to me."

Leaning on Nelia, Musonius looked at me like Agamemnon about to sacrifice Iphigenia. "What else can I do, Gaius? The *princeps* himself has given me an order."

"But ... but you're my friend—"

"A criminal has no friends," Domitian sneered. He had dismounted and come to the top of the short flight of steps leading up to the portico. Agricola's men threw me to the ground in front of him, much more roughly, I thought, than our act required. I could feel that one of my knees was badly scraped.

I looked up at Domitian and launched into the crucial part of the drama. "Please, Caesar, don't do this. I'll do anything you want. I'll give you ... anything."

Domitian laughed harshly and shook his head. "You're a sniveling coward after all, aren't you? What do you think you could give me that I couldn't just take from you?"

"I'll give you ... the girl." I lowered my voice, but not enough that his soldiers couldn't hear me. "She's what you're really after, isn't she?"

Domitian grabbed me by the hair, pulled out an ivory-handled knife and pressed it to my throat. Before I could grab his hand I felt a sharp prick and a warm trickle of blood. Off to my left Nelia gasped. Agricola hadn't mentioned this in his plan.

"If you say another word," Domitian hissed in my ear, "I'll kill you right here."

"In front of all these witnesses?" I said softly, making him glance over his shoulder at his soldiers, who were still mounted. "How many of them will you have to kill then?"

Still clutching my hair, he pulled me to my feet and dragged me into the house. Aside from a half-hearted grab at one of the pillars in the portico, I offered little resistance. Getting him away from his men was a key part of Agricola's plan. Domitian wasn't particularly strong, but I knew I had to pretend to be weaker and more frightened than I actually was. I knew how the play was supposed to end. Domitian didn't.

We stopped just inside the house, at the foot of the stairs leading up to the room where Agricola and I watched Domitian's arrival. The slightly open door and the stairwell provided the only light. To my left was the door to Musonius' library, where Tacitus was stationed. Being in the house emboldened me. I knew Agricola was on the stairs, out of sight beyond the landing, waiting to step in like a *deus ex machina* and rescue me.

Domitian threw me against the peeling paint of the wall, clamping one hand on my throat and waving the knife in the other. "Where is she, Gaius Pliny?" He pressed his face to mine. He had eaten something heavy with garlic on his trip up here.

"Where is my mother?" I gasped.

He relaxed his grip and stepped back, my blood staining his hand. One corner of his mouth turned up. His knife remained at my chest level. "So we're going to bargain. Well, your mother is in your house in Rome, under guard. No harm has come to her and none will, I assure you. I have no reason to harm her, or anyone else in your house, as long as I get what I want."

"And how will you explain to your men that they have to slaughter a girl? Or will you do it yourself, like you killed that mason, Maxentius?" Agricola had urged me to get Domitian talking about his crimes when he thought no one else was listening.

"The mason?" He snorted derisively. "A falling brick hit him on the head. It was an accident. You said so yourself, in front of witnesses."

"That was before I found out where he was working—in your crypto-porticus. The only way he could have been hit by a brick in that underground passageway was if the brick was in someone's hand."

"And you think I have nothing better to do than stroll around randomly killing my workmen? Do you still believe I was trying to test you?"

"No, you were trying to protect yourself." I pressed the edge of my tunic against my throat to stop the trickle of blood.

"Protect myself from a mere workman?"

"A workman who knew a secret that could pull your power right out from under you. He was starting to talk about it in a tavern—an unknown descendant of Agrippina, a bearer of Caesar's blood. One of your spies heard him, so he had to be silenced. And you had to do it yourself. You couldn't explain to someone else why you wanted him killed."

"I have learned there are some jobs I can't hand over to anyone else." He sounded almost proud of himself.

"Such as killing your brother?" It was a stab in the dark, but I saw, from his quick intake of breath and the hardening of his expression, that it had hit the mark. "Was he the first man you killed?"

Domitian lowered his knife and rolled his eyes in disgust. "Dear Titus, the 'favorite of the gods.' I got so tired of hearing everyone call him that. What's worse, he was our father's favorite. If I had waited for him to die, I would have been old and gray before I ever got near this power. Yes, I'll admit it. When he was weak with a fever I held a pillow over his face. It didn't take long."

"Was killing Maxentius easier than killing Titus?"

"Yes." Domitian seemed to be enjoying his confession. I was, I realized, the first person to whom he could boast about his crimes. "Maxentius didn't suspect a thing, even when he saw the brick in my hand. I was pretending to examine its quality. I asked him about his work. When he turned to point at something ... well, you've figured out the rest."

"Did Regulus help you?"

"He stood look-out. But it won't do you any good to know these little secrets, because you're going to die very soon yourself."

He grabbed my tunic and pulled me toward him. "Is she really a descendant of Caesar? Are you sure of that?"

"Her veins are a veritable aqueduct of imperial blood."

"Unlike mine, you mean." He shoved me back. My head bounced off the wall and I slid to the floor. "How did you find her?"

I rolled onto my side, grabbing the back of my head and feeling for the place where I was sure my skull had cracked. Agricola could step in any time now. "I followed the only lead I had, that letter of Agrippina's that you gave me. Musonius was the only person mentioned in it who was still alive, so talking to him seemed the logical place to start."

"That was my first instinct, too. But I couldn't come out here, asking questions. You could."

"So you already knew of my friendship with Musonius?"

"Gaius Pliny, there's nothing I don't know about you. I know your mother's favorite color and the name of every slave in your household."

"Then perhaps you can tell me which one is Regulus' spy."

"Are you sure there's only one?" He smirked at my look of dismay. Crouching over me, with his knee on my chest, he thrust his knife in my face again. "We're wasting time. Where is the girl?"

The more pressing question for me was where was Agricola. As I understood his plan, he should have made his appearance by now. How long was I supposed to hold Domitian off?

The sudden confused sound of angry men's voices from outside surprised Domitian. "What's that?"

"That, Caesar," Agricola's deep, imperious voice said at long last, "is my thirty men surrounding your six." He stepped down from the stairs, sword drawn, and blocked the door out to the portico.

"Agricola! By my father's ghost!" Domitian stood, but slowly, like a man in full control of a situation, or one who knows the outcome has just passed inexorably beyond his control. "So that's what this is all about. You're finally going to kill me and take power yourself."

"That's ridiculous," Agricola said, but he looked embarrassed, the way men do when they're caught in what they thought was a clever lie. "We're just trying to protect the young woman you want to kill."

Velleius stepped in the door and saluted Agricola. "Everything is secure, sir."

"And there's Velleius, your *fidus Achates,*" Domitian said, almost relaxing, as though he no longer had anything to lose. "Now it's all clear. Gaius Pliny, do you realize how badly you've been duped?"

I scrambled to my feet, still clutching my head. "What are you talking about? Agricola has been protecting me and my family since your Praetorians attacked me in the Forum the night before last."

When Domitian turned to me the confusion on his face seemed genuine. "Praetorians attacked you in the Forum?"

"Yes. They weren't in uniform, but one of them dropped his sword. It had the Praetorian insignia on it."

"A Praetorian sword dropped. How convenient!" Domitian pursed his lips and nodded like an orator who's heard exactly what he needs to finish off his opponent in court. "Are you aware, Gaius Pliny, that Velleius' brother is a centurion in the Guard? He can get a Praetorian sword any time he wants one."

I looked at Agricola, for the first time unsure of his ultimate plan and my role in it. Since the moment Velleius arrived at my home, everything I had done had been at Agricola's direction. Suddenly his protection looked more like entrapment. He had cut Nelia and me off from any support but his veterans, then maneuvered us into an isolated spot where he knew Domitian would come after us with only a handful of men. He had refused to return to Rome or even to consider fleeing from here.

"He's just trying to turn you against me," Agricola said calmly. "I have no intention of harming him, let alone overthrowing him." I wished I could read his face better, but what little light we had in the narrow space was coming from directly behind him.

"Oh, don't be ashamed of your plan," Domitian said. "It's perfect, especially since it must have been crafted rather hurriedly." He seemed to be taking this all as a joke. If not for Agricola's sword, I think the *princeps* would have patted him on the shoulder. "You can't overthrow me unless you can find someone who has a stronger claim to power than I do. Ironically, acting on my request, Pliny finds exactly what you need—a descendant of Caesar's. The people will rally around anyone with a drop of old Julius' blood in their veins. You can rule through her until you can father a child by her and establish your own dynasty. You already have the name—*Julius* Agricola. All you need is a bit of the right Julian blood. Will you become ... Julius Agricola Caesar Britannicus? That has a nice ring to it."

"I'm quite content with my own name," Agricola muttered.

"You'll feel differently when you're living on the Palatine. Have you married the girl yet?"

"I can't marry her."

"Of course you can," Domitian said. "Just divorce that little bag of bones you're married to now."

At the insult to his wife, Agricola raised his sword, then lowered it again. "But Nelia's husband might object to her marrying someone else."

"Her husband? Who—?"

Agricola nodded at me.

Domitian swung around and thrust his knife out in front of him. "You, Gaius Pliny? Since when?"

"We were married this morning."

"Are you to be the puppet in this scheme then?" Domitian's eyebrows arched. "How long do you think you'll survive once Agricola has the senate and the army behind him?"

I stepped back, to get as far from Domitian's knife as possible. "I just wanted to guarantee that Nelia had some protection, some standing before the law." At least that was what I had thought I was doing when Agricola raised the possibility of Nelia and me getting married this morning. But what if Domitian was right? Now that Agricola had him trapped, did he still need me as bait?

Domitian took a step toward me. "You fool, she has Caesar's blood. She's a direct descendant of Augustus. What more protection does she need, damn it?"

"That's exactly what she needs to be protected *from*," Agricola said, causing Domitian to spin around and face him again. "She knows what happened to the rest of her family and how dangerous it would be for her and her child if anyone else discovered that she bears Caesar's blood."

"She has a child?" Domitian gasped.

"She's carrying one," I said.

"Hmm. And thirty men to my six, you say?"

Agricola nodded. "And your men have been disarmed."

Domitian sighed heavily and shrugged his shoulders. "Then I guess there's no hope for me." As he spoke the last two words he lunged at Agricola. The general, as surprised as I was, barely had time to get his sword up and parry the thrust of Domitian's knife. He pushed the *princeps* back, and Domitian stumbled into me, knocking us both to the floor, with Domitian on top.

Agricola stood over Domitian, who bowed his head and covered it with his arms. I could feel him quivering and became aware of a warm wetness seeping through the imperial tunic onto mine.

Raising his sword, Agricola said, "In the words of Catullus, Caesar, hail and farewell."

It will probably take me the rest of my life to sort out the whirlwind of emotions that rushed through me as Agricola's sword arced upward. Domitian was a cold-blooded killer, a tyrant, and a coward. He had murdered his brother so he could usurp his place. He had killed an innocent workman in cold blood. How many more people would he slaughter? I could prevent that by simply letting Agricola's sword fall.

But, as the sword descended, I rolled over, pushing Domitian out of its path and leaving me on top of his sobbing hulk. The sword clattered loudly against the mosaic tile of the floor, gouging out chips.

"No!" I shouted. "You can't do this, Agricola."

"Are you mad?" Agricola roared. "This is the only way to save Rome." He had turned now so that half his face was in the light, half in shadow. He was breathing heavily and his eyes seemed to glow.

"How will this save Rome? Domitian murdered to seize power. Will you be any better if you kill him?"

"You know me, Gaius Pliny. You know I could never be the sort of ruler this wretch has been." His sword hung idly by his side now, but it seemed to twitch with eagerness to strike again.

I tried to keep my voice low. "I know you're an excellent commander, my friend, and a generous father. But power can corrupt even the best of men."

Tacitus emerged from the library and stopped, whether in amazement or just waiting to see how the drama ended, I couldn't tell.

"Are you in on this?" I asked.

Before he could answer, Agricola laughed. "He knows nothing about it. I couldn't trust this to a man who can no more keep a secret than a sieve can hold water."

The sword began its upward arc again. "Move, Pliny. I must do this."

I stiffened and tried to judge if there was room for me to dodge again, but we had rolled up against the wall. "You'll have to kill me first."

"Then, with the most profound regret, I'll do exactly that. I can't turn back now."

"Of course you can," Tacitus said. "You haven't done anything you can't undo." He began to edge toward me until his father-in-law lowered the sword and pointed it at him.

Agricola laughed harshly. "Spoken with the naiveté of youth. Do you think Domitian can let me live after I've gone this far?"

From beneath me Domitian, with his arms still covering his head, whimpered, "Yes. Yes, I can. I'll … I'll do anything."

"You'll *say* anything to save your miserable life," Agricola said.

"Any of us would," Musonius' voice said. The door swung all the way open behind Agricola and Musonius stood in it, outlined by the sunlight. Over his shoulder Nelia's head was barely visible. "However miserable it is," he went on, "it is our life, and no one else has the right to take it from us."

Agricola turned, raising a hand against the glare. His sword was still poised at shoulder level. "Don't interfere," he growled.

"I just did," Musonius said softly. "Must you kill me now, too?" The old philosopher held out his hand.

Agricola looked from Musonius to me and Domitian. His breathing grew heavy. Then he raised the sword over his head, gripped the handle with both hands, and plunged it toward Musonius like a dagger. Nelia screamed.

Before I could react, Agricola drove the blade into the door beside Musonius' head. Musonius never flinched. With a deep groan Agricola let go of the sword and stepped back. As though some strength inspired by madness was ebbing out of him, he seemed to shrink. He sank down on the stairs, his elbows on his knees and his face in his hands. Hercules must have looked like that when he awoke from the mania that led him to kill his children.

Or was this more of Agricola's act?

Domitian crawled out from under me, his head still drawn down into his shoulders, like a child who wasn't quite sure the thunderstorm was over. "You just signed your death warrant, Julius Agricola," he said, his voice barely more than a hiss. "As soon as I return to Rome—"

Musonius closed the door and stood against it. Reaching over his shoulder he clasped the handle of Agricola's sword with both hands and, with surprising ease, pulled it out of the wood. "No one is leaving here, Caesar, until we have negotiated some kind of truce and guaranteed the safety of all concerned."

"I won't negotiate with anyone," Domitian said.

"Then I'll give this back to Agricola." Musonius raised the sword.

Domitian looked around, but the two doors were blocked by Musonius and Tacitus, the stairs by Agricola. And I had picked up his knife. "Now I know how old Julius felt that day in the senate. You, Gaius Pliny, with the knife in your hand, will you strike the first blow?"

I handed the knife to Musonius. "What are you proposing?"

"We must insure that no harm comes to you, or to Agricola, Tacitus, or Nelia and her child."

"I give you my word on that," Domitian said.

"But we have no way to hold you to your word," Musonius said.

"We all heard him confess to murdering Titus," Tacitus said. "If he breaks his word, we can charge him before the senate."

"He'll deny everything," Agricola said without looking up. "And his toadies in the senate will never vote to convict him."

"What if they saw a written confession, with his seal on it?" I suggested.

"Excellent!" Musonius said. "And not just one copy. Each of us should have an identical copy, written in Domitian's own hand and sealed with his seal. Everything we need is in the library here."

He took a step toward the library, but Domitian folded his arms and backed up against the wall. "What do I get if I sign such a thing? All I've heard is how you'll protect yourselves. How do I know you won't bring forward this child with Caesar's blood in a few years?"

"I will sign a statement," I offered, "that, after careful investigation, I have determined that there are no living descendants of Caesar's family."

"And I," Musonius put in, "will likewise attest that Nelia is the daughter of my cousin Fulvia and her husband Lucius Cornelius Catulus, both deceased. We will see to it that she lives quietly, away from Rome, and will never challenge your authority."

"As her husband, I can guarantee that," I said, wondering how I would ever do it.

"But someone is bound to find out the truth," Domitian said. "What will I do if they rally around this child and rise up against me?"

Looking up for the first time, Agricola said, "I will stand with you, Caesar. You have my word on that."

"The word of a man who just tried to kill me?" Domitian snorted.

"You're still alive, aren't you?"

Domitian nodded. "All right. Let's sign these damn things and be done with it. And I need a fresh tunic."

"But," Agricola said, his voice hardening, "understand this as well. Regardless of what documents you or I may sign, if *anything* happens to Nelia and her child, or to Gaius Pliny or Tacitus or Musonius ... I will not rest until I have impaled your head on a pike and thrown your body into the Tiber."

Gaius Musonius to his dear Gaius Pliny, greetings.

With the most profound sadness I write to tell you that our beloved Nelia died in childbirth during the night, in spite of all your mother and your woman Naomi could do for her. The child was born a bit early and the birth was a difficult one, the most difficult Naomi says she has seen. I'm sure she will give you a full account when she returns to Rome. The child is a boy and is doing well. One of my women is nursing him.

This is when philosophers are supposed to write treatises of consolation, isn't it? But I can find no words. Early this morning I even read Cicero's consolation to his wife when their daughter died, looking for comfort, and found it utterly vapid. What words can avail when something like this happens?

My daughter and her husband will take the child with them when they return to Syria and raise him as their son. As much as I hate to expose my daughter to the possible danger, I see no other solution. They do not know the boy's true heritage and have sworn to me that they will never tell him that he is not their son by birth. As you know, I agreed to bring them here and introduce Nelia to my daughter only on condition that Nelia keep her identity a secret. Your mother and Naomi have not revealed anything, as far as I know, but I'm not sure they will be able to accept that the child is going to be sent away.

How many secrets can we keep, my dear Pliny? The five of us who confronted one another in that stairwell are only mortal vessels. Eventually one of us will crack and the truth will leak out—the truth about this child and about many other things. I'm an old man. I don't expect to live long enough to have to cope with all the problems that could arise. You, on the other hand, are young. I'm afraid you will be living under the shadow of what we've learned and done for the rest of your life.

We will hold Nelia's funeral on the day before the nones. If you're here, you will be welcome. If you choose not to attend, we will understand. Laberius will bring your mother and Naomi back to Rome after the funeral. I plan to bury Nelia's ashes at the foot of an old bridge on my property. She loved that spot because the bridge has some Etruscan writing on it. I think it's also where she met Marcianus and probably where she conceived his child. He, incidentally, has joined the army, his father tells me. Nelia's rejection of him made him so despondent he wanted to get far away.

I have not made a copy of this letter, and I urge you to burn it at once.

Given by my own hand on the 3rd day before the nones of December

I read the letter for the fourth time since it arrived an hour ago, brought by a slave who had ridden his horse into the ground in his haste. Then I dropped it into the charcoal brazier that provided what little heat my tablinum enjoyed. Outside the sky glistened, cloudless but cold. Around the house my servants were putting up candles and greenery—decorations for the coming Saturnalia. This letter should mean they would have to come down and be replaced by signs of mourning, but I wasn't sure I wanted to alert Domitian to Nelia's death.

My wife is dead, I reminded myself. As a Stoic I was supposed to accept whatever happened with indifference—*apatheia*. When my uncle died, I felt sadness, but I was able to get up and resume my life. Why did I feel now like I just wanted to sit here in the gloom by myself? Why couldn't I be indifferent?

My wife is dead. But what did that mean? Of all the unusual marriages in Rome, ours must have been one of the strangest. Nelia died giving birth to another man's child, a man who didn't even know he had gotten her pregnant. My mother, unable to understand why Nelia couldn't live in Rome, had spent the last three months at Musonius' house. Now she had lost her 'daughter' for the second time. She would never recover from this loss, I was sure. Nor would Naomi. What would my house be like with two women living in permanent mourning?

If I was going to be there for the funeral, I had to leave almost immediately and try to get to Musonius' villa before dark today. My mother would never forgive me if I didn't come. I had planned to go up there in a few days anyway, to be on hand when the child was due to be born.

During the time that Nelia had been at Musonius' villa I had made three trips to visit her. On the last one, almost a month ago, I was pleased to renew my friendship with Artemidorus, Musonius' son-in-law, whom I first met in Syria.

I poked at the ashes of the letter to make sure it was being entirely consumed.

In the time we spent together I came to realize I did not love Nelia in the way I want to love a woman if she is to be my wife. We certainly shared respect and admiration for one another. In addition, I was fascinated by her—by her strength, her vitality, her intelligence. We had read Agrippina's original memoir together as Nelia translated it.

But she frightened me in some way, too. I could imagine how one of Agrippina's numerous lovers must have felt when he was with her: *This woman is amazing, but can I survive being with her?*

While I would never have divorced Nelia, I suspect she would have left me eventually, or taken on lovers. She made no secret of the fact that she never felt I was exciting enough. 'Dangerous' was her word. But, for her sake, I stood between a power-mad general and a quivering *princeps* and lived to tell about it.

Not that I really can tell anyone about it. Nelia herself never knew exactly what happened in that gloomy stairwell. Musonius, like the chief priest in a mystery cult, shut the door on her and swore us all to secrecy. He's certain Domitian will ultimately seek his revenge because we saw him humiliated, even to the point that he urinated on himself.

So far, though, we've been safe. Agricola bought a villa close to Musonius' and retired from Rome. Some of his veterans work the land for him. Others have settled on small farms nearby. Domitian knows Agricola could call up a considerable force in a short time. He has left us alone and seems content to concentrate on finishing his grandiose house on the Palatine.

I got up, stirred the ashes of the letter once more, opened the door to the tablinum, and called to my steward. "Demetrius, I have to go to Musonius' house."

252

CHRONOLOGY
(All Dates A. D.)

14/15 Agrippina the Younger born

27/28 Agrippina married to Domitius Ahenobarbus

37 The future emperor Nero born

39-41 Agrippina in exile on Pandateria

41-54 Reign of emperor Claudius

54 Nero becomes emperor

55 Nero's second consulship. His colleague is Lucius Antistius Vetus

59 Death of Agrippina (March)

62 Antistius Vetus governor of Asia; his daughter is married to Rubellius Plautus

65 Antistius Vetus and his daughter commit suicide

66-73 Jewish War against Rome

68 Death of Nero (June)

69 Year of the Four Emperors (Galba, Otho, Vitellius,Vespasian)

70 Fall of Jerusalem

73 Fall of Masada (last Jewish fortress)

69-79 Reign of Vespasian

79-81 Reign of Titus

79 Eruption of Vesuvius (Aug. 24-26); death of Pliny the Elder

81-96 Reign of Domitian

GLOSSARY OF TERMS
(All Dates A. D.)

Agricola: Gnaeus Julius Agricola, father-in-law of Tacitus. Agricola had a distinguished career as an army officer and provincial official. He extended Rome's conquest north into Britain before he was recalled by Domitian in the summer of 83. He died in 93. Tacitus mentions a "persistent rumor that he had been poisoned. We have no definite evidence. That is all I can say for certain" (*Agricola* 43). Sounds like the premise for another book.

L. Antistius Vetus: He was consul with Nero in 55 and was governor of the province of Asia in 62, the year before Julius Agricola, Tacitus' father-in-law, was a minor offical there. His daughter, Antistia, did marry Nero's cousin, Rubellius Plautus. Antistius urged Rubellius to rise up against Nero, but Rubellius would not. Antistius and his daughter were forced by Nero to commit suicide in 65.

Argos: In mythology a watchman with extra eyes, varying in number according to different versions of the story. He was killed by Hermes and his eyes were used to decorate the tail of the peacock.

Aureus: A gold coin. Until Nero's day the aureus was reckoned at 42 to the pound, compared to 84 to the pound for the denarius. Nero devalued the aureus to 46 to the pound.

Catacombs: Burial sites which originated near pagan cemeteries on the outskirts of Rome. Burial of the dead within the walls of an ancient city was prohibited because the area within the walls (the pomerium in Rome) was considered sacred to the city's patron deity.

Cognomen: See "Names" below.

Exhedra: An outdoor eating area, usually located toward the rear of the garden of a Roman house.

Fasti: Originally lists of days which were considered propitious for public business (dies fasti) and days when public business could not be conducted (dies nefasti). They later came to include names of consuls, lists of priests, and records of triumphs. Several fragmentary lists survive.

Fidus Achates: Achates was the loyal companion of Aeneas in the *Aeneid.* He seemed to be everywhere Aeneas went.

Golden House: Nero's extravagant villa, built after the great fire of 64. It was not a single structure but a series of buildings, lakes, and green spaces stretching across the center of Rome, somewhat analogous to New York's Central Park but reserved for one man and his courtiers. Vespasian opened it to the public when he took power and built over most of it during his reign. The Colosseum sits on what was the main lake of the Golden House.

Impluvium: A basin sunk into the floor of the atrium of a Roman house. Rain drained in through the hole in the roof of the atrium, was collected in the impluvium, and channeled into storage tanks. Long after the homes of most wealthy Romans were connected to the aqueducts, they continued to build their houses with this old-fashioned "convenience." The impluvium was often decorated with colorful tiles or ornamented with statuary.

Latrina: A Roman toilet. Both men and women usually performed all bathroom functions sitting down. A Roman bathroom could be unisex because both genders wore long robes with no undergarments. They could sit down and cover themselves while using the toilet. In public toilets persons picked up a stick with a sponge on the end of it as they entered. When they were finished, they used the sponge to clean themselves, then dipped it in a stream of water running around the edge of the toilet and returned it as they left. In smaller toilets old pieces of papyrus were often used for cleaniness. The poet Martial jokes about cacata carta, "shitty sheets" of papyrus. Public toilets and those in the homes of the wealthy had water constantly flowing beneath the seats to remove waste. Smaller latrinae were essentially indoor outhouses, which had to be cleaned by slaves. Human waste served several functions. Urine was used by tanners in curing leather. Excrement was used as fertilizer.

Liquamen: A commonly-used sauce made of pulverized fish and fat. Yum!

Musonius Rufus: Stoic philosopher, known as "the Roman Socrates." He lived from ca. 30 to 101/102. He was exiled several times and was closely associated with Rubellius Plautus, a relative of Nero's who was put to death in 62. Whether Musonius wrote anything himself is uncertain, but some of his teachings were collected by his students, such as Epictetus. Pliny knew Musonius' son-in-law, Artemidorus. Some scholars have noted similarities between Musonius' vocabulary and precepts and those of the New Testament.

Names: A Roman citizen's name usually consisted of three parts. The actual name, the nomen, was the middle name, as in Gaius Julius Caesar. It indicated the family to which the man belonged. In this case Gaius would be the praenomen ("first name") and, since there were so many men with this name, a cognomen would be added, the name by which he was known or distinguished from all the others. When a man was adopted, as Pliny was, his biological father's name was usually incorporated into his name. Thus Pliny became Gaius Plinius Caecilius Secundus, with the Caecilius being his birth father's name. Women were given a feminine form of their father's family name, e. g., Julia, Cornelia, Livia, etc.

Nomenclator: Wealthy Romans usually had one servant whose primary job was to be a kind of social secretary, knowing everyone who was worth knowing in the city. He would usually walk close to his master as they passed through the streets, ready to whisper a name in his master's ear if the master did not recognize someone who greeted him.

Piscina: A pond in the peristyle garden of a wealthy Roman's house where fish could be kept until they were ready for the table. Because of the expense of beef, pork, or meat from other large animals, the Romans ate a lot of fish. That obtained from the markets was often of poor quality. In one of his satires Juvenal complains of being served fish so old and tough it must have crawled from the water to his plate.

Princeps: From the earliest days of the Republic the Roman Senate was led by its eldest member, the *princeps senatus,* the "first man of the senate." It was his privilege to speak first on any issue presented to that body. When Augustus came to power this title was extended to him as the "first man" of the Roman state. Since the emperors of the first century wanted to downplay the military basis of their rule, they preferred this civilian title.

Rubellius Plautus: Rubellius was one of a number of relatives of Augustus in the fourth generation. His grandmother was Livia Julia, daughter of Antonia the Younger, daughter of Augustus' sister Octavia, and his mother was Julia, granddaughter of the emperor Tiberius. His descent from Julius Caesar was as close as Nero's, since both were descendants of Octavia, just through different daughters. Rubellius was admired as a Stoic philosopher, but Nero forced him into exile in 60 and ordered him to commit suicide in 62.

Tablinum: Room off the atrium of an upper-class Roman house where the master of the house kept his papers and accounts, analogous to a modern home office.

Topiarius: Wealthy Romans often took pride in their gardens. A skillful gardener was a valuable asset. In one of his letters Pliny describes the hedges of one of his estates. They were cut to spell out his name.

Triclinium: The dining room of a Roman house. Guests reclined on their left elbows on couches set around a table where servants placed food. The typical arrangement was three couches per table, with three guests on each couch, but Ovid and other writers make it clear that more than three people often occupied a couch. By the first century A. D. women reclined alongside men. The middle couch was for the most important guests, with the "low" position on that couch for the guest of honor. That put him closest to the host, who occupied the "high" position on the "low" couch.

Trigon: A ball game often played in the courtyards of public baths. We have no sure knowledge of how it was played, but it seems to have involved three players standing in a triangle and throwing a ball to one another. Points may have been scored if an opponent could not handle a throw. Ovid wrote a book about Roman games, but it has not survived.

Vigiles: As large as Rome was, it had no regular police or fire departments. Augustus established a corps of nightwatchmen after a fire in 23 B. C. At first it consisted of a few hundred slaves, but after another major fire in 6 A. D., he turned it into a body of 7,000 freedmen, divided like the army into cohorts and centuries and commanded by tribunes, under the overall leadership of a Praefect appointed by the emperor. Since the Romans had no effective fire-fighting equipment, the vigiles, who were stationed in the various regions of the city, patrolled the streets and tried to get people out of buildings in case of fire. The Praefect of the vigiles eventually took on some quasi-judicial functions.

villa rustica: Most Roman aristocrats had homes in the countryside. Pliny describes two of his in his letters. Most of these country estates had fields where crops were grown, but a true villa rustica was a working farm, not just a place for a rich man and his family to escape the noise and the summer heat of the city.

Praise for the first Pliny mystery:

ALL ROADS LEAD TO MURDER

"Wonderful historical mystery set in the Roman Empire during the early Church and St. Luke's timeframes. . . helps the reader experience what it was like to live during Roman times. ... superb use of setting and characterizations. Historical figures come alive in his expert hands. – Bob Spear, *Heartland Reviews*. Rating: five hearts

"Superbly crafted, wonderfully written murder mystery ... thrilling detective story meticulously backgrounded with accurate historical detail. – *Midwest Book Review*

"The colorful characters, both fictional and historical, are well blended to reveal the sordid web of money, greed and ruthlessness hidden behind the facade of civilization. One hopes to see Albert Bell's Pliny again." – Suzanne Crane, *The Historical Novels Review*

"Superlative job of leading the reader into his Roman world. A winner all around!"– Margaret F. Baker, *Past Tense*

"Masterful blend of history and mystery. ... wonderful book. with splendid characters, vivid history and a fair and puzzling mystery. I heartily recommend it." – Barbara D'Amato, award-winning author of three mystery series, Past President of Mystery Writers Internationals and Sisters in Crime International

"Rich and rewarding read, in the tradition of Lindsay Davis' Marcus Didius Falco books or Steven Saylor's Gordianus the Finder ... succeeds both as an historical document and as a mystery. ... colorful tapestry depicting the sights and sounds, the smells and tastes that reproduce a lifelike portrait of the world of two millennia ago." – Jack Ewing, *Wicked Company*

"Bell promises us a series, and this reviewer for one looks eagerly forward to the next installment!" – Irene Hahn, Romahost, About.com

ALBERT BELL is a literary renaissance man. His previously published works include: nonfiction, historical fiction and mysteries. His articles and stories have appeared in magazines and newspapers from *Jack and Jill* and *True Experience* to the *Detroit Free Press* and *Christian Century.*
Dr. Bell has taught at Hope College in Holland, Michigan since 1978, first with an appointment shared between classics and history; and, since 1994, as Professor of History and chair of the department. He holds a PhD from UNC-Chapel Hill, as well as an MA from Duke and an MDiv from Southeastern Baptist Theological Seminary. He has been married for 40 years to Bettye Jo Barnes Bell, a psychologist; they have four children and a grandchild.

Bell discovered his love for writing in high school with his first publication in 1972. Although he considers himself a "shy person," he believes he is a storyteller more than a literary artist. He says, "When I read a book I'm more interested in one with a plot that keeps moving rather than long descriptive passages or philosophical reflection." He writes books he would enjoy reading himself.

Visit the author's website at:
www.albertbell.com

When the body of a mason is found in the library of current Princeps (first citizen) Domitian, Pliny the Younger is asked by his mother to find the killer. At the same time, Domitian orders Pliny and his friend Tacitus to find out if there is a real heir to the throne. Their exploits in Syria (All Roads Lead to Murder) have reached the ears of all in Rome, and they now have the reputation of being competent detectives. Readers will delight in the duo's tracing of Caesar's blood line; walking with Pliny through his daily routine is entertaining, too. Outstandingly researched and laden with suspense, this journey into ancient Rome by history professor Bell could be one of the masterpieces of the historical mystery genre. Lindsey Davis and Steven Saylor will hold readers over until the third casebook of Pliny the Younger publishes. Highly recommended for all collections.

-- Jo Ann Vicarel - *Library Journal*

INGALLS PUBLISHING GROUP, INC
PO Box 2500
Banner Elk, NC 28604
Phone: 828-898-3801
FAX: 828-898-4930
bookkeeper@ingallspublishinggroup.com
www.ingallspublishinggroup.com